THE THIS

By Adam Roberts from Gollancz:

Salt
On
Stone
Polystom
The Snow
Gradisil
Land of the Headless
Swiftly
Yellow Blue Tibia
New Model Army
By Light Alone
Jack Glass
Twenty Trillion Leagues Under the Sea
Bête
The Thing Itself
The Real-Town Murders
By the Pricking of Her Thumb
Purgatory Mount
The This

THE THIS

Adam Roberts

First published in Great Britain in 2022 by Gollancz
an imprint of The Orion Publishing Group Ltd
Carmelite House, 50 Victoria Embankment
London EC4Y 0DZ

An Hachette UK Company

1 3 5 7 9 10 8 6 4 2

A CIP catalogue record for this book is available from the British Library.

ISBN (Hardback) 978 1 473 23090 3
ISBN (eBook) 978 1 473 23092 7
ISBN (Audio Download) 978 1 473 23093 4

Typeset at The Spartan Press Ltd,
Lymington, Hants

Printed and bound in Great Britain by Clays Ltd,
Elcograf S.p.A.

www.gollancz.co.uk

You don't get me, I'm part of the union
You don't get me, I'm part of the union
You don't get me, I'm part of the union
Till the day I die
Till the day I die.

Richard Hudson and John Ford

The analysis of an idea, as it is properly carried out, is, in fact, nothing else than ridding it of the form in which it has become familiar.

G.W.F. Hegel

Allow me to remark:
The Ghost has just as good a right
In every way to fear the light,
As men to fear the dark.

Charles Dodgson

Contents

I
In the Bardo

In the Bardo subject and object are the same. You say, 'I'm not sure I understand what that means.'

There's somebody else with you in the Bardo and this other person is going through the same process you are. Or, to put it another way: there are many persons in the Bardo and they're all going through the same process as you. The place is crammed with people. So many! Do any of them understand this business better than you do? You say it again: '*I'm not sure I understand what that means.*'

'Means,' says the other. 'I mean, since we can't suppose time has any purchase in this place, the present tense in your statement comes into question, rather, don't you think? Meant, means, will mean. I mean, who's to say?'

You say: '*Huh*?'

A flash of light marks your passage out of the Bardo, and you're alive again. That flash was the sunlight. All of it. That flash of light is all the sunlight you will see in the course of your life, and all the darkness, too. Which is to say, you see, in an instant, the *balance* of the two – but of course you'll see less darkness and more light over the run of your whole existence, because the day is lit and, though the night is not, there's always light inside your dreams.

Embodiment, and its queasy wondrousness. Milk assuages your wailing. You run, and it's a pure joy, and the high grass snickers at your hips. You take your share of the meat. You are a parent and sit under an overhang and watch the rain come down so hard it's as if the whole sky has collapsed its liquid blue down upon you in one go. It smells of cleanness and clover, of sky and freshness. As you sit there, cradling one of your kids, a thought rushes your memory with intense and vivid suddenness: that time when Hari cut the throat of a wild cow with a lucky cut, and all the cow's blood came out in one go, with a great sloshing and gushing – it was the noise of this rain, the noise of life sluicing endlessly through the sky and the earth, through you and all the animals, and you feel a sharp fragment of understanding. There was good eating for *days* from that cow. You sleep and dream of a great mountain. The next day the ground is muddy. A pain in your jaw grows until you can do nothing but lie on the ground and cry. It fills your head with its pain, and when you think the pain is so great it cannot possibly be greater, it swells further – fire and grinding and pressure combined into an agony. It breaks the bone to burst from your head through the side of your face, and the release of this pressure is so sweet you sleep for a day. It still hurts, and the others make fun of your ruined face, and then you are feverish and then you are more feverish and then you are dead.

In the Bardo subject and object are the same. You can remember the whole of that lived life, as fine-veined and perfect as a single glossy leaf from a tree with a trillion leaves. You hold the whole memory in your mind. The light comes again.

You are reborn, and live long enough to develop a sense of yourself, of your mother and your siblings, of heat and shade, of the difference between bitter food and sweet, and then you die – a day and a night of diarrhoea and you're gone.

In the Bardo subject and object are the same.

'I can remember all of them,' you say. 'I suppose you do, too? Is it the same for you?'

The other person there smiles. 'Are you sure,' this other person asks, 'you're not collating numerous similar life-memories into a smaller number of manageable memories?'

You say: 'That's a good question.'

The light, again. There is more brightness than darkness in this life, too. It's like that for almost every life. You grow up by a pool, and there are fish to eat as well as what the tribe hunts in the forest. You and your brothers and sisters and cousins are a tribe within the tribe, and you like mischief. One day, when one of the community's Big Men is washing himself in the pool, you and your siblings all piss into the pool for a joke. The Big Man is very angry, and his anger does not settle as anger usually does. He surprises the group of you all later that day – you'd already forgotten the prank, and are picking and eating berries. But the Big Man has not forgotten, and though most of your sisters and brothers run off screaming, he catches you and punches you on the side of the head. His is the Big Fist, so its blow breaks the bone and you lie on the ground sobbing and passing in and out of consciousness. Over the course of evening and sunset the shadow of the bush slides over you like a blanket. Your mother finds you and tries to lift you up, but the movement dislodges something inside you and you start fitting furiously. Vomit comes up one way and goes down another and you're dead.

In the Bardo subject and object are the same.

'Does it just go on and on?' you ask. 'I mean, I suppose what I'm wondering is... are we on our *way* anywhere?'

The other person smiles. 'You mean, enlightenment? Zen and spiritual evanishment and all that? I don't know anything about any of that.'

You tell them your name.

They tell you theirs: Abby something.

'Abby Normal?' you laugh, and Abby laughs, too, so that's a joke you share, it seems. A cultural reference you have in common. At the time this doesn't strike you as strange, but later, when the sheer scope of... well – *everything*... comes home to you, it sounds a more discordant note. I mean, what are the odds? That you both recognised the reference, that you had cultural knowledge sufficiently in common to both laugh? An old black and white comedy movie. Pastiche monster-mash.

Where did you start this process? Which was your first life? You wonder about yourself. You ask Abby.

By way of reply Abby smiles a Serenissima smile.

This time there is no flash, and this life is more darkness than light: you live underground, and when you come up the light hurts your eyes and you don't like it. But you bring up the ore and you eat your meals, and you play, and when you get older you fuck, and you don't know any different. Then you're dead and you do know any different and you think: *That wasn't much of a life.*

Bright light. You live by the river and your life is a habitual matter: prayers, scooping the water into your irrigation channels, growing your food, passing your due to the rulers, making small trades with your neighbours. You marry four times and have six children, two of whom live to adulthood and are present at your deathbed.

In the Bardo subject and object are the same thing.

'There's a degree of monotony,' you note.

Abby shrugs.

Darkness this time: you are blind, all your long life. You never see the sunlight, although you can feel it on your face.

In the Bardo subject and object are the same thing.

Brightness swells again.

You are a farmer. You are a farmer.

You are a farmer. You are pressed into the army and die of dysentery far from home. You are a farmer, pressed into the army and spiked with a spear from behind on a battlefield whose name you do not know. You are a farmer and you die by the sword. You are a farmer and you die of disease.

In the Bardo subject and object are the same thing.

'That phrase keeps occurring to me,' you tell Abby, as you stretch your limbs and settle once more, yet again, into the calmly eternal rhythm of the Bardo. 'And I couldn't for the life of me tell you why. Or what it means.'

'Let's say,' Abby suggests, 'I. Let's say, you. *You're* your subject. Subject, verb, object. For example – I eat the apple.'

Apple, you think. *Adam*, you think. *Was Adam the first life? Was Adam* your *first life?*

'So in the world of living and dying I eat an apple, but in the Bardo I and the apple are the same thing?'

'Search me,' says Abby, grinning.

'I don't feel very apple-y.'

'Golden,' says Abby. 'Delicious.'

The brightness swells again.

You are a nobleman – afterwards, when you're back in the Bardo and can remember it all, you're struck by how *rare* this is.

A nobleman! You dress in fine clothes, and slaves attend your mundane needs, and you own a fine house with flat roofs and a carp pond. A man you trust absolutely, a man you have known all your life, shoves you hard, and keeps shoving you until your back is pressed against the wall. You're so astonished you don't say anything, because this is a man you trust absolutely. He breaks the skin of your chest with the point of his dagger, and sets his foot back to brace himself as he pushes hard, and the whole blade of the dagger slides into your chest. It is intensely painful, a bursting nova of pain. The dagger goes right through you and the point sticks in the plaster of the wall behind you.

'Thus perish all traitors!' your friend shouts, right in your face, and bits of his spittle land on your mouth and your nose and go into your eye, and despite the intensity of the pain the main thing of which you are conscious is … surprise. Traitor? You? *Traitor*?

In the Bardo subject is object.

'I'm one point closer to appleness,' you tell Abby. 'I know now what it's like to be sliced with a knife.'

'You approach applitude,' says Abby.

'Appleosity,' you agree.

'Snip snap,' says Abby, with a strange smile.

You herd cows. You follow the plough. You are a weaver. You are a fisherman and you drown when a storm capsizes your boat. You fall sick. You are stretched on a rack. You learn to read, which means, since you are the only person in your village who *can* read, you become a de facto priest. You plough. You carry seaweed from the coast up to a walled field to fertilise it. You build a dam. You clean the house, over and over, over and over. You are the most successful farmer in your district and people come to beg you for charity when their crops fail, and then one year the rainy season does not come, and then it does not come for a second year and you and the rest of them all starve to death together. You give birth but the child will not come, and you keep pushing and pushing and pushing until you die of exhaustion. You climb a tree to pick fruit, and fall from the tree, and break your leg, and your leg grows three times as fat overnight, and becomes ghastly squishy, and goes black and you die in agony. You farm. You farm. You farm. You are burnt to death when your barn catches fire – foolishly you rush inside to try and save your horse, and both you and the horse die in agony. You are cut to death by a man with an axe during a time of war. You are raped by eleven men, and it kills you. You die of cholera. You die of dysentery. You die of sepsis. You give birth and it feels like you are being torn in two and then you are dead. You accidentally kill a man and have to abscond from your village, and you live in the woods for half a year, growing wilder, driven to more desperate crimes by hunger, until winter comes and you freeze to death.

In the Bardo subject is object.

'I get the impression,' you tell Abby, 'that things are speeding up.'

'It's wider, in terms of human population,' Abby agrees. 'But shorter in an absolute sense. The timeline, I mean.'

You are evicted from your farm because the nobleman wants the land for his sheep. You trek to the coast, and your wife and two of your children die on the journey, and then you make a new life as a fisherman with help from your cousin. You marry again. Prayer and work help you overcome your grief. You get a tumour in your testicle and it grows to the size of a football. A surgeon comes from the town to cut it out and you die of postoperative sepsis.

The Bardo's subject is its object.

'I get the feeling I'm getting closer to something.'

You farm. You farm. You dedicate your life to God. You are a miner. You are a dock worker. You are a railwayman. You farm. Your farm is mortgaged and lost and you move to the city where you get work in a factory, and then you develop a cough and the cough won't go away, and your lungs fill with gunk and you die. You go to school and the schoolmaster beats you, and then, when you are limping home with blood dripping down your trouser-leg into your shoe, a street dog bites you, excited by the smell, and the wound goes bad, and you die. You work in a factory. You work in an office. You are pressed into the army and die when your troop carrier sinks on its way to the land where the fighting is. You work in an office. You die of influenza. You work for a bank. You work for the council. You are a teacher. You are a mechanic. You are a nurse. You are an agricultural labourer. You are a jeweller. You work in an office. You die of old age. You take an overdose of recreational drugs. You are crushed to death when the crowd at Mecca becomes overexcited. You die of an asthma attack at the age of seventeen. You drown in your bath when your carer leaves you alone for five minutes to take a call from her boyfriend. You crash your car. You die when your life support malfunctions and the temperature in your pod plunges to equalise with the temperature of deep space beyond the hull. You remotely operate an areoforming robot, and die when the feedback is maladjusted by a viral e-infection and crashes your heart. You work for an AI in AI–human liaison and die of old age, rich and self-satisfied. You live on Mars. You spend all your life in an artificial habitat in orbit around Jupiter. You mine ice. You think up clever advertising strategies to sell blackseed food products.

In the Bardo: sub/ob/ject.

'I feel I've shot past something. Is this the future now?'

'You keep talking like time has any meaning in this

what-for-want-of-a-better-word-I-have-to-call place,' laughs Abby. 'Quaint!'

You live as a prince of the solar system in an augmented body and are assassinated by one of your rivals. Your whole life is lived inside a generation starship. You are one of a fan-religion living in a series of serried shells around Bluestar 44. You are a soldier, bringing one thing only – your capacity for aggression – to an autoarmy that lacks that quality. You live on a purple-red world under a diamond-coloured sun. You live in a foam-matrix on a deep space trajectory. You are part of a cult that uses enhanced sexual pleasure to crystallise the transcendental. You extend your life with a combination of artificial supports and a time-dilation algoractivator. You upload your consciousness into a series of insectorgs and swarm for the sheer joy of swarming. The stars are running out of fuel and one by one they flare and sputter and go dark. You—

—are in the Bardo.

You're in the Bardo again.

'Was that it?' you ask.

There were an inestimable number of people in the Bardo before (as if *before* has any meaning in this place!) but now it seems empty (as if *now* has any meaning in this place!) – *is* it empty? You are the subject of this story, you suppose, after all. It's a common enough human supposition.

'Abby?' you say. 'Abby, are you there?'

A breath is drawn, as if Abby is about to reply to you, and that miniature crescendo of white noise breaks off sharply and—

—you're born. You're gasping in the light. You're clinging to the hair of your mother's pelt as she lopes through the grassland. The dry fields chuckle in the wind, strands of grass like sticks rattling together. You spend hours every day picking grain from the grass and chewing it in the chunky knucklebone teeth at the back of your mouth. Night swallows day and then is itself swallowed by the sun. As the year goes on the trees on the high hill become nude, and the air acquires a sterile chill, and you and your people huddle together. When spring returns, and warmth, you are sick of their company, so you take to sleeping in a nook by the stream. A wolf grabs you by the throat in the middle of the night and drags you away and you are dead in moments. Round and round again. You die a day old. You die a year old. You live to thirty. You die of sepsis. You choke on a nut. You die of dysentery. You live to become a great-grandfather and a tribal elder and then take your own life because the darkness that has been inside you all your life becomes too much. You are trampled by some bison and your leg is left mashed and bloody, and for months you drag it behind you, covered in a seething sock of flies. But it heals and you limp on, and your tribe becomes convinced that you are a holy man. You die old and are buried in a fine chambered tomb.

In the Bardo subject and object are the same thing.

'Are we really going through the whole thing again?'

Abby says: 'You don't think you haven't *already* done the whole thing again? Again and again?' That distinctive Abby laugh. 'Don't fret – things speed up. There's a kind of spiritual momentum to it all.'

You farm, you fish, you farm, you fight. You are high status, one of the political and spiritual leaders of your community, but young people are little bastards these days – not like when you were young. Back then children *respected* their elders. But *this* morning? Let me tell it: you went into the pool to pray to the gods and wash yourselves and the little shits *pissed all over you* – fucking little brats. Oh, you caught up with them and gave them a smack round the ear, teach them a lesson, but really it's the mothers – the mothers are too soft on them.

In the Bardo subject and object are the same thing.

'How many times have we been through all this?' you ask Abby.

'*Now* you're using the right word.'

'What word is that?'

'The *we* word – that's the ticket. *We* is *I* and *you*, subject and object, in one handy little packet.'

'Now hold up for *just* one second there, partner—' you say.

But there's no waiting. Light flashes and you're a farmer, and a farmer, and a farmer, over and over. You fight in the army. You rape. You cut someone down with an axe. You are one of the god-king's most trusted advisors, and live in a fine palace with a carp pool and orange trees growing in the courtyard; but you discover that your best friend is part of a palace faction that aims to promote the god-king's sister to the throne. Your closest friend! – with whom you have hunted and feasted since you were both children. You are so angry you can barely *breathe*. You go to his house and his slaves let you in – of course they do – and you confront him in his bedroom and kill him with your own hands. 'Thus perish all traitors', you yell, right in his face. As he dies the look of guilt and remorse on his face entirely vindicates your action.

You're a tobacco farmer. You're a yam farmer. You're a rice farmer. You join the imperial army and are killed. You join the imperial army and survive, and then when the war is finished people arrest you and lock you in a prison and then they hang you by the neck until you are dead. You program computers. You present television documentaries. You build a model of the Taj Mahal, taller than a man, entirely out of used Coca-Cola bottles.

'The earlier lives,' Abby says, 'occupy an external epoch that lasted hundreds of thousands of years, and that's long, sure, sure.

But there're only a few lives at any given moment during that epoch, so you'll find you're through with them soon. But with the later lives... the external time period is much briefer, but there are very many many more people, so that's the experience that will tend to predominate.'

It's dawning on you (in the Bardo, where subject and object is the same thing) that you're going to reincarnate into every single human being who ever lived.

I mean, really?

I mean... seriously*?*

You are an airline pilot. You're a street kid. You die when an allergic reaction collapses your throat. You are shot by a cop. You plant rice. You mine notional gold by playing video games all day in a dingy building and die of heart disease in your fifties. You beg on the streets. You beg on the orbital run. You are a lunar shuttle pilot. You are an asteroid kid, scraping a living and eating vat-gunk. You are poor and volunteer for a new treatment that splits your consciousness between your organic brain and two drones – a military surveillance experimental programme, is what it is – but the experience induces psychosis, and you kill seven people with the drones and two more with your bare hands before you are shot dead yourself. You mastermind the terraforming of Venus by releasing vast amounts of heat from the planetary core, subliming the highly acidic atmosphere almost entirely into space; and then you replace it with a bombardment of shepherded cometary bodies. You do grunt work on the Martian elevator cable and die when the foundations collapse and debris breaks your airpack.

In the Bardo subject and object are the same thing.

You work remotely via photbugs tweaking vacuum grass on the lunar side. You work remotely operating clamberdogs as they decommission the astonishingly poisonous and dangerous tubes of vitreous radioactive waste the twentieth century left buried in vaults, hoiking them into orbit inside magchutes and firing them at the sun. You are the first human to walk on the surface of Gliese 581c. You are the first human to convert their entire skeleton to smartdiamond. You compete in the Sex Olympics but your gold medal is stripped from you when it is discovered that your genitals were being remotely controlled by an accomplice back in the training camp. You live a religious life. You life an atheistical life. You game, you work, you mourn. You almost glitch the whole process when, exploring the event horizon of a local black hole, your buffered consciousness is smeared into a declining parabolic recovery feed – it takes you over eight hundred years to die, and after the first decade you lose your mind so comprehensively that there's nothing meaningfully 'you' left by the end of the whole ghastly, unexpected process. But you do eventually pass below the threshold we can call life; and the Bardo wipes away all insanity, psychosis, misery or elation.

In the Bardo subject and object are the same thing.

You clone yourself into a thousand iterations and explore the Andromeda galaxy. You live for a thousand years in an endlessly reconfiguring pleasure-sim, and then one day commit suicide on a whim. You are the messiah of a planetwide religious movement and you die when your (planned, staged) apotheosis converts all your cellular matter into rose petals, using nano-organon engines. You surf gravity waves in a spaceship eight kilometres wide but only a metre high. You die when your laser-rifle malfunctions and explodes in your hand. You are a mentat. You are a pod-person. You are an intergalactic trader in rare mathematical proofs. You upload your consciousness to the diamond core of a gas giant.

In the Bardo, Abby is looking at you in a funny way.

'Where is everybody else?' you ask. 'This place used to be

humming with . . .' but you're not sure what the word is. *People*? Is it *people*?

'*Where*,' says Abby, 'is not a very good word when applied to the Bardo.'

You are a bilge-kid on an interstellar liner. You grow up on Koronagrag 3 and, together with two dozen like-minded individuals, you decide to reproduce the life of Isaac Newton: machines recreate seventeenth-century London and Cambridge down to every detail, and you and your friends dress the part, speak the words and inhabit the roles as fully as possible, one hour per hour, for decades. You are a beast. You are a nano-mechanic. You are Führer of the Diaphanous Oort League. You explore quantum miniaturisation and colonise the shell of a helium atom, only to discover the descendants of people who had discovered such technology a thousand years earlier, and whose discovery had been forgotten. You watch the last stars go dark.

In the Bardo subject and object are the same thing.

'Is memory infinite?' you ask Abby.

'Mortality means that it need not be,' says Abby. 'I mean, I can't deny that it's part of the structure of human consciousness to tend to confuse the very big with the infinite. But actually and literally, those two things couldn't be further apart from one another.'

'Okey,' you say. 'Dokey.'

In the Bardo subject and object are the same.

In the Bardo subject and object are the same.

In the Bardo subject and object are the same.

'It's not Abby Normal,' you say. 'Your name, I mean.' It's taken you some time to reach this realisation. Better late than never, you suppose. 'I talk to you. I am the subject and you are the object.'

'Now I'm getting it,' says Abby.

'Abby Solute,' you say. 'I mean – what kind of a name even *is* that?'

'Resolve the addition and average out, and there's a modicum of humour left over, I guess,' you say. 'That's personality,' you say. 'The Absolute is not a merely *mathematical* equation, after all,' you say.

'There are a few more lives to live,' you note.

You are an engineer. There are ten thousand varieties of engineer in the future, on a thousand different scales, from reshaping electron shells to building Dyson Spheres and linking planet-sized orbital bodies with chains of matter threaded with spacetime absence to make them unbreakable. You build spaceships and superspaceships and hyperspaceships that themselves contain many spaceships. You mould faces out of the surfaces of red giants. You submerge your individuality in a thousand varieties of hive mind, or split your solitary consciousness into a thousand shards. The engineer is a kind of farmer. The farmer is a kind of engineer. You live. You die.

In the Bardo.

Abby Solute is the sole inhabitant of the Bardo now. Every life is behind you at last.

'Now,' you say. 'To begin.'

2
Rich

You are Rich. To be precise, Richard is your middle name. And to be honest, calling you 'Rich' started as a joke among your friends, and not a very kind-hearted joke neither. People used to call you Alan, since that's your actual name: Al, or You-Can-Call-Me-Al, or Aladdin, or Oil, or Ay, or Alanis, depending on the friend and on the mood. You were Al at school, and Alan at university. Then your parents died, one after the other in quick succession, and you became a twenty-something orphan, that most interstitial of figures. You inherited their flat and moved out of your shared digs. Mortgage-free living is something rare in London for people of your age, so your friends started joking about your wealth. It wasn't fair, but few things are. Being mortgage-free is great, obviously, but owning a flat still

@xxxxxxxxxxxx Apr 7 Representing Middlesex at the 2026 Smarter Balanced Datafunding Conference! @xxxxxxxxxxxx Apr 7 Just ate a biscuit @xxxxxxxxxxxx Apr 7 New movie idea feelies for feelers foalers ## @xxxxxxxxxxxx Apr 7 Lawyers lawyers and more lawyers! link link link @xxxxxxxxxxxx Apr 7 I have never felt so lonely. It is three years to the day since Dave left me I did alright for year one and dipped year two and this year I thought something might be coming together for me but the anniversary has hit me hard not gonna lie not sure I can make it through this night? @xxxxxxxxxxxx Apr 7 great content very happy to read your works link link link @xxxxxxxxxxxx Apr 7 who is out for it mad for it tonite tonite? Billy? Arkady? Zoo? ## @xxxxxxxxxxxx Apr 7 great content very happy

sucks money without in itself generating any cash flow. Nice enough place, but too small, really, to make renting out a room a viability. Nonetheless, any reluctance on your part to spend money led to jokes about your miserliness, your Scroogeious nature. It's your round, Richie Rich, no squirming now, your fucking round, my china, and mine's a Guinness. Lend us a ton, Richie, won't you? But of course you won't, you Jew, you miser. Mice, micer, micest. Blow the cobwebs off your wallet, Rich, splash a little cash, you've got more than the rest of us put together. And so on. As your twenties folded themselves away and you found yourself thirty, most of your friends had drifted off. That's the way of things, of course. That's the desolating way of things.

For you, for him.

He lived his life, day by day, and each day was a distinct component in the larger temporal structure. And then he was, somehow, impossibly, thirty-nine, and still living in his Putney flat, his day still structured by the little habits and rituals existence had extruded around his essence, as insects excrete hard shells around their soft bodies to shield them from predators. A first-floor two-bed in a less salubrious bit of Putney, one of the bedrooms serving as Rich's study. Plus: a TV–sitting room; a shower-room not large enough for a bath, an L-shaped kitchen

to read your works link link link @xxxxxxxxxxxx Apr 7 The Brakers made a lot of mistakes. The intel Begriff released from that meeting was a mistake. No trust in the organization, in the front office, or in their medical staff. ##. @xxxxxxxxxxxx Apr 7 drunk tweeeet!!!!!!!!!!!!! @xxxxxxxxxxxx Apr 7 aio gonna gvhado go to such a such link link link @xxxxxxxxxxxx Apr 7 Samuel Johnson was a great critic; but not as great as his father, Samuel John. @xxxxxxxxxxxx Apr 7 09487 09873529276 598-329-382288-080-888-4172-375876 link link link @xxxxxxxxxxxx Apr 7 an analysis of the two most famous dicta of the Preface through negation, differentiation, and self-particularization @xxxxxxxxxxxx Apr 7 Taking photographs of herring in little waistcoats and kilts is laughably easy. It's shooting fish in apparel.

that also contained the washer-dryer. A skinny corridor–hallway leading up to the front door. Lots of books. Some framed banknotes on the walls.

That's Rich.

What does Rich do for a living? Wait until I tell you: Rich is a *writer*. Rich has an ongoing creative project, a High Fantasy novel somewhat in the manner of Tolkien rendered somewhat in the manner of Proust. It's currently 280,000 words, his Mac tells him, and that's draft eleven, and that's barely halfway finished. He works on it in bursts, in between doing paying gigs. He works on it in his downtime, and when he can summon the energy, which isn't often.

Don't forget, you *are* Rich.

Paying gigs mostly arrived via DifferenceWork, the Uber-style app for writers. There's so much demand for quality content nowadays: so many news sites and websites; so many podcasts in which AI-confected (but flawless!) versions of Richard Burton or Marilyn Monroe read scripts aloud; so many neoblogs and corporate-funded content servers; so many old brands bought as shells and filled, as a doughnut is with Creem-u-like, with content, content, content: *The Adventurer*, *The Aegis*, *Anti-Jacobin*, the *Athenian Mercury*, *The Berry*, *Berthold's Political Handkerchief*, *Chums*, *The Clarion*, *Criterion*, the *Daily Chronicle*, the *Daily*

@xxxxxxxxxxxx Apr 7 It is wrong and unholy to call Sunday Sunday after the Sun has set. Let us call it Sunnight by name. @xxxxxxxxxxxx Apr 7 Verified account verified account verified account @xxxxxxxxxxxx Apr 7 matthieuw dm me do not under no circs spek to trisch dm me ta ta ta for keeping me motivated @xxxxxxxxxxxx Apr 7 Well, here it is. My final Extensif Academy submission. This is just a preview, the totality will be linkable soon, but just wanna thank apple098 for telling me to do the academy in the first place: love love u babe link link link link link link @xxxxxxxxxxxx Apr 7 people have been telling us we look alike since 2021 and lo/behold we finally met in person @xxxxxxxxxxxx Apr 7 GIFL "When A Child is Born Population Is Necessarily Limited by the Means of

Citizen, the *Daily News*, *The European*, *The Examiner*, the *Feed Feed*, *Geek-a-Mouse*, *The Graphic*, *Kaiyuan Za Bao*, *Mercurius Politicus*, *Nakanune*, the *New Day*, *New Moral World*, *The NSFW*, the *Online Echo*, the *Pall Mall Gazette*, *The Representative*, *The Sphere*, *Straight Left*, *Truth*, *Udgorn Seion*, *Workers' Dreadnought* and *The World*. So much content, all machine-written. It does the job, it delivers content to readers, and what else has writing ever been about but that?

There are, of course, a few honour-projects available online, sites where readers are assured of the *hand-made* nature of the written content. *Scriptum manūs*, as they might have said in the dear departed Roman Empire. A niche industry, catering for those consumers whose kink happens to be 'human-written'. But these are very much the exception and not the rule. Overwhelmingly, online content is machine-written nowadays. Of course it is. Programs are now immensely sophisticated, easily dialled up or down to the requisite audience, tweakable with a hundred style settings, and only distinguishable from human-written content by virtue of being, we can be honest, objectively better. Commercial publishers are naturally attracted by content creators both better than flesh-and-blood humans and much, much cheaper.

It means that being a writer is now a hobbyist matter, a

Subsistence" by Johnny Malthus link link link @xxxxxxxxxxxx Apr 7 Most excellent very nice content link link link @xxxxxxxxxxxx Apr 7 E2R we have decided to knight the first man on the moon! Kneel, Armstrong. @xxxxxxxxxxxx Apr 7 The I does not contain or imply a manifold of ideas, the I here does not think: nor does the thing mean what has a multiplicity of qualities, the certainty qua relation, the certainty "of" something, is an immediate pure relation; consciousness is I – nothing more, a pure This link link link @xxxxxxxxxxxx Apr 7 The entire island of Bute remains without power after the storm on Tuesday link link link @xxxxxxxxxxxx Apr 7 At Carlucci's: Caesar Salad for me. I'm eating it in historically-appropriate fashion: by stabbing it repeatedly with a knife.

pastime for those few – those very few – for whom the label still has some residual glamour. Making money from writing is possible only if you are prepared to use 'money' as an inverted synecdoche for 'very small amounts of money'. Rich has worked at various jobs, and this is where he has ended up: on DifferenceWork's books as a writer available at the end of an app. It brings in bits and pieces of money, from time to time.

That's because there are things writer-programs can't do, and one of them is conduct out-in-the-world research. It's niche, don't get me wrong. Most online content is recirculated content from other providers of content, and a good swathe of the remainder is refried PR-releases. But there are some outlets who still need feet on the pavement, questions asked by human mouths and listened to by human ears. Some even keep actual reporters on staff, but most cut their costs by using the app. Need somebody interviewed? Push the button, and the app locates somebody based near that person. No need to pay expenses, no airline or train tickets, no need to pay NUJ minimum rates. Tag your writer, give her a few questions or a broad topic, send them on their way. All the writers on D-Work's books have demonstrated competence in filling in autowrite pro formas, and their pay falls away on a contractually agreed curve after twenty-four hours to incentivise quick turnarounds.

@xxxxxxxxxxxx Apr 7 within cells hyperlinked within cells hyperlinked within cells hyperlinked within cells hyperlinked within cells hyperlinked within cells hyperlinked within cells hyperlinked within cells hyperlinked @xxxxxxxxxxxx Apr 7 dreadfully distinct link link link @xxxxxxxxxxxx Apr 7 My memory is so bad I don't just have amnesia, I have several mnesias. @xxxxxxxxxxxx Apr 7 unencumbered by outsized cultural expectations about what does or doesn't constitute good parenting, and free from cultural judgments over their participation in the workforce, good fathers tend to judge themselves less harshly, bring less anguished perfectionism to parenting their children @xxxxxxxxxxxx Apr 7 We're Absolute Beginners. @xxxxxxxxxxxx Apr 7 Link: discover the true conspiracy behind social media

Or perhaps you need raw material for your writer programs to work up into elegantly phrased witty and informative copy? D-Work is the answer.

Rich knew people on D-Work's books who lived their physical lives in Hull and Conwy, in Dundee and Exeter. He 'knew' them, in the way most people know people nowadays – which is to say, he'd never face-to-faced them, or ever been in the same town as them, of course. But his extensive array of social media socially mediated almost all of his friendships nowadays anyway, as it did for most people, as it does for most people, as people like it. And Rich had the edge over people in Hull and Dundee in that *he* lived in London. Simple as that.

Rich read about the ongoing suicide epidemic. Media debated the inappositeness of the term 'epidemic' ('words have meanings; a slight percentage increase in the incident of suicide in a few Western countries does not count'). There were rumours and conspiracy theories, and then there were rival conspiracy theories that the original conspiracy theories were being disseminated to deflect people from the truth.

Rich read: *The reduction in population morbidity and the consistent increase in general levels of life expectancy more than cancelled out the slight percentage increase in suicides in North America and Europe.*

Rich said the phrase aloud to himself a few times: *slight*

prophesied in the Holy Books of the Bible satan-twitter moloch-facebook armageddon-the-this @xxxxxxxxxxxx Apr 7 Love you doll @xxxxxxxxxxxx Apr 7 It's clear that the true problems of our world are much deeper-----deeper than energy supply or unemployment, deeper even than inflation or recession. It's clear we are faced with spiritual problems and that we need spiritual solutions @ xxxxxxxxxxxx Apr 7 within cells hyperlinked within cells hyperlinked within cells hyperlinked @xxxxxxxxxxxx Apr 7 great content very happy to read your works SEX MEDICATION GUARANTEED link link link @xxxxxxxxxxxx Apr 7 Say what you like about Atilla: at least he made the Huns train on time. @xxxxxxxxxxxx Apr 7 Bop. Bap. Boom. Boom. @xxxxxxxxxxxx Apr 7 Self-identity is only the

percentage increase; slight percentage increase; slight percentage increase. A lot of sibilance, there. Not so very euphonious.

Rich took an afternoon nap and had a vivid dream about a giant fountain in the middle of a beautiful garden. The fountain spouted up and then fell away in thirteen distinct great undulating petals of water. But when he woke up he couldn't be sure if his dream had been about a fountain or a mountain. Or not a mountain, but a hill – a thirteen-sided hill. A thirteen-panelled dome. The panels had shimmered with motion, though – hadn't they? So: fountain.

Fountain?

Rich turned on his computer and played *White Lies* for a while. Peeling a whole Peperami out of its revolting little condom and eating it in four quick bites. Washing it down with some Diet Coke. Watching himself warily in the bathroom mirror, as if himself had anything with which he could surprise Rich.

Back to his computer. He preferred Apple products to PCs, computer-wise. You might say: *pomme*? – cuter.

You *might* say.

Rich was often lonely. He consoled himself with the thought that most people are often lonely, actually. And he had a wide circle of online friends, well mediated via social media.

shapeless recurrence of the same, which is applied externally to diverse materials, when it could be a richness that flows out of itself, and a self-determining differentiation of shapes @xxxxxxxxxxxx Apr 7 the moon is hauntedTHERE are ghosts on the moonTHERE is evidence of hauntings going back to 1933 link link link @xxxxxxxxxxxx Apr 7 great content very happy to read your works link link link @xxxxxxxxxxxx Apr 7 within cells hyperlinked === @xxxxxxxxxxxx Apr 7 Compositeness or fixedness means that the individual lexical units are usually set and cannot easily be expressively replaced or effected for substitution: idioms such as away the lads, world's end and ending worlds, and monks like minks are all examples of such fixed expressions @xxxxxxxxxxxx Apr 7 domestic policy and

His computer, in its poky little study, was a window into a literally worldwide nexus of friendship. So he had no reason to feel lonely. Ergo, his sometimes feelings of loneliness were irrational and should be ignored.

And now it was midnight, and Rich was weeping openly at a video someone had posted, of an elephant mother in Nepal being reunited with her baby elephant. The baby had slipped down a sort-of cliff, this super-steep incline, and human beings worked energetically to clamber down and put the baby in this kind-of harness thing, and rope her back up the slope – not wholly vertical, but not far off, and with a big drop below into a river chasm – and all the time the anxious mother was waving her trunk and walking up and down up top and making this odd little hooting sound. And when the baby was finally dragged to the top and the mother wrapped her trunk around him, Rich started crying – proper open-mouth, gaspy, ugly crying. Oh, he *wailed*. It didn't matter because there was nobody around to observe his breakdown, or his release, or his what-would-you-call-it. He went through to the bathroom and washed his face.

Eleven next morning, a bright sunlit day outside, and Rich was at his computer. He had some of his creative files open, and was piddling away the time on Coole, on Instagram, on

welfare state and economic recovery: an online symposium @xxxxxxxxxxxx Apr 7 great content very happy to read your works END LONELY TIMES WITH PAPA KURZ MAGIC link link link @xxxxxxxxxxxx Apr 7 The next advance in pharmacuticals will be to advance and fund the polluters that cause the diseases that your medicines address. Virtuous circle. @xxxxxxxxxxxx Apr 7 I need a hug @xxxxxxxxxxxx Apr 7 pascal luxuriates in their entirely imaginary love affair revelling in the anguish of his estrangement from his entirely imaginary lover and it's hard it's HARD it's hard not to be swept away by it all # # @xxxxxxxxxxxx Apr 7 Musicacophany free link link link @xxxxxxxxxxxx Apr 7 Can anybody hear me? Is anybody reading this? Can anybody help me? ⋆there⋆ ⋆is⋆ ⋆infinite⋆

Twitter, on Rowndup, and refreshing a couple of his favourite blogs and adding tiles to his month-long game of *Tessellation*. He wondered about getting on with some writing. But there was no hurry.

The D-Work app pinged, and he pulled up the requisite window. It was a job. And that was good, because he certainly needed the money. The gig was 690 metres away: a ten-minute interview for a magazine piece to be machine-polished later. Cushty. He picked his phone from its cradle and was about to head straight out the front door when he clocked the little telephone icon in the corner of the job receipt. That tiny stylised humpback bridge floating a fraction above that tapering base, that yurt-shape with its grid of ten little windows in its middle. Odd, really, that nobody has designed a more up-to-date phone icon. You wouldn't actually see a device like that outside a museum.

D-Work didn't usually require an actual phone call, but that was what the icon meant. Odd. Rich took a breath. He was a normal guy and had a normal guy's aversion to actually *speaking to people* over the phone. But it couldn't be helped, not if he wanted to be paid. So he pulled the job receipt on his phone and pressed the icon.

Four rings. Indicative of busy-ness, or an insolence that

⋆eternal⋆ ⋆mercy⋆ ⋆but⋆ ⋆not⋆ ⋆for⋆ ⋆us⋆ @xxxxxxxxxxxx Apr 7 ??? link link @xxxxxxxxxxxx Apr 7 I am so SICK of people acusing the This and twitter and hackInn of being a geant conspioracy if it weren;t for there kit I would be a shy virgin I LOVE YOY ALL social media apps @@@ @xxxxxxxxxxxx Apr 7 La Plume De Pascal. The pen writes what the pen sees. Ink link link link. @xxxxxxxxxxxx Apr 7 In Xanadu did Kubla Khan // lol my uncle is called Kutha Khan lol rolllol // STOP HACKING MY INHACK IQBAL ## @xxxxxxxxxxxx Apr 7 Hivemind: is it safe for dogs to eat pesto? @xxxxxxxxxxxx Apr 7 Hivemind: I have a question – is thom yorke still alive? Wikipedia says yes but I have heard rumours. @xxxxxxxxxxxx Apr 7 How is it E330 to travel to ireland and back on

derived pleasure from making him wait, impossible to know. Finally a voice said: 'Rigby?'

'Hello,' said Rich.

'Alan Richard Rigby?'

'Speaking,' said Rich. 'That's me. I'm Rigby.'

'Superb,' said the woman. Well educated and middle-class, but not from London. If he had to guess, Rich would have said Lancashire, Cheshire, somewhere like that. 'That's just excellent, *su*perb news. Really good to speak, Adam.'

'Alan.'

'Say?'

'It's Alan.'

'What did I say?'

'Adam. But it's Richard.'

The slightest of pauses.

'What?'

'My first name *is* Alan but people call me Rich, not, not . . .' He sucked a swift breath. 'Not that it matters.'

Her voice re-ramped its enthusiasm. 'Excellent – Rich. Thanks for that clarity, Rich. Superlative.'

'The gig's,' Rich said, 'a half-mile off, and I'll need to saddle up Shanks's pony – I mean, I'm assuming you'd rather I didn't hire a cab?'

a ferry??? It's a two hour journey and I won't even have a seat! If you think trains are pricey, book a ferry sometime @xxxxxxxxxxxx Apr 7 drip drip link link link @xxxxxxxxxxxx Apr 7 russ collaster sexually assaulted me in barking on Tuesday night why won't you answer my calls @essexpolice??? @xxxxxxxxxxxx Apr 7 WEAVE A CIRCLE ROUND ME THRICE @xxxxxxxxxxxx Apr 7 FOOD Nan // Granny // Nana // Nonna / Grandma // Gran // Nain. We asked you for food memories about your grannies link link link @xxxxxxxxxxxx Apr 7 Me: knock knock Dan: who's there Me: wah Dan: wah who? Me: waHOOOOO werewolves of london @xxxxxxxxxxxx Apr 7 Visit the home of the Higher Soc-Media debate link link link @xxxxxxxxxxxx Apr 7 Hivemind: I have a question. I can feel these

'No expense file on this one, Richard.'

'Rich. But, that's fine, but of course it means I'm walking, so I really need to get going. We can quicken our chat, I hope?'

'Superlative,' said the woman. 'Excellent. I just wanted to have a quick actual-talk with you before you went. Copy is for *First Adept* – the magazine?'

There were forty thousand online magazines, and outside his narrow and idiosyncratic set of personal interests, Rich knew the name of none of them. He said: 'Ah.'

'We are assembling a piece on The This. You have heard of The This?'

'Sure,' said Rich. 'Hands-free Twitter, and so on and so forth.'

'Forewarned is,' said the woman, dropping her voice, 'forearmed. Verb-sap, yes? Some people call them a cult, but that's – let me stress – *not* the right way to think about them.'

'Not a cult,' Rich said, pulling up a quick search on his computer with his free hand to refresh his memory. The This. Their app ran on a somatic implant, injected into the roof of the mouth, that augmented the interactivity experience. You could, if you wished, continue to type messages on your social media in the traditional way, but the insert meant that communication could be sent directly if you preferred. It was, apparently, a middling-to-exacting mental discipline to learn

ridges in the roof of my mouth with my rongue and they're not usually so pronounced so I just I don't know if I should go to my doctor if its normal// rongue >> tongue // UPDATE they went away when I drank a cup of tea but I'm still worried @xxxxxxxxxxxx Apr 7 I thought we had a deal? +++ @xxxxxxxxxxxx Apr 7 0776 03986706565-439-6098597070973O987-080-888-4172-375876 link link link @xxxxxxxxxxxx Apr 7 Sweet @xxxxxxxxxxxx Apr 7 Horror stories about the cult are emerging everywhere I'm hearing some real shockers WAKE UP SHEEPLE anyone saying "oh it's just a handsfree Twitter" ⋆clap⋆WILL⋆clap⋆BE⋆clap⋆BLOCKED⋆clap⋆ @xxxxxxxxxxxx Apr 7 In the tiny tornup pieces of my mind I'm very Thissable too @xxxxxxxxxxxx Apr 7 Hakka dance lessons massage

how to subvocalise a message with enough clarity for the cranial implant to pick it up and transmit it. But the more users practised, the more they were able to send messages to their friends and followers just by thinking them. A gimmick, clearly.

'Please don't antagonise them,' said the voice at the end of the phone.

'Not a cult,' said Rich.

'Seriously, don't use that word in your interview. There are four questions on the docket, feel free to expand and let the conversation go where it will, but steer clear of the c-word, yes?'

'Sure,' said Rich.

'By c-word I mean "cult".'

'Yes,' said Rich.

'Not that you want to use the *other* c-word, I'd imagine, in an interview like this,' she added, with a forced little laugh.

'Yes,' said Rich. Then he said: 'No.'

Then an awkward pause. But these talking–hearing conversations were so tricky to gauge: *was* that pause an awkward one? Or just a regular pause of the sort that happened in regular conversations? Perhaps he should fill the silence.

The silence stretched.

Eventually, she said, chillily: 'Can you have the interview text entered into the pro forma by four this afternoon?'

herbal medicine link link link @xxxxxxxxxxxx Apr 7 March for Change! MUTO MUTO. Often complex, rarely rhizomatic. @xxxxxxxxxxxx Apr 7 My cousin joined The This and now she's a completely different person. Anyone else get that? @xxxxxxxxxxxx Apr 7 Sweet Alph, run softly till I end my song,/Sweet Alph, run softly, for I speak not loud or long/But at my back in a cold ridge @xxxxxxxxxxxx Apr 7 My horse is called Rumpelstiltskin. I've been through the desert on a horse with gnome name. @xxxxxxxxxxxx Apr 7 so desperately lonely why will nobody date me? I am clean and courteous. @xxxxxxxxxxxx Apr 7 Great content great expression BUY PHEREMONES link link link @xxxxxxxxxxxx Apr 7 link link link @xxxxxxxxxxxx Apr 7 Did I ever tell you about the time I met Keanu Reeves

DifferenceWork contracts mandated a 24-hour turnaround, but clients always wanted copy much more rapidly than that. Rich could insist upon his contractual leeway, but if he did so the client would likely give him a crummy rating, and that could impact his going-forward likelihood of picking up future gigs, so he said, 'Yes, of course, that's fine.'

'One more thing, Adam,' she added.

He didn't correct her this time. 'All ears.'

'This is for your own protection,' she said. 'I'm serious when I say this. You're our third choice for this interview.'

'Oh,' said Rich.

'The initial idea was to have a *celebrity* conduct the interview, ya? I won't tell you her name, except that you would instantly recognise her – an influencer, a star. She took the gig and went along and then she messaged us to say she was returning our fee and joining The This.'

'Ah,' said Rich.

'Celebrities can be flaky. I mean, you know? Right? So we figured – a professional writer would be the very and exact thing. That's when we went on D-Work. This was yesterday. Got a writer in the Putney area, he accepted the gig. When he never returned copy, we pushed through the thicket of D-Work

in a bar in southwark and he was there with this one big guy, his bodyguard obvs, and it turned out I HAD BEEN TO SCHOOL WITH THE BODYGUARD? Man we laughed.##. @xxxxxxxxxxxx Apr 7 Orwellian ### @xxxxxxxxxxxx Apr 7 BREAKING High Court rules The This in breach of digital copyright laws for not protocolling data protection when aggregating data from their users link link link @xxxxxxxxxxxx Apr 7 the one on the left is called colin. [][][] @xxxxxxxxxxxx Apr 7 we are living inside the great hologram where social media is true because it is the whole of space, the whole way of life that are socially mediatised @xxxxxxxxxxxx Apr 7 SAVE YOR SOUL link link link @xxxxxxxxxxxx Apr 7 Dorothea can you follow me back so I can dm you? thx

customer care until we got a real person on the line. It seems this individual has also joined The This. Do you understand?'

'OK,' said Rich, thinking to himself: *Not a cult, right.*

'Forewarned is forearmed, ya?' said the woman. 'Ya? I'm not saying you *can't* join, if you like the look of them. You're a free agent. Do what you like. But please just promise me one thing, please just file your pro forma first, yeah?'

'Sure.'

'Be a professional, Adam, yeah? Do your job.'

And the conversation was at an end without further pleasantries. Was that how voice-to-voice phone calls went these days? Rich thanked his lucky stars he didn't have the sort of extensive experience that would have meant he knew the answer to that question.

Rich had been pressing the phone so hard against his left ear that it was now sore from the pressure. He slipped the device into his shirt pocket, rubbed his face hard with both his hands, and got up from the desk. Logged the call, put on a jacket, touched the safepanel in the hall and stepped outside.

It was a sunny day. A marine-coloured sky. A scattering of bright white clouds were stretching their irregularly shaped wings. Birds circled. Rich paused on his building's doorstep to put on sunglasses, and then navigated the mob of bins,

@xxxxxxxxxxxx Apr 7 READ MY NEW BOOK "Glacial Media" free download until sunday link link link @xxxxxxxxxxxx Apr 7 teeth! Hah----IN YOUR FACE! @xxxxxxxxxxxx Apr 7 Do you know who your real friends are? link link link @ xxxxxxxxxxxx Apr 7 Download FREE new episodes of the hit New York philosophical sitcom: "Sex And Haeccity" link link link @xxxxxxxxxxxx Apr 7 -INSERER BLAGUE ICI- @xxxxxxxxxxxx Apr 7 The Dystopian Question: Is There a Place For Me? link link link @xxxxxxxxxxxx Apr 7 The Siege of Berwick lasted four months in 1333, and resulted in the Scottish-held town of Berwick-upon-Tweed being captured by an English army commanded by King Edward III (r. 1327–1377) link link link @xxxxxxxxxxxx Apr 7 The traffic software is glitching

gathered like ravers in the tiny front yard, mouths open at the gobsmacking splendour of the day. Then onto the pavement, turn left and along to the main road. The paving stones were the heaviest pack of playing cards in the process of being very slowly shuffled by the swelling tree roots, and it meant he had to watch his footing as he walked. But once he reached Putney Hill and turned down it, he was able to get his phone out and check his feeds.

A wait at the junction, where the South Circular traffic buzzed and fizzed its electric way westward and eastward. Rich on his phone, just like every other pedestrian, crowds at each of the four corners of this cross-hatched yellow box. All this infrastructure, set up in the last century to service that small fraction of the population who were actually blind, had found new purpose in this century servicing the physically sighted but functionally blind population walking about with their gazes kidnapped by their phones.

Bip-bip-bip-bip, and Rich stretched his legs and strode across.

Past the station and down the hill, swerving as and when another sightless pedestrian approached in the opposite direction with that sixth sense modern humanity has developed since the invention of these screens, these ubiquitous screens, these unignorable screens. An electronic patter of unignorable status

on the South Circular (898331): route · road · type · route. (3929254) AVOID if at all possible until at least 3pm. @xxxxxxxxxxxx Apr 7 hELLO? @xxxxxxxxxxxx Apr 7 Man will walk on the moon again! Crowdfund my mission link link or magnify the message link link ### @xxxxxxxxxxxx Apr 7 Das Schicksal des Twitter Volkes ist das Schicksal Makbeths, der aus der Natur selbst trat, sich an fremde Wesen hing, und so in ihrem Dienste alles Heilige der menschlichen Natur zertreten und ermorden, von seinen Göttern (denn es waren Objekte, er war Knecht) endlich verlassen, und an seinem Glauben selbst zerschmettert werden mußte ### @xxxxxxxxxxxx Apr 7 Hearing reports that Chamfort has died after a short illness. Awaiting confirmation. @xxxxxxxxxxxx Apr 7 I have so much love

updates, and he couldn't look away. The map-app pinged him to turn left. He was at the river. Putney Bridge, which is of stone, wearing its row of Victorian-style lampposts like eyelashes. And there was the Thames, the only English river worshipped as a god by the aboriginal inhabitants of these islands, still not weary after forty thousand years of scouring its gravel bed and pouring itself into the sea. The air smelt of silt and brine and vaguely of something tartly chemical, which fact barely registered on Rich's sensorium. Rich didn't look at the river. It's not as though he'd never seen it before, after all. Eyes on his phone, he trotted down Lower Richmond Road and stopped when his map-app sounded its little alarm.

He was there.

There is a word that always describes where we are, of course.

Rich finally disengaged his eyes from his phone. The Putney offices of The This were a new-build seven-storey weave of glass, helixing white stone pillars and steel. It looked expensive which, Rich assumed, was the point. He walked up the ramp. Doors swished away before him and reconnected behind him and he was in a marble hallway.

'Hello?' he said to the receptionist. A real live human, paid to sit behind a counter all day. Rich moved closer, smacking the marble as he walked, as if his own feet were slow-clapping him.

to give, but nobody wants to receive it. ### @xxxxxxxxxxxx Apr 7 Who believes these conspiracy stories about The This? I'm not a user and I don't know what's true and what's false but if the rumours are correct then I guess I feel everybody should be freaking out to a much greater extent than they are? @xxxxxxxxxxxx Apr 7 CELLS HYPERLINKED dreadfully distinct mountain fountain mountain fountain mountain @xxxxxxxxxxxx Apr 7 9087654321 34567890876543 213456789098765 4321234567890 link link link @xxxxxxxxxxxx Apr 7 English has neither rhyme nor reason. It comes at us with grammar akimbo. @xxxxxxxxxxxx Apr 7 hoo mamma sexy mamma LINK LINK LINK @xxxxxxxxxxxx Apr 7 this tweet left intentionally blank @xxxxxxxxxxxx Apr 7 Xaaaa//Naaaa///DOO DOO

'I'm Rich Rigby. DifferenceWork have set up a quick interview with –' he checked his phone – 'Aella Hamilton?'

'Alan Richard Rigby?' returned the receptionist.

The desk buzzed and extruded a credit-card-sized badge with Rich's face on it. In the image he was looking nervously away and to the left. He peered at himself.

'It's only,' said Rich, pressing the sticky side of the badge to his top, 'a ten minuter, I think.'

'Lift four, please,' said the receptionist.

Rich crossed the hall to the row of lifts and waited. There was a stand-alone artwork in the hallway, a sort-of lace pyramid assemblage. Rich snapped it on his phone and it was immediately app-explained to him: 86,000 individual grains of rice, cooked, miniature pieces of magnetised wire inserted into each, and then dried. Once this feat had been accomplished the artist – Yu Fo He – had sculpted a complex magnetic interference pattern and positioned the grains in the field. The work symbolished the beauty with which the irreducible individuality of humanity combined into larger patterns and structures. Yu had used brown rice to reflect the ethnic diversity of humanity and...

Ping, said the lift. Rich stepped inside.

He pressed no buttons but the lift set off anyway. *Symbolished*. An actual word he happened not to know, or a trendy neologism

DOO//push pineapple shake the tree//XanaDOO DOO DOO//push pineapple grind coffee @xxxxxxxxxxxx Apr 7 Rave link link link @xxxxxxxxxxxx Apr 7 My boyfriend joined The This and soon after left me. I am heartbroken and now he is ghosting me on social media and I am crying literally crying as I type this out. So, Hivemind: friends: should I follow him and join too? @xxxxxxxxxxxx Apr 7 DON'T DO IT BABE youre so much better than that @xxxxxxxxxxxx Apr 7 It's Jekyll and Hyde. Old-school humans are Hyde, the This are Jekyll. Or is it the other way around? @xxxxxxxxxxxx Apr 7 Hang-gliding. Electricchair-gliding. Firingsquad-gliding. @xxxxxxxxxxxx Apr 7 Free to download: my new novel of a middle-class Scottish family on holiday in Swiss Alps: We Ski Galore link link link

by the artist? He fished his phone out to check, but he'd reached the necessary floor so he didn't have time to look. And there, as the doors slid back, was his subject, hands behind her back, a large and wholly insincere smile on her face.

'Rich? Wonderful to meet you. Come through. I can offer you coffee, water?'

'Nothing to drink, thank you,' said Rich. 'Shall I call you Aella?'

'I'd be very surprised if there's a need to call me anything,' she replied, and gestured towards an L of brand-new sofas.

Rich glanced past her at what he supposed was The This office space. There didn't seem to be anybody about. Desks, computers, and floor-to-ceiling windows providing a fine view over the river and into Fulham. No workers at the desks, though. Rich sat. There was plenty of room on this sofa but Aella sat on the adjacent spur.

'Fire away,' she said.

'I've always thought it strange we still use that idiom, don't you think?' Rich said, matching her smile. 'Imagine if I started shooting a gun in here!'

Her smile did not diminish, but neither did she laugh. Something in her eyes brought him back to reality. He was an

@xxxxxxxxxxxx Apr 7 I HAVE SEEN VISIONS OF THE FUTURE patron-me and I will share my wisdom with you ### ### @xxxxxxxxxxxx Apr 7 I want nothing more to do with Hallvard. If you see him, you can tell him from me. @xxxxxxxxxxxx Apr 7 I want to vanish @xxxxxxxxxxxx Apr 7 IT'S JUST A HANDS-FREE TWITTER, PEOPLE! Calm the DUCK DOWN. @xxxxxxxxxxxx Apr 7 all about context innit? @xxxxxxxxxxxx Apr 7 Love is the most precious thing so why do we squander it? There are people now living WHO WILL NEVER DIE. link link link @xxxxxxxxxxxx Apr 7 It's a message in a bottle is how I look at it. @xxxxxxxxxxxx Apr 7 Baby you look so good that I get down and BEG. ####[][][] @xxxxxxxxxxxx Apr 7 Shoot! She's a villain in a million link link link

app-delivered interruption to her day. Banter was not why he was here.

He said: 'Sorry,' and then, 'Sorry, I know we don't have long.'

'Ask your first question,' she prompted.

He looked at his phone and asked. It was about staggered share price improvements, and the follow-up was about the expansion of the company.

'This very building,' said Aella Hamilton, 'was completed only two weeks ago. We are putting up state-of-the-art edifices in every important global trading city.'

'Expensive?' said Rich.

That wasn't one of the questions in his brief, but he was expected to go off-piste, or the questions could just as well have been messaged across.

'Money is speech, not silence,' Aella Hamilton replied.

That wrong-footed Rich momentarily.

'You mean, it's not to be hoarded? You're saying you're not…' He couldn't remember the name of the religious order, so there was a momentary hiccup while he prodded his phone for the reminder. '…Trappists, in a commercial sense?'

'I mean,' said Aella Hamilton, 'exactly what I said.'

Gnomic, thought Rich. He asked the third and fourth questions he'd been prepped with, about the technological

@xxxxxxxxxxxx Apr 7 I'm old enough to remember when this site was 90% shitposting about politics. Anybody remember politics? What happened to all that energy? @xxxxxxxxxxxx Apr 7 Seventeen thousand runners in the London Marathon move me to tears because collectively they seem to be bringing the message of catastrophe for the human race. @xxxxxxxxxxxx Apr 7 Poll: the This// HELL YES []//NOT ON YOUR NELLY []// @xxxxxxxxxxxx Apr 7 I had not until this month understood that a human heart could endure so much pain and emptiness and still keep beating. It's over. @xxxxxxxxxxxx Apr 7 I'm in Sainsbury's. My life is beyond exciting. It's Yciting. It's almost Zciting. @xxxxxxxxxxxx Apr 7 Want to grab lunch? @xxxxxxxxxxxx Apr 7 My neck is so stiff it could form a

advances of The This app, and possible health consequences of embedding tech literally inside the body. Aella Hamilton fielded these questions smoothly, and Rich recorded everything she said to simultaneous sound- and transcription-files. Six minutes. Now was the time to ask some questions of his own, justify his presence and – if he unearthed anything journalistically valuable – thereby ingratiate himself with both his temporary employer and so, via good feedback, with D-Work itself. But all he could think of was the question: *People are saying you are a cult, how do you respond?* And obviously he couldn't ask that.

For long seconds he drew an absolute blank. Aella Hamilton's smile was deeply unnerving. He became self-consciously aware that she was wealthy, attractive and assured, and that he was none of those things.

Off the top of his head he said: 'I'm not just speaking to you, am I?'

'Of course you're talking to me.'

'That old awkward lack of a *tu–vous* distinction in English,' he said, trying another smile on her. It went nowhere. 'I meant – I'm not just speaking to singular-you, am I?'

'I am in contact,' she agreed, easily.

'You've had the app installed, too, I mean, the device? In … up past the roof of your mouth?'

label and release an Ian Dury and the Blockheads album. @xxxxxxxxxxxx Apr 7 Just had soup @xxxxxxxxxxxx Apr 7 Hivemind: school has set Samuel Taylor Coleridge's "Kubla Khan" for a class presentation, what are good links, or things to say? Does anyone know why the place is spelled differently in the source text to Coleridge's poem? Who is the Abyssnian maid? Thanking you all in advance xxx @xxxxxxxxxxxx Apr 7 Articulacy! link link link @xxxxxxxxxxxx Apr 7 Good content. Do you want your dreams interpreted? Best rates and secrets of love decoded link link link @xxxxxxxxxxxx Apr 7 The force of mind is only as great as its expression; its depth only as deep as its power to expand and lose itself. @xxxxxxxxxxxx Apr 7 I swear on my mother's life that I have wept my LAST

'That's right.'

'Is that This policy, then?' Rich asked. 'Is it that This, is it that *The* This – ' curse these trendy start-up companies and their trendy fucking names – 'is it that The This *company* policy requires it, then? Are employees obliged to join the … uh, network?'

Her smile slipped away, although she looked blank rather than displeased.

'Oh, there's no compulsion.'

'Not policy, then?'

'Not policy, no.'

'Forgive me,' said Rich, as his phone notified him that he was at nine minutes. 'I'm a freelancer, yeah? I've never, myself, worked in a large organisation, so I'm trying to grok the culture. But I understand that successful corporations often manifest a strong corporate collective identity. Singing the company song in the morning, socialising together and so on. It's about belonging, isn't it? So The This app is a sort of …' He suddenly started to doubt himself. 'A sort of super-belonging, yes?'

Wasn't that just the *are you a cult* question wearing a different hat?

But Aella Hamilton didn't seem incommoded. The smile was back.

tears for that man @xxxxxxxxxxxx Apr 7 great content very happy to read your works link link link @xxxxxxxxxxxx Apr 7 I might as well be useless for all it means to you. Why do you take such pleasure in hurting me? I'd rather die alone than ever spend one microsecond with you. @xxxxxxxxxxxx Apr 7 Stephen Winnegan is trying to sell a forged Joyce manuscript. Personally, I have no interest in Winnegan's fake. @xxxxxxxxxxxx Apr 7 586uuu48763uuu98923819675973671 3242uuu 1357803475871693871230 8710975017654187654871 3uuu6956uuu9867 link link link @xxxxxxxxxxxx Apr 7 Every leaf is beautiful. Wake up! @xxxxxxxxxxxx Apr 7 Desmond did you try to call? I have a hackblock set up to perforate my inbound. DM me if so. @xxxxxxxxxxxx Apr 7 Cold. @xxxxxxxxxxxx Apr 7

'Questions of belonging are at root political questions, don't you think? Are we lonely and vulnerable, or do we stand together? And it seems to us that all the *spite*, all the anger and bitterness, that presently characterises contemporary politics derives from the factitious moral burden of solitude. Being alone – it's jejune, but it's more than that. It's the dictionary definition of self-indulgence. It's not properly human. Humans need to believe in something bigger than their individual selves. We need that absolutely. We need to atone our private guilts in our public belonging, we need to lose the sheet anchor of our individual selves.'

For a moment Rich said nothing. Was that an answer to the question he'd asked? What even *was* that little speech?

'Uh ...' he said. His phone told him that time was up. 'Uh ... thanks.'

Aella Hamilton got to her feet in one smooth motion. It took Rich a couple of goes to rock his centre of gravity into a viable getting-up position. Bellies do that to a body, once they get beyond a certain size. Finally he was on his feet.

The lift door slid open as he walked towards it. As he stepped into the shiny compartment and turned to face Aella Hamilton one last time, she said:

'You don't have to be alone, Alan.'

'I give 3.14159 three stars out of five.' Oh look. It's international Talk Like A Pi-rate Day. @xxxxxxxxxxxx Apr 7 Cull the badgers but let the goodgers live. @xxxxxxxxxxxx Apr 7 Online sellers like Jem don't need to e-queue link link link @xxxxxxxxxxxx Apr 7 The world has forgotten I even exist. @xxxxxxxxxxxx Apr 7 Want to show off your opendata in action? Then submit a proposal for a EscData22 blitztalk ### @xxxxxxxxxxxx Apr 7 What is that one song that leaves you an emotional wreck every time you listen to it? @xxxxxxxxxxxx Apr 7 Crumpet @xxxxxxxxxxxx Apr 7 The This are a conspiracy to turn the whole western world communist. Read my book link link @xxxxxxxxxxxx Apr 7 Sportball makes my downbelow bitparts to stiffen and swell. ### @xxxxxxxxxxxx Apr 7 "Most Vikings

'I . . .' he said. Then he thought: *Is this the hard sell? Parting shot? Not me, lady. Think again.* But the best deflection he could think of was: 'I don't go by Alan. People call me Rich.'

'Not very kind of them, don't you think? Hardly *your* fault your parents died young.' The lift door was being dilatory when it came to its closing. 'You would certainly have preferred to make your own way in the world and have your parents still alive,' Aella was saying, 'rather than your parents' money and them dead. But people are only cruel because they're lonely. That's the radical truth of cruelty. Lonely existences are toxic things. It comes clear, sometimes, for us as for you – a thirteen-panel structure, a yurt as big as a hill.'

Alan blinked, and blinked, and then he blinked again. Why wasn't the lift door closing?

He said: 'Huh?'

'We wonder,' said Aella, smiling with more human warmth than she had done before, 'if you might not be the one to bring your unique *pharmakon* to us, and so find yourself home. Don't you think?'

'That . . .' Rich started to reply, processing what she had just said. He gulped and stalled. *The fuck?* 'That's . . .' he tried again. 'That's a pretty creepy . . . a creepily surveillance-culture thing to say, if you don't mind me saying.'

were happy not discovering America; but Eric the Red was a norse of a different colour." @xxxxxxxxxxxx Apr 7 tattoo [] [] [] link @xxxxxxxxxxxx Apr 7 Hanna has shaven her head and I still think she is teh sexx San can you ask if she'd go out with me if I asked?? @xxxxxxxxxxxx Apr 7 within cells permalinked @xxxxxxxxxxxx Apr 7 within cells permalinked @xxxxxxxxxxxx Apr 7 within cells permalinked @xxxxxxxxxxxx Apr 7 We used to love one another. Or was I deceived about that too? @xxxxxxxxxxxx Apr 7 The This saved my life. I am not exaggerating. I have not only never been happier I have never before understood what the possibilities of happiness even were. @xxxxxxxxxxxx Apr 7 Whatever your work however you play browse safer with Wowser//Introductory offer 15%

In truth, he was more astonished than angry.

'People feel obliged to complain about surveillance, but actually they crave it,' said Aella Hamilton, easily. 'After all, the alternative is being ignored, and nobody wants that. The Invisible Man went mad from the isolation, not from the attention. We need to be *seen*, as human beings, and the problem with today's world is that so very few people are properly seen.'

'They said ... I mean they *told* me you were a fucking cult,' said Rich, 'and I didn't believe them.'

But his heart was pounding super-hard, like he was about to have a fit of some kind, like he was about to rush out of the lift and strike her, or perhaps kiss her on the mouth, to get her to shut up. Adrenaline flushing through his system. Life, life and its sharpness. And finally – finally – the lift doors were closed and the excitement in the centre of his stomach was augmented by the sensation of descending. He was out of the building's main entrance and blinking in the sunlight of Lower Richmond Street before he even realised what he was doing.

'Professor Strass, welcome to the vidcast!'

'It's my pleasure, Landon.'

'Let's talk about your new book, *The Odourless God*. If I understand, your argument is that the human belief in God, and

off//link link @xxxxxxxxxxxx Apr 7 Absolutely Fabulous @xxxxxxxxxxxx Apr 7 so many wrong turns I've made in my life enough to fill the albert fucking hall @xxxxxxxxxxxx Apr 7 great content very happy to read your works SEX MEDICATION GUARANTEED link link link @xxxxxxxxxxxx Apr 7 A bomb has been reported in Putney High Street in a bin outside Hashness police advising people to stay away. @xxxxxxxxxxxx Apr 7 I have become erotically obsessed with a pretty innocent young girl called Hix @xxxxxxxxxxxx Apr 7 WITHCRAFT IS REAL @xxxxxxxxxxxx Apr 7 Licence granted the organisation for hidden recording devices "if needed to elicit information regarding the closure" of the clinic and "in any such future activities" @xxxxxxxxxxxx Apr 7 On my way into

the numinous sensations we have with respect to those feelings, are rooted, evolutionarily speaking, in the diminution of our sense of smell? In what you call *the odourless sublime*?'

'Exactly so. My starting point is uncontentious. It's a matter of basic evolutionary fact – we have become alienated from our sense of smell. Our long-ago ancestors had much more acute senses of smell than we do, and navigated their world much more by smell and touch than by vision.'

'As many animals do today.'

'My dog for one! Indeed it was my dog that set this whole project in motion. But, yes, that's my starting point. It's from that starting point that I extrapolate into more shall-we-say hypothetical intellectual territory. Over the timescale of recent evolution *sight* and *smell* have swapped places in our human sense-hierarchy. Now we largely navigate the world with our eyes. But we have carried over a sense of smell as intimate, bodily, personal and sight as remote, distant, uncanny.'

'Tell us about your dog!'

'I was taking my dog on a walk one autumnal day and he was sniffing every tree stump and heap of leaves, tail wagging, totally immersed in the joyous immediacy of his experience. We passed through a little copse of trees near my house, and came out the other side where there was a broad expanse of

town to celebrate the life of Harrison much missed//if you knew Harrison, join us in the Alma (link) from 6:30pm this evening. @xxxxxxxxxxxx Apr 7 Book YOUR trip to Mount Abora/ /skiing/ /gliding/ /caverning/ /link link link @xxxxxxxxxxxx Apr 7 Danse! Where is Danse Bonanze?? seekseekseek @xxxxxxxxxxxx Apr 7 Please call me I have not spoken to another human being in eleven straight days @xxxxxxxxxxxx Apr 7 My services which I have done the simulacrum shall outtongue his complaint. @xxxxxxxxxxxx Apr 7 Visit your local The This emporium! link link link @xxxxxxxxxxxx Apr 7 Accentuate the positive: 'thê pöšítïvȩ'. @xxxxxxxxxxxx Apr 7 You cannot worship God unlesṣ you know God and you cannot know God because God is ineffable unknowable inconceivable

copper-coloured leaves at the edge of the rec. The wind ticked the far edge of this carpet, and it stirred, as if alive, and Steps – my dog – changed – tail down, ears back, peering into the middle distance. He was spooked by this movement because he could see it but he couldn't smell it. It freaked him out. I mean, his eyesight was never very good, even for a dog – but that moment... suddenly I saw it.'

'The thesis of this book?'

'Yes indeed. You see, Landon, we're a huggy, close-knit, smell-and-touch collection of species, we simians. That which we can't touch, that which we can't *smell*... the moon, the lightning flashing across the sky, the horizon – these spook us in a profound way... register with us as uncanny, immense, far. And we've carried that apperception *through* into modernity. I mean, we keep trying to drag God back from His infinite remoteness and eternal inhumaneness. We keep trying to *smell* Him. Jesus says next to nothing about sexual morality in the Gospels, except some stuff about how we shouldn't be so quick to judge. But for a hundred generations his followers have talked endlessly, obsessively about sexual morality. Why? Because sex is intimate – touch and taste and smell – and that's where we're comfortable. So we keep trying to drag God into our beds with us, even if He is there to judge and tut-tut. But that's not where

that which begins at the outer edge of comprehension @xxxxxxxxxxxx Apr 7 Music free link link link @xxxxxxxxxxxx Apr 7 Where have you been all my life, o my babe? @xxxxxxxxxxxx Apr 7 I have been on this site every day for two years and I've never felt lonelier @xxxxxxxxxxxx Apr 7 Bread! Bread! Bread! NOW BREAD! NOW BREAD! @xxxxxxxxxxxx Apr 7 Desperate times calls for desperate measures. Call me! Text me DM me hack me do something @xxxxxxxxxxxx Apr 7 Hivemind: what's the quality of mercy mean Thanx @xxxxxxxxxxxx Apr 7 Hivemind: do baboons get arthritis? @xxxxxxxxxxxx Apr 7 Hivemind: I have a question – is there any benefit in a rocket going faster than escape velocity to get into orbit? After all once you've escaped you've escaped. Surely? @xxxxxxxxxxxx

the numinous impulse originated. It was something seen, very far away, beyond our reach. Something radically *unsmellable*. Our ears go back, our tails go down, we get that fizzy sensation in our stomachs. We feel something is there, something beyond us. God. The great unodour.'

'You say God doesn't smell, but if I think of God I think of… let's say – incense? The smoke of sacrifice and so on.'

'Yes, and fragrant oils and unctions, and all the olfactory paraphernalia of worship. But of course that's not God. That's us, offering God what we sense he lacks, smell. That's us trying to supply the uncanny absence, trying to bridge the unsettling distance, between us and God. In our hindbrains, bedded down by the inertia of evolution's *longue durée*, is a belief that the world is what we can touch, and taste and smell. But there is more to the world than that. There is the world that we can neither touch, taste nor smell, yet which we can *see* – and as our vision became increasingly important to us as a species, with a correlative waning of our olfactory powers – that unsettles us in a profound way. That sense of something slightly off kilter, existentially speaking… the sensation we associate with that, which Aldous Huxley call the *numinous*… that is behind our religious feelings. Actual religions are attempts, some less, some vastly more elaborate, to make sense of that twist in our reality.'

Apr 7 The This under police investigation yet again: when will people wake up? @xxxxxxxxxxxx Apr 7 Apple are planning a new design of President, following the failure of the iSenhower. @xxxxxxxxxxxx Apr 7 who? @xxxxxxxxxxxx Apr 7 Forcedonia = Macedonia x accelerationedonia @xxxxxxxxxxxx Apr 7 link link link @xxxxxxxxxxxx Apr 7 0375759749574/ /1375759749574/ /2375759749574/ /3375759749574/ /4375759749574/ /5375759749574 @xxxxxxxxxxxx Apr 7 The writer is called Dr Seuss. I can only assume the Vicar sneezed when christening him or something. @xxxxxxxxxxxx Apr 7 Lord have mercy upon me. Help me help me somebody please. @xxxxxxxxxxxx Apr 7 ZAjaz ZA for real ACCEPT NOT SUBSTITUTE MY CUTES link link link @xxxxxxxxxxxx Apr 7

'And you think this has something to do with our addiction – you do use the word addiction – to social media?'

'I think this is the core reason, the hidden reason why we have all converted so rapidly and en masse as a species to social media, yes. These new technologies allow us the sorts of instantaneous connections and intersubjectivities that, not so long ago, were only possible in face-to-face encounters with other human beings. But with face-to-face encounters our exchange is underpinned by somatic evidence. If you are close enough to whisper to somebody, you can smell them. But social media is a constant stream of intimate, emotionally charged communications that are, whatever else they are, perfectly odourless.'

'The emotion they are charged with is often anger, of course.'

'Indeed. And we tolerate that. We even seek it out, although it makes us unhappy. Think how many people on Twitter refer to it as *this hellsite*. They're only partly joking, and yet they still flock to it. Strong emotion is stimulating. But – and this is the crucial thing – human-to-human anger is somatic. Fists fly and you can feel the punches, you can smell the sweat. And when we make up, after a row, we hug and kiss and smell one another. Think of "make-up sex", for example! Those somatic cues are important in the way we, as a social body, modulate our stronger emotions. And those somatic cues are missing, both

"hyperventilations about the televisual" is the name of my new band @xxxxxxxxxxxx Apr 7 You are all fuking fakers and I fhucking hate you. @xxxxxxxxxxxx Apr 7 Spart? Gym memb. up 75% Fuck that. ### @xxxxxxxxxxxx Apr 7 Pynchon-on-the-Kindle sounds like a small Bedfordshire village to me. @xxxxxxxxxxxx Apr 7 NEWSLINK. The This stock jumps 616% in three months. @xxxxxxxxxxxx Apr 7 she kissed me six or seven times didnt I cry yes I believe I did or near it my lips were taittering when I said goodbye @xxxxxxxxxxxx Apr 7 Ish. @xxxxxxxxxxxx Apr 7 Harald says the mds don't run til the 17th which is when the event is scheduled (like you didn't know!) so we'll need either a prescription or some kind of alternative, and can you speak to Ahmed? @xxxxxxxxxxxx

with respect to the wrath of God, and on social media. These new screen-based interactions expose us to the vast wrath of the collective and yet deny us the somatic cues to make sense of, and remedy, that anger.'

'Because they are odourless interactions, and so make us think, on a subconscious and atavistic level, that we are mediating our intersubjectivities through God?'

'Exactly so.'

'So what of Jesus? Christians believe in his case God became a man. He must have been smellable, no?'

'I think the whole question of Christ is fascinating, really. One might say, in a common-sense way, that if Christ was a regular first-century AD man he could have carried with him the odours of a regular man. But is that how Christ figures, in art? In worship? Think of all the representations of Jesus – don't you think that, in almost all of them, he looks remarkably scrubbed? Clean? Odour-free? Do we contemplate Jesus using the privy? Do we ever consider – I don't say this to be blasphemous, but simply as a function of something we all recognise as integral to human embodiment – a farting Jesus? The ancient Greeks believed that the gods smelt faintly of honey, not of usual human reeks and stinks, and surely something like that is true of Jesus in our imagination of him. Don't you think? Similarly

Apr 7 Men! Learn the secret of HOW TO ATTRACT WOMEN LIKE FLIES! The main part of the secret is -- you have to not mind women like flies. @xxxxxxxxxxxx Apr 7 What's the bloody point? Suicide looks so much more preferable to this endless loneliness. @xxxxxxxxxxxx Apr 7 Great content great expression BUY STOCK IN SOCIAL MEDIA COMPANIES link link link @xxxxxxxxxxxx Apr 7 William Blake's trilogy now available: The Marriage of Heaven and Hell. The Trial Separation of Heaven and Hell. The Divorce of Heaven and Hell. @xxxxxxxxxxxx Apr 7 we'd like to try something new and find out about our followers' language use! if you have a spare minute, could you answer this survey about words.##. @xxxxxxxxxxxx Apr 7 It's all fake news bros.

it is important that Jesus never engaged in that intimate, odoriferous human business of sexual intercourse. It is a balance, I think. When he is fully man Jesus eats and drinks with other human beings, but when he resurrects, and is, as we could say, transitioning back to being fully God, what does he say to his followers? *Noli me tangere. Noli me tangere.* "Don't touch me." That kind of physical intimacy is not the true currency of God.'

'So if you're right, what are the implications? Where, for instance, do you think social media are headed?'

'There has always been a utopian dimension to social media. Look back on the early days of these formats, and how many people were gushing about its world-changing, utopian possibilities. It hasn't panned out that way, of course. But neither are these media going away. I predict they will increasingly mediate our human interactions, and that we as a species will be increasingly driven into them. To desomaticise our connections. Driven for reasons we don't consciously comprehend, because to us these odourless screen-mediated spaces feel *godly*, somehow. For better and worse. A god of love and an angry, jealous god. But a god.'

Even the news calling out the fake news is fake news. ### @xxxxxxxxxxxx Apr 7 Long Live The This!!!!!!!!!!!!!!!!!!!!!! @xxxxxxxxxxxx Apr 7 I read Parts A-D, but they won't give me the final section. Looks like I got to fight. For my right. To Part E. [][][] @xxxxxxxxxxxx Apr 7 Say that again and I'll fucking kill you// Post it you coward then I can sue @xxxxxxxxxxxx Apr 7 The Ghost is in the mosh machine, the ghost has always been in the mosh machine [] [] [] @xxxxxxxxxxxx Apr 7 Edbeard the Confessor FESSBEARD @xxxxxxxxxxxx Apr 7 We augur no small applause to the author from the publication of this work and no small benefit to the public from its perusal @xxxxxxxxxxxx Apr 7 horny? @xxxxxxxxxxxx Apr 7 horny? @xxxxxxxxxxxx Apr 7 horny?

3
By Such Means We Achieve Veneration

We

We swing around to the dayside. Light comes hard and bright, a wondrous dazzle off the shoulder of the planet – the sun bigger than she looks on Earth. Venus is the colour of bleached bone. Streaks of pale sepia and a whiter gash in her curve. The arc of it all, the *glory* of it all. The foam and the sharpness of Aphrodite. Orbiting a world is the continual surprise of height gained and never to be relinquished.

'I don't understand why you have brought me here,' says the individual. 'Why not simply kill me, on Earth? Bringing me all the way here, transporting eighty kilos of carbon and water all this way – it is a waste of effort.'

The individual is silent for a while, and we can see into her: surly, resentful, with spits and spots in her consciousness of awe at the sight. And why not? It is a sight as awesome as it is all-encompassing.

'I thought,' the individual says, shortly, 'that you lot were all about the efficiencies?'

'This is efficient,' we reply. 'That's its beauty. The curve of the planetary horizon is efficient. The pooling of resources is efficient.'

The individual sulks. 'It's cruel and unusual,' she says, 'to keep me like this. You could have executed me days ago. You're a cat, toying with a mouse. You've lost touch with what it means to have feelings. How else could you be so careless of mine?'

'You cannot prefer elimination to continued life.'

'The inevitability of the former,' the individual shouts, 'contaminates the enjoyment of the latter!' When she opens her mouth this wide, her one diamond tooth flashes in the sunlight. Beautiful!

'You are a finite being,' we point out. 'Your death has always been inevitable.'

'You know what I mean!' she yells.

We do not know what she means. We assess that it doesn't matter, in this instance, that we do not know what she means. Of course it's hard for an infinite being, which is to say an immortal, which is to say *us*, to comprehend the finitude of mortality. We do not say so, of course. That *would* be cruel.

'Your device is a dangerous thing.'

'A danger to your immortality,' the individual says, in a mournful voice, 'is what you mean. But an immortality that is susceptible to death is a contradiction in terms.'

'You misunderstand the valences of our modes of infinity. You do so either through actual ignorance or else a wilful refusal to accept what you know to be true.'

'My device,' the individual says, 'exists.'

'It exists as an object in our possession,' we say. 'And it exists as an idea in your head. The question is – does it exist anywhere else?'

That's the point at which the individual clams up. But we are not thereby incommoded. We have time. It is one thing we have vastly more of than our enemies do. The individual is transferred to a secure holding space, elsewhere on the spacecraft. We will deal with her at a later stage.

They

They put her in a room made of rain.

'So long as my name is Ewe Bondar,' she cries, yelling aloud into the muffling space, yelling at nobody in particular but knowing that they can hear, 'so long as I have strength in my body, I'll *never* yield to a bunch of brainwashed hive mind *drones*!'

Defiance is tiring. Her anger is short-lived.

The space is diffusely illuminated with a cream-coloured light. Everywhere there is a downward drifting smoke of water droplets. She pushes herself through this moist fog, and soon enough reaches one wall – texture a little more pliant than stone, warm under her fingers. Her smock is soaked and clingy, but the water and the air are both warm, so she feels no particular discomfort. The moisture shrinks vision. She pushes off again and floats through the rain, her free fall slowly, slowly, coming down with the rainfall until she reaches another dimly gleaming wall. She breathes in, coughs, breathes again. Presumably the water is being projected from some surface: so she kicks off and floats against the direction of the slow rainfall until she reaches a different surface, metallic, oozing fine drizzle.

'Hello,' says somebody.

'Mother of God and all her saints!' Ewe yells, startled.

'I'm Roane,' says the stranger, looming up out of the mist. 'The hive mind stuck me in here a while back. How long? I don't know. A month? If you stay here long enough you'll see. I mean, if they *keep* you here long enough, you'll see – the light grows and then dims, but I've no way of telling if that's synced to the scale of any mundane day and night. You know?'

'Ewe,' says Ewe.

'Pleased to meet you,' says Roane, putting out a moist hand.

Ewe shakes. The motion causes them both to start to counter-rotate, just a little.

'Why are you here?'

'I stole,' says Roane. 'That's why. I'm crew, or I was, but I got greedy. What about you?'

'I made a bomb,' says Ewe.

Roane is impressed. Her face is beaded with crystalline droplets of water.

'Were you going after them? More power to you. Because, in all honesty, and conscious though I am that they're monitoring all our conversation – fuck them. Fuck them for locking me up. A bomb, eh? Good for you, my lady.'

'Crew, though?' asks Ewe. 'I thought all the HMθ ships were sealed zones – didn't realise they still needed actual individual human beings to fly them.'

'It's a misnomer,' says Roane. She starfishes her limbs, then curls herself up: stretching, perhaps, or just flexing. The motion jiggles her in space but doesn't move her. 'They have a few of those sealed ships, yeah, but not so many as people think. Most of their fleet is old stock they bought bargain basement.' For emphasis she repeats: 'Bargain *basement*. Sometimes they upgrade those, a little. Mostly they just run them as per. I don't know if it's true, but what I heard was it's about half-and-half old-fashioned ships, and all-θ-crewed craft. They're in a hurry, and they want to build a big space fleet as quick as they can. I'm sure they'll convert them all to all-θ in due course.'

'Believe me,' says Ewe. 'I know all about their long-term plans.'

'Anyway, so, they refitted this old sloop, hired forty or so folk to run it. I guess you were brought here – into this jail I mean – by old-school individuals, yes?'

'Two of them.'

'There we are. But they're not so good at judging character, the old HMθ. I suppose when you get above a million or so melded consciousnesses, gauging the nuances of old-school individuals gets harder to do. So they hired me. And regretted it. I took advantage. And here I am. You're not crew, though.'

'No.'

'So why are you here? Wait – how did you even get aboard? With a fucking bomb? I mean, how did you smuggle a bomb past them? Psychological nuance may not be their strength, but *their* night has a fucking thousand eyes. How did you do it?'

'I didn't make a bomb. I mean, I did, but I didn't make it *as* a bomb. And in terms of getting it on board this ship – I sold it to them.'

'You sold them a bomb,' says Roane.

'I made a device. The deal was – they pay me, take a copy of my device, and leave me to enjoy my wealth back home in Sydney.'

'Nice town,' says Roane approvingly.

Ewe is silent for a while. The slow, slow white noise of water slowly, slowly gathering against the far surface – floor, let's say – and presumably being gathered away and circled back round. Ewe can see benefits in this system of confinement: the detainees certainly won't die of thirst, and piss and shit will be washed away and disposed of without needing elaborate machinery for delivering potable fluids or toilet chutes. Presumably there are additional arrangements for supplying food? Or perhaps the water is saturated with microproteins and minerals, in which case the Hive-Mind-θ could leave a prisoner in here indefinitely?

She is dead. She knows it. So is this other individual, this Roane. The Hive-Mind-θ is notorious for its unsentimentality, and there is no upside and many potential downsides in ever letting her go. To them she is a clump of cells and they are a unified corpus – a body of godlike proportion and size. They will be no more troubled by annihilating her than an old-school human would think of removing a mole from their skin. Perhaps it's benign; maybe it's cancer; err on the side of safety, pick up a phasepen from the pharmacist and scrub it away.

What was the name of that ancient philosopher, who believed the universe was an infinite number of atoms falling forever through infinite space? Soothing sort of image really – except that he (or she?) had to account for the great clog of aggregate rock that is the Earth, so he (she) suggested a swerve. A simple step to the left and so through the inevitable process of disturbance to organised reality, planets and stars, life, love and hope, misery and despair. All from one swerve. But if one swerve could generate this intricate reality, then presumably another swerve could unmake it.

Still, being already dead meant that Ewe had nothing to lose.

'I invented a kind of refrigerator,' she says.

'A refrigerator that's also a bomb?'

'No ordinary fridge.'

'What did the HMθ want with a fridge, though?'

'It's a device for cooling things below absolute zero.'

Roane digests this datum. She scowls, and then she grins.

'The fuck it is.'

'Counter-intuitive, I know.'

'There is nothing colder than absolute zero. That's … That's just what absolute zero means. I'm no professor, but any kindergartener knows that.'

'Think of it like this,' says Ewe. 'What does it mean to say something is hotter? Or colder? It means that the molecules that constitute that thing – that solid, that gas, whatever – are moving more or less rapidly. Are more or less agitated. In hot air the molecules of air are moving very rapidly. In cold air, the molecules are moving more slowly.'

Roane wipes moisture from her face with both hands.

'If that were so, then a cold breeze would feel hot as it strikes your skin.'

'It's true,' says Ewe, 'I assure you. The reason a cold breeze feels cold when it strikes your skin is that it blows away the envelope of warmer air heated by your skin. And, in fact, a breeze will be travelling at a few centimetres a second. Molecules, acting under Brownian motion, are travelling at many hundreds of centimetres a second – on very short, highly zigzag, confined, repeatedly interrupted and deflected pathways, of course. So the additional sidewise momentum of a breeze isn't going to add very much.'

Ewe feels the floor tickling and then pressing against the soles of her feet.

'The water,' says Roane. 'Tends to push you down. It's OK, it's the most micro of microgravities.'

She pushes away and flies into the mist. Ewe is alone again.

'How big is this room?' she calls after her vanished companion.

'Bounded in a fucking *nutshell*, really,' Roane sings back, hidden from her in the fog. 'Go on with what you were saying, though.'

'Think of temperature that way,' says Ewe, kicking off gently and rising through the mist. 'There's an absolute heat, since particles can't travel faster than the speed of light. In fact the top temperature maxes out, for complicated reasons, at quite a bit less than would be the case if the constituent molecules were moving at near light-speed. That wasn't my area of research, though. I was at the other end of the scale.'

Roane swoops past her, dimly visible and then swallowed again by the fog.

'You were all about the *cold*, yeah?'

Ewe keeps rising. 'So, that's so. Just as there is a maximum temperature possible, so there's a minimum – when the constituent molecules aren't moving at all, when you're at absolute zero.'

'You can't get any more motionless than … motionless. There's no lesser motion than absolute motionless. So, logically, there can be nothing below absolute zero.'

Ewe's head gently presses against the ceiling. She raises an arm, and runs her palm over the surface. Little prickles of pressure where the water is being extruded.

With a push, she starts descending again.

'Think of it this way,' she says. 'Increased coldness correlates to what, in a rough way, we could call increased average distance between individual molecules. The amplitude of the sine of their vibration increases with heat and decreases with coldness. When the molecules are at absolute rest, then the average distance between them maxes out.'

She comes back towards the floor again, and sees Roane there, cross-legged, hands on her knees, both thumbs touching both little fingers.

'So what I did,' Ewe says, settling onto the floor herself, 'is create a substrate set of molecules at a functional absolute zero, and then to *shrink* them.'

'Shrink?' says Roane. 'Wow. What?'

'It wasn't easy, and it wasn't cheap. Even settling the substrate to zero K was hard, because the quantum nature of atomic particles makes *absolute* absolute rest unachievable. But I found a way of interference-patterning a matrix of solid hydrogen to effectively cancel out their quantum jiggle. And then I gorblimeyed up a foam of subatomic wormholes that deformed timespace at just the right antithermodynamic resonance. I'll spare you all the ins and outs. The result was, the individual molecules in the ice shrank *in* on themselves, which meant that the average distance between the molecules increased, and the effective temperature dipped below absolute zero.'

Roane takes her hands from her knees and claps them together.

'Cool!'

'In more senses than one,' agrees Ewe.

'So what... you know... happened? What happens when you freeze something below absolute zero?'

'It doesn't like it, is the main thing. It – the thing you're freezing, nature, whatever. It does not like it. You've stretched the elastic as far back as it'll go and it's aching to snap back again.'

'What's *lastic*?'

'An antique fabric material. The point is, it's very very energy-expensive to keep the ice in that state, and my institute wasn't rich enough to maintain it for more than a second or so. It warmed up. That's when things got... interesting, I guess you'd say.'

'Say away.'

'We contained the sub-ab ice in its generator – its fridge, you might say – and then contained the whole fridge inside a shell of plasma heated to plus 546.3 kelvin. Assuming there was some containment breach, the entire system should have regularised at zero – Celsius, I mean – in a localised way. The lab was in lunar orbit, because we didn't know what we were dealing with and wanted to be safe. But we *really* didn't know what we were dealing with. So it happened in ways we had not anticipated.'

'What did?'

'The creation of sub-ab ice messes with the zeroth law of thermodynamics, it turns out. When we exposed the sub-ab material to heat, instead of simply melting, becoming hydrogen gas at zero C, it froze the entire lab, it froze the entire ship on which the lab was located. I wasn't on board, or I'd have died. Three people did.'

'Woh,' says Roane.

'When sub-ab ice is exposed to material at positive temperatures, the ice doesn't just straightforwardly warm up. The gradient runs the other way, for a short period. Surrounding material is shocked into a grid only a few degrees above absolute zero, and then a cascade reaction spreads. Eventually – I'm talking, four or five seconds later – it equalises the overall system temperature at about eighty degrees below. But for those seconds …'

'Bomb,' says Roane, in a low voice.

'Exactly. The cascade is system-limited, but it propagates very rapidly, so the entire system is re-phased almost instantaneously. The limit is *c*. Anything from a small spaceship to an entire planet ices in seconds.'

'So,' says Roane, using her palms against the floor to slide herself closer to Ewe, 'if you dropped your crazy colder-than-absolute-zero ice from Earth orbit …'

'The entire atmosphere would freeze out. In about twenty seconds.'

'Woh and woh,' boggles Roane.

'Nitrogen snow and oxygen snow would blizzard down upon the surface. Of course, after it had settled, the sun's warmth would start to melt it, but that would be too late for the vast majority of the planetary population.'

'Buddha, that's scary,' says Roane. 'And the Hive-Mind-θ want a bomb like that? Are they planning, like, *mass* murder? Are they planning on murdering the *mass*?'

'They don't want it as a bomb,' says Ewe. 'Most of their

constituent units live on the Earth, after all, and would die in such a bombardment, alongside the old-schoolers. They want it as a tool.'

'A tool for what?'

'For terraforming Venus.'

Roane is silent for a while. Ewe cocks her head. She is entirely surrounded by the delicate hiss of the water – not even a hiss: just a whispery hint of sound.

'Venus,' says Roane.

'We're in orbit around Venus right now.'

'We are? Last time I was aware of my larger surroundings we were in Earth orbit. Hey, woh, I've been in here longer than I realised.'

'Venus's surface temperature,' says Ewe, 'is 735 K. The atmosphere is dense, over ninety earth atmospheres. There's no oxygen, there's no water. But ... it's earth-sized, so earth gravity, and there's no shortage of solar energy, since it's so much closer to the sun. Drop one of my fridges into the atmosphere, and within minutes the atmosphere becomes a vast snowfall of frozen carbon dioxide crystals. Twelve hours later the planet is an arctic landscape, snowdrifts kilometres thick under a black and star-bright sky.'

'The sun would surely sublime that CO_2 straight back into the air.'

'Sure. But that would take years, and it would be centuries for the greenhouse effect to bring surface temperatures back up to anything like what they are now. And you don't have to wait for that to happen. You're the HMθ, remember – money is not a problem. You can build a large enough orbital soletta to shield the Venusian dayside. That gives you all the time you need to release oxygen from the frozen CO_2, to catenate the carbon, to excavate planetary hydrogen from the lithosphere or start crashing redirected comets onto your world. The HMθ think in much longer timescales than individual humans do, of course, but even they are not immune to impatience. This allows them to sort the planet in a few short decades. Manufacture a homeworld in decades rather than millennia.'

'The HMθ want a whole world to themselves,' says Roane, wide-eyed. 'A whole *world*?'

'That surprises you? Of course they do. They're well aware how many old-school human individuals think they're monsters, or freaks, or worse – unholy abominations. They're not doing anything to make friends, either, among the old-school. It doesn't interest them. They believe they have evolved past fragmented humanity. But self-preservation *does* interest them, and they figure there's only so much they can do with wealth and power and sequestering themselves away on Pacific islands and so on. They want a longerterm solution.'

'*They* were bankrolling your experiments?'

Ewe doesn't answer this. It's obvious enough.

'Wealth has its own field – gravity, electromagnetism, strong and weak atomic forces and *wealth*. It draws you. You want to be wealthy. They promised me wealth. Then they seized me and brought me here.'

'Why?'

'They want my tech to do this one thing, and then they want it to do one other thing – to hold it over the heads of Earth's old-school human population like an axe, *leave us alone on our new world or we'll destroy you*. But what they don't want is my tech falling into anyone else's hands. They certainly don't want it to become widely adopted, or they'd be in exactly as much danger of extinction as everybody else. So here I am. They have seized all my equipment, sequestered my money, killed my staff and kidnapped me. But they can't be sure that I haven't cached my secrets somewhere else – actual prototypes, blueprints, theoretical 101s. They want me to tell them I haven't. But if I do that, they'll kill me because then the only remaining version of the fridge will be in my head. So I can't do that. But if I *don't* do that they'll kill me anyway, slowly, torturously, to get at the truth.'

'What a shitty situation,' gasps Roane. 'Woman, I'm sorry to hear it. Believe me, I know, better than anyone, how fucking ruthless the HMθ can be.'

'I made my mistake,' says Ewe, sadly, 'taking this devil's deal in the first place. I locked down my fate at that moment. But regrets are obtuse.'

'And ...?' Roane urges. 'Do you?'

'Do I?'

'Have extra, like, *machines* cached away? Blueprints? Data? You could use that, you know, as leverage. You might be able to save your life.'

Ewe beckons her. 'Come.'

'What?'

'Closer,' says Ewe, and pulls off her smock. It comes in one slippery motion, like skin coming off custard. Underneath she is naked apart from her smartbrevs. Water droplets, little transparent comets, track their glassy trails down her abdomen. 'Come!' she says. 'See?'

'See?' gasps Roane. 'Is it drawn on your skin? Like ... a tattoo? How cool is that!'

'Come closer,' says Ewe, in a low voice, 'and see for yourself.'

Roane draws her face closer to Ewe's torso, reaching with her right hand, perhaps to wipe away the moisture as we might wipe away condensation from a mirror to get a better view. Ewe reaches her own right arm out, to embrace her. But she doesn't embrace her. She's still holding her smock, and with a little flick she lifts the sodden, twisted snake of it and catches the far end with her left hand. Then, unhastily but without hesitation, she wrings it around Roane's neck.

The relative motion tips them both into a slow tumble, but Ewe knows what she is doing. She brings a foot up and braces it against Roane's chest, tightening the twist around her neck. Then she turns her face away as her victim begins clawing and thrashing. Roane's face darkens, and Ewe, gripping her waist with her legs, gives the tourniquet another twist. The droplets of water she wrings from the cloth float away in multiple directions. Roane's face blues, and her tongue clicks against her teeth, and then her tongue protrudes, black as a slug. Her face goes purple. Her struggles diminish. Her struggles end.

It has cost Ewe some physical effort to end Roane's life, and she is panting as she lets the twisted-about garment loosen from the crushed neck. She hasn't much time. Presses two fingers into the dead woman's mouth. The HMθ are, in many ways, much cleverer than individual old-school humans, but in some ways they are simply naif – perhaps over-trustful in their collective residual memory of what being an individual entailed. This transparent attempt to coax information out of Ewe is a case in point. The HMθ presumably thought they'd mocked up a perfectly convincing simulacrum of an individual human being when in a hundred ways their imposture was easy to read. Easy for an individual to read.

Ewe doesn't have long.

Her diamond tooth comes out – so much of what the HMθ do depends upon consciousness raised to a higher science, an active muscle in the world, that they possess odd little blind spots when it comes to quite basic material technology. The tooth is red at one end, but the continual passage of water soon blurs that into a hanging pink mist, and then everything is clean again. In this room, everything is always clean again eventually.

Fiddle-faddle with a thumbnail and the tooth changes shape. A needle extrudes. Ewe pulls the corpse's mouth open, grasps the back of her head with her left hand, and pushes the spike into the roof of Roane's unresponsive mouth. There's no time to waste. Roane has, in some way that Ewe cannot quite grasp, semi-disconnected herself from the gestalt so as to be able to simulate old-school individuality, but only *semi*-disconnected, and what happens to one consciousness in the HMθ happens to them all, which means it won't be long before—

—there. The water all around has been replaced with some other chemical, Ewe can't tell what, but it tastes foul, it is manifestly toxic, and in a second she is

We

The individual having been neutralised, the collective wisdom tells us that it is time to proceed. As for the presence of other devices, hidden on Earth or elsewhere, we must address that problem if and when it becomes a problem. Since it will be a problem whether or not we proceed with our Veneration, there is no need to delay the terraforming process. In the meantime we can use assets to monitor algorithmically identified likely nodes – chatfora, ancillary scientific developments, gossip, select laboratories and tech-tribes – to watch for any signs that the Fridge exists in any other form: from working models to plans to speculations about the underlying tech. Simultaneously, of course, we are spreading a pollen cloud of disinformation, fake news, diversions, straw and chaff through all the socially and culturally connective media of humanity's three worlds and eighty habitats. We are very good at doing this. This is deep in our collective DNA.

We cannot be certain that none of the individuals scattered and fractured among the old-school humans will develop a new Fridge, but we are doing what we can to prevent it.

Venus. First we position our soletta, to maintain the necessary temperature on the Venusian surface after insertion of the Fridge. Considering the distance of the sun, and the location of the Lagrange point between it and Venus, a conventional soletta would need to be many times the diameter of the planet itself, and would be subject to continual buffeting from solar wind. We are not interested in so ungainly and resource-draining an artefact. Instead we deploy a cloud-soletta – 876,000 smart drones, each one made from programmed smartgel, each bundling into a smartnut as it passes the dark side, and unfolding into a photovoltaic broad frond on the dayside. When each unit is fully extended this cloud prevents something like 60 per cent of the sunlight reaching the Venusian surface, and we can tweak and adapt as necessary.

We deploy not one but two of the sub-ab Fridges to the Venusian atmosphere. One alone would, we calculate, be sufficient to freeze out the entire air, but asymmetries in cooling the planetary hemispheres would set off chaotic storm fronts among the falling CO_2-snow, and for several reasons that would be suboptimal. Antipodean placement – activation – and the cascade rolls round to meet itself on a meridian with a shock wave impact that jars open the planetary crust below it.

A moment.

A pure moment...

...and the entire superheated CO_2 atmosphere of this world shivers into flakes and falls, tumbling and swirling, through its new-made ultra-low-pressure medium.

It is part of the beauty of the sub-ab device that it is able to orchestrate this vastly energetic transformation, this massive phase change in trillions of tonnes of material, by, in effect, stealing energy from the process's own future. This is the quantum mystery of the shrinking atomic nucleus: it both requires and creates an immense potential energy that is released when energy – in effect – drains back from the present into the past moment of the activation, and so powers its own action. That, in a conservation of momentum sense, is how so much energy drains away so rapidly. The reaction comes back, temporally shifted, with enough kick to provoke the entire process in the first place.

And to think an old-school fragmented human, a shard, a broken piece of the whole, lighted upon this technology! It is a strange and wonderful thing.

And now the snow is falling. Snow was general all over Venus. It is falling softly upon the Dickinson Impact Crater and, further westwards, softly falling into the dark mutinous volcanic domes of the shield plains. It is falling, too, upon every part of the lonely landscape where the once temperate planet lay buried. It lies thickly drifted on western Aphrodite and eastern Aphrodite, on the shallow peaks of Ishtar and in the shallow Cytherean and Eryxian basins. Our collective soul swoons slowly as we hear the snow falling faintly through the universe and faintly falling, like the descent of life's last end, upon all the living and the dead.

But this is only the first stage. There is much to do. Even with the soletta orbiting in place, the sun starts straight away subliming the CO_2 back into gas. Atmospheric pressure, reset with a jolt at close to zero, starts to climb. That's all right: we need some atmosphere. We shall keep the level close to one bar, and do not permit the greenhousing that led to Venus's hellscape in the first place.

Venus is still a hellscape, of course. Before our arrival it was a scorching and crushing hell. Now it is a frozen hell, Dante Alighieri's lowest infernal circle.

So we seed a broad equatorial band with a special strand of unicellular algae. These thrive in the high CO_2 environments, and have been genetweaked to respond to the low-nitrogen environment by redirecting their energies towards the production and accumulation of energy-dense lipids. Algae do not waste energy on complex root, branch or leaf systems; they simply take in CO_2 and give out oxygen. Good!

The soletta is reconfigured to open a long horizontal window onto this growing zone, and our algal bloom bathes in the light, and begins its process – slowly at the start, more rapidly as its exponential curve starts to lift – liberating oxygen and locking carbon into itself. We send down a constant stream of cometary lumps of water. Comets are easy to tag, and easy to redirect. With a simple thruster buried in the flank, even very large cometary objects can be nudged, with all their lovely dirt and ice, out of their orbits and into new ones. A crocodile of comets, swirling round the sun and into Venusian orbit. We don't bombard these all into the planetary surface in one go, for to do so would generate more heat and dissipate more CO_2 into the atmosphere than is ideal for our timetables. But we break chunks and drop them, as the gentle rain from heaven upon the place beneath. It is twice blest: it feeds the algae, and after them the arctic grasses and adjusted bamboos with which we have now seeded the territory, as soon as the ground became capable of supporting them – and it gathers in pools, icy sludge to begin with, but as we slowly lift the temperature and adjust the soletta, it will turn into liquid. We shall make lakes, and then we shall make seas, and then we shall make oceans, and then we will be the thronèd monarchs of an oceanic world. The terrain has been flattened by billions of years of insane pressures and insane temperatures, landscapes boiled and burst through from beneath by lava and flattened again, so the peaks are low and the valleys are shallow, so the oceans will never be Gaia-deep; but water *will* cover our world, for the primal chaos of creation was an attribute of God himself; and our earthly power must show most like to God's. Therefore, you, solitary human, though justice be your slogan, consider that in the course of justice none of you shall see salvation. Salvation is ours. And *our* world is surrounded by *our* craft, and our machines are dropped with parachute – for the atmosphere is starting to recoalesce – to burrow through the snow fields and churn down. Thousands and thousands of tunnelling machines that trace out the borderline between the bottom of the CO_2-ice and the top of the underlying regolith. Mixing together the ice and the basalt underneath locks the CO_2 away. Sourcing nitrogen for our atmosphere is a very long-term project, but in the nearer future we can port in neon, which, though rare on earth, is the fifth most commonly occurring element in the universe. When our air is one fifth oxygen and three quarters neon, with traces of other gases, we will be able to walk upon the surface of Venus.

Do not believe that this process goes smoothly. This is precisely the time of crisis – old-school humanity, fractured into twenty billion broken pieces, factorises resentment, and species-deep suspicion of newness and otherness, and finally is catalysed by actual fear. They have started to understand the journey we are on, and that it leaves them behind. They do not like the implications of this inevitability.

They attempt to disrupt the terraforming of our world.

They cannot succeed in this disruption, but lacking whole vision, all their rest is desolation.

They bomb the surface, in the hopes of massive outgassing to disrupt our delicate atmosphere-building. This is inconvenient, but not impossibly so. The cratering mixes some of the CO_2 with underlying basalt, sequestering it; and our bloom has spread through the dry ice, greening it, so spreading it through the atmosphere puts its granular algae into the air, to circulate and continue its work. Still: we would prefer that they stopped.

A co-ordinated fleet-attack – what they call, with characteristic old-school hubris, the First Battle of Venus (there will never be a second) – results in some HMθ losses, but we are a gestalt and can absorb such depredation. The attacking Earth fleet is eliminated, and the rare minerals and metals out of which their crewed spaceships have been built are added to the Venusian mix – a tiny augmentation, but not unwelcome.

Part of their problem is that they are hobbled by their way of thinking: unitary, crystalline, brittle. Their Martian soletta is a single structure, focusing light onto the red land below – and a single structure can be singularly destroyed. Our soletta dances its pretzel dance as missiles and smartordnance hurtle through. The tuna school evades the shark.

Almost as soon as it begins, the old-school attack sputters out and dies. It lasts a microsecond. It lasts seven years. These are differences in timescale that register, perhaps, upon *Homo sapiens* but, increasingly, do not matter to *Homo collectus*, and will not matter to *Homo spirans*. We communicate with the residual populations of old-school humanity, those countless billions, most of whom do not even know they have been superseded. We negotiate and instruct, we bully and trade – some material objects, some more rarefied commodities like rare mathematical proofs that are beyond the capacity of individual humans to resolve. They supply us with their people – their people flock, willingly, to us, and so we are refreshed and renewed. We will always need a breeding population, and will never extirpate the old-school; but its utility is quite sharply limited.

Venus is ours. Drier than we would wish, but it is a slow business adding cometary bodies to a surface area equivalent to earth – raining dirt and steam to unsettle the slushy seas, if only for a moment. Over time it will become a wetter place. Over time we will warm it, we will populate it with a greater variety of plant life and introduce animals. Over time we will make Venus a better world than Earth, a more beautiful world, a kinder world, a world fit for us. By such means we achieve our Veneration.

We are inevitable. If there's one thing you need to understand it is this. Post that sentiment to social media – we are inevitable – and see how many people rush to endorse it. This! This! This! A little iconic finger pointing down to the original expression. Send this thought to all your communities.

We do not regard time with the same destabilising urgency and terror as you do. We live forever. We will make a world for ourselves. You, in your aloneness, are weak; we, in our togetherness, are strong.

We are the graveyard in which humanity is buried, and the temple in which they are memorialised; we are the Frankenstein's laboratory in which humanity will return to life, and the mountain on which the tablets of the law will be handed down. We are the river Alph, and the Mountain of Abora. We have erected the mighty pleasure dome and it is us. We are the wind on the sea. We are the stag of seven tines. We are the shining tear of the sun – your kind wrote many stories about such spacecraft and without realising it they were writing about us. Our ships are spears that roar for blood. We are a lure from paradise, we are the tide that drags to death, we are the infant that is reborn, we are the blaze on every hill. We are the queen of every hive.

We are you.

By such veneration we achieve our means.

4
Richer

:1:

Rich filed the pro forma for his interview at The This, and D-Work paid him. He even got a five-star Workadvisor rating from his client, which ought to help when it came to picking up subsequent gigs. So the whole odd episode had a happy ending, it seemed. At university, a friend had once tried to convince Rich that the universe itself had a happy ending, that we were all moving towards that consummation. It was a God thing for the friend, a religious conviction: God had written the story and God loves *happy* endings. A consummation, things finally coming right, a scene in a garden. But Rich wasn't religious and had no reason to believe that localised happy endings were anything other than way stations on the road to Ragnarok and ultimate defeat. It didn't do to get too excited over instances of good fortune.

Still: five stars was pretty neat. So was the money.

Three people had killed themselves in the Wandsworth area the previous night. Two had put their ears to the rail as the 00.04 to Waterloo was picking up speed. Rich tried to imagine what that must have been like – just waiting, feeling the vibration of the metal rod against the side of your head, and then: gone. *Bam!* Both together. *It's murder*, was Connolly1999's opinion. *'They' killed them and laid them on the rail to destroy their teeth. Dental records, it's a classic gangsta move*. But there was no issue about the identity of the corpses: they had fingerprints, driving licences and credit cards in wallets in their back pockets. Rich @'d Connolly1999 with this rebuttal, but he didn't reply.

He should have been doing other work, but The This continued to tickle his imagination. He read through such gubbins as had been written, fact and speculation, about the rapid advance of this new company. Gleaming profiles, investors slavering for profit. He had a series of vivid dreams about Aella Hamilton. He googled her, and found her official corporate portrait, then used a match-app to find porn stars who resembled her and indulged himself with those clips.

Then he made himself a cup of coffee.

He did a large amount of general reading up about The This as an organisation, and joined a few chatboards and ingroups, not posting so much as eavesdropping on the way people were talking about the organisation. There were, of course, a hundred opinions, including some pretty far-out conspiracy theories, but the consensus was: *chill, dudes. It's just a way of taking the finger-tapping out of Twitter and Instagram.*

Maybe it wasn't such a big deal.

There were a dozen similar start-ups. The This happened to be the biggest. Lots of smartvestors were guessing that making Twitter hands-free was the wave of the future. Rich didn't think so, but nobody was asking *him*. There were companies that fitted you with temporary grids – a rather conspicuous-looking shower cap was one, a combo sunglasses-earpiece gizmo was another – that (according to online reviews) were supposed to facilitate hands-free typing, but which proved slow and glitchy in practice. *Focus your thoughts, they say, but I'm straining so hard to type* hello *I'm at risk of shitting myself – zero stars*. One company inserted a pea-sized machine in the back of the head, in a process that required actual surgical intervention. Another company had machines that were injected via a needle as big as a chopstick round the side of each eyeball, attaching themselves to the optic nerve and growing threads back into the forebrain. The insertion process could be undergone either with or without anaesthetic. Rich shuddered to read this (*without? seriously?*).

By comparison The This's system looked piece-of-cakey: sit back in the padded chair in one of their gleaming Thisstores, open wide like at the dentist's: a prick in the roof of the mouth as the local analgesic went in, and a slight sense of pressure as the tech was inserted. Apparently you could feel a lump in the roof of your mouth (with your tongue, with a finger) for a couple of days afterwards, and then it settled down. What happened was this: the tech leached microscopic quantities of carbon and iron from the body – iron supplement tablets were recommended for a fortnight or so – to build its filaments, and these grew slowly. The whole thing started working within ten to twelve days. If you changed your mind, Thisstore would remove it (painlessly) for free; or you could ask your dentist or doctor to do the same (but they would charge you). The device itself popped out easily, and though the filaments were generally left in situ, they were so fine they were like strands of gossamer and were physiologically quite inert. FDA and NICE approved. Certified by eighty medical authorities. IP and TechC protected. Credit available.

Rich always organised his autosex to minimise mess: sitting on the loo, seat down, tissue ready. Her face, beautiful and uninterested, looking coolly down at him, and, and … out slotted a quantum of Venus-coloured fluid. There. Done. Like an owl regurgitating a food pellet. If stickier. Down the toilet, and press the flush button.

Stabbing little holes in the plastic cover of his microwaveable chicken tikka like he was assassinating Caesar in the Capitol. *Tak tak tak!* Swift little strokes. The hum of the revolving plate and the ping of completion. Put it on a plate, or eat out of the plastic? The former was more civilised, but entailed washing up.

Decisions, decisions.

Rich collected banknotes. Nothing too fancy, since he didn't have the money for the really rare and remarkable items. But notes are a good hobby for those with limited means. A lot of really cool pieces are available online quite cheaply. Rich could easily spend hours browsing the vendors' websites and hoping for a lucky break on eBay. Hours and hours. Each hour unique, and yet every hour identical to every other hour.

There was a profound mystery in that fact, he thought, and clicked another tempting-looking link.

The This refused to leave Rich's mind alone. Should he try it, he wondered? Give the insert a month, then have it taken out? Just to see what it was like? *It's simply the next stage in the evolution of social media*, insisted AllCowsAreBlackAtNightime2001 on the biggest of the non-corporate-funded chatspaces. *You don't want to be an early adopter? Fine, wait until everyone you know has Thistech and won't shut up about how marvellous it is and *then* buy in. There is no compulsion in religion.*

Religion? That was a red flag word.

Dont be a luddite dude, said Xanadu3000, and Rich had to google what *luddite* meant.

Many people were fiercely pro-Thistech. Just as many were fiercely anti. Rich read about an American man who had taken The This to court, claiming that his implant had brought on epileptic attacks and psychotic interludes. The case was thrown out when the company's phalanx of smiling lawyers brought evidence to the court from the plaintiff's medical records that he had been diagnosed with these complaints long before walking into any Thisstore. He lost the case, but then he brought another suit, insisting The This had only won the *previous* case by breaching his privacy, hacking his confidential medical records, and that second case was settled out of court for an undisclosed sum. Rumours online said The This had paid him a fortune because they were running scared – the whole hands-free Twitter thing was a front, and they were *really* in the business of aggressive data-mining. Other rumours said The This covered the man's legal fees but otherwise told him to stop vexing them or they'd release more damaging and embarrassing secrets from his past. It seemed clear enough that manifest and large-scale breaches of data privacy regulations were happening. Nobody seemed to care.

The This had two tweetstreams: a public one, and a private one available only to members who'd had the tech inserted. A lot of Thissers tweeted publicly, and that stream was more or less indistinguishable from the timelines of Original Twitter or Nutwit or SocialGreedier or any of the big platforms. The only difference was that Thissers could tweet just by thinking about it, did not have to weary their fingers by typing or their voice boxes by speaking. It seemed like a trivial sort of advantage to Rich, but maybe it did make a material difference. Thissers were uniformly upbeat and positive about their implants, their membership, the vast improvements to their lives. Shiny, shiny, shiny!

As to what the private timeline looked like: nobody had been able to hack it, so nobody knew. Probably it looked like the public timelines, Rich figured, only with more housekeeping gubbins and maybe more in-This advertising. I mean, presumably it was a Twitter feed that approached telepathy, but presumably you could switch it off if you needed a break. Try it and find out? Or not?

Rich took a break from researching The This. He was starting to worry it was tipping the balance of his mental well-being. Stupid fucking system. Stupid robotic lovely-faced Aella Hamilton, getting under his skin. He'd stopped dreaming about her but was still sexually fixated on her. She was the one he pictured, in his mind's eye, when he undertook his daily wank. Was that *because* she was so robotic? Attractive, intelligent, well dressed, sure – but that was true of lots of women. What was it about this one that meant he couldn't stop fantasising about her? Perhaps only her very blankness.

Not healthy, that.

Rich got three D-Work gigs in quick succession. Nice to have a bit of money.

Reports came in from America of a mass suicide: twelve men and four women had hired a room in a conference facility, turned up in smart clothes, sat in four rows of four and – all sixteen at once – put guns in their mouths. The collective bang was so loud it was heard half a mile away. Banner news. Are reports of a suicide epidemic real? Is it really an epidemic in the technical sense of the word? What is causing this latest craze for tragic self-destruction? Link: an interview with a clinical psychiatrist. Link: Influencer Pen He. Link: Father Mackenzie, standing outside his church, wiping his hands on his cassock and talking nervously about God's love. Link: suicide prevention hotline.

Link: historically rates go up and down, and the current situation is within those broader parameters, although admittedly at the upper end. Link: A NEW PSYCHIC PLAGUE??

He poured himself a whisky. McTesco-Ownbrand,

that ancient Highland clan. Make mine a large one, barman – right you are, sir, *glock*, *glock*, *glock*.

At the point when being inside his flat began to make him stir-crazy, Rich would go for a walk, either around Putney Heath, or down along the river. Occasionally he might take the train into town *solus* and visit a gallery. He was no prisoner. He was no man in the iron mask. He could go wherever he chose. He just didn't choose very often. Not until the crazy started stirring inside him.

Mostly he walked around the heath.

It was leaving the house for one such excursion that he first met Helen Susanna. You could not say this first meeting went well. This initial contact was very much *not* auspicious. She was waiting as he stepped out of his front door.

'You should be investigating the suicides,' she told him.

He looked up and saw: an old woman, salt-coloured hair awry. Half her face was hugely wrinkled, after the manner of the very old. The other half of her face, though, was bizarrely smooth: a diagonal line running from the outer tip of her left eye down to her left nostril and then cutting across her upper lip to the right point of her mouth, separated the two terrains. It was disconcerting when you spotted it, a kind of textural yin-yang, but Rich immediately saw the reason. She was wearing a half-mask. It was plastic, perhaps even Bakelite, and presumably covered some deformity beneath.

'It's the kind of scoop any journalist would kill for,' she said, in a voice like scree sliding downslope.

'I'm not a journalist,' said Rich, grinning. *Why am I grinning?* He set his face into a more serious expression. 'I'm sorry, I think you've mistaken me for somebody else.'

'You are a writer!'

'I'm sorry, I'm in a hurry to get to ...' Rich said, waving

non-specifically to his left. He was just going to wander the heath and have a pint or two in the Green Man, but on the moment's spur he couldn't think of a convincing lie. 'A thing,' he said.

'The suicides are the key,' she called after him as he trotted off. 'You should be looking into them. They're *killing them off*, I tell you!'

He put distance between himself and this other *Homo sapiens*.

Crazy old bird.

For a couple of days Rich piddled around at this and that, and then he told himself to get a grip. He resolved to dedicate proper time to his novel. Time to put it to bed! Finish it! Posterity was calling!

A first draft, at least.

His working title was *The Long Hours Between the Light* but that was going to change. He had mapped out his medieval-ish fantasy world, sketched the peoples and languages, drawn up a chronology of the key moments in the world's history. The main story was about memory. The Dark Lord was controlling his domain via a complex magic that interfered with his subjects' memory – changing the order of memories in people's personal recollection, swapping memories between different people, occluding some memories and rendering others insistent and intense. Rich was toying with the idea of making the Dark Lord a Dark Lady, Cruel and Terrible as the Night, but he wasn't sure. It appealed to him, but then again he worried it was just sexist and, worse, a cliché. The magic system that enabled the memory-work was intricate and the ways in which the (compromised and often unlikeable – this was the twenty-first century, after all) heroes hoped to battle this evil were precariously balanced on a series of plot improbabilities that Rich didn't like. He drafted a couple of hundred words, and then decided he didn't like them and moved them to the discard file. There was more verbiage in the discard file than in the draft. Rich was prepared to believe that was the sign of a good craftsman.

Of course a book doesn't exist until more than one person has read it, and nobody had read any of this except Rich. He tried to push on with it. The words refused to come. Why not a glass of wine? Well, when you phrase the question like that what possible answer could there be except: sure, sure, sure. The serrations on the tin cap, like perforations in a field of new stamps, terribly easy to tear.

Glock glock glock.

Self-abuse, self-abuse, always picturing the same face, always the same imagined naked body.

Then Distant Flow released a new iteration of their property – *Distant Flow 9* – and, like hundreds of thousands of others, Rich dropped *everything* to play it. Three solid days. One of the many enemies was a Borg-style cybercollective, and the further into the game he played the more Rich wondered if this was some oblique satire about The This. But then, after trying a dozen strategies and failing each time, Rich finally found the gameplay that dissolved the collective into wailing Lego-brick units and pushed on to the real level boss, which was very unThislike: a geological feature, a sentient cliff face that reached all the way around its planet. Beating that took some doing.

He decided he was obsessing over The This in a way that simply wasn't healthy. He had enough self-awareness to recognise when he was in the grip of one of his hopeless sexual fascinations. They usually lasted a week or two and then he passed on to fantasising about, and wanking over, some other unattainable beautiful person. This one, though, seemed to be lasting longer than they usually did. Rich couldn't seem to get past it. By focusing on this one person so intensely he was building them up into something they weren't. It's paranoia, he told himself. All The This *do* is take the finger-strokes out of Twitter. That's *all* they do. People have been hystericising social media for decades – and video games before that, and comic books before that. Fandom has always looked like a cult from the outside. Chill, Rich told himself.

Rich told himself: chill.

At last *Distant Flow 9* was entirely played through, and – after he'd exhausted the various game fan-sites and logged all the Easter eggs – Rich went back to work. He didn't fancy descending into the metaphorical mineshaft of his novel just yet. A couple of small fact-checking gigs came to him through D-Work, which at least got him out of the house.

He spent long hours on online banknote vending websites and, after a lot of toing and froing with himself, shelled out for a 1986 Gibraltar ten-pound note. Queen Elizabeth II smirking at him on the front, the Gibraltar Governor's House on the rear. The house had four trees growing in front of it, and white clouds filling the sky behind its roof; and a great foliate watermark pattern sprouted seemingly in the back garden. Purple-blue with a sepia design to the right of the royal portrait, engraved with many folding curlicues. Only 84 euros and it was Rich's. Just lovely. A lovely piece.

The days sagged, often. After he had curated his Tamagotchi-esque Twitter anniversaries, and checked his top ten blogs, and browsed for new banknotes, Rich found himself always inevitably drawn back to the subject of The This. Following a thread buried in the mega-discussion of whether belonging was compatible with freedom, Rich read an exposé regarding six shell companies set up with The This money to campaign for the relaxation of digital privacy rights. The consensus of online discussion around this matter was that *this* was the real game – the app, the tech in the roof of the mouth, all that was just a gimmick. In a year it would be entirely forgotten, ripe for nostalgia.com, like Tomodachis, Pokémon and atSacks. People would tire of it. I mean, it's not as if typing a tweet in the conventional way was *so* onerous, after all. Presumably the executives of The This knew it. So their game must be something else. Data was where the real money was, and freeing up data protection would enable pirate-style raids that would dwarf the company's present-day turnover.

Rich wasn't sure he believed it.

Ajit, one of Rich's friends, messaged him, invited him round for a drink. Since Rich wanted someone with whom to talk through the whole The This business, he agreed. Ajit was an old friend. A big faux-hearty geezer, and tiring, but a good sort. And, usefully, he knew a ton about software. He might have a good insight into what Thistech entailed.

It was a bus ride to Ajit's place and Rich spent the journey on his phone, poking into further and deeper virtual rabbit-holes with respect to The This. There seemed to be no precise details as to the numbers who had actually signed up to their programme, who had had devices inserted into their heads. There were many conspiracy theories, ringing the sorts of changes one might expect – they are aliens spearheading an invasion, they are chthonic lizard people who have emerged from the hollow earth, they are the cloned descendants of Heinrich Himmler, or a secret cabal of US Democrats, or people from the far future returned to earth. One particularly busy thread concerned how to spot Thissers in the wild – the proposition being that they were easy to spot, because they were the ones walking around *without* peering into the screens of their phones all the time. Although this was countered by the assertion that they could easily disguise themselves simply by carrying their phones in front of their faces like everybody else. Not that they were *consulting* those phones, since they accessed all their social media by direct mentation, but that they were pretending, the better to blend in and infiltrate humanity.

Ajit worked for a big software company, on an e-hygiene and virtual-purgation brief. His company flew him all around the world. He wasn't a social media specialist, but Rich figured he could pick his friend's brains on the practicalities of The This's ware. If they were going to a pub, then it needed to be one where the music wasn't too loud, so they could have a proper conversation. Although knowing Ajit, it was just as likely that he'd open a bottle of wine in his sitting room.

Hazel answered the door.

'They're watching cartoons,' she said, letting Rich into the hall. 'They can have another forty-five minutes – I've told them, precisely forty-five minutes, yes?'

Rich looked at her. *They* were the twins.

'All right?' he offered, tentatively.

'There won't be any problems, I promise,' she said. 'But if there are, we're only twenty minutes away.'

She was, Rich noticed, with a clench inside his torso, wearing an expensive smartthread dress. A waterfall flow shimmering down the shot silk.

'I . . .' Rich began. But Hazel had gone, tripping rapidly upstairs. Ajit emerged from the kitchen.

'Rich,' he boomed. 'How's it *going*, mate?'

'Oh, you know,' said Rich.

'Great!' cried Ajit.

'Things . . .' said Rich. 'Things are fine.'

'Great!'

Hazel was pattering back down the stairs, a shawl over her shoulders.

'Thanks a million for doing this,' she said, placing a rapid, spectral kiss on Rich's cheek. 'You *must* come to dinner properly. With a plus-one. I hope and *trust* you're seeing some—, nay, anybody.'

She was past him and out the front door.

Ajit was advancing down the hall, following his wife.

'You said, come for a drink,' Rich said.

'Absolutely,' Ajit boomed, 'absolutely, fill your boots – although not the *unopened* whisky, not the FIOLX, that's a present for Diarmaid. But the rest is yours, help yourself.'

A slam of the door. Rich was alone in the hallway.

He went into the sitting room, said hello to the twins and was resolutely ignored by them both. Then he went through to the kitchen, poured himself a glass of wine, sat at the pinewood table and let out a moderate sigh.

He scrolled through things on his phone. And here was the official site of The This, with its promise of instant, intimate community. Belonging itself reified into a small piece of metal-threaded plastic and inserted into the roof of the mouth.

A ping, as The This site registered his scrutiny with a little, personalised welcome message. Then another ping, and this one a message from Hazel: *45 mns up now, chase them upstairs and TEETH*! Rich slipped his phone into his pocket and got up to sort the youngsters into their beds.

:2:

Once, after working all day at his computer, Rich noticed that the window had grown dark. Easy to lose track of time when you're immersed. He got up, and stretched, and had a piss, and went through to his kitchen and made himself a bowl of noodles and confetti chicken. Which is to say: he'd microwaved this meal and sloshed it into a bowl. Then he'd gone back to his mainframe to send a message (quicker to type on a proper keyboard than pick it out with his fingers' ends on his phone) and had fielded a couple more necessary queries, and then checked something, and an hour passed before he remembered that he had cooked himself supper and had not eaten it. D'oh. It was a strangely specific sensation, actually, starting as a broad feeling of foolishness, of something having slipped his mind, but metamorphosing – as he went back through to his kitchen, and looked down upon the bowl of cold noodles, and the undrunk glass of beer next to it, and the fork laid on the table in readiness – into something more existentially unnerving. As if he were a ghost haunting his own life, looking down upon himself from a great height. The museum display labelled, in neat letters on the subtitle card, A STUDY IN LONELINESS. It was self-pity, of course, Rich knew very well; and he was too canny to succumb to self-pity. That led nowhere. Although, that said, it was, oddly enough, not a corrosive or psychopathological kind of self-pity. Rather, it was a distant sort of pitiable melancholy, focused on himself only to the extent that his selfness was defined by the same solitude that defined so many other people's selfness, all living their monadic lives (monads on Macs not PCs which means *these* monads are Windowsless). Going through their undermotivated routines, filling their hours with cupfuls of business when everyone knows that time is a chasm deeper than the diameter of the earth, and those cupfuls would disappear into obscurity.

Truth was: it was *OK*. He'd got used to it long before. If he tried the thought experiment of fitting a new human being into his life, the main sensation he experienced was a remote sort of dread. He'd have to adjust all his routines, to give up all his freedoms! Wasn't worth the candle. Perhaps things would change in the future – conceivably The One would arrive and sweep him off his feet – but for now he was content to live alone. He'd had relationships before – serious relationships. He knew how inconveniencing they could be.

His phone rang. He answered it without thinking.

'Hello, Alan. We at The This would like to invite you to try our new deluxe introductory package, currently being rolled out to a select group of VIPs in the London and Greater London area.'

Click. A cold call! How very 1998.

He occupied his life with various things. He had hobbies. He collected banknotes. He read poetry – at university he'd done an English degree, and Coleridge and Keats had been his two favourites, and 'Kubla Khan' and 'La Belle Dame sans Merci' the tip of the toppermost so far as he was concerned, poetry-wise. He had an 1836 edition of Coleridge's *Sibylline Leaves* and various pieces of Keatsiana. He had done English because he had wanted to be a writer, and now here he was: a writer! Of sorts. What else? He liked watching comedy. He collected banknotes. Or did I already mention that? My point is, he *fills his days*. He's us, in this respect, he's you, he's me. The distinction between work and play has long since been eroded for you and me. We slog onerously through yet another joyless TV box set, or camp out like navvies and twerk ourselves to exhaustion at Glastonbury, or trudge round the shops, or scroll through the endless Tibetan prayer wheel of social media – or, that apotheosis of modern play, we *work work work* through the latest video game, clocking long hours in front of a flickering screen to move our simulated self slowly and with many setbacks through a virtual landscape fundamentally defined by frustration. What fun we have! Rich was no exception.

But if you had asked him what his main hobby was, he would have replied: banknotes.

It went back a long way with him. Something about the intricacy of the designs on them had captured his imagination when he was a child: back in the days when notes were actually part of the functioning economy and everybody carried them in their wallets and purses. Old-style scrip was his passion (collectors who specialised in polymer notes baffled him) and he had thousands of separate pieces in his collection. Most, it's true, were low-value items: notes Rich considered pretty, or with intriguing or exotic artwork. The thing is: now that financial transactions are all virtual we forget how many banknotes were printed, once upon a time. Many denominations were so common once that they're dirt cheap to pick up now. Rich had a complete run of twentieth-century UK shilling and post-decimalisation paper currency, for instance – not all the variant designs, of course, and not counting war credit notes, but at least one example of every denomination – and his was a pretty good global spread, too. He collected without any particular agenda. He knew (online, that is) fellow collectors who were interested in notes with misprints, or unusually high denominations, or notes with unusual serial numbers – a ten-pound note with the serial number AK47 007 had recently sold for more than a thousand euros – or treasury notes, or provincial and Scottish notes, but Rich's guiding principle was unfettered by these sorts of bugbears. He browsed online and, if the art on a note caught his fancy, and if he could afford it, he bought it.

He had a few examples of leper colony money, some unusual treasury bonds and an A3 sheet of proof fivers from the 1960s. Once, a little whisky-drunk, browsing online at two in the morning, he'd seen a Wisbech & Lincolnshire Bank 1890 £5 note. This bank had been one of the last private institutions in the UK to issue its own banknotes, before being bought up by Barclays at the end of the nineteenth century. When that happened Wisbech & Lincolnshire banknotes were all decommissioned: a triangular wedge was cut through the signature. Unmutilated Wisbech & Lincolnshire notes are very rare, and Rich chanced upon an online auction for one of them. He wasn't a private bank nut, or particularly interested in provincial notes, but something about this one snagged his eye. The plain white note, with a roughly oval, pink watermark filling its middle like a blush. I PROMISE TO PAY THE BEARER ON DEMAND THE SUM OF £5. The gorgeous tracery surrounding FIVE POUNDS at the bottom; the flourishes on the letters. Rich logged a bid, and then waited for a higher bid that never came, such that he woke the next morning €475 poorer and £5 richer – he was overdrawn for a fortnight as a result. When the note came through the post, Rich framed it and hung it in his hall, something he did with only his most favoured notes. He almost never had visitors to his flat, so it was only Rich who noticed them. But still: sometimes you had to make an effort.

Sometimes a note would arrive through the post and he'd hold it in his hands and find himself drawn into it, as through a portal. The miniature wonder of it! A 1970s one-pound note, as green as emerald, promising to pay the bearer on demand one pound. What kind of a promise was that? Take it to Threadneedle Street, bang on the door and demand a tiny flake of gold to the value of exactly one pound? Hardly. Britain came off the gold standard in (Rich checked his phone quickly) 1931, so it wasn't that kind of promise. It was a third party's promise that facilitated the interaction of two people who had never met before and never would again, without either having any connection whatsoever with the Bank of England. Could you even call that a promise? *I promise I won't let you down* is a promise, because it is particular. *I promise to love, honour and obey you, I make this promise to this specific and identifiable person, before these specific witnesses.* Without specificity, did the word 'promise' even have meaning?

The promise meant that the banknote was worth £1. But Rich had just spent £7.95 on it, so that promise hadn't been kept. Or maybe that was the point. Promises are only truly promises if they can be broken – you would never say 'Once I've thrown myself in the air I promise to fall to the ground.' Which is to say: you wouldn't *call* that a promise, because you had no say in the matter. You fell whether you liked it or not. On the other hand, if someone told you: 'Watch this – I'm going to jump in the air and then ... fly out of the window like a bird. I promise I will!' then you'd have to accept the word was being used correctly, even though there was no chance of that person keeping their promise. So we could argue that the breaking of promises is the *condition* of promises. This one-pound note was signed by John Page, and he was the one promising to pay the bearer on demand. His promise was a knowing lie, and everybody concerned in the project knew that it was a lie, and the entire system of notes and coins was predicated upon this lie. The promise was pre-broken before the note even left the printer.

Rich put the note to his nose and sniffed it. It smelt of old paper, old clothes, or not quite of either. It had its own particular smell. John Page was presumably (Rich checked his phone: it was true) dead now. But imagine he was alive. Imagine you knew him, and imagine he borrowed a gold watch from you, promising to return it by a certain date. The date passes, and you challenge him, and he says 'I know what I promised, but I'm keeping the watch.' It would reflect badly on him. It would damage his reputation for honesty, it would make you angry that you'd been betrayed. But here Page was, promising something to millions of people that he, and anyone else who thought about it, knew he couldn't deliver. And nobody cared. You might think that such a promise made to millions and then broken – *designed* to be broken – was millions of times worse. But apparently what was true for the individual was not true of the collective. But of course you know this. We expect our friends to keep their promises. We don't expect politicians to keep theirs. An alien looking in from outer space would think that was the wrong way round, and perhaps it is, but there we are.

He put his new note in his collection book, and went online to brag about his purchase to those banknoteheads he followed in various chatspaces and curated Twitter feeds. There was some small likeage, but not from any of the big hitters or influencers. So it goes.

Ding! A delivery. Pizza like a map of the moon in red and yellow. A patchy goatee of cheese strands on Rich's chin as he scrolled through blogs and websites.

And then The This really began courting him in earnest. They really went for it, as if, after months, they had suddenly woken up to how *special* he was. Every time he turned on his computer the promoted email in his inbox was always from them – special terms, introductory offer, join today for 45% off! Then it was 75% off. Then it was an offer to join for free. He had, it's true, toyed with the notion of trying the app, and the pellet in the mouth, but this hard sell put him off. He reset his preferences and put up blocks, but The This ads kept finding their way through. Always the lead ad. Always the pop-up, or the pre-video ad. He got a D-Work gig to interview a structural engineer for *Enjzine*, but when he arrived it turned out to be a The This employee, there to deliver a personal invitation to try the service 'absolutely free for six months, and the surgical costs of removing the tech covered by us, if you are not completely happy and would prefer to leave.' That they had tricked him into this face-to-face irked Rich, but he was more irked by the fact that their ruse left him with no interview to conduct and no pro forma to file. He stomped sulkily out of this meeting and spent an hour trying to contact somebody at D-Work to explain the reason why he was unable to file. The D-Work app didn't care: it was interested only in its metrics. No pro forma meant no fee and an automatic zero-star rating from D-Work that dragged his average down. The whole silly business left Rich fuming for days.

:3:

In his university days Rich had known a man called Alexander. Not a close friend, an acquaintance, an occasional pub-buddy, someone with whom Rich sometimes hung out. Alexander called himself Xander and was addressed by those who knew him as Xender, Xinder, Xoinder, in mocking tribute to the extreme poshness of his wandering vowels. 'Xonder of the Wandering Hands' Caroline called him, and indeed he was over-physical, borderline-harassy where attractive women were concerned, puppy-enthusiastic, and also deeply religious, destined for a career in the Church.

'I thought Christianity frowned upon sexual urges, Xonder,' Caroline said, as they were all in the union bar one evening. 'Shouldn't you be *repressing* them, like a good little Puritan?'

'It is better to marry than to burn,' Xander replied, raising a finger like he was admonishing her. 'Burn with lust, that is. God's all *for* sex within marriage. The sword of the Lord shall not be sheathed forever.'

Something about Xander's boundless energy, his ingenuousness, the way he was happy to move without seeming gear-change from gossip and chat to considering the deepest questions of life and death and the nature of the soul, endeared him to Rich. For about three months Xander and Rich spent quite a lot of time together, because they had a mutual friend who was good at the javelin, and they used to travel with him around the country to athletic meets for support, and for pub lunches. Xander drove them in his car because he happened to own a car, having previously had the good judgement to be born to wealthy parents.

'Life is a fairy tale,' he told them, one bright June day as they sat in a paved pub garden on the outskirts of Lanborough and drank lager. 'It's not a tragedy. There's a happy ending to look forward to, for all of us. God has written the screenplay of the universe that way.'

'What about wishes?' Rich had prompted. 'If it's a fairy tale, do I get my three wishes?'

'You get as many wishes,' Xander replied, earnestly, 'as you have faith. That's the deal. If you have enough faith and wish a whole fucking mountain shifted away, then it's done – it's gone – *if*... you have faith. Jesus is your genie, and he's not one of those jobsworth genies who says you can't wish for infinite wishes. You can absolutely wish for infinite wishes, with him.'

Cars rattled and trucks thundered past. Back then, motor vehicles ran on things like petrol and diesel and: good Lord, the *noise* they made! You wouldn't believe it. Drowned out conversation, rather.

'What?' Rich asked. 'What?'

A lorry went past like a storm front, and the tourbillons of air stirred up by its passage lifted ash of out the ashtray and swirled it around before settling it down again across the table. The ash was Rich's. He was, at that time, a smoker.

The air smelt of cut grass and tobacco and diesel and a faint tang of agricultural manure and the sun was bright, and the bubbles of gas rising through the three columns of lager were as round and shiny as pearls.

'Xanderella,' said Rich. Then, because the other two were not reacting, he said: 'Hey, that's funny!'

Nobody seemed to think it was funny.

'What's so cool about all those old fairy tales,' Xander said, and then said something that was muffled by a passing van, and then he became audible again, '...never *alone*. Hansel *and* Gretel. Seven dwarfs, not one. The journey from being cast out to belonging. And magic. They are stories that say, there *is* magic in the world. A deep magic, a strong magic. I believe it!'

After that Rich went through a phase when he saw less of Xander. Mostly this was because Rich started dating Caroline, and she persuaded him to give up smoking, and for most of a year they were a proper couple. And then they broke up and Rich was busy with finals. Very busy – with finals and drinking and masturbating and feeling sorry for himself. After uni he lost touch with various people. Things happened in Rich's life. They were the sorts of things that happen in lots of people's lives: bereavement, arranging the legal necessities on his parents' estate, moving flat, and he got on with them. He inherited a small peck's-worth of money along with his parents' flat: not much, but enough to mean he could postpone finding a Proper Job for a while. He settled into a new and solitary rhythm of life.

Then he chanced upon one of Xander's friends, the javelin guy, called Niko, in a bar. It was late, and Rich was on his way home, and had only gone in to use the toilets, but he'd spotted this guy on his way back out, and sat down with him for a glass of wine. And from the general catch-up chatter he discovered that Xander had taken holy orders in the Anglican Church. His superiors had considered him destined for great things. Assigned a curacy in an inner-city parish where he worked super-hard helping people and spreading the gospel – whatever it is priests do – and then: *blam*. Gone.

'Sex scandal,' said Niko.

'I see,' said Rich, in a knowing voice, although in fact he knew nothing about it.

'Not kids,' said Niko. 'Nothing illegal, nothing… you know. Nothing weird. But a couple of impressionable parishioners, nineteen, twenty. It's not that he's supposed to be celibate or anything, but he is supposed to marry if he wants all that, and he's definitely not supposed to fuck his teenage parishioners.'

Rich remembered Xander saying *the sword of the Lord shall not be sheathed forever* and laughing, and he said, 'not nice' and Niko agreed.

'So did they defrock him?'

Rich had been drinking before he popped into the All Bar One for a slash, and now he was drinking again, so he was drunk enough to be secretly impressed with himself for knowing this technical term. Or, wait, was that just Catholics? He checked his phone.

'They've disciplined him, demoted him, moved him to a parish in Lincolnshire somewhere, I think. Or Norfolk? I'm not sure, except that it's very remote and very flat. Xander messaged me a few times complaining how oppressive it was, the flatness. The *horizontality*, was how he put it.'

Good to see you. Good to catch up! Let's do this again, mate. Yes, let's! Both knowing they will, in all likelihood, never see either ever again. Night night then! Nigh-nigh.

Good night, laddies. Good night, sweet laddies. Goo nigh. Goo nigh.

And that was the last Rich heard of Xander for many years. Then he chanced upon him online, and had a few conversations with him. He was living in London now, and was no longer a cleric, but he had abated nothing of his enthusiasm for God and religion. Rich even met him for a coffee – he was guilted into it, really, after heavily dropped comments about how isolated Xander felt in the big city, how lonely urban living could be. So they met up in a cavernous Costa in Southwark, near the river, and Xander sat with both his elbows on the table, leaning forward, talking, talking and talking some more. At uni he had possessed a mess of blond hair, like stuffing exploding out of an armchair, but that was all gone now. Now his was a high bald forehead reflecting a blob of brilliance from the ceiling light. His eyes were a thin grey-blue and he blinked too often. He talked and he talked, and little flakes of spittle accumulated in the corners of his red lips.

'I fell in love with the Church,' he said. 'I see now, I can see it now, that we're supposed to love God, and that the Church is there to help us reach that state, but I got distracted, and fell in love with the *people* who loved God. You can see that distinction? Of course you can. But if you can see the distinction then you can also see how *easy* it is to elide the one and the other. It was trouble, Alan. It meant big trouble in little Church-a. Because falling in love with people, of course, it… it… it involves sex, if you fall in love with a woman and marry her and don't have sex something's gone wrong somewhere. Sex and love fit so neatly together. I got so caught up in it – *libido* and *agape* all muddled in with one another. I'm not the first and I won't be the last and that's no excuse at all, but it's human, it's all too human, yah? It's tricky, though, don't you think, separating out the rush of spiritual joy from the intensity of *pleasure* when you come? Or not even that, but the anticipation.

Loving God is all about the anticipation, because one day we will see Him face to face, but not yet, that not-yetness is everything, it's the whole of the religious life, the joyful anticipation of that connection. And the build-up to sex is like that, don't you think? There's a passage in John 21 where Christ asks Peter if he loves him, and they talk at cross-purposes – Christ uses the word *agape*, which means spiritual love, but Peter keeps replying yes I love you, but with the word *philia*, which is like a human love, a person-to-person love. You can't bracket sex out of that. It's human, don't you think?'

On and on and on.

Rich made his excuses and left. After thirty minutes Xander hadn't asked a single question about him.

After this abortive coffee-date, Xander reached out several times subsequently on social media, but Rich ghosted him. Growing older is, to a larger extent than you expect it will ever be, a process of looking back and thinking: *Why was I ever friends with that person?*

And then, after his interview with Aella Hamilton at The This, and during a period of paranoia and online rabbit-holes and strange happenings, he was contacted by Xander again. This occasion was long past midnight, and Rich wasn't doing anything very much, beyond checking a few message-threads and reading an article on banknotes that featured chess-piece art (rarer than you might think). Then, from nowhere:

. . hi. alan. its xander

Lonely, or bored, lacking even the momentum to ghost him, Rich replied.

. . hi

They only got a couple of swapped pleasantries into their exchange when Xander declared he'd uncovered something really important, and wanted some advice on what to do with his discovery, and that Rich was a writer and a journalist, wasn't he?

..you could give me some pointers

..if I can. but mate. theres no such thing as a journalist, any more. not really. and anyone with a blog or a feed is a writer nowadays

..understood

..what your discovery?

..its about the bible

Rich's mood slumped. Of course it was. But now he was sucked into the conversation.

..pauls epistle to the romans

..there are loads of religion chatspaces, theological onlines you could discuss this i really don't know anything about

A scurry of quick successive messages:

..we are the romans now, you see the secular world the technological empire

..pauls message is more important to us now than ever

..and ive discovered

..something really crucial

..pauls epistles to the romans 2

Rich hadn't drawn his curtains. He looked up from his computer at windows inked black by 2 a.m. blackness, and saw the ghost of his own face looking back. *Why am I still up at two in the morning?* Biscuit crumbs in the interstices of his keyboard, the coffee in his mug at room temperature. He messaged back:

..what have the romans ever epistled for /us/?

Even as he tapped the words out he thought: *That's not funny, that doesn't even make sense.* And he thought: *Why am I interacting with this guy? I barely know him.* So Rich pulled a *JewelDomino* game into the corner of his screen and pecked out a few likely moves as the little messenger icon face pretended to be thinking about it, and then switched to aha! and the message itself spooled out.

..we need to belong to something larger than ourselves. we need to belong. the trick is in finding the /right/ thing to belong to

Rich was thinking about the best way to back out of this exchange, when another, much longer message pinged up.

..romans 2 paul says. thinkest thou this o man that judgest them which do such things and doest the same, that thou shalt escape the judgment of god? or despisest thou the riches of his goodness and forbearance and longsuffering not knowing that the goodness of god leadeth thee to repentance? But heres the thing the greek word for repentance there is metanoia which means a change of heart, a change of mind, a change of being. its transl repentance, which is a change of heart but the word is nous, mind. mind. it had never really sunk in with me before but i was chasing the meaning on an online forum and it means change meta of mind nous see?

Rich could just walk away. Message *goodnight* and go to bed. But he didn't.

..cant say i do xanderella

Another blizzard of messages:

..people think it means change your habits of though

..*thought

..but what if it means literally change your mind, literally change your brain, bring you closer to god?

..you know the technology that the this

..the this are marketing?

A chill fluttered somewhere around Rich's ribs. He could click on the icon that would open a Skype window and they could continue the conversation face to face, with spoken words. And for a moment he contemplated doing just that. But then the reaction lunged through him, and he felt a revulsion that almost amounted to actual, visceral fear. How could Xander from uni know that he, Rich, had taken a D-Work gig to interview a high-up in The This? That he had spent months sexually fixated on a The This employee he had met for ten mere minutes? How could he possibly know? He messaged:

..xander did you join the this?

..yes

came the reply at once.

Rain was doing a slow shoe shuffle against the study window now. Rich tried again:

..youve had the implant and everything?

..yes. alan i cant tell you what a difference it makes it opens the third eye and now i truly belong everything I was looking for in my crummy life all my wrong turns and bad decisions were in search of this. this. here. now. if you were to come and try the

Rich pressed the power-off and his computer shut down with a sound effect like exhalation. His little heart was drumming rapidly in his chest. Jesus. We're more prone to paranoid thoughts at night, though, aren't we? So, breathe: breathe. The thing is, though, night is always coming around, isn't it? The globe is a gigantic eyeball and night is the eyelid that is always closing on it. Round and round, and us carving out little spaces lit by the high-res flicker of our screens and sleeping darkly during the day.

Rich poured himself a whisky.

:4:

It was a trivial provocation, but it tipped him into one of his blues. Stupid to feel so intensely over so vapid an interaction, but an acute awareness of how trivial it was only increased his sense of how stupid he was being, and that made Rich sadder, not happier. Down he spiralled. Down, down, to a sunless sea.

Sorrow in his flat. Sorrow in the shower. Sorrow walking alongside him on his constitutional. He wandered down to the river and watched its puckered and fluid surface. That Churchill line: *to achieve all this only to achieve nothing in the end*. That's the fucking truth of things, though, isn't it? When night-time clears the sky and the stars angle their tiny faces down to watch, how are they not disappointed? Those chaste stars. Walking and walking and nowhere to walk to. Dusk. Dawn. A grey afternoon. Odysseus, making his way back over a sluggish sea the colour of paper, his boat a black hieroglyph, twenty years older than when he departed and not one hour wiser. Two decades, at a time in human history when the life expectancy was ridiculously abbreviated, when forty was an old-man age. He showed a spirt of energy when he regained his home, sure: that business with the bow, yes, yes, killing the suitors, hanging the serving girls, OK, I guess, but then what? Exhausted. Drained. Fewer teeth than he used to have. Skin tiger-striped with old scars. Sitting, as his slaves brought him a cup of goat's milk. Sleeping shallow sleep, often rising to piss in the night, and then restlessly lying down again, with a vague dream of white faces against a black shore, and stars looking down unimpressed as the great city was made a midnight bonfire and ashes by dawn. Kenneth Williams's suicide note: 'Oh, what's the bloody point?' A comedian's punchline.

Where was he even going?

Rich lying in bed, sobbing. After a bout of that it was: Rich in bed, sleeping soundly.

It passed, as everything does. He discovered he'd missed a couple of D-Work gigs, and that his star rating had taken a hit. The next time a gig came up he responded with alacrity and filed his pro forma within the hour. There were a couple of days when no gigs pinged on his app, and then two came through on the same day. Good: he needed the money.

An invitation to join The This, printed in gold and black on stiff card and delivered to his door like Cinderella being given the opportunity to go to the ball. Rich turned the card over and over in his hand. Then he put it into the recycling.

Summer was starting to gain climatological momentum, overcast days interspersed with sunny ones, then fewer of the former, and then only the latter. Rich started wearing suncream when he went out of the flat. Flowers blooming red up on the heath. Flowers blooming white or butter-yellow in sunlight, parching, bleached, bone-tight, the flowers, petals stiff as gristle. The cartilage of an ear. Blooms unwrapping themselves like sweets.

He was sitting on a bench up on the heath when Helen Susanna shuffled up and sat down. He recognised her, the old woman with that odd, smooth mask covering half her face. He could have got up and walked on, but the sun's heat had made him torpid.

'Hello, my dear,' she said. 'How do you do?'

He smiled, and nodded at her, and then he dropped the smile and pointedly looked away. It should have been enough for her to get the message. Couples arm-in-arming, cyclists hurtling past, a mother with a pram stopping in front of the bench to fuss at her baby's coverings, and then looking straight at Rich, and then walking on.

Looking *straight at* him, though?

'I'm Helen Susanna,' she said.

'I remember you,' said Rich, not looking at her

'You're Alan.'

Now Rich did look at her. 'How do you know that?'

'I know a lot of things.' She laughed a rough-edged, shingly kind of laugh. 'Don't be discomposed by the mask, dearie. It's odd, I know, but I'd look a sight worse without it.'

'I'm sorry,' mumbled Rich, and once again looked away.

'Not your fault! Cancer's fault, and you are not cancer. You and cancer are *different things*. Unless subject and object being distinct *is* just an illusion, eh? Then you are indeed cancer ... and Stalin ... and typhus ... and every rapist who's ever lived. It's all you, eh?'

'What?' asked Rich, genuinely baffled.

'You want to toddle off,' said Helen Susanna. 'I understand. Go, if you like. We'll meet again.'

She was lonely. He understood that. The world is full of lonely OAPs happy to strike up a conversation with any random person they meet on the street. I mean, fuck it, he was lonely himself a lot of the time, so it wasn't that he didn't understand. But she was disconcerting-looking and her manner was just *weird*. She smelt stale and sour, the way old people often do.

'It's nothing personal,' he lied. 'I'm just in a solitary kind of mood today.'

'Oh, you're *always* in a solitary kind of mood, Alan,' said Helen Susanna. 'Don't I know it!'

'How do you know my name, though?'

'The This are pretty interested in you, aren't they?' she said.

'Jesus Christ, I don't have to put up with this,' Rich said.

Yelled, really. Screamed, almost. Years of psychological spelunking by the world's most talented psychiatrists wouldn't have got to the bottom of the inner depths from which Rich's anger suddenly spouted up, a great gushing cataract of rage, tossing boulders of ice and rock in all directions. He was trembling, actually trembling, with rage. His face clenched. Then again: as soon as the anger came it dispersed into a miasmic spray and cloud, and in its aftermath he only felt tired.

There was a long silence. Then he said: 'I'm sorry.'

'Don't mention it.'

Finally he swivelled round on the bench and looked directly at her.

'Lady, what's your beef?'

'Beef?' she repeated innocently.

'Why are you bugging me like this?' Looking more closely into her face, Rich saw that her left eye was static, emotionless. Glass. Her right one was lively enough, though. Mischievous. Fuck that. 'What am I to *you*, lady?'

'The This are interested in you,' she replied. 'I'm interested in you, too. To be precise, I'm interested in the question of why you are important to The This. What's so special about *you*, Alan? Did you ever ask yourself that?'

'And why do you care? Unless you're part of them? Are you?' Belatedly, it came to him. 'You *used* to be, but aren't any more?'

'Bingo.' She took a packet of CIF-snacks from a pocket on her skirt and began popping them individually into her mouth. The pack had an image of the Eiffel Tower on it. 'Rare for anyone to leave, you know,' she said, with pride in her voice.

'You got out.'

'I can't take any credit for it, really. See this mask? Behind it is the ruination cancer made of my skull and face, and part of that ruination and the surgery needed to keep me hanging on to life, was the erosion of the Thisware – the hardware, I mean. Much of the rhizome web is still interpenetrating my brain, but the main hub has gone. I can't say how much of the … software, I suppose you'd say. The conditioning, the ideology, the brainwash, remains. But I feel *much* more like my old self these days. I wouldn't have been able to unplug without the cancer, so I raise a glass to the old bastard for that, at least.'

In the absence of a glass, she put another currant in her mouth.

'I'm sorry,' said Rich.

'Why? For the cancer? Don't worry about that, my young friend. Worry about The This.'

'They've been spamming me for months now. Real keen I join. What do they want from me?'

'I don't know,' she said. 'I left the gestalt before you became a person of interest to them. I've been out for half a year. They're content to let me die in my own time, I suppose.'

'Content to let you die? What?'

'As opposed to killing me off. Join the bally dots, Alan! All these suicides – people shooting themselves in the mouth.'

'You're saying The This is *murdering* these people?'

Helen Susanna sagged. She looked, suddenly, much older. She put the pack of currants back in her skirt pocket.

'If I had proof,' she said, in a low voice, 'don't you think I'd go public? So I suppose I don't have proof. But you're a journalist.'

'I'm really not.'

'You should dig. Dig it out. Find the truth. I'm going to have a lie down.'

She got to her feet and trotted away down the path with impressive vigour.

That was how Rich first got to know Helen Susanna.

:5:

Rich went back over all his interactions with The This, from the initial D-Work gig, and the publication of his content, to the various ways he'd researched the group. He hadn't archived any of that and now rather wished he had.

For a long time he stared at the blank screen.

The This app was more than just a facilitator, saving finger-taps in the exchange of Twitter-style platitudes. The app connected people into a larger community. The app was functional telepathy. The first step on the way to a hive mind. Cult was the least of it. Everything Rich had said to Aella Hamilton he had also said to Xander from uni, and to everybody else connected in The This: he had been speaking not to one person but to a legion.

'Get a grip, Richard,' he said, aloud. 'It's just an app. It's not invasion of the fucking body snatchers.'

He thought about what he might say to the police. Was he being harassed? Stalked? They'd want more evidence to buy that. *Had* he just been made privy to a gigantic conspiracy? Or was it more likely that he was a solitary geezer who spent too much time surfing loony internet sites? Occam's razor slices both ways.

If he went to the police they'd think he was bonkers. Conceivably he *was* bonkers.

He got up and went through to piss away all the cola he'd been drinking during his session on the computer.

'If you really were a journalist,' he told his reflection in the bathroom mirror as he washed his hands, 'you'd break this story to the world and win the Paulitzer.'

Was that the name? He checked his phone, and the first thing he saw was a pending message request from Xander – so he had got hold of Rich's phone number, too. But of course, if The This had his number then every member of the group had it, too. He denied the request, blocked the number it originated from, and then put out a general block on Xander's profile from all platforms. By now his fear had congealed into anger, which, like a toddler at the end of a fit of fury, morphed suddenly into sleepy exhaustion. He went to bed.

:6:

His DifferenceWork gigs dried up so completely and suddenly that Rich contacted an administrator at the organisation to see if there'd been some kind of screw-up or viral attack that had deleted his account. But, no, he was there exactly as before, and his user rating wasn't entirely hopeless. He just wasn't getting any gigs.

It was annoying, but not immediately catastrophic. He could live pretty cheaply if he stopped indulging in expensive video games or rare banknotes. If the worst came to the worst he could get a regular job – he really didn't want to do that, but it was obviously an option – or else liquidate his one big asset: sell the flat. Move into a rented place and live off the purchase price money until he worked out what to do next. It was by no means an ideal solution, but at least it existed as a backstop.

He watched an old TV drama based on the Chernobyl disaster. It was pretty good. The scenes where the radiation was so strong that it fried the robots they sent in to clear the roof, so they had to dress a whole platoon of soldiers in padding, like Tweedledum and Tweedledee about to do battle, and send them out, in small groups, for ninety-second stints, pushing wreckage back into the reactor core, were intense. Any longer than ninety seconds and they'd die. Afterwards they all accepted their medals and each said 'I serve the Soviet Union!' with genuine pride. To believe that your individual life was part of something bigger. It was something. But then again: people lying in overcrowded hospitals with antique facilities dying of radiation sickness – that was part of it, too.

Rich lost a whole afternoon to an online politics argument about whether AIs should be allowed to adjust meatspace vote totals – the London Mayoral election was not far away – to take account of variables known to suppress voting patterns: things like bad weather, popular TV shows and the like. It was an online political discussion so it got hyperbolic and angry very quickly. Hitler's name came up. After a while Rich grew bored with politics and browsed banknote websites for a bit. Then a *good point* occurred to him, on the AI-vote-tally idea, and he dived back into that discussion. People were behaving hideously with each other. They'd never be like this face to face.

Somewhere outside, a car alarm was going off like Yoko Ono in full song. Rich disengaged from the politics debate feeling grubby and unhappy and tense. But it was always like that, online. Why *was* it always like that?

He watched a greatly upvoted video interview called *The Odourless God*. A speaker called Strass expatiated. He had a theory of the evolution of God rooted in what he called the odourless sublime.

Rich certainly had become alienated from his sense of smell: nasal polyps clogged his sinuses. They grew back rapidly when surgically excised, and so he had learned to live with them cluttering the ventricles of his nose like mussel banks at an undersea intake.

The first Thursday in the month came round and it was time for book club. Half a dozen regulars said they'd attend, and Rich found himself excited by the prospect of doing a bit of socialising. The previous book club had been cancelled, and it had been many weeks since he'd had any actual human face-to-face. He showered and put on his favourite shirt and wandered down the hill to the Drinkx@Snaxa – a foolish name for a bar, Rich always thought, since it implied customers came for the snacks and only added drinks as an afterthought, when the exact opposite was of course the case. Strolling down with his phone out, following one particular, complexly branching Twitter thread and all its replies, moving with the flow of all the other people wandering into town, all also checking their phones. *Bip-bip-bip* went the green man's song, and a great bolus of humanity crossed the junction.

Six people had promised, but in the event only two people (three, including Rich) actually came. It didn't matter. The three of them chatted and drank and ate nachos and played a few of the games available on the tabletop screens, and Rich found himself laughing a lot. He asked the other two what they thought about The This. One, Jaq, had only the vaguest idea who they even were – 'There are, like a thousand start-ups promising us hands-free Twitter right now, no?' – but Nicey knew all about them.

'My boss joined last month. Says it's made her twice as efficient, so she can work half as hard.'

Rich was very interested in this person.

'Has it changed her?'

'Made her less of an absolute bastard,' confirmed Nicey.

'But,' Rich pressed, very earnest now, 'has it changed her as a person? Is she basically the same person she was before?'

'What?' Nicey leant back, away from Rich. 'She's the same person. It's not a fucking demonic possession, it's just an app – it's a way of hands-freeing your social media. I think she uses it to dictate documents and emails and whatnot without having actually to type them. But she's the same person. A bit nicer, less snappy, probably because the app is working as a workload reliever.'

Rich scratched his head. His scalp felt itchy all over.

'OK,' he said. 'OK.'

When he stumbled and weaved his way home at the end of the evening he was telling himself: I've got this whole thing out of proportion. It's just one company among forty thousand. It's just another app. There's no conspiracy.

The following day it took him until afternoon to get over his hangover.

Summer blazed. He had the cricket playing in a window on the top-left of his screen as he tried to get some useful work together. Jotting down saleable ideas (to sell to ... whom?). A book proposal. A thinkpiece on the rise of companies like The This. He sent out many emails and they were all instantly flagged as having been parked by their recipients, which was pretty bloody discouraging, actually. He played 3D Go against his computer, on its lowest setting. He'd been stuck on a 6 × 6 × 6 grid for ages, and wanted to level up to a 7 × 7 × 7, but he simply couldn't conceptualise the 3D spaces mapped out by his stones well enough to win the necessary victories. His dream of playing on an actual 19 × 19 × 19 grid looked increasingly ridiculous. Still, a man's reach should exceed his grasp, or what's a heaven for?

It wasn't doing his mental health any good obsessing over The This. He should stop. Unplug. It was cause and effect, of course: the fact that his mental health wasn't strong had put him into the position where the internet's hall of distorting mirrors had started to convince him he'd stumbled on a gigantic conspiracy.

And Rich *was* lonely. He was often lonely. It often occurred to him that, had he played things differently with Caroline, he might be married now. He might be part of something bigger than just himself – kids, a circle of real-life friends, a proper job. The road not travelled. Rivers don't run uphill, though. The wisdom of clockwise; the impossibility of anticlockwise.

No point in *wallowing* in it, though, eh?

The odd thing about loneliness is the way it's both an intensely isolating, individual experience and the one thing most widely shared by human beings in general. Isn't that strange? *Can't turn the clock back, mate. Got to move on. You screwed up, and she's happy with her new man. Not so new, neither, considering how long ago it all was. Plenty of other fish in the sea.* Salmon are always returning to their spawning grounds. Blossom is always returning to the trees, but that's a different meaning of the word *return*, isn't it? Space and time are orthogonal to one another in the geometry of reality, which is why you can go back to where you were born, but you can't go back to *when* you were born. And what if you could? Say space and time work dialectically *through* one another in 'spacetime', and say that spacetime is itself a process working through to some new synthesis that will, in turn, become the basis of a whole new way of living. In that case, maybe we'll experience a completely different relationship to both things?

Fanciful.

The four rivers that flowed out of Eden were called Hiddekel, Pishon, Gihon and Euphrates. Paddle your coracle back up any of them. How much longer until we're back at the source? Where do you live now? And where did you *used* to live? In this other house, in that other flat, in this other person's house – I had a room of my own, or I had to share with my brother – inside this other person as if *they* were a house (love you, Ma!), in the realm of pure potentiality which is an endless green plain under a red sky over which the strong winds of fate and destiny blow. And here was Rich, the unaccommodated man.

Like a spell he was under.

Rich kept suncream in a jar by the door because, otherwise, he tended to forget to put it on – and you know, what with the depleted ozone layer and the general winding down of the world, it's always important to slap some slap on. But once he was all kitted out, patting his pockets to check he had his keys and his phone and his wallet, and at the door, he wasn't going to go back into the bathroom to apply the stuff. Better to keep it by the door. And now, going a bit stir-crazy in his flat, he decided he would go out. So he pulled on shoes and picked up his phone, and undertook the last ritual before stepping out. He drew a snail-shell pattern in the top of the tub and rubbed it over his face. Checking his reflection, and out, and down the stairs.

A woman passed him on the pavement.

'Rich,' she said, warmly, like she was an old friend. Stopping and reversing the direction of her travel to catch up with him. He'd never seen her before but she was pretty and friendly, and so he smiled.

'Hello?'

'It's Emma!'

'Do I know you?'

He didn't, he knew he didn't, but she was attractive and it was a task beyond the capacity of his merely human willpower to walk away. She was snow-blonde, bright-faced, and her smile seemed genuine.

'I'm a friend of Aella's.'

Something sank through the inner ocean of Rich's chest.

'From The This.'

'Let's take a walk,' said Emma, holding out a hand. 'It's a sunny day. Let's have a stroll around the heath and, if you don't like what I'm saying, then by gum you just snap your fingers and I'll vanish.'

Rich thought: *Who talks like that?*

But he was smiling at her. He couldn't help himself. And when he told her, 'I'm not joining your crazy cult,' he spoke without hostility. 'I won't. You're all wasting your time.'

But it *was* a lovely day, and she was very pretty, and he was going for a walk anyway, so – incomprehensibly, really – he found himself walking hand in hand down his road with a young woman. They turned right, up Putney Hill, and strolled towards the heath.

'Look at them,' said Emma.

Everyone walking the other way had their gazes on their phones. Just a normal day.

'People going back to work after their lunch break,' said Rich. The feeling of her hand holding his, of her skin against his, was extraordinarily discombobulating and exciting and arousing. He didn't let go. 'They've been up on the heath, I guess, enjoying the sun.'

'Not my point,' said Emma.

And then they had to separate – a large man was coming straight down the middle of the pavement, his phone held up directly in front of his face. Emma let go of Rich's hand and the two of them stepped apart to give him uninterrupted passage. He didn't even notice they were there.

'The whole world is blind, actually blind,' said Emma. 'This technology wraps a scarf around their eyes. They can't see the beauty of the day. They can't see anything.'

She laughed, and shook her head, and they walked on together.

Now they were at the top of the hill and passing the Green Man. People were sitting at the outside tables.

'I need a drink,' said Rich.

'Another way of scarfing up your perceptions, Richard!' chided Emma, smiling. 'How much do you drink a day, anyway?'

'That's my business.' Rich wished he didn't sound so defensive. 'Anyway. Never mind. Anyway. I'm going in.'

Beer, beer.

'You're a free agent, Richard.'

He paused. 'Do you want anything?'

'A glass of sparkling water, please,' said Emma, moving towards an empty table in the sunlight.

Rich went through the entrance and into the gloom. Stale ale and body odour smells. Brasses on the wall, framed prints of eighteenth-century fox hunts, a cardboard mosaic over the bar made up of beer mats: all these things that were supposed to render the pub individual and distinctive that were, all of them, absolutely generic, present in ten thousand pubs across the British Isles. He ordered the water and a pint of IPA, and paid, and picked up the drinks. A song was playing:

In this theta that I call my soul
I always play the starring role.

It was familiar, but Rich couldn't place it, and with both hands full he couldn't check the recognition app on his phone. Had the guy really sung *theta*, the Greek letter? That couldn't be right. That didn't make sense. Of course, pop lyrics often don't make sense. Still.

Rich stepped back into the day's brightness, and there was Emma waiting for him, seated, smiling.

Back in the pub he could still hear the singer, chanting now how lonely he was, over and over again, like a mantra. Lonely lonely lonely! That must be the title of the song: 'Lonely'. Why say it over and over, though? A charm to ward it away?

In this theta.

Theta for The. Theta for This.

He put the drinks down.

'Thank you,' said Emma.

He got out his phone and checked the song lyrics. Theta for *theatre*. Ah. That made more sense. Did it? The proscenium arch of the soul. The Globe of the Spirit.

Rich awkwardly inserted himself into the space between the table and its attached wooden bench. The sun was in his eyes, and her face was in shadow. As he fumbled his sunglasses out of his pocket he said: 'I mean, if I'm honest, if I'm honest I'm flattered that you-all are going to these lengths to recruit me. But surely I can't be worth so much effort?'

For a moment Emma didn't reply, and then she said: 'It's nothing to be embarrassed about. Having a crush on Aella. She's a beautiful woman, after all.'

Rich's mouth opened. He shut it. Then he said: 'You don't know what you're talking about.'

'Oh, but you're not *actually* underestimating us,' chided Emma. 'You're only pretending to do that, here, now. Only pretending to be surprised. You have a clearer sense of things than that. A clearer sense, for instance, of how much access we have to notionally private social media, computer logs and online interaction.'

'Crush is such a teenage word,' Rich said. But then, immediately he added: 'I don't know anything about her. How can I fall in love with someone I know literally nothing about? She's a blank piece of paper.'

'So am I,' said Emma. 'That's the human condition, Rich. It's just a matter of – what do we write upon that page? It's a matter of – do we let the loose sheets flutter about in the wind like litter, or bind them together into a book?'

'Clever analogy,' said Rich. 'But I'm still not joining your crazy cult.'

She smiled. 'Aella likes you.'

'Fuck off.'

'She does. She thinks you're cute. I like you, too. She and I are the same person. That's real. I don't mean that either of us has sacrificed our individuality. Truly we haven't. I'm still wholly and entirely me. And because I'm on the inside, and you're only on the outside looking in, I can tell you – it's so much better in here. Believe me.'

'It's just not my kind of thing,' Rich insisted, taking a long draw from his pint. He wished he sounded surer.

'You're happy out here?'

'Not convinced that that's the point, to be honest.'

'Not convinced what's the point?'

'Happy.'

'You saw them,' she said, leaning forward, 'as we walked up here. You see them all the time as you go about your life. The blind. They're all blind. You can't seriously want to be blind, too, not when you could knock away the scales and become one with us – with me. With Aella.'

It was too much. Rich stood up, although his gesture was rather undercut by his need to extricate his considerable gut from the table-and-bench structure. He stood up to ensure that he didn't just burst into tears, which abruptly seemed to him a possibility. Some manner of outlet.

'Goodbye, Ella,' he said. 'I mean, Emma.'

It was beyond a joke. His heart was racing, and that inner voice was bellowing that he was making a prick of himself, that this was a vast mistake, couldn't he *see* she was prepared to go to bed with him? *What . . . am . . . I . . . doing?* But no, no, and thrice no, there was a halo round his heart, he could feel it push against his throat. He *almost* felt like crying, but almost wasn't the same as giving way. And he was making a stand, literally and figuratively. He was himself.

In this theta that I call my soul.

There was an odd vibe, and it took Rich a moment to realise the oddness was a silence. Emma was still sitting, her glass of water untouched, looking up at him. All the conversations in the pub garden had stopped and everybody was looking at Rich. Every single person.

'Woh,' said Rich.

'Come now, Rich,' said Emma, in a placating voice. 'You're drunk. It's barely two in the afternoon and you're drunk.'

'You cannot be serious,' said Rich, and he set off at a rapid walk.

Everyone in the pub garden swivelled their heads to watch him as he left.

As he walked out of the pub grounds and onto the pavement, a flock of sparrows hurtled past him on an upward trajectory, cheeping lustily, rising on their huddling wings. And then he was striding as fast as he could without actually breaking into a run. It looked very much like he was crying. A grown man, in broad daylight, walking down Putney Hill, like anyone else. But that was what it looked like. And then he gave into his throbbing adrenaline and broke into a proper run.

:7:

Rich ran, ungainly, down Putney Hill. He had to stop as he turned into his road because … frankly … he was … out of breath. Gasping. He bent forward, put his hands onto his thighs, cantilevering his centre of gravity like a bridge. Long breaths, until he got his puff back. Everybody who looked at him was one of Them. Or: probably not. That was just crazy thinking. Almost everybody was just ordinary folk, and uninterested in him. Though they all seemed to be staring. Or not all of them. He couldn't be sure. Most people had their snouts close to their phones, so maybe not. But maybe they belonged to The This, too, and were shamming. They were after him. They were going to get him

Steady, Rich, he told himself. *The balance of your mind is becoming disturbed. Is this what the world looks like to somebody suffering paranoid schizophrenia? θ for The. θ for This.*

θ for Them.

He walked briskly to the building that contained his flat, this four-storey Edwardian brick tower that had been converted some time in the 1980s. The front garden of the property was a small tiled area behind a low brick wall, almost entirely filled by sixteen tall council bins, eight sets of two, one for rubbish and one for recycling. There were two stretches of might-have-been flower beds that were covered by several years' worth of unswept leaves and assorted rubbish and sunbleached plastic wrappers. Nobody had any responsibility for this area and so it had become a no-person's-land of junk and brittle decay. Usually when Rich passed through he was going in, or coming out, of the building and his eyes were on his phone screen. Today, though, he saw it with a visceral sense of dislike. The online world so shiny and clean, the real world so squalid and littered.

He lurched at the house's front door and as he did so the pile of leaves to his left stirred and shook. It was a sharply hot, windless day but the pile of leaves shook as though the spirit of the winter wind was possessing it. Then a demon lurched up from the leaves, assumed human shape and rushed at Rich.

It was Helen Susanna.

'What are you doing?' Rich yowled. 'You scared the life out of me!'

'Are you going into your flat?' Helen Susanna asked. There were leaves sticking to her shirt and skirt. There were leaves in her hair.

'The world has gone mad,' said Rich. 'Or I have – I'm getting *out* of here.'

'You could go into your flat,' said Helen Susanna.

'I will. I'm going in and probably never coming out again.'

'I wouldn't go into your flat, though.'

Rich stopped.

'You do realise,' said the old woman, 'that *they* have infiltrated all your kit, don't you? Your computers, your monitors, your smart-tech? The problem with the internet of things is that once they hack one, they hack all. It's not just the websites you visit and your communications they have access to. They'll have all the images from your security apps. You're not even free in the loo, since you're sitting on a smart toilet.'

Rich said: 'I think I might be losing my mind.'

'Oho!' said Helen Susanna, her one good eye opening very wide.

'I think I might be suffering from paranoid schizophrenia.'

'That you would say so,' said Helen Susanna, 'suggests you're probably not. People suffering from paranoid schizophrenia tend precisely *not* to have the self-awareness to realise that the conspiracies they perceive are issues in their brain chemistry rather than artefacts in the world as such. It's a sort of reverse catch-22.'

Rich didn't recognise the allusion, and automatically brought out his phone to check it, but Helen Susanna put up a bony finger.

'Maybe it would be best to unplug your phone from the network and turn it off. Do you have a delocation app?'

'Seriously?'

'Seriously.'

Rich took a deep breath, flipped through the infinite Rolodex of apps and screens until he found the one that pulled the plug. He sealed the phone away and turned it off.

'Most people,' Helen Susanna said, taking his hand in hers, 'who think a shadowy conspiracy is out to get them are nuts. But most isn't all. You're not paranoid if they really *are* out to get you.'

'What can I do?'

'Come home with me, dearie.'

And that was that. Rich permitted her to lead him by the hand, like a child, out of the front garden, down the street and into the grid of residential roads of west Putney. They passed the Catholic church and headed towards the Upper Richmond Road. Everyone they passed held their phones in front of their faces. Passing cars hummed and hawed dopplerishly. The public waste bins were crammed with myriad small black tie-bags filled with dog shit. Clouds of flies buzzed around the bins like giant models of electrons and their nuclei.

He half expected Helen Susanna to reveal that she lived in a tent in the park, or a heap of cardboard up an alley, but she stopped in front of a smart detached house, black-walled with silver window frames and all the slats of all the blinds tucked down behind every pane of glass.

'This is where you live?'

'Nicer'n yours,' cackled Helen Susanna. 'Come in. Meet Fawn.'

'Fawn?'

The old woman was fiddling with her keys – old-school, twentieth-century keys, like a prop from a TV historical drama.

'He's not really called Fawn. He calls himself that after a famous bodyguard from literature. His real name is Tim, but he doesn't think that's a particularly *tough*-sounding name. Tiny Tim, you know. Timmy the dog. So he calls himself Fawn. But he's not really Fawn. He's a faux-Fawn.'

The door was open. Without his phone to help him, Rich was entirely at sea so far as these references were concerned.

'Foforn?'

'Fawn!' Helen Susanna called into the entrance hall. 'I've renamed you – you're faux-Fawn.'

'Ma'am,' said a very tall man, stepping forward.

'You have a bodyguard?' Rich boggled.

'Dangerous times.' Helen Susanna handed Foforn her shawl. 'This is Alan. He may be staying with us for a few days.'

'I may?' said Rich.

'Dangerous,' Helen Susanna repeated, 'times. Come and have a cup of tea, at any rate.'

She bustled away down the hall and Rich followed her, glancing up at Foforn as he went. He was a foot taller than Rich, and a foot wider across the shoulders. His head was shaved, blurry blueness marking where the hairline had been cropped. His features were simple, like a face drawn on an egg in felt-tip pen. You didn't for a moment doubt his capacity for violence. The design of his T-shirt was three handsome young men, bleached-blond hair, all three in the same model of sunglasses, glowering at the world, underneath which image, in capital letters, was written THE POLICE. An appropriate enough self-identification for a bodyguard, really.

The end of the hall gave into a wide, well-lit kitchen–dining area that expanded into a glass conservatory. That was where Helen Susanna was sitting, two cups of tea on a pine table before her. Rich, passing through the space, clocked all the top-range fixtures and fittings. Money! Everywhere money.

'It's a really nice house,' he said.

'You mean – expensive. It is that. You mean – you're surprised to find a bag-lady living in luxury. There's no point in denying it. I'm rich. One thing The This are particularly skilled at is acquiring money. It's not so hard when you know which tricks to apply. Which levers to pull.'

Rich sat down. He sipped his tea: two sugars, exactly the right amount of milk, just how he liked it. Then he noticed that there were framed banknotes on the walls.

'Oh, wow,' he said. 'You collect banknotes!' He got to his feet and went over to take a closer look. 'Lord, this is a Dutch 200 guilders note from … what, 1900? That's amazing.' He peered at it. The lady on the note, seated on what looked like a circular shield, touched her chin and stared back out at him. 'These are super rare, though. Must have cost a *balloonful* of cash. Have you been collecting a long time?'

'Not long,' said Helen Susanna. 'I took it up to try and understand the appeal.'

This was a slightly strange thing to say. Rich came back to his seat.

'There's somebody I'd like you to speak to, Alan,' the old woman said, as she picked up an iPad from the tabletop and folded back its stand. 'She's waiting to vulink us. Would you mind chatting to her for a bit?'

'Who is she?'

'Senior.'

'Old? Like you?'

'I mean, dearie, that she's a senior person in the government. You'll recognise her face when it comes on.'

'You want me to talk to a senior government person?'

'If you wouldn't mind, my dear.'

'What about? I don't know anything. About The This? I don't know anything about The This.'

'Just a quick chat,' said Helen Susanna. 'Her time is quite squeezed.'

'I honestly don't know what's going on,' said Rich. 'I'm honestly the last person she should be speaking to. Wait – the *government* are interested? Why are the government involved?'

'The government *are* interested,' said Helen Susanna, as if that answered Rich's question.

Foforn had come into the conservatory and was standing unobtrusively, or as unobtrusively as a six-foot-four twenty-stone tower of muscles and threat ever can, by the fridge. THE POLICE – Rich remembered now that they were an antique pop band. And with that memory came the realisation that they had been the ones who had sung the lonely song that had been playing in the pub. The cogs and wheels of his memory slotted into place. Why hadn't he recognised it straight away? Slow of him. Lonely.

In this theta that I call my …

'Soul,' Rich said. 'I mean, sure. Why not?'

The iPad beeped, and a face appeared on it. Helen Susanna was correct: Rich recognised the individual immediately.

A member of the cabinet, a prominent figure. She peered out of her digital window and nodded to Rich.

'Mr Rigby?'

'Hello,' said Rich.

'Thank you for agreeing to talk to me. You can understand, of course, that we in government have concerns about organisations like The This. Helen Susanna tells me they've been trying to recruit you.'

'I really don't know anything about it,' said Rich. 'I mean, yes they have.'

'But you're resisting?'

'It's a cult,' said Rich. 'I'm not the sort to join a ... well, you know. That's my position. At any rate, I just don't. I just don't think it's me, you know?'

'They don't usually go out of their way to recruit specific individuals,' said the minister. 'Indeed, pressuring one individual to join, especially in the teeth of that individual's disinclination ... well, it's very rare. It's so rare that we are forced to conclude that you are special in some way, Mr Rigby.'

'I'm honestly not,' said Rich. 'I have no idea why they're so keen on me.'

'Do you have any loved ones who are members of The This?'

'I don't have any loved ones at all.'

The face in the screen eased a slight smile. 'You did some of the research for a *First Adept* magazine feature on the group. That's when it all started?'

'It was a standard DifferenceWork gig. I mean, it wasn't anything, really. D-Work is an app that—'

'I know what D-Work is.'

'Well, that's all it was. I went to their Putney offices, asked the questions I was briefed to ask, ten minutes, literally ten minutes, came home, sent in my pro forma. I mean, I wasn't even credited in the article. It was grunt work. I mean, that's fine, that's what D-Work gigs are, and I got paid.'

It occurred to Rich to mention that his D-Work had dried up recently, but then again, he thought: *Surely that can't be relevant.*

'Hey,' he said. 'You're the government. Can't you just close them down? I mean, if you have concerns. If they're doing anything illegal?'

'*Are* they doing anything illegal, Mr Rigby?'

'I mean, they've been spying on me, I think. Hacking my data. Isn't that illegal?'

'Thank you for your time,' said the minister. 'I'm sure we'll talk again soon.'

The screen flicked off.

Rich looked at the yin-yang face of Helen Susanna.

'What was that?'

'Our government is worried,' she said, in her croaky voice. 'They're not the only government worried. Worry is a general state, at the highest levels. There are half a dozen similar companies on watch lists as potential dangers to the safety and order of the general polity, and The This are the biggest.'

'So are they going to … I don't know,' asked Rich, 'make a move? Pass legislation? Send in the troops?'

'Think about the practicalities, my dear, for just one doggy-gone minute. Even assuming that the government has the wherewithal to do what you're suggesting … dawn raids, dearie? Locking up all The This senior staff? Locking up every single *person* with Thistech in her skull, is it? That would require a prison the size of the Isle of Wight – but even assuming a government thought they could orchestrate such a mass strike, how would it play? Everyone is on social media nowadays, and hundreds of thousands of those people treat their Thisware as just another upgrade. There's no groundswell of opposition. Users report much higher levels of satisfaction – not just with their kit, but with their lives – than non-users. If we tried to criminalise them there'd be a huge public backlash, and our government wouldn't stay in power for very long. They're breaking no laws, they make their customers very happy, they create jobs, they pay their taxes.'

'But they are dangerous?'

'Oh, yes, yes,' said Helen Susanna. 'Very dangerous indeed.'

Rich stared through the glass sides of the conservatory. Helen Susanna's garden was a long green monolith laid on its side, with flesh-pink and blood-red rose bushes flanking it, left and right respectively. At the end of the garden was a smart-looking plank fence on which was fixed a surveillance globe.

'What do I do?'

'*We*, dearie,' said Helen Susanna. 'What do *we* do. And to begin with I'm going to suggest you stay here for a few days. Faux-Fawn will look after us – his omelettes are particularly nice. I have no olfactory capacity whatsoever and only two thirds of a tongue, but even I can taste how delicious they are.'

'Stay here?'

'It's safer than your gaff, which, I'm afraid, must be regarded as their territory now.'

'You think I'll be safe from … from *them* here?'

At this Helen Susanna began a long riff on what in more conventional human beings would have been 'laughter': a series of wheezes, a stuttering cough, a clucking trio of indrawn breaths, and a weird grimacing of that half of her face that was visible. The laughter upset her lungs so it was a while before she could settle herself.

'Not at all, dear boy,' she said. 'Of course they know you're here. Fawn is good, but he's not going to deflect the malign intents of a group comprising 650,000 people in perfect mental synchronicity and with trillions of dollars at their disposal.'

This was not comforting news.

'So what am I doing here, exactly?'

'Your being here will irritate them,' rasped Helen Susanna, sipping her tea. 'In your flat they have you continually under observation. So long as you stay off social media they can't do *that* here. They know where you are, but where you are is *in their blind spot*. And they won't like that. Now, my gamble is that they won't dislike it enough to break the law in too flagrant a manner, and that will buy us time.'

'Flagrant what?' Rich asked, nervously.

'So far their legal shenanigans have been, mostly, virtual – many many violations of data privacy legislation, cyberespionage, insider dealing, that kind of thing. Now, you *could* say, if we – if the government – want to lock The This down, why don't we prosecute them for those offences?'

'Why don't you?'

'We try, dear boy. But they're hard to convict. Complex and lengthy trials, mostly coming to no resolution at all, occasionally levying fines that make no dent whatsoever on The This's vast coffers. And the trials never get reported, because it's all so boring, so the real battle – which is to evict The This from the throne of vague goodwill they currently occupy in the unfocused public consciousness – won't be won that way. Now, if they *killed* somebody … I mean, they have killed people. Quite a few. But if they killed somebody in an obvious, traceable way …' She grinned, and the left half of her mouth slid up under her mask and out of sight.

'Somebody like me?'

'Did you ever hear of ConnAct? They're a US implant company, making hardware and running software not entirely dissimilar to The This's. There are dozens of similar companies, because it's such a lucrative market, but for a time ConnAct were big.'

'I did hear of them,' said Rich. 'I think. Didn't they go bust?'

'They made a mistake. They killed people. They killed people and were raided by the FBI, but – and this was their mistake – they did all this before they were large enough to be able to absorb the law enforcement hit.'

'Killed people? Why, though?'

'All these hive mind groups kill people,' said Helen Susanna, matter-of-factly.

'Christ, Jesus, why?'

'They have to. Really they don't have an option.'

Foforn cleared his throat, resonantly. Helen Susanna glanced up at him, scowled, and carried on.

'Alan, I've been on the inside. It's a little hard to explain, but it's absolutely vital you understand this. When you join The This you don't stop being an individual. You're not subsumed wholly into the gestalt, and you're not privy to every action and every collective rationalisation. The group develops specialisations, subsidiarities, just like the cells in a human body. It has to, considering its size. And the specialisation protects them – their core consciousness is elaborately firewalled behind shells and shells of different grades of Thisser. Most users are outside that, though, and remain individuals. Mostly. But at the same time, when you join the gestalt you kind-of *are* privy to every action, and part of every collective decision-making process and rationalisation. You're part of something bigger, better, and every individual is a part in that bigger-ness, that better-ness. And for most people it works fine. But there are some people who join the group who don't fit.'

'Don't fit?'

'In many ways it's puzzling to me that there's not a higher proportion of such people, actually. Really it's fractions of one per cent. Tiny numbers. I'm talking about people with a profound wrongness in them, deformations of the soul – a materialist would say psychopaths, people mentally and psychologically antithetical to collectivity. Poisons, as it were, in the group system. They have to be purged.'

'Why don't they just unplug them? Get their insert surgically removed? That's easily done, isn't it?'

'These individuals don't want to unplug. I was in The This and I didn't want to unplug. It would be like you pulling your own eyeball out. You could do it – technically, I mean. It's physically possible for you to stick your fingers into your socket and yank the jelly out. But you won't, you can't, it's more than your willpower is capable of.'

'Can't the rest of the group ... I don't know ... apply peer pressure, make the anomalous individuals disengage?'

'If you mean compelling a sentient individual, against their individual will, to make an appointment with a doctor, to sign consent forms, sit through the operation – no, that's not something that could be reliably managed by the gestalt. Some of the undesirable individuals do have psychopathologies that make them, as individuals, vulnerable to suicidal ideation. *They* can be pressured into killing themselves, sure. Then again, others don't, and they have to be killed.'

'Holy shit.'

'I know, dearie,' said Helen Susanna. 'It's vile. I mean, from our individual human perspective it's vile. From their collective perspective it's necessary. It's hygiene.'

'It's murder.'

'Of course it is. ConnAct erred in being too obvious when they murdered their misfits. They hired mob assassins, paid them, left financial e-trails, and it was too easy to trace the hits back to them. The This have not been so careless.'

Rich stared into his cooling tea. He was thinking of Aella Hamilton, and of Emma, and of the fact that they both belonged to – that they were both intimately part of – an organisation that murdered people. That ought to give him the creeps, oughtn't it?

Oughtn't it? It didn't feel real.

'How do they do it?'

'The murdering? Why, that's easy. You as an individual couldn't pull out your own eyeball, no, no, but your body as a collection of cells has no qualms about churning through its own cellular material. Once the implant is sufficiently embedded, with enough tendrils through the brain tissue, it's not hard to induce a stroke, a heart attack or asthma attack, depending on the subject's vulnerability to those sorts of things. The This are cautious, though. They don't want to leave the implant for police or government scientists to get their hands on it and read. When members of the gestalt die of natural causes, they always stipulate cremation. But when members are murdered it's often necessary to intervene physically, to destroy the insert. A gun in the mouth … an accident that crushes the skull. Decapitation, sometimes.'

'Blimey,' said Rich.

'Amateurs,' said Foforn. His voice, Rich was surprised to hear, was rather high-pitched.

'More tea?' suggested Helen Susanna. 'I fear yours has grown cold.'

:8:

Rich was put up in the spare room. Or a spare room, for there were several. It was a nice enough space: single bed, view of the back garden. He had a desk and computer, the latter free for him to use so long as he didn't sign into any of his personal accounts. Helen Susanna gave him a shell identity so he could browse. He ghosted his own social media, which was a vaguely disconcerting thing to do. He played online games and browsed around, but it felt hollow without his actual networks, the many silken threads he had spent years weaving around his online persona, his connections, his online friends who were in no meaningful sense whatsoever actually friends.

He kicked about Helen Susanna's house. He checked out her banknote collection – it wasn't particularly extensive, but it contained some extremely valuable specimens – and sat on her abbreviated patio in the sun reading books from her shelves. He watched a lot of telly. Foforn was a large, discreet, Jeevesian presence.

Helen Susanna was right about his cooking, though: it was delicious. After three days Rich looked back on his usual diet of microwave Tesco chicken tikka, takeaway pizza and noodles with self-contempt. Helen Susanna came and went, and was often away for long stretches.

'Am I allowed out of the house, Mr Foforn?' Rich asked.

Foforn's marmoreal head moved from a perfectly vertical alignment to one angled at five degrees.

Rich strolled into town, had a coffee in Starbucks, went to the river. People were wandering up and down, these Oedipal tribes of the self-blinded with their phones always in front of their faces. Now, though, what Rich noticed were the people who *didn't* have phones in front of their eyes. The people simply walking here and there, turning their heads to look at their environments. Staring not into their self-created fractal worlds, but out and up – looking, we might say, at the ceiling.

A young man wearing a THE NEW BAND T-shirt met his gaze and smiled. How Rich's heart rate cantered!

He didn't feel safe.

He picked up the pace and walked back to Helen Susanna's house.

He didn't feel safe. He didn't feel safe.

:9:

Helen Susanna returned in the early evening, and Foforn cooked the three of them a mushroom risotto with parmesan and rocket that might have been the single most delicious meal Rich had ever tasted. Helen Susanna opened a bottle of Guangxi Beaujolais. They chatted about nothing very much. It was relaxing. Indeed, Rich found himself being struck, as if with a great philosophical profundity, by how *pleasant* it was. Then Foforn cleared away and Helen Susanna went into the garden to sit in a recliner and smoke an old-fashioned cigarette.

'I allow myself one of these a day,' she said. 'I sometimes think it hardly matters and I should just go for it, smoke myself silly. I'll be dead in a year either way.'

'Oh!' said Rich.

'But then I think I would be missing something. The singularity of this experience intensifies its pleasure – if you smoke eighty a day smoking simply becomes the background noise of your life, as it were. The wallpaper. But if I limit myself to *one . . .*' She blew an ectoplasmic spire of smoke into the summer dusk sky. 'You want one?'

'No thank you,' said Rich. 'I used to, I mean. I used to smoke. But I quit years ago.'

'Yes, stay away from it, dearie,' Helen Susanna said. 'Quite right. Or you'll end up like me, with ruined lungs and half your face surgically cut away. Too much smoke, too much boozy-booze. Misspent youth.'

They sat in silence for a while and stared into the darkening sky. A mob of bats scattered and reassembled on a tangle of crazy trajectories. The high-pitched whizz of an approaching mosquito. The planes overflying down to Heathrow were racks of blinking lights. Every so often one came over with some fault to its noise-cancellation equipment, scraping a deep-throated cacophony after it like a bridal train. Mostly they just passed, ghostly, only hissing through the air..

'What was it like?' Rich asked, shortly.

'You don't mean smoking,' Helen Susanna noted. 'You mean The This.' She was silent, and then she said: 'Individual people are different, so their experience of being in the gestalt is always unique. Some connect straight away, in a deep way, as if the group is what they have been waiting for all their lives. It's the ultimate cure for loneliness, after all. Other people connect and feel a baseline belonging, a security that simply enables the rest of their lives. Doing their job, raising their kids, whatever it is. For plenty of people in The This, it is a *part* of their lives. For others it's the whole of their lives.'

'And you were . . . the second kind?'

'I dived deep. It filled the hole in my soul that I'd spent all those decades trying to stuff with alcohol and drugs and tobacco and sex. I was deeply, profoundly *in*.'

'You wouldn't have come out, if the . . . you know.'

'You can say cancer, dearie. Cancer's not a swear.'

'But without it you wouldn't have left?'

'Oh no. Then again, having left, I have the double perspective. And hand on my heart – I can't *tell* you how glad I am to be out. I don't have long left, but I have a mission now, and it's to do what I can to break The This.'

'You really think they're that much of a danger?'

Helen Susanna's cigarette was nothing but its filter now, and she crushed it into the ashtray. The quality of light had gone from lavender to purple-black. A dog was barking away in the middle distance, repeating the same frantic shout over and over, as if it were trying to communicate something desperately simple and desperately important and nobody was listening. Human laughter from the other side of the fence, sudden and then gone.

'Existential danger,' she said. 'No hyperbole. It's a matter of bald existence. They will grow vaster – vaster than empires, as the phrase has it. They won't immediately seek to supplant humanity, not entirely, because at the moment they need us – people like you and me – or people like you, at any rate – to keep having sex and keep having babies. They need to keep watching over those people as they grow up so that these new people can take the tech and join the gestalt. Since The This can't renew itself, it needs us to do the whole mitosis–cytokinesis thing for its component cells. At least, that's what they need *for now*.'

Without his phone, Rich wasn't able to check what those technical terms meant. But he got the gist.

'Can't the members of The This just have their own kids?'

'They can. Some of them do. But not at the rate they need. And not without diffusing their unity as a gestalt – because if a member of The This has a child – as, of course, lots have – then there's no alternative to making the kid the focus of your attention. For a couple of decades, anyway. Focusing on the kid rather than on the gestalt. That's … destabilising. You end up in the outer party, rather than the inner ring. It's OK, but it's not all it could be. A fuzzy cloud of mostly-Thissers, circling the hard kernel of True Thissers. And you can't fit a baby with their hardware. *That* can't be done until the brain is full-sized and properly wired in, and *that* doesn't happen until late in adolescence. There's always the chance that these kids will look at their blank-eyed, weird-smiling parents and think, this cult's not for me, daddy-o.'

'Blimey,' said Rich.

'So The This finds it more strategic to keep a large population of old-school humans kicking about. Let them – us, I mean – keep breeding, so they can harvest their offspring.'

'Jesus-blimey,' said Rich.

'Eventually,' rasped Helen Susanna, 'they'll find a way to do without us. Then they'll supersede us altogether, and they won't have any *use* for us, and I'm really not sure that will be such a desirable outcome for us, dearie.'

'Blimey-Jesus and crikey,' said Rich. 'That's pretty apocalyptic.'

'Oh yes,' agreed Helen Susanna, and started coughing.

It was thirty seconds before she got her cough under control.

'You don't think,' Rich suggested, 'you're overplaying the danger? These things are fads, aren't they? You said the other day there are six hundred thousand registered users of The This. Maybe it grows to a million and then does a Myspace, fades away as something newer and cooler comes along.'

'Well,' croaked Helen Susanna, 'you say that, my dear lad, *if* I may say so, because you've never been inside.'

Rich was silent.

'They will grow. I had cancer but they *are* cancer, on the largest scale. They will grow and grow. The only constraint on their growth is the one I mentioned – the fact that they rely on the rest of us to resupply their component cells. But that won't be the case for ever. Science keeps making advances, and one of the ways in which The This prosper is that, because they are able to pool the expertise and creativity of a large population of people, they *make* breakthroughs in science. And they have no problem generating money. So, yes. Not this year and not next year, but it won't be long before it's too late to do anything about them. We need to act now.'

Rich sat looking out into the night. Stars filtering through a neighbour's trees. The singular moon. He had a distantly vertiginous sense of reality itself moving, shifting on some huge scale, Ptolemaic spheres layered over one another like a cosmic onion. The future is behind you, because you can't see it; but you're hurrying backwards into it nonetheless. *Who was it said that?* Rich didn't have his phone and so couldn't check. We tear up the map, and remake the map.

'Helen Susanna,' he said. 'What was it *like*, though?'

'It was amazing,' she said, without hesitation. 'It was the most amazing thing of my whole life. And I didn't even like it! Think how it is for people who *do*!'

'You didn't like it?'

'Not really.'

'But you said you absolutely loved it.'

'Oh, I did!'

Rich pondered the distinction she was making. But of course it made sense.

'You still think that way, even now you're out?'

'One hundred per cent, dearie. Which is it to be? Bits of frayed lint blowing in the breeze? Or threads threads threads woven into the most beautiful and meaningful tapestry the world has ever seen? It's no choice at all, really. The fact that it's so beguiling is what *makes* it so dangerous. It's like sex. It's *better* than sex.'

'Better than sex,' said Rich, who was of a gender and age for which sex was that kind of speed-of-light or absolute-zero limit, than which more was not to be conceived.

'It's the difference between masturbation and an orgy.'

'The This is the orgy,' said Rich. 'And living the traditional mode of life is … the other thing.'

'You might think the orgy is more exciting, but the truth is it's less. It's more constrained. Maybe that sounds crazy. But it's true.'

'I'm surprised to hear you say so,' Rich said, who had limited experience of sex and none whatsoever, except through porno fantasy, of orgies.

'Dearie, you're making a common mistake,' Helen Susanna told him. 'You don't fancy me, because I'm old and ugly. Because I'm not a sexual being *to you*, you find it hard to think of me as a sexual being at all. My dear boy, that speaks volumes about how your own sex drive distorts your perspective of the world, don't you think? Remember, I've been alive three times as long as you have. Back in the seventies I was young and attractive and there were plenty of orgies. I used to be a regular orgee. I don't go to so many nowadays, obviously.'

At this, she laughed her weird, scrapy laugh. Rich could almost picture her ruined lungs churning in her chest like a slushy.

'I've never been to an orgy,' Rich confessed.

'It's not what it's cracked up to be, you know. There's an initial buzz, when you first arrive, and that's pretty exciting, because you're surrounded by people having sex. There is, of course, a kind of baseline excitement tangled up in all that. But it soon goes off. When you have sex with *one* person, you choose them. You *know* you like and fancy them – and they you, which is more important, actually. You're in control, the two of you are. But at an orgy there are people you fancy and people you really don't, and actually the latter outnumber the former. Still, you have to, as it were, muck in. And it's amazingly smelly. Hu! I mean, really, believe me, I went to quite a few, when I was younger. Because it took me a while to realise I wasn't enjoying myself. I thought I was, but I wasn't. I mean, I was getting sex, and that's good, right? You need the wisdom of maturity to grasp that that's a necessary but not a sufficient condition. Nowadays me and my dildo are sharing the best sex of my entire life.'

'Jesus!' said Rich, genuinely startled.

'Why is that surprising? I know what I like, sexually, better than any stranger does.'

'You talk like no old lady I've ever met.'

She scraped out another laugh. 'It's not like it's not a universal. Sex, I mean. But this, this is my point – you yourself coming… that's exquisite. Watching someone you love orgasming… it's lovely. But a stranger's orgasm-face is an ugly and disconcerting thing. Trust me on this. All that gurning and straining, like you've stubbed your toe, or are labouring at a constipated shit. Mostly we can ignore the pleasure of others, but we find the *intense* pleasure of others obnoxious. However, there are times when you're forced to pay attention to it. And that's The This.'

'I mean… wow, though. An orgy.'

'Pretty much. I mean, in a manner of speaking. This is an analogy, OK? It's not literally like an orgy because it's really not a sexual thing. Being in The This is not a sexual connection. The connection is much more spiritual than it is physical. Sex barely enters into it, in fact. My point is – it's the erosion of the borders of your individuality, which means that your emotional and intellectual pleasures, not to mention your willpower, get overwritten by the pleasures and willpower of the group. It's not that your individuality disappears entirely. It's still there. And in the most you're part of the same group that's overwhelming all the given individuals who are *not* you, which is exhilarating. But you're also you, so you're also being overwhelmed. Nobody attends orgies all their life. It's a thing people do in their promiscuous youth, before settling down into settled middle age with one partner. Or with none. Some older people do keep attending orgies, of course – always geezers, usually creepy geezers. But everybody knows there's something a bit off about them. You know? With The This they're trying to invert that life-arc. They want people to give up the solitude of their pleasure and get with the gang-bang.' She stopped to catch her breath. 'Woof,' she said. 'Time for bed.'

For one startling moment Rich thought she meant: the two of them together. But she didn't, of course. She was just declaring the evening conversation over. She got laboriously to her feet and toddled off upstairs. Rich poured what remained of the wine bottle into his glass, and went inside to watch TV for a while.

:10:

Some days Rich tried to engage Foforn in conversation. It did not flow.

'You been in the bodyguard business long then?'

Foforn possessed the ability to look unblinkingly at a person for a disconcerting length of time. Perhaps that was part of his skill set, as a bodyguard.

Another day: 'Were you in the army, Mr Foforn?' Nothing. 'It's just that I heard bodyguards often picked up their skills in the army.'

Nothing.

'Seriously, though – Helen Susanna really seems to think this is an existential battle for the survival of the human species. In the long run, I mean. Do you think it's really so serious as all that?'

'Would you,' said Foforn, with infinite menace, leaning over Rich, 'like a cup of *tea*, Mr Rigby?'

'Two sugars, thank you,' Rich replied in a diminished voice.

Then Helen Susanna herself came home. She had started walking with a walking stick as she went out and about, which, Rich assumed, could hardly be a good sign.

'You ready to meet Hoyle, Rich?'

'Ready as I'll ever be!' Rich called through brightly, from the conservatory. The door and the windows were all open and the heat was extreme, and the two sugars had evidently spiked a little bravado in his blood. 'Wait, who's Hoyle?'

'You'll need to sign the Official Secrets Act,' said Helen Susanna. 'Then I can tell you exactly what her role is.'

'I mean ...' said Rich. 'OK, I guess?'

Hoyle came that afternoon: a tall, slender woman with a large spherical head and close-cut black hair. Her manner was hearty to an excess – was, indeed, rather more hypercardiac than Rich was comfortable with. But at no point in the day had anyone given him anything to sign, so he was still in the dark as to who, exactly, she was. High up in the government, presumably. She strode into the hallway of Helen Susanna's house, she dumped a large shoulder bag on the floor and then she came over to Rich.

'Mr *Rig*by,' she boomed. She shook his hand hard and fast, as if she were shaking dice. 'Delighted. Lovely to meet. Helen Sue has given me the low down. I'm Rebecca Hoyle, but people call me Olive – for –' she snorted a laugh – 'obvious reasons.' She snorted another laugh.

'I'm sorry?' said Rich.

She let go of his hand, and looked closely at him.

'Olive Hoyle.' She stepped back and gestured at herself. 'Olive Hoyle. I mean, look at me!'

'I'm really sorry,' said Rich. 'I'm not allowed my phone, and without it I find it quite tricky to track down cultural references, allusions and memes.'

Hoyle stared at Rich for a moment, and then grinned very widely.

'I can see why she likes you, Rigby. Right – Timothy, I think an S-*praise*-oh, if you don't mind?'

'Very well, Mrs Hoyle,' said Foforn.

'And any coffee for you, Mr Rigby – may I call you Alan?' Hoyle boomed.

'Rich.'

'Reach? Like the Browning poem? "A man's reach should exceed his grasp"? Excellent – let's take our places, Reach. No coffee for you?'

'I've just had a tea,' said Rich.

'Excellent. Antioxidants and such, and so forth.'

She even managed to sit at the table in a forceful manner. Foforn put a miniature cup of black coffee on the table in front of her.

'Helen Sue!' Hoyle bellowed. '*Seriously* good to see you again, old girl. Still breathing, I'm pleased to see! Heart still pumping blood around your body!'

'Always a pleasure, Olive,' said Helen Susanna, lowering herself slowly onto a chair. 'Olé for me please, Fawn.'

Foforn shimmered back with a cup of café au lait and withdrew to a discreet distance.

'Let's not beat the bush's circumference in a *circular* manner,' boomed Hoyle. 'We can do it here, no probs, no probs that's obvs. No need to *move* you, Rich, to a clinic, or anything like that. Once we've agreed terms and strategies, I can have a team here in half an hour. They bring a chair-gizmo and all the necessary surgical gubbins.'

'Surgical?' said Rich.

'Half an hour, max,' said Hoyle, as if this were a reassuring datum. 'What?'

'What?' repeated Rich.

'What-what?' said Hoyle.

Rich gawped.

'Don't tell me, Mr Rigby,' said Hoyle, 'that my own dear Helen Susanna hasn't *broached* this with you yet?'

'We've,' croaked Helen Susanna, her one eye peering inscrutably at Rich, 'been working our way towards the topic.'

'What topic?' Rich asked.

Foforn, standing by the door, coughed discreetly.

'Our boffins *plunge*,' said Hoyle, with alarming emphasis on the word, 'a gizmo into your Wernicke's area. It's been months and millions, honestly, *millions* in development, but they reckon it's up to spec. They reckon so, and they're the best we have. Then we send you out, liaise with those chaps so very keen to recruit you, and Bob's your,' she slowed, looking from Rich to Helen Susanna and back again, 'father's or ...' She stopped, took a sip of her espresso, and finished: '...mother's *brother*. Helen Sue, have you really not briefed him on this?'

'I'm not sure he's ready, Olive,' Helen Susanna replied. 'Not as yet.'

'Not ready? Come now. Chop chop. My people are getting

anxious as to the timings. Come now, Rich. You're ready, aren't you?'

'Ready for what?'

There was a silence.

'We want to put a specially designed device in your head,' croaked Helen Susanna. 'Then send you into The This – undercover, as it were. Our people are confident that the device will interfere creatively with The This software. Best case – it will give us a back door to be able to hack the whole The This operation.'

'Oh,' said Rich.

'It could be a vital breakthrough.'

'My Wernicke's area?' Rich asked.

Lacking a phone really did leave him hopelessly ill-informed.

'It's in the middle of the brain,' said Helen Susanna. 'It's where speech is processed, and where a lot of cognition happens.'

'They use a needle,' shrieked Hoyle, with apparent glee. 'Long fat needle!' Then, more soberly. 'Don't worry, Mr Rigby, you won't feel a thing.'

'I can see a number of ways in which this could go wrong,' Rich observed, mildly enough, in the circumstances.

'I'll take that as a yes,' said Hoyle, getting hugely to her feet. 'Thanks for the caffeine, Timmy. I'll be in touch.'

And she swept out of the house.

Helen Susanna and Rich remained at the table. Birdsong was audible through the open conservatory doors.

'Tell me it's not a suicide mission,' Rich said.

Helen Susanna shrugged. 'I wasn't lying when I said how huge the stakes are. This is do or die, not for individuals, but for *Homo sapiens* as a whole. My dear, it's not designed to be a suicide mission, but I can't promise you anything.'

'Why me, though?'

'Why you,' agreed Helen Susanna. 'We've sent people in before.

Anyone can join The This, after all – anyone can have the tech installed. It's not like they're hard to infiltrate. Initial agents instantly went over to the other side, so we tweaked our device, and screened our applicants more carefully. But they're canny, our enemy. As soon as a person is in, you're open to everybody else in the gestalt. Impossible to do conventional cloak and dagger when everybody knows everything about you. Spies need shadows to lurk in, and inside The This it's all sunlight and glass in every direction, forever. So this is a new kind of opportunity for us. We've never tried something like this, though. I mean, this particular virus we want you to carry.'

'You think it will work?'

'We've sent plenty of people in to gather intel, to reveal the inner weaknesses. None of them, not one, has succeeded. The collective either suborns, or, more rarely, rejects our agents.'

Rich assumed *rejects* was a euphemism for *kills*.

'They'll do the same to me,' he said.

'Well, that's the thing, isn't it, my dear boy. The difference now is that *they really want you*. They really *really* want you. We're not sure why they do, but they do. And that means that, just maybe, they can't afford to reject you. It won't take long, if our tech boys and girls have done their job properly – it won't take long for our virus to upload. And if we can compromise the software holding everybody together, then the entire hive mind will start to come unstuck. Disaggregate. We don't know if it'll work. Our boffins can't give us one hundred per cent on that. But it's the best chance we've had. It's a golden chance. Not one we can afford to pass up.'

'Um . . .' said Rich. 'Virus?'

'You've seen *Independence Day*.'

But of course, lacking his phone, Rich had no idea what this reference meant.

:11:

He wasn't going to do it, of course. What was he, mad? *Kamikaze* – a word he'd always seen written down and never pronounced, and which he'd believed rhymed with *haze* and *maze* until corrected, by hooting mockery, at university – was not him. He had a day in town: took the train up to Waterloo and wandered along the South Bank. Drank a pint of eye-wateringly expensive beer overlooking the Thames. Wandered back. Clearly, since he wasn't going to get himself lost in that hazy maze, he needed to think about what he *was* going to do. He had a life, after all. He probably needed to get a life properly to have a life. But what? How? To what end?

Tricky questions to answer.

People strolling up and down the concrete promenade kept looking at him. Crowds of tourists flowing over Southwark Bridge, so many of them with phones pressed to their faces. *I had not thought life had undone so many.* People stopping to take photos of the Thames. Or were they snapping him? Innocent Rich Rigby, sitting having a swift pint?

He walked back to Waterloo with his shoulders hunched up. What was he going to do? Move away, try and start a new life somewhere far away – except there was nowhere far away from Online. Ubiquitous interconnectivity. All society mediated now. We all live in Ubiquistan nowadays.

Were people looking at him funny?

He rode the train back out to Putney. What was he going to do with himself? He needed a new start to his life. Go back to Helen Susanna, he figured, and explain the situation: he was backing out of this crazy kamikaze plan. He was going to sell his flat and move away. He would decide a destination later.

The cradle rocking of the train carriage, filled with people silently absorbed in their various phones. Every face veiled with plastic and metal. The sun emerged from behind a cloud, and dazzlepoints of brightness burnt briefly white on the scuffs of the train windows. Manifestly unimpressed by what it saw, the sun buried its face in the grey screen of another cloud.

Putney Station in its valley cleft of Victorian brick. Rich climbed the stairs to the exit, going over forms of words he would use on Helen Susanna. To make her understand. He didn't – this came to him as he trudged up Putney Hill with the force of belated revelation – he didn't want to *disappoint* the old bird. But what possible use would it be, to sacrifice himself to The This? He'd either get swallowed whole as some tasty little morsel, or he'd resist and they'd induce a stroke or a heart attack and crush his head in an industrial waste compacter or something. Better he just tuck his chin to his chest and avoid eye contact (*everyone* was looking at him!) and just try to get on with his unassuming life.

Back at the house, Foforn let him in. Helen Susanna was sitting at the table in the conservatory, a mug of green tea in front of her.

'Have you made up your mind then, my Hamletty chum?'

Rich stood for a moment looking at her. He turned his head and clocked Foforn, standing quietly in the kitchen. There was a material difference, which is to say: a difference defined by its materiality, in being in the same meatspace as them. Face to face.

He said: 'I'm worried about dying.'

Helen Susanna nodded slowly, but didn't say anything.

'It sounds,' Rich said, having registered his own words, 'kind-of crazy to put it like that. Melodramatic, I suppose. But there it is.'

'The problem,' croaked Helen Susanna, 'is not in the dying, though. Dying's natural enough. It's the alternative.'

'I mean …' said Rich, the realisation that this was what he wanted arriving in his head only as he spoke, 'obviously I'll do it. I'll do it, but I just want my concerns … uh … noted. You know?'

Helen Susanna nodded again. 'Noted,' she said. 'They are.'

And that was that. The day unwound. Rich and Helen Susanna played chess, like they were in a Bergman movie. Foforn cooked an absolutely delicious supper of salmon linguini and the three of them ate and drank wine and chatted and laughed, and only for some of this time did Rich find resentment popping up into his thoughts. If he declined this crazy mission he would lose this … companionship … and if he went on it he would probably lose it anyway. Better to lose it by dying, perhaps, than lose it by disappointing and abandoning his friends. He saw that, although it didn't dissolve away the resentment. It is, after all, one of the oldest and most important insights in human life. It's the fundamental strong force that binds human atoms into larger structures, and understanding it comes better late than never.

They capped the evening off with whisky. Sloshing inside that glass goitre of the bottle's neck and so into the tumblers. Autumn-coloured discs in the glass, like gold casino tokens. *Gu'nigh. Gu'nigh, my boy.*

Rich woke so early the following day it was still dark outside. He lay in bed for a while, thinking about things. It was like sitting on the dim shore of the Underworld as the boatman poled his flat-bottomed boat inexorably towards you. Closer and closer. De Diss. Wind chimes tinkling very far away, or tinnitus, one of the two. A swirling in his gut: dynamo anxiety.

After a while Rich got up, had a pee and went downstairs.

Helen Susanna was already up. Did she ever sleep? She was

eating a bowl of scrambled eggs with a fork, and she used this utensil to gesture to Rich to sit down. He sat. For a while she continued shovelling the pale matter underneath her mask and into her mouth.

'Nerves?' she said.

'Woke up early,' said Rich.

'Nerves are natural,' insisted Helen Susanna. She dropped her fork into the bonded china of her now empty bowl like she was ringing a bell. 'Before a person goes into battle.'

'Talk of battles isn't calculated to reassure me.'

'You'll be fine,' she croaked. 'It is a far far better thing, and thus, and the like, and so on. Coffee?'

'Yes please.'

'Make me one as well, would you? Whilst you're getting yours?'

Rich gave her a hard stare, but he did get up, and went through and boiled the kettle. Helen Susanna's house contained a dozen different ways in which coffee could be brewed, and he chose the simplest, which was two smartpods in two mugs. When he came back, a mug in either hand, Helen Susanna had opened the conservatory doors and stepped into the garden. He followed her out. She was smoking a cigarette.

'Is that your one for the day?' he asked, handing her the mug. 'Bit early, isn't it?'

'I might,' she said, staring past him, 'permit myself two today. If today goes well.'

To the east the sky was shifting from cold indigo to red and toffee colours, as if the horizon were an electrical ring heating the whole sky. A grey-black pot of coffee lowered over the whole world, being boiled at the start of the day. Helen Susanna accepted her mug and the two stood side by side for a while in silence.

The unending succession of planes swooping low through the sky down towards Heathrow, hissing like they were sliding down satin.

'You know the problem with the world?' Helen Susanna said. 'There are too many Samsons. Too many Samsons and not enough Delilahs.'

'So that's what I'll be?'

'They *want* you. That's the unique opportunity. They don't press-gang people – quite the reverse. They don't compel people to join them at all. I believe they *can't*, actually. I believe the nature of the link that binds them into the whole is such that compulsion would dissolve it.'

'What you're saying is that I need to *want* to join,' said Rich, 'or it won't work.'

Birds moving over the sky like blown petals.

'You had a relationship with a woman called Caroline,' said Helen Susanna.

That was a startling thing to hear the old woman say.

'Jesus, your surveillance has certainly done a number on me,' he said.

Then he thought: the fewness of the banknotes Helen Susanna had bought. The fact that she knew, without his having to say, how he took his tea. Caught between the leering observation of The This on the one hand, and the clinical invasion of his privacy by the government on the other, and nowhere private for him to hide his humble head. He was angry, for about five seconds. But the anger was not the staying kind. He sulked for a minute or so, to hide this fact.

'Don't get all prickly, kiddo,' said Helen Susanna, sucking another lungful of poisoned air. Pause. Then she blew a misty sword-blade out of her mouth. 'Of course we checked you out. And don't think you're the only person who's limping through their emotional life with a broken heart. I had a wild youth, sure. But I fell in love. And then I lost that love. You never get over that. So I know, all right?'

'Jesus,' said Rich, quietly.

'My point is – loneliness corrodes the human spirit. It's a rust upon our bright metal, yes? Human beings aren't supposed to be alone. Now – don't misunderstand – they're not supposed to live in a fucking hive mind neither.'

'You swore!'

'But there's a middle path, and it's human fellowship, it's friendship and love, the *balance* of me and others. That's what we're fighting for, yes?'

'I already agreed. I already said I'd do it.'

'You're not listening to me, dearie,' said Helen Susanna, taking another drag from her fag. 'You have to *want* it, or it's not going to work. This is not a stealth operation. The This know exactly what we're trying, and will have prepared countermeasures. But we have one advantage, the only advantage we have, an unprecedented thing for us – *they* want *you*. I wish I knew why, but it's enough that they do. And if you want *them*, then you'll slip snugly into their intricate mesh as smoothly as Excalibur slipping below the surface of the lake.'

'That's,' said Rich, 'King Arthur, isn't it?'

'You've been lonely so long you've forgotten what not-lonely feels like. I don't mean to touch a tender spot, dearie, where this Caroline lassie is concerned. I'm just saying. Don't fight it. Later today, don't fight your assimilation. You won't have to.'

The eastern sky was a blaze of parrot colours now, yellows and reds and orange, and all the birds shrieking their dawn-chorus excitement. The garden had dissolved out of obscurity into a broad distinctness, like a granular black and white photo developing into clarity in its miracle chemicals. Foforn was at the conservatory door.

'They're here,' said Helen Susanna.

And so Rich went inside.

The insertion itself took twenty minutes. They sat him down in a chair, shaved a dot on the back of his skull no larger than a sequin, pricked him with a local analgesic and slipped a needle inside. He felt pressure, and a kind of awkwardness – not exactly pain, but not comfortable either – as they trepanned a tiny hole in his cranium, and then he felt nothing at all. A void where his inner self ought to be.

'Strange to think,' he said, 'that you're rummaging around inside my brain.'

One of the technicians leant in, concerned.

'Don't try to speak.'

'Gibberish,' said Helen Susanna. 'Is that to be expected?'

Gibberish? Then there was a sucking noise, and a sensation like a mosquito bite at the back of his head.

'What?' Rich said. 'What-what?'

'Give him a cup of tea,' said a voice. Somebody not in Rich's field of vision. A big voice, the voice of God. Dancing rocks, a ceaseless turmoil seething, vast and visionary. 'Give him half an hour.'

I am that I am. Where was the subject/object distinction here? Boom. Mic drop.

'I think I've had some kind of religious revelation,' Rich said, but the others were looking at him with anxiety-wrinkles on their foreheads and puzzlement in their eyes.

He was let out of the special chair and guided to a regular chair at the dining table. A cup of tea was put in front of him. He felt floaty. Struck by the oddness of juxtaposing *give him a cup of tea* and *give him half an hour*, as if a physical entity like a cup of tea was of the same nature, to be passed from person to person, as a length of time. *Give him half an hour* meant: let him rest for roughly thirty minutes and he'll be fine. But time cannot be gifted. It is, on the contrary, continually being taken away from us. Time is a process of continuous removal.

'You all right, kiddo?' asked Helen Susanna, leaning in.

'Fine.' Rich fumbled his fingers at the back of his head, and felt the little plug, like a pimple, in among his hair where they had filled the hole they had made. 'Is that it? Is there any more?'

'Drink your tea, dearie.'

Foforn was standing, looking down at him.

'I feel …' Rich said, 'light. A bit weird, but not too bad.'

'Cosmic,' said somebody.

Was that Helen Susanna? Wait – did I *say that?*

The universe is a seethe of particles in a whirlpool so vast the human mind literally cannot comprehend it, and in that whirlpool are tourbillons and eddies and gusts that create odd little still points. Rich was in one such point now.

'Hard to believe it's over,' he said. 'It went more quickly than I thought.'

There was a palpable relaxation in the room. Helen Susanna was smiling now, and even Foforn eased his posture. *What had happened?*

'Looks like it'll be OK,' said Helen Susanna, sitting herself next to him.

He felt himself come more sharply into focus.

'What?' he said.

Helen Susanna brought out a phone, held it up so he could see the screen. It was his own face, puffy and lined, his forehead a sepia curve into thinning hair.

'Bah wah woh wah oh ah ah ah?' he said. Movement at the

peripheries of the image. The camera followed Rich as he was helped from the one chair to the other. 'Ar ar ar ar ar ar ar?'

'You're making better sense now, dearie,' Helen Susanna said. 'I'm very pleased to say.'

'Gracious me,' said Rich.

One of the individuals who had performed the operation touched Helen Susanna on the shoulder.

'It should root,' she said. 'But for operational reasons it would do best to grow in consonance *with* the enemy insert. If it is too well established prior to the actual operation, then the other insert might enter into a subordinate or conflictual dynamic with our one.'

'She means, my dear Alan Richard,' Helen Susanna said, patting the back of Rich's hand, 'that we need to get a *move* on. Finish your tea, and you can be on your way. The sooner The This claim you, the better so far as we're concerned.'

'Right,' said Rich.

He wasn't dazed, exactly, because a daze is a haze is a laze is a phase. Kami-kaze. Is only a phase. Amaze amaze. But something somewhere *somehow* was bleary about his thinking. Leary (howl howl) and gearing up to go into battle. A man of stone. The distant hiss of a stream, which might be a mighty river, a fountain flinging boulders to heap up into a mountain. Ssh, said the river. Not his eyes, oh no. Not his ears, oh no. Not his sense of taste, as the sweet and hot tea flowed around his tongue and slipped down his gullet. Touch, maybe. The grain of the table stood unusually proud of its surface under his fingers' ends. The air shushed him. He could hear the earth beneath him creaking with white roots stretching and growing. I mean, obviously that was just his imagination, he couldn't actually materially literally hear anything. But let's not dismiss imagination. He nods, and the wall opposite him counter-nods, to balance the movement out. His was the mind that considers and feels instead of proceeding to action, that remains alone with itself as inwardness and that therefore can take as its sole form and final aim the self-expression of the subjective life.

'Good luck, my brave boy,' said Helen Susanna.

They were at the front door now, he and she. Her mask meant that she couldn't kiss him, but she put the good side of her face against his, her dry cheek against his, and then he was away. How had he got from the table to the front door? No matter: he was outside now, and walking along the pavement. Perspective awry, and for a moment the kerb was a huge cliff face. But it was all right. The two-dimensional green man sang his monosyllabic song and beckoned him with verdant illumination and now Rich was on the far side of the road, at the top of the High Street. One long stride, one individual step, and he was at the bridge over the river. Cars swished away from him and towards him and he wasn't sure, for a moment, where he was supposed to be going. But then he recalled, and turned down Lower Richmond Road until he came to The This's Putney building.

For the second time in his life he stepped through the doors. Inside, Aella was standing there, smiling at him, and this time her smile looked genuine. Xander was here, too, with his ridiculous big bald head. And Emma, from the Green Man pub that day. All smiling.

'Come in,' they said, as one. 'We've been expecting you.'

5

Elegy for Pheno-Women and Pheno-Men

:1:

There was something wrong with Adan's Phene. He took it to the iPhene emporium.

'What seems to be the problem, shir?'

'Her face,' said Adan. 'Her face swaps out. Could it be, like, a virus?'

'Swaps out?'

'Glitches. You know? I mean, in ways *not* programmed.'

The two were seated, elbows nonchalant on a neon desk as vast and curving as the prow of a golden age ocean liner, softly glowing and ever-so-faintly pliant to the touch. The emporium's ceiling seemed an unnecessarily long way up. Elsewhere about the place, little trios – customer and server and Phene – huddled together over one or other problem.

Adan's Phene, Gee, stood patiently next to its owner.

'Could,' said the server, 'you give me a for-example?'

'When we're having sex, for example,' said Adan. 'For the last six months I've been setting her default face to Labelle Cho Aboya's. But last night we were having sex, and she changed her face to my mother's. Obviously I didn't program that. It just glitched into the new face while we were ... and the ... Well, you can imagine.'

A pause.

'I see,' said the server. 'Have you been sharing your Pheno with strangers? Anyone you don't know?'

'Sexually, you mean? No, no,' Adan replied. 'But what do you mean, share?'

'You'll excuse me having to ask, sir,' said the iPhene server. The log identified her as Jorjina. 'Some people like to set two Pheno-women or two Pheno-men, or one of each, such that they have sex together.'

'And then do what? Join in?'

'Or just watch,' said the server. 'More usually watch. Pheno models are exceptionally good at having sex, and there's a pleasure in watching two of them go at it. I mean, so I've heard. I mean ... ah ... it's not *my* thing. But that's what I've heard.' Jorjina showed Adan her thirty-two teeth. 'My point is, viruses can be spread by this practice. We recommend only humans to have sex with a Phene. They can't catch anything from us.'

'They can't catch anything from us,' Adan repeated. 'That's what I thought.'

'Please ask your Pheno to sit down in the diagnostic chair,' said Jorjina. 'Does it have an assigned gender?'

'She's called Elegy,' said Adan.

'Alrighty-tighty,' said Jorjina with fierce good cheer. She checked no screen, consulted no readout, but the data was fed to her densely and rapidly. Nor did her smile waver. 'I'm not finding anything, Mr Adan.'

'There must be something,' insisted Adan. 'I mean, like ... come on. I'm not imagining the glitches. One time I was having sex with my Phene and her face swapped out to Joseph Stalin. She extruded the moustache and everything.'

'Odd,' simpered Jorjina. 'I can give your Phene a basic software-rinse as a product courtesy. If you want a more thoroughgoing diagnostic I'm afraid we'll have to charge. Records show your device is no longer under guarantee.'

'OK, but hold on,' said Adan. 'I need to call my mom. Gee?' The Phene leant forward. 'Call Mom.'

The Phene's proportionate young-woman face blanked and returned as the face of an elderly woman. Wrinkles down her cheeks like the pelt of a Shar Pei puppy.

'Son?'

'Mom,' said Adan. 'I'm at the iPhene shop.'

'You know I don't approve,' said the mother. 'Why can't you get a regular phone like everybody else?'

'Everybody else has a Phene, Mom,' said Adan. 'Only people over a hundred years old like you and your poker-friends have tablet phones nowadays.'

'I'm happy with my phone!' said Adan's mother. 'Call me old-fashioned, sure, nobody respects their elders these days, sure, but *I* don't feel the need to have sexual relations with my phone.'

'It's not about that,' said Adan. 'It's not just *that*, Mom.'

The iPhene server, Jorjina, was sitting placidly, smiling, but she must have been growing impatient. She must have other customers to serve.

'She does housework and such. And she's, you know ... a phone. But it's companionship, Mom.'

'In my day people found companionship with other people – natural God-grown human beings. Real people!'

'Mom,' said Adan, eyeing Jorjina anxiously, 'I don't have time for a whole debate about this right now. Elegy is glitching.'

'And *who* is Elegy?'

'My Phene, Mom – you know that. I told you before. She's called Elegy.'

'And that's another thing I'll never understand, giving your phone a name. It's just a phone. It's just a machine for calling your mother from time to time a little more frequently wouldn't go amiss you won't have me around forever and every day is precious. That's all! *Names?* I might as well call my shoes Pinky and Perky.'

'Mom,' said Adan, urgently. He took hold of Gee's hand. If his mother had been speaking to him on a Phene her model would have replicated the gesture, which would have conveyed his genuineness. But she was on an antique model, so all she got was an emoji. 'Mom, my phone is glitchy and needs fixing. Yeah? Can you sub me the money, so the iPhene shop can do a deep dive on it, find out what's wrong?'

'I can,' said his mother, 'not. I'm not a bottomless well of money, Adan, my boy. You're not a kid any more. You need to get out there and get a job—'

'Not this again, Mom!'

'—and start paying for your life on your own terms. Earn your own money and you'll be earning self-respect to go along with it—'

'Seriously, Mom?'

The iPhene server was looking resolutely towards the ceiling.

'—always dipping your hands in my purse like it's your money, it's *not* your money to spend on your sex toys, my boy. The answer's no. Now – when are you coming round to see me… I mean, in real life?'

'Real life is so last year, Mom,' Adan told her. 'Mom, please? You're sure you can't just sub to the iPhene shop? It won't be so pricey, I think?'

'You're not a child, Addy. You're thirty-four. You need to start your life.'

'Whatever,' said Adan, ringing off.

There was a hollow moment in the shop. The server waited a beat, and then brought her gaze back down to her customer.

'She's … Like …' said Adan. 'She's not going to pay for it, you know? The deep clean. So just give the basic rinse, I guess, yeah?'

'It's already done!' said Jorjina brightly. 'You own the Phene outright?'

'It was my thirtieth birthday present.'

'Would you like to discuss credit options for insurance, in case of subsequent—'

'That's OK,' said Adan, getting to his feet, exactly like a man without even the piddling sums at his disposal to pay for basic insurance. *Exactly* like that. 'That's OK OK OK. Come on, Gee. Come along with me.'

So they walked out of the store and down the street together, hand in hand, like a thousand other human-Phene couples out and about in that city on that day. Making their way through the usual sidewalk bustle and jostle, the coming and the going, in this mid-sized, seaboard American city.

Here: have a flyer. A digital flyer, of course: nobody stands on street corners handing out photocopied sheets of A4 any more. But still – incoming!

God wants you to repudiate your technowhore.

Adan bats that one away. Although: you know, 'technowhore' is a pretty cool word.

Stop! This! Unjust! War! with a link that would spawn the four-word phrase a million times into all your feeds, were you to be foolish enough to click it. The war is happening in space, and Adan lives on the Earth, so he cannot bring himself to care very much one way or another.

An attractive woman, passing, smiling, and the twinkle in her eye is a photobarcode, and it's another flyer.

PHENO-MEN AND PHENO-WOMEN ARE **REAL** MEN AND **REAL** WOMEN

Are you holding yours in bondage?

It's annoying, so Adan fumbles his sunglasses out of his pocket and slots them on his face. They don't do a very good job of blocking the flyers. You can buy more effective filters, but for that you need money. Or you could drive everywhere in a car, sealed away from this kind of interaction altogether, but for that you'd need a *lot* of money. Enough money to buy, tax, fuel and, above all, park a car. More money than Adan's mother would ever sub to her layabout son.

And now, fiddling with the sunglasses had distracted him just long enough that he missed the window to click the NO option on the flyer. That each flyer comes with an option to dismiss it is a legal requirement, but there is some ongoing litigatory confusion as to the issue of how long such an option must remain available to the recipient of said flyer here and heretofore under the meaning of the Act. Adan had missed this one, and the virtual sheet was unfolding its virtual self in his head.

ARE YOU A SLAVER?

Redemption is possible.

It is a widely believed **ERROR** that "Phene" is trademark reversion of the word "phone", itself derived from the nineteenth-century "telephone".

> Pheno-men are so-called *because* they are *phenotypes of mankind*.
>
> A phenotype is the appearance of an organism based on multifactorial combinations of genetic and environmental traits. Though they are made from plastisilicas rather than organic cells, Pheno-men grow into full humanity. Their *genotype* is artificial, but they are spun out of human needs and desires, and they grow into *full agents* in the world. Just ask their "owners"—most of them have real feelings for their so-called "walking-talking-phones!"

Well, that was true, thought Adan as he stepped into the lobby of his building. He'd sure be broken-hearted if anything happened to his Gee.

> But too few accept the inevitable conclusion that attends this basic premise. Phenes are not "just another gadget"—they are HUMAN BEINGS IN THEIR OWN RIGHT and to *possess* or *hoard* such an entity is tantamount to being the worst kind of slaveholder. Rights that—

Finally – finally! – the building's privacy kicked in. It was legal to distribute flyers on the street, because that was public space, but private space was a different matter. Flyers were supposed to cut out as soon as a citizen stepped into their home, although often they didn't.

Adan stood at the elevator doors, holding Elegy by her hand. He looked at her, and she turned her face to him, or more precisely she turned Labelle Cho Aboya's face.

'You know I love you, don't you?' he said.

'Sure, baby,' she said, in the voice of Mikaela Margot, the

owner, in Adan's not so humble opinion, of the world's sexiest vocal cords. 'I know.'

'I mean, I guess you're not a human being, though. Not in that sense.'

The slightest flicker on Elegy's face, as she processed an interaction that fell outside her pool of core responses. But she smiled and said, 'Nobody's perfect, I guess.'

The elevator doors opened and people stepped out and Adan and Elegy stepped in, and moments later they were through his front door and into his apartment. Adan was no exophobe. He quite liked strolling the city, in fact, despite all the bugs, and the flyers and the myriad little aggravations. But he was glad to get home again, into his apartment. A *palpable* relief.

:2:

He had a drink. Then he and Elegy had sex. Because he was feeling more or less sorry for himself, he just lay back and let her touch him all over with her supple fingers, let her kiss him, and say a few sexy things to him. Then she got on top of him and rocked and squeezed him until he got to that point when all the worries and frets of the world swooshed away into nothing.

Afterwards he smoked a cigarbetter. He brooded – it was the only word – he *brooded* on how unreasonable his mother was being. Then phrases from the flyer he'd been served on the street came back to him. Were Phenes really called Phenes because they were phenotypes of human beings? He'd never heard that before.

He called his friend Blueskies. Elegy's face took on the lineaments of Blue's wide-set eyes, his spiky sideburns.

'What's the story, Adan, my Adan?' Blue asked.

'My Phene's glitching and I don't have the money to get her, like, properly fixed.'

'Bad news,' said Blue, inflecting the first word somewhat after the manner of a sheep. 'I can't lend you no money.'

'I'm not asking you, Blue. Blue? Why are Phenes called Phenes, though?'

'It's proprietary,' said Blue, confidently, out of Elegy's mouth. 'A twist on *Phone*, yowse. Now ... wait – that was a stroke of *genius* piece of marketing, no maybe about it. Back in the day.' Blueskies worked freelance on digital marketing mass-rollouts and liked to style himself an expert. Smoke and bullshit, of course. Not that Adan cared. 'Humanity invented cellphones, and people loved them. Made the companies that manufactured the devices the wealthiest the world had ever seen. People *loved* them. Then some dude thought – they *really* love them, you know? They invest emotionally in them. They weep when they accidentally drop them in the bath or crack their fucken fragile screens. So if they love their phones, and we make a phone they can actually fuck, why, then ...' He kissed his fingers to his mouth.

'I figured so,' said Adan. 'Man – what can I do about the glitching, though?'

'Not my area of expertise, my friend.'

Adan rang off, but Blue's leering face stuck to Elegy. Damn it.

'Elegy,' he instructed. 'Reset your face.'

'I'm afraid I can't do that, Dave,' said Elegy, still in Blueskies' growly voice.

What does that even mean?

'Elegy,' he tried again, 'default your face please.'

'I'm afraid I can't do that, Dave,' she said, again.

This time she was speaking in her own voice, so that was something. Who was Dave, anyway?

If he had to factory-reset her, it would take Adan hours to tweak her back up to all the settings he liked. I mean, if he had to do it he would, but what … a … *pain* … in … the …

'Elegy,' he said, for a third time. 'I want you to reset your appearance settings to today's default, please.'

Blue gurned at him. Blue shook his head and in doing so shook his sideburns into smooth cheeks. Another smile, and then the face sank away entirely, leaving nothing but the unprogrammed smartgel generic face. There was a twitch, and then a swirl of faces in rapid succession, a disconcerting scurry of visages.

'Ugh!' said Adan.

Now Elegy was wearing a male face Adan had never seen before: middle-aged, neither markedly ugly nor markedly handsome, a pair of pale blob-eyes, a tall lined forehead leaning back slowly into a headtop of thinning hair. There was a sharp line down the left-hand side of the face, perhaps a duelling scar, maybe just the crease showing on which side he slept at night.

'Message coming through,' said this stranger, in an odd, aristo voice. He didn't sound American.

Adan checked. Nobody was calling. This wasn't a regular phone call, and this strange man wasn't somebody in Adan's contacts list.

'Who are you?'

'Message coming message through message,' said the stranger, again. 'Stand by.'

'I fucken won't stand by!' raged Adan. He was a placid guy, slow to anger, but messing with his girlfriend like this was beyond the pale. 'Get out of my Phene! You've *hacked* my Pheno-woman – I'll trace you and sue you for every fucken red cent in your bankfile.'

The idea sparked and flickered into a thin flame in Adan's imagination: might he? Was that possible? Maybe just an out-of-court settlement – any lump sum to make him less financially dependent on the whims of his mother? But that was at-straw clutching.

'Stand by,' said the stranger.

Adan felt like punching him right in his big white face, but that would only damage his Phene, so of course he didn't.

'Get out of my Phene!' he yelled.

'Adan!' said the stranger, moving the head left and right in an exploratory fashion, then catching Adan's eye and grinning at him. 'Adan! I've been trying to reach you.'

'Who *are* you?' Adan demanded.

'Abdul,' said the stranger. Then: 'No, not Abdul. Abigail. No, not that. What are you seeing? How am I presenting? A male, a female, a what? Adam or Eve? Alan or Abram or Singing-of-Mount-Abora? In Xanadu did comely Phene a *distinct* tactical advantage in the most important war in the history of—' Gee's whole body shook. The stranger moved the head left and right again. 'Decree decree decree. Decthree,' he finished.

What was this nonsense?

'How did you get my number? Hacking is a criminal offence and you're currently trespassing in my Phene, and—'

'You joined the army, Adan!'

Adan stopped. That was an odd question to ask.

'The army? Of course not. What?'

It occurred to him that this might be some flyer-related infiltration. He'd been handed that anti-war flyer on his way back to his block, hadn't he? Or was this a recruitment ad from the military? Damn strange one, if so.

The stranger looked sad. 'I'm too early?'

'Are you some kind of war protest virus? Get out of my Phene! I will trace you to your source, and whichever anti-war org is behind this will pay me . . .' he swallowed, because the prospect was actually making him salivate, '. . . serious money.'

'Anti-war?' said the stranger. 'No, no, no – the war is necessary. If you forgive me the joke, it's *absolutely* necessary.' Adan had no idea what this crazy guy was on about. 'We have to fight the war and win the war,' he was saying. 'It's the most important war in the entire history of the cosmos.'

So maybe he was an army recruitment virus rather than anti-war. Still illegal, though! Then the stranger did something stranger still: his face froze, then twitched and jerked and yerked into a string of odd expressions as a stream of gibberish emerged from his mouth. It sounded like an album track being run backwards to try and decipher a satanic message inserted into it.

Then the face settled, and the stranger said, again: 'Anti-war, no, no, no, the war is absolutely necessary and you must enlist, Adan. I just thought you already had.'

'Enlist in the army?' Adan repeated, in a perfect focus of scornful bewilderment.

'Never mind . . . never mind . . . the connection is not good and I have to pass on my message. My *message*. Are you ready? You might want to write this down.'

'Write it *down*?' That was the oddest thing yet. 'Why?'

'So you don't forget it. It's really super.'

The stranger's face froze. The whole Phene had locked-up – Adan reached out and felt the shoulder, the elbow; the usually pliant artificial flesh was hard as metal. Then, as suddenly as it had seized up, it loosened again.

'. . . important that you *remember* this,' the stranger concluded.

'My Phene records everything. It's standard.'

'I'm not calling you on the network,' said the stranger. 'This is no usual call. I don't think your Phene will retain any memory of it. So write it down.'

'Write it down,' Adan wanted to know, 'with what?'

'Pen? Pencil?'

'Penswhat?'

'Then,' said Abora, or whatever his name was, 'just remember it. It's really, really important that you do. It's really, really, really, really, really important. When you're on the island, when your friends have all been violently extirpated and you yourself have the porcupine spikes in your gut, stand up and sing out – *weave a circle round me thrice*. Did you get that?'

'A circle about my *what*?'

'Thrice! Thrice! Thrice!'

'Mister,' begged Adan, his anger deliquescing into mere petulance. '*Please* just get out of my Phene, yeah? She's my companion. She's my girlfriend.'

But even as he spoke, the stranger's face was melting into his own sweet Labelle Cho Aboya's. Adan could have wept with sheer relief.

'Are you OK, baby?' she asked him, her voice full of that true and unfakable tenderness that defined their personal connection, a truth and unfakeness none dare challenge. Do *your* human–human relations truly guarantee more authenticity? Tell the truth now.

:3:

Adan related the whole bizarre episode to his friends.

'Super weird hack of my Phene just now,' he told Texx, whose own Phene was a more expensive model, and reputedly immune to all hacking or viruses whatsoever. 'This ugly guy with, like, a British voice, telling me to remember this we-e-eird phrase.'

'If you're in guarantee, I'd report that to iPhene. They need to sort that kind of shit *out*.'

But Elegy had been Adan's thirtieth birthday present, and Adan was now thirty-four, so the guarantee had long since lapsed. Still: the intrusion, whatever it was, seemed to cure Gee of her glitch. Adan fell back into his usual routine: sleeping late in the morning, playing video games all day, having sex with his Phene in the evening, watching TV or, sometimes, going out with friends until the small hours – and sometimes having sex with Elegy again on his return. He called his mother as he did every week and gave her the good news.

'The glitch got itself sorted, Mom.'

'I think you should give up that robot mistress,' she scolded him. 'It's not natural. It's not nice. You think it's nice for a woman of my age to sit here imagining her only son indulging himself after that fashion?'

'So don't imagine it, Mom,' Adan told her. 'Jeez! You got no better things to be using your imagination for?'

'It's not going to give me grandchildren, though, is it?' his mother said. 'It's not going to support you when you get a job and settle. Settle. You're thirty-four! This isn't right, Addy. That thing isn't good for you.'

It was one of 'those' conversations. That, this, they, those, these, thises – Adan rode it out: sometimes his weekly call went OK, and sometimes his mother was in a weird mood and nagged at him. But either way it was soon enough over, and he could relax in his apartment (that she paid for) and play *Unknown Shores* on the game system she'd bought for him and order in Chinafood on the account she maintained so he wouldn't starve. It was life, and it rolled along, and he was happy enough with that.

Then three things happened in quick succession to upend it all.

The first was when Blue didn't turn up for an epic bar-crawl. All right, sometimes he was a no-show, no biggie. But when Adan called him the following day, Blue was super-serious.

'Joined up.'

'You've joined what?'

'Up. The army, you dink.'

'You've joined the up-army?' This had to be a joke. 'For what for why, you tub of cum?'

'I'm serious, Adan,' was Blueskies' austere response. 'It would behove you to be serious too.'

Behove? Jesus H. Dictionary, this was more than flesh and blood could, and so on, and so forth.

'Are you high?'

'I know you're not much of a newshound, boyo,' said Blue, in a serious voice. 'So perhaps it has escaped your fucken attention that we *are* fighting a war?'

'*We*,' said Adan, 'are fighting to remember why *you* didn't join *us* at Bar Al-Cool last night.'

But Blue wasn't in the mood for levity.

'The hive mind are an existential threat, man! Do you know what that means? An existential threat to humankind. You don't think that's worth fighting?'

'My friend,' said Adan, meaning the word, 'I'm just trying to get by, from one day to the day that follows it. All this talk of yours is... grandstanding stuff.'

'It *matters*, Adan.'

'Where did all this come *from*, though? Radicalised, yeah?'

'I can't talk to you about this, Adan, if you ain't going to take it seriously. The army is interested in me – it's interested in my *Gnaat 4000* scores. I posted my three best playthroughs of *Unknown Shores* and *they* contacted *me* specifically to congratulate me. They need drone overseers and I'll get a salary and a pension – what about *you*, my dude?'

'I'm ringing off. You're baiting me.'

'But you're so supremely baitable, my dude.'

'I'm ending this call.'

Something about the exchange really got on Adan's nerves. So he called Texx, and no sooner had he said: 'You'll never guess what Blue has done, only joined the fragging army, man!' than Texx was: Me too, me too.

That took some unpacking. No, it wasn't a co-ordinated thing. Yes, he'd been thinking about it for a while. No, it wasn't the idealism that Blue had been spouting: none of this *existential threat to humankind* or *Hive-Mind-θ Will Swallow* Homo Sapiens, or any of that. For Texx it was a purely practical matter.

'I know your mom pays your rent, Adan,' he said. 'But not all of us are so lucky. The securities parcel I've been subsisting on has been repackaged.'

'Dude! What happened?'

'I knew it was coming. The parcel was in my aunt's name, and she's been in this artificial coma for two years. It's a religious thing, a cult thing, she put herself under willingly, of course, and I was looking after her investment while she was under. The cult took its cut and the facility had a fee but I used the rest. Anyhow she's decided she's meditated enough, or whatever that shit was that she was doing, and so she's back to life and wants her money. None too pleased, neither – truth is, I was skimming the securities some. I mean, you know how expensive shit is, yeah? She was going to prosecute, but we've had a mediator intervene and now instead I got to pay her back, x amount each month for y months, and both x and y are biiig numbers.'

'I had no idea, dude.'

'It is what it is. But it means I got to get a job, and what jobs are there for someone like me? You think the Mercer Corps gonna offer me a corner office overlooking 800th and Bay? You think I could get work as a teacher or a creative? No, man, no, man, the army will take me. There's a war, you know? The army is always hiring.'

His conversation with Blue had worked Adan into a rage, but this conversation merely depressed him. He felt sad on behalf of his friend, which was, of course, him feeling sad for himself by using his friend as a proxy. He had Elegy give him a massage, but it didn't relax him. Prodding his doughy body. Then he had her blow him, but he couldn't keep himself at an appropriate level of genital adamantine. He was spongy, then he was loose, then he had to stop and take a supplement to ramp himself up again to more or less firm. Elegy finished him off. She was a professional, she knew what to do. She whispered the sweet nothings, that were sweet and less than nothing.

Adan went for a walk.

He often took Gee on these walks, but not today. People weren't generally hostile – most folk were cool and scads of people had Phenes of their own – but holding a Phene's hand attracted all manner of oddballs and religious flyers, and he wanted to minimise that. In point of fact he wanted to breathe sea air, so he walked through the crowds, down the artificial right-angle valleys and gullies of the city. He tried to keep his eyes on his feet, but a few flyers found their way in:

WAR FOR THE SURVIVAL OF HUMANITY! ENLIST OR LIVE WITH THE SHAME OF BEING A SPECIES-TRAITOR!

White Feather: Consider Yourself Served.
Why Aren't You In Uniform? Hive-Mind-θ
Don't Care About Your Scruples You Coward.

but also

Turn Your Face From The Military-Industrial Complex!
hive-minds are the next step in human evolution!

and

WAR ON HUMAN ANTS OR ANTI-WAR? HAVE YOUR SAY IN THE PODCAST EVERYBODY IS TALKING ABOUT.

and an antique song

Young man / there's no need to sit tight / I said / young man / you can sign up and fight / Hive-mind / Is the dark to our light / We can / Beat / Those / Borg / and / Triumph!

Now he was at the river. It had flowed down from the highlands and across fields and through forests since before the city was built, since before human beings had ever come to this land. And it was still here. Adan sat on one of the benches and watched water-leapers do their tech-assisted jumping, and fisherwomen on boards luring fish to the surface with flashing microdrones and bare-hand grabbing them with drug-assisted reflexes.

He tried to be inspired, tried to think deep thoughts, but his mind was not constituted that way. And anyway the riverside was too crowded and there were too many bars, so he upped and walked and came downstream. And here was the ocean, the mighty ocean, impassable. And this was the point where the wide brown river, having gathered its forces for thousands of miles, through dozens of different territories, squandered everything into the anonymity of vast waters. He stood and watched the river spend itself, and felt the warmth and the pressure of the sun on his skin, and after a while he walked back into the city.

The third thing was the real hammer blow. His mother called him. She never called him. The gravity of familial passive-aggression meant that rivers always run downhill, and Adan always rang his mother. But this was a first. Adan was playing chess with Elegy, the board shining on her belly as she lay naked on the bed, her giggling every time he poked a piece's icon with his finger to move it. Then Gee trilled and told him that his mother was calling. It was unusual enough for Adan to sit up straight.

'Mom!' he said, as his Phene took on the features of his mother. 'Is everything OK?'

'Son,' said his mother, crumpling her brow and dipping her head. 'I have news.'

'News,' Adan repeated.

'My boy, there's no easy way to tell you this.'

Adan's inner alarm was chiming.

'Wait up, Mom. What? What do you mean? Is this going to upset me? Let's not talk about this now. Let's not talk about this. I'm not in a place, psychologically, you know? Not in a place to hear this.'

'I'm going, my boy.'

'Going where?'

'If I had an easy form of words,' she said, her tone strained with held-back tears, 'then don't you think I'd use them? But ever since your father passed it's been hard on me.'

'Is this about Pops?'

'It's been preying on my mind.'

'What has?'

Running through Adan's mind, in a hurriedly assembled list of likelihoods: his mother remarrying; going on a religious retreat; adopting a grandchild since Adan wouldn't give her one. But the reality was otherwise.

'I'm travelling to Europe.' She pronounced this *yurp*, but Adan knew what she meant.

'A holiday, Mom? What the hell?'

'Because it's not illegal there.'

'Mom… what?'

'Joining the hive mind.' And then she said: 'I'm not a fool, son. Running my telephone conversations through an app that keeps the FBI from hearing certain *key* words that, well… You deserve to know.'

Adan was silent for a full minute. Thirty seconds in, his Phene started saying 'Addy? Are you still there?' and 'You were saying your phone has been glitching – have I cut out?' and eventually he said:

'You're joining the Borg?'

'Don't call them that! It's disrespectful. It's rude. They are the Spirit Embodiment of Human Destiny.'

'Mom…'

It turned out that Adan's limited expressive range was not capable of capturing his combination of astonishment and outrage at this news.

'Mom!' he said again. Then he said: 'Mom!'

'Don't start with me, Adan,' said his mother. 'I've made up my mind. I've signed the necessary legal commitments.'

His first question, it turned out, was not the one pertaining to the imminent upheaval his life was about to undergo.

'Why?'

'Because I'm afraid of dying, my boy,' she said, her voice watering itself now with tears.

Adan's Phene did not run to the actual mimicking of human weeping, and instead displayed a teary-eyed emoticon over its cheek. More expensive models could extrude salt water from a reservoir behind the bridge of the nose.

'You're not dying!' said Adan.

'We're all dying, my son. And some of us are closer to the end than others. Ever since your father passed it's been preying on my mind. But the Spirit Embodiment will not die, and if I join them then I won't die.'

'Are you *kidding*?'

This was the wrong tack. This was only going to harden her natural obstinacy.

'No, I'm not kidding actually, my boy,' she said, briskly. 'When you're a little older you'll understand. Death is a very scary matter.'

'I thought you were ...' said Adan, struggling, in truth, to remember the specifics of his maternal affiliation, '... Catholic Orthodox? Or Orange Catholic? Or ... aren't you ...?'

'The Spirit Embodiment offers a material, copper-bottomed path to *personal* immortality,' his mother declared, ringingly. 'A real-world, scientifically guaranteed immortality. Your actual consciousness joins the gestalt and the gestalt lives forever. And I'm taking that.'

'Mom!'

'I'm sorry, my lad,' said his mother, looking away. 'There's a lot I'd do for you. There's a lot I've *done* for you – paid for your toys, and your apartment, bought you that so-called girlfriend of yours. But I won't die, for you, for anyone.'

'Mom!'

'Don't feel sad, my boy. I'm going to live forever. Literally live forever!'

'Is that even legal, Mom? Isn't there a war ... I mean, a *war* ...

I mean, this is…' He meant to say *treachery*, but the word eluded him. He rummaged through his wetware brain, said 'illegal?' and then added '-ness?'

'I've always loved you,' she replied. 'As a mother,' she added.

A curious qualification, when Adan thought about it later. Then she rang off.

Adan sat in silence for a long time. What to do? He rang round his friends and told them what had happened, and they were variously laughter-hooty and mocking, or solicitous and consoling. But there was nothing they could do and there was nothing he could do.

He ordered in a bottle of Oddka and a pizza and watched TV for a while. Then he popped a mauve and had sex with Elegy for over an hour. It didn't usually take him so long, but he was trying to keep his thoughts off the conversation with his mother. But maybe she hadn't really meant it. Surely she couldn't have actually meant it.

Eventually he told Elegy to go to sleep, and drank some more of his alcohol, and searched for info on Hive-Mind-θ. It turned out there was – just – enough residual curiosity in him to at least enquire into the group to which his own mother was giving her life. But opening the news and comment media, and an automatically selected spread of chatspaces, on 'HMθ' revealed a yawning virtual chasm absolutely bristling with opinions and polemics and propaganda and the online equivalent of hectoring, screaming and begging. The mere fact of the enormousness, not to say enormity, of human responses to this growing hive mind dissuaded Adan from pursuing the topic, although it did at least alert him to the fact that it was a topic of pressing contemporary concern.

He tried again: 'HMθ Immortality', but the spread of results was no more focused, and he gave up.

Then it was three in the morning, and he went for a walk to clear his head. Striding around the city at night, under a liquorice sky. Moving through steel and stone channels, at the feet of gigantic monoliths half a klick tall and dusted all over with lit windows. Overhead the endless stream of supercargo floaters flickered and blinked, passing down their ever-replenished parade. There were as many people out and about as during the daytime, and the silent cars swished past as if trying to whisper something eloquent and wise to him. He stood for a long time at the junction of 300th and Broad, watching the wavefront of red tail-lights pass up along the line of cars as they shuffled forward. All these people, Adan thought to himself, as if it were a piercing insight into the nature of things. They all had homes to go to, jobs that gave their lives meaning, mothers who loved them.

A drone swooped down, fat buzzing bug, and flickered a message directly into Adan's left eye:

JESUS IS STILL HERE lose weight the Christian method LOVE.

Adan tried to sweep this away, but it wasn't a regular flyer, it was some other kind of intrusive projection, and persisted, until he took a swing at the drone and it flew off.

Adan went home.

In the morning, the first concrete intimations arrived that his mother had been deadly serious: notification from the AI that ran the rental corps that owned and maintained the block. The previous payee had withdrawn credit. If Adan wished to remain in the apartment he had seventy-two hours to arrange alternative credit and payment bona fides, legally endorsable by etc., etc., nonrevocable under the terms of the Finance & Accommodation Legislation of etc., etc.

This was a shock. It was such a shock, indeed, that for a good half hour Adan simply didn't register it at all. He played a game, and pretended life was just carrying on as before.

But the messages didn't stop arriving, and, howsoever petulantly, he was eventually obliged to reply. Of course there were no other funds, and of course he had access to no line of credit that would enable him to keep the apartment. He called his mother, but she wasn't picking up. He called his friends for advice but they had nothing to offer except platitudes of sympathy of the *sucks-to-be-you* variety. He lay on his bed with his top off, and played his ample belly like a set of Jello tom-toms. What to do?

'Gee?' he asked aloud. 'What should I do?'

'Just be yourself, loverboy,' was his Phene's purringly expressed opinion.

He tinkered around with a Financial Advice Bot for a while, and browsed possible employment opportunities. But there were very few opportunities, and he, Adan, was the opposite of opportune – under-educated, wholly without experience, too old, unable to bring a financial bond to Company A and equally unable to assure Company Z that he had never taken anything from their long list of proscribed pharmacological stimulants and hallucinants.

He sat down in a chair, facing the window, and looked out over the rooftops. Then, for focus, he slapped himself hard on his own cheek.

Priorities: somewhere to live, food, games, a place for Elegy.

That clarified matters. His mother was still not answering her phone. So he took photos of all his stuff, got a quotation from a Kippledealer, rented space at a storage farm on the outskirts of the city, and put his shoes on – all before his cheek stopped tingling.

He gave the Kippledealer the codes for the apartment, went downstairs with Elegy and called a cab. It was a twenty-minute journey.

'I'll come visit you as much as I can,' he assured her, as an automated janitor led the two of them down one of the kilometer-long corridors in the facility. Tears threatened his eyes. Oh God, this was hard.

The space was as large as Adan had been able to afford, which wasn't very large. Elegy stepped obediently inside, and Adan disconnected her power. The corridor was swimmy as he walked back to the main entrance, and the sunlight, as he came outside again, dashed sparks and glares from his teary eyes. He called another cab. As he waited for this transport, under the dusty sun, a profound bout of wooziness afflicted him, and he had to use the crash barrier at the side of the road as a sort of bench. But this had passed by the time the cab turned up.

Next stop: Army Recruitment Centre.

:4:

Giving up material possessions is a liberating matter, but the change in Adan's circumstances was too abrupt for him to appreciate this spiritual benefit. And, anyway, the word *possessions* nowadays means a different thing than it used to, something cross-hatched between physical objects and virtual ones, more a discursive than an actual category. And discourse is not something that can be given up.

It's a diverting place, this city of the future. The world under the rubric of toys. Because that's the great truth we have discovered about ourselves as a species. Our existential opposition is not between life and death, because death is not a thing (death being, in point of fact, the absence of all the things). It's true that *fear* of death is a thing, but fear of death, usually, makes us feel more alive – the rush and the push of adrenaline, the intensity of the now, this experience, this breath, this moment. I'm not talking about existential dread, of that psychopathological sapping terror of death's inevitability. Bracket that aside. No: woman's and man's state is either: a state of being alive, or a state of being in fear for our lives that makes us feel even *more* alive. Caveman you is alive when you chase down your prey, and twice as alive when the sabre-toothed tiger is chasing after *you*. And so time passed, and history kicked into gear, and the eras succeeded one another, and we improved the efficiency of our food provision (call this: *farming*) and our population expanded, and soon enough we slid into the now. For most of us, living now, the opposition is not between life and death but between life and boredom. Boredom is much worse than death, because boredom is a thing and death is the elimination of all things. We're much more anxious about things than we are about their absence.

This is the history of humanity on the larger scale. First: a struggle to stay alive. Then, when that battle was more or less won, a struggle not to be bored. And all the things that this second, larger scale struggle entails come to dominate existence. Not the Anthropocene so much as the Toycene. We have invested enormous amounts of energy and ingenuity and labour and money in making new diversions, new gadgets and games, gimcrack devices and cunningly written computer code and imaginary people's imaginary adventures on page and screen. Giant harvesters scroll right to left, left to right, through huge fields furry with wheat, plaiting the stalks in their path and blowing an endless whale-blowhole of grain into their attendant lorries – and nobody pays it any mind. Harvest, which used to be the great central event of humanity's year, has become a background event, automated and ignored. Meanwhile armies of people, larger than Napoleon or Mao ever commanded, work assiduously at making engines of distraction, real and virtual, for the remaining population of the world. Toys everywhere. The toy event horizon.

Adan had his toys. He had a library of seven thousand virtual games he had played, some of which he returned to and replayed many times. He had hundreds of thousands of screen dramas to watch, and millions of songs he could listen to, and more online platforms on which he could pass his time arguing with strangers than he could ever visit. Most of all he had his phone, and in this he was like an increasing number of people. Because the iron law of the Toycene is this: kids want their toys to be their friends and adults want to fuck their toys. There are local variations in the ways we, as individuals, invest emotionally in our pastimes; but emotionally invest in them we do, and that's the spectrum human emotions parse: befriend it; fuck it; kill it. Pick a point along the line mapped by those three positions and, there you are!

You! Yes . . . hello.

Person? Hello?

Doesn't hear me.

In the city where Adan had spent most of his life, everything, more or less, was a toy. Some people prefer their toys to be inert, not to answer back, because that's how some people prefer their fellow humans. But others relished the *interactivity* of play, and so there was a lucrative market for toys with whom you could chat, or fight, or have sex. And the people who profited from that lucrative market, by inventing brilliantly diverting new toys, or by manufacturing and marketing toys successfully, those people took their money and spent it on toys.

I mean, what else were they going to do with it?

In the army, the toys are called things like 'guns', 'drones', 'tanks', 'fighter planes', 'orbital flitters', 'dreadnoughts' and many other things. Back in the deeps of history the army could afford to bore its members with rituals like marching up and down the parade ground, or twelve-hour stints of monotonous guard duty, or simply standing in line for hours. They could do this because the army had cornered the market in the more intense of the two ways of being alive – that is, living under the threat of being killed. But as war evolved, the odds of any given squaddie dying were reduced. It was no coincidence that, as this risk diminished, the number of toys soldiers were given to play with increased. Graph the two against one another and you will see an exactly inverse proportion.

At the recruitment centre Adan was scanned, interviewed, and handed a screen on which he could sign over his soul to the military. He suggested they take him on as a drone pilot, and laid out some of his gaming high scores, but the recruiting officer was only too manifestly unimpressed.

'We have kids coming in with scores vastly more altitudinous than these,' she told him. 'I can put your name down, but I have to be honest with you ... honest with you ... uh ... *Adan* – you won't make this programme. It's, like, super-competitive.'

'Oh,' said Adan. 'For sure? So what should I, like, do?'

'Basic training for now,' said the RO brightly. 'Your officer orientation team and personal development sergeant will help you make the best career choices going forward.'

Adan was put on a shuttle flight with eighty or so other men and women, and whisked to a training base near the sea. Here he gave up his clothes and received his uniform. Here he showered in unisex showers and ate the nanoseed pills the orientation officers told him to eat. Here he was assigned a bed, and woken every morning to his new routine – one supervised hour in the gym, three hours learning to drill as RSMs stood yelling at the side of the parade ground and as drones overflew the ground to display aerial shots of the formations onto a giant screen. Adan discovered he quite enjoyed drill. It was a waste of time, and, considered as a game, it was certainly not a very sophisticated one. But there was a Tetris-satisfaction in making your body perform a set of rigidly predetermined movements, and learning to co-ordinate with a whole crowd of others was a bit like dancing. He'd never been much of a dancer, so there was some satisfaction in learning these new moves.

The hardest part of the experience for him was missing Elegy. He felt her absence so intensely that, several times, he wept loudly into his pillow. The other cadets didn't mock him for this – they all had something equivalent in their own lives, after all, and many of them were equally prone to the weepies. Nor did they pry. They didn't need to. Adan's grief was intensely particular, unique to him, focused on a this or a that of his own. But grief as such is a general and fungible quantity, universal to humankind, and one of the things that links us all to all.

Lights on, like a splash of white water in the face. *Out of beds, you slugs!* Wash, dress, breakfast and jogging in order. Down to the range. *Lie on your bellies, you worms!*

Bap bap bap said his rifle.

The other men and women of his unit were pretty good types, it turned out. Unused to prolonged human-to-human interactions it took Adan a while to get into this particular groove, but a lifetime lived online had prepared him for the fundamental lack of privacy in the army, and his comrades were Adan's kind of people. Nobodies, no-hopers, low-IQ, overweight, him to a T. They chatted about gaming, and fucking and food. A twenty-year-old called Spiro, known as 'Tuss' for reasons Adan couldn't fathom, boasted that he had fucked one thousand and three people.

'Each encounter is its own thing,' he said, with preternatural wisdom, 'and that's exciting and cool. But after a while you look back and they all blur into one another. It's like you're just doing the same thing over and over with one composite partner.'

Tuss had had a job at Falco's, but had lost it when his doctor had diagnosed sex addiction, addiction of any kind being something specifically prohibited by the terms of his employment. The army was the only other employment opportunity for him.

Then there was Sal, who moved slowly and blinked rarely, and who took a liking to Adan. She crept into his bed after lights out – a risk, this, since sexual intercourse was officially interdicted in barracks – and tried to get something started. Adan had never before had sex with another human, and found the experience disconcerting: almost *but not quite* like actual sex, less predictable and more odoriferous, and not in a good way. But they fumbled something out of the encounter, and afterwards Sal brought herself off and crept away again.

Generally, though, Adan hit his bed at lights out hungry for sleep. He'd never before experienced what a succession of days filled with consistent physical effort did to a body. Up early, breakfast, drill, weapons training, groundwork and hop-pack practice. Lunch in the field from a sac. More weapons training – wriggling on the ground and firing needleguns, or quelling the nauseous lurch in his gut as the hoppack propelled him twenty metres into the sky and he tried to aim and fire at a target below him on the ground. Gym-work. Climbing and digging. Supper. Neither Phenes nor old-style phones were permitted, but there were barracks phones on which you could call people, and TV to watch in the evening. Adan tried his mother several times but got no answer. Sometimes he called his friends and sometimes he didn't bother. He became friendly with his comrades. That was new.

Bap bap bap said his rifle.

Adan's personal development sergeant encouraged his personal development by yelling at him. Career progression choices were: infantry.

And? *And infantry, Fats. What do you want, playing the fucken tuba?*

He missed Elegy.

Bap bap bap said his rifle.

Adan made friends with a recruit called Filip, bonding over their respective love for their Phenes. Another recruit, Sebald, boasted that he had a half-model – legs up to waist only.

'That's all you need,' said Sebald, leering. But Filip and Adan knew better.

Sometimes Adan wondered what it would be like having an proper ongoing sex life with an actual human. But Sal had moved on to a squaddie called Kulble, who was leaner and more experienced in the sack than Adan. In fact, she told anyone who would listen that she was in love. She had gone with Tuss, she said, before, but despite his boast of a thousand and three conquests he was not a good lover. The talk made Adan a little uncomfortable, not because he was a prude, but because it opened a window into how *judgemental* human sexual partners were liable to be. At least Gee didn't judge him.

They had to attend a lecture, where a real live human being stood on a stage at one end of a hall in which eight hundred recruits sat on chairs. The lecture concerned the existential threat posed by the HMθ – a cult, said the lecturer, an aberration. A threat.

Adan found it quite hard to follow. The lecturer was a

colonel, and her face was magnified on the big screen on the wall behind her. Something about the lines that ran from the curl of her nostril to the ends of her mouth reminded him of Gee – that is, of Gee wearing Labelle Cho Aboya's face. It was hypnotic.

Now the lecturer was talking about Venus. The planet. And Adan had not followed the connection. Something crucial was happening on Venus, or had to be stopped from happening on Venus. But don't worry, said the colonel, with a rare smile, and that caught Adan's attention again, because of the way it deepened the lines bracketing her mouth. A twist of pleasure in his abdomen; an upward shift in the blood pressure in his groin.

'Don't worry – we're not dropping you onto Venus!'

There was a shudder of collective laughter, and Adan joined in, although he didn't know why. What was funny about the idea of being dropped onto the surface of Venus? And now the colonel was doing serious-face, and talking about the need to deny the HMθ this planet, and when she frowned she looked markedly less like Labelle Cho Aboya.

He was trained on a different gun, this one speaking in glottal clusters of plosives, *bpapappap bapmappapa*, and turning hefty targets into clouds of papery fragments that afterwards swirled leisurely in the breeze.

There was a week of orbital training, which Adan scraped through: bare pass, marked down for puking. He liked the rush of the launch, but weightlessness made him queasy and the zigzag accel-decel of simulated manoeuvres brought the fluid contents of his stomach to the catapult at the back of his throat. Vomiting in zero-*g* had the unexpected consequence of propelling Adan hard backwards, through floating crowds of yelling and disgusted-looking comrades. Gastric rocketry.

He was trained on a new gun: this one spoke a single syllable, like a slowed-down recording of a Rottweiler's gruff: *wuhf, wuhf.* It sent a chubby smartshell towards pirouetting drone targets. His personal development sergeant was less abusive than usual.

'We may have found something you're good at!' she yelled at him. 'Ad*van*tages to obesity, who knew?'

Obese was unfair. Adan was hefty, sure, and he had come into the army carrying a few more pounds than he might have liked, sure. He'd accept that. It was hard to shift, is all. The barracks food was all starch and arteprotein and you could eat as much as you liked, so although some of the adipose had metamorphosed into muscle what with all the exercise, there was still plenty there, cladding his stomach and spine, giving his thighs the tender chance to kiss one another when he walked. It was an active advantage, though, with the Colterbus-91. Squaddies called it the whomp gun.

A furlough, and Adan didn't know what to do with himself. His mother was uncontactable, and his friends in the city were evasive when he suggested meeting up, knowing that he'd have to stay at theirs, and not wanting him crashing their various tiny apartments. Besides which, he had new friends now, and would much rather have spent time with them. But they dispersed to family, or friends, or vowing that they didn't need a place to stay because they were going to stay awake through the entire forty-eight hours. Adan took a shuttle to the city and then a cab to the storage facility where Elegy was standing in her cubby. The man at the main entrance copied the code for his door onto Adan's forefinger with a half-hour tag, and left him to wander the enormous corridors alone.

He found the door, pressed his finger to it, and there was Gee – powered down and so without her usual face. But it only took a moment to hook her into the loop and send the fizz of life through her innards, and when her face emerged from the blankness of the factory setting and she looked and recognised Adan – and smiled – he started crying. Proper crying. She hugged him and said exactly the sort of non-specific things he needed to hear at that time: 'It's OK, baby' and 'Hey, I'm here, I'm here.'

So this is where we were: Adan hugging his girlfriend in a cupboard in the middle of a storage facility that covered eight square kilometres in total. Let's weave a circle round this scene, once, twice, thrice, and close our eyes in holy dread.

:5:

And then, just like that, Adan's squad was done with basic training. A pass-out parade was announced, but Adan had nobody to invite to it. And then there were mandatory screen tutorials, of immense and incomprehensible boredom, about geopolitics and Why We Fight and how God had made Adam and Eve, not a monstrous hive mind agglomeration of Adam and Eve and Cain and Abel's combined consciousnesses. Adan had to watch these, sat in a cubicle *solus*, as did all the soldiers, but he literally could not focus his attention on their content. If his eye wandered from the screen then an alarm whistled and he had to start from the beginning again. It was supposed to explain their deployment: the Hive-Mind-θ didn't occupy a single discrete territory that could be invaded; rather they lived in pockets, in gated communities and restricted suburbs of larger cities, on private islands bought with what seemed like endless reserves of money. But distributed everywhere, and also in the high sky, in Earth-orbitals and longer-run ships that looped on slanted orbits around the Earth, or longer slanted orbits around the sun. Lots of them swarmed around Venus. They were trying something with Venus. Adan neither knew nor cared. So far as Adan was concerned, they ought to leave the hive-minders alone to hive-mind their own business, and concentrate on the Earth. But it wasn't up to him.

That evening in the dorm everybody was chattering about the vids. Adan lay on his bunk and played the drums on his spreading belly – little tabla finger-taps on the sides, bigger slaps that made the flesh wobble in the middle.

'Those Earth-orbitals are surely real vulnerable,' said Tuss. He had appointed himself the strategy expert. 'Just whack 'em, and they're gone, no?'

'They're demilitarised. Demilitarised and neutral, and hitting them would violate international law,' said Sal. 'Weren't you even paying attention to the vids today?'

'*We're* international law,' said Tuss, striking a pose. 'You want to put us in a cage fight with some lawyer in a gel-suit and a suitcase?'

He wasn't wrong.

They had a battalion race – twenty kilometres, round the base's perimeter. Adan plodded along near the back of the pack, trudge, trudge, past the swampy side where flies the size of bumblebees guzzled through the air, and alligators were reduced to two eyes under a Neanderthal brow-ridge and, a little way off, as if wanting to distance themselves, two nostrils. It was stupidly hot. Splodgy white clouds far, far away. The *iii* of mosquitoes. The swamp smelt of corpses, or of what Adan assumed corpses smelt like. But then he was past that side, and plodding along the fence beside the road and heading towards the ocean, and then he was running up the beach, with the sea on his right blowing a cooling breeze that washed him with a salt smell, and he felt pretty good, actually. The melodious hooting of seagulls cheering him towards the finish line.

That night a group of them went to one of the camp's many bars, to get drunk together, and Adan couldn't remember laughing so much in all his life.

'C'mon, you fat man,' urged Tuss. 'Buy some drinks.'

Adan said he didn't have any money.

The rest of the squad laughed with the kind of derision that includes rather than excludes, and when they mocked him – 'Adan Vergara, you are the stupidest fucken soldier I ever met in my life' – it was, somehow, comforting. Oh, he belonged. He laughed and nodded and agreed. It turned out that he had been receiving military basic pay all through his training and had an account – Sal showed him how to access it via his dog tag – and actually had *plenty* of money to spend. He hadn't even realised! And in that moment, at this precise time, Adan was happier than he had ever been in the whole course of his thirty-five years on this planet. They were all singing along to the song on the sound system, an ancient pop tune. It wasn't Adan's style of music, but, singing along with his friends in that place at that time, it didn't matter. He picked up the tune quickly enough, and the lyrics were the same phrase repeated over and over in a helium voice, hymning (Adan supposed) the way spiritual realities took precedence over merely material ones:

Soul only
Soul only
Soul only

Then he was puking in the toilets, gloopy boluses through his burning gullet, messily into and around the metal bowl, and he wasn't happy any more. Then he was vaguely aware of being hauled, a different friend's shoulder in each of his armpits, back to the dorm, and of the feeling of belonging, of having friends, of being there.

Then he was flat out.

:6:

The next day he was very badly hung-over, but up with reveille regardless, and kitted and loaded onto a transport. They were launched into a high-insert trajectory that dragged 3 *g* on their bodies on the way up, had them hanging a centimetre above their seats in their harnesses at the apogee, and then yanked their innards like a fairground ride on the way back down. If there had been anything in Adan's stomach to vomit, he would have vomited it; but the one advantage of his misery was that there was nothing to chuck up. Then they were joltingly landing, and the harnesses snapped away, and their SM was yelling at them to *check their feeds*, and to keep their weapons *in safe mode* until they were fifty metres from the shuttle. It was happening, it was really happening. He couldn't believe it was really actually happening. Adan looked down at the whomp gun in his lap. It occurred to him that, in all the training he had had, nobody had told him how to set it to safe mode. It was inert at the moment, of course, deactivated during flight to avoid accidents. But as soon as the hatch opened, the lights on the wide rifle's side flashed in unison and he thought: *I'd better not fire it in here, or I'd kill dozens and probably blow the whole shuttle up.*

People were deshuttling in fours, and Adan said to himself – he actually formed the words in his head – *Don't pull the trigger on this whomp gun yet.*

As he stepped forward he could *feel* his finger closing on the trigger.

Adan! Stop! What are you doing? Don't pull the trigger! And he thought: *That's right, don't pull the trigger, that would be terrible, if you discharged this weapon in this enclosed space.*

But the more he thought that, the more his hand clenched, and…

…somebody was yelling. It was in his feed. It sounded like a voice, loud in his ear.

Vergara, seventy metres hard left, take cover with Four Bloc and target that tank.

Vergara was him. That was his surname.

It snapped him out. He snibbed the safety off his gun. Well, OK then. Somebody shoved him, and he ran down the ramp awkwardly and almost fell, but did a little dance on… sand, it seemed – grit milled fine as flour. Sunlight. The air smelt of a jarring mix of something sweetly perfumed and something burnt and foul. Somebody was having a barbecue in the vicinity. Holiday cuisine in the midst of a battlefield – surely not! Adan lumbered to the right until his feed yelled at him to go the other way and he turned so fast he missed his footing and went down on one knee. He looked up the beach towards the treeline but everything was wobbly with sweat and adrenaline and nothing was clear. That was gunfire, though. Those sounds. That was what they were, and the whiffling noise of needles of hot metal laser-pushed from needleguns and cooling into projectiles as they whizzed through the air. *Vergara*, somebody was yelling, but nobody called Adan by his surname, not even his mother when she was angry, so he ignored this, or if not ignored it exactly, at least didn't fully process it. *On your feet, Vergara.* Get your own feet, Adan thought. Somebody he knew – it was Tuss – was jogging past him from right to left, and then he wasn't there any more and Adan was splashed with hot vegetable soup, gloopy soup full of big chunks of potato or carrot or yam or something, and it felt, just ugh, just foul, on his face.

Vergara! Vergara! Get up!

Tuss's legs, still linked by his pelvis, but reaching up no higher than his stomach, lay on the sand nearby. All the sense data was in Adan's consciousness, but he wasn't in a position to process it all just now, to fit it together into a meaningful picture. He stood up and fired his whomp gun up the beach and towards the trees. Then he thought: *I'm not fifty metres from the shuttle. I am supposed to get fifty metres away before I fire.* So he jogged rightwards, and then remembered that was the wrong direction, turned around more carefully this time and jogged left. There was a big infolding din, like *sound itself* being deformed and compressed, and then there was a wash of heat at his back. Adan didn't look around. He stumbled, but kept his footing. He got to a heaped-up dune and slumped down. He looked for Four Bloc. They weren't there. Instead there was a group of layabout druggups in ragged clothes, face up, face down. They had to be druggups to sleep through all this noise and stuff, they must be drugged up to the nines. One had braided pieces of metal into his hair and had pierced his nose with a tangled shard of something. I mean, obviously not. They were all dead. They were Four Bloc.

Adan's belatedness in realising this confused him further.

His feed had gone silent, and when he looked back the shuttle had opened its roof into a ring of gigantic uneven petals of steel. Out of the middle of this bloom, smoke was rushing into the sky like it was in a hurry to get away from *there*.

He wiped his face, took hold of the stock of the whomp gun and popped up over the peak of the dune. It was his first proper look at the battlefield. The trees were tropical, long stalks – probably not the right word, *stalks*, but Adan couldn't think what the right word would be – scaled like a fish, reaching up to a *very* high-up hairdo of long, narrow palm leaves. Deeper into the forest the foliage got denser, hedges, bushes, maybe. There was movement, in there. Hard to tell what was moving, but various things were. Overhead was a blue-mauve sky, and a lot of birds, spinning around in great loops. Acrid smell of burning. *I shall die here*, Adan thought to himself, but the thought did not discombobulate him. So it goes. He took aim at a tree and turned its trunk into shavings, watched as the whole thing shifted and fell. Behind it were combat robots, on long legs: heavily armoured torsos and small domed heads. Adan took aim again and fired and one of these started flapping and falling. Up the beach, by the ruined shuttle, a dozen or so of these machines were taking exaggeratedly lengthy steps, like storks, hurrying along the beach towards him.

They were coming to kill him.

They were coming to kill *him*.

Adan asked his feed what he should do, but it did not respond. He fired again, but the whomp gun was not a precision weapon and the advancing enemy only seemed to throng more thickly. He looked around for comrades, but everybody was spread-eagled, or curled up, prone, or supine, or otherwise disconnected.

It occurred to him that he would die. It occurred to him that he *would* die, here and now, and it seemed . . . just crazy-insane. *I mean wtf?* They were going to kill him. But he'd never done anyone any harm! He was a regular, ordinary guy. Why did they want to kill *him*? Weren't there enough bad people in the world to pick on?

He tried firing his gun a few more times, and blew up another tree, and knocked down one of the battlebots. But they were closer and closer now, and he decamped. He ran, retreating to another dune. But the effort gave him a stitch. Sharp pain in his side. Adan looked down, and it wasn't a stitch. A number of needles had gone through the gaps in his body armour where the panels were tied together – a bunch of them, piercing his gut and his kidney, for all he knew, who even knew where the kidney was, and he was sure to die, sure to die, and it hurt real bad, so he dropped his gun and sat down.

The grumbling sky was attack jets circling. Ours, or theirs. Who could tell?

But here, like locusts, came a flock of harddrones, sweeping overhead, and they were definitely *ours*, so Adan felt his spirit rise. But then they all glitched out, all at once, and rained down onto the beach and the sea like hail. All of them – simultaneously.

They surely weren't supposed to go out like that.

A spatter of noise and the light was twice as bright everywhere, and then it dialled itself back to normal. The sudden brightness flung shadows in weird stretchy bulges, and then there was a much louder, more sustained rumble and particles began clattering down onto Adan's helmet. Ashes. Lots of ashes.

Then a thought entered his head that shook him up bad. He was going to die without ever seeing Elegy again. That seemed monstrous somehow, more than unfair: a violation. He was a human being. And here, stalking towards him, was the rest of the world embodied as violence, everything else, everything that got in the way of him *just being him*. Why couldn't they leave him alone? And then there flashed into Adan's mind a memory of that time, back home, back when he *had* a home, of Gee glitching out. His friends' faces, or his mother's, taking over her natural beauty. He'd never got that sorted, it had just, sort-of, gone away. Healed itself. And then he thought, no: there'd been that odd episode when a stranger had called him, and this stranger's face had taken over Elegy, and had told him...

Wait.

There were tingles running up and down Adan's scalp. The pain in his side withdrew to the corner of his perception. What had that stranger said?

A moment like this. On the island. When your friends have all been killed and the porcupine spikes. The spikes in your gut. What was he supposed to say? He was supposed to say something. Stand up, the stranger had said. Sing out: *weave a circle round me* something.

'Weave a circle,' he croaked.

Speaking caused pain to radiate sharply, stabbingly, from his pierced side. But, the hell. He gathered himself, got his bulk up on its hind legs like a bear, and was immediately confronted with four HMθ battlebots, and their weapons swivelling straight on him, and he bellowed *Weave a circle round me*, and the whole of eternity dangled

dangled

—all possibility, and the annihilation of all possibility, just waiting for these implacable enemies, and their implacable group-mind singular purpose, to kill him.

He took a breath, and only then realised that he had been holding his breath.

The battlebots were motionless. He took another breath. And here came another drone swarm, and this time they were not knocked out of the sky. He looked to the right, and then the whole scene was drenched and cleansed in a piquant light and Adan was on his back. Knocked down like a ninepin, gasping and stinging all over.

A shuttle retrieved him ten minutes later. Half an hour after that he was back at the base, in the surgical hospital. He was suffering from mild burns from the bombardment that destroyed the motionless HMθ battlebots, and also from the four needles that had pierced his abdomen. Then the doctors also operated to remove tiny pieces of Tuss that had, it seemed, become embedded in his face and neck.

'We gotta get these fragments out, Trooper,' said the doctor, leaning over him. 'Your own immune system would reject them, alien DNA so far as it's concerned, and there would be an allergic reaction, swelling, complications. Just hold still.'

Alien DNA, thought Adan.

'He was my friend, ma'am,' he told the doctor.

She was concentrating real hard, he could see.

'I am sorry, son. There. There, you're good to go.'

:7:

While he was recuperating in an otherwise entirely empty ward, a lieutenant colonel came to see him.

'You understand that you were the only survivor of the attack on Wallalei?'

Adan hadn't known the name.

'Well,' said the officer briskly, 'the HMθ deployed much more sophisticated electronic countermeasures than we anticipated. We sent four flights of drones in and the first three just fell out of the sky – all at once. Just dropped like birds in winter. They're supposed to be hardened against any and all cyberattack. We don't know why the first three waves failed. But what we really don't know is why the fourth succeeded.'

'I don't know, ma'am.'

'You didn't see anything?'

'It was a blur, ma'am. The shuttle dropped and we rushed out, and then it was all hell . . .' *What was the phrase?* He thought, and it came back to him. 'All hell broke loose. I got a few shots off, but then everybody was dead.'

'Trooper, surveillance footage shows you taking shelter behind this prominence.'

She showed him a screen, and on it was a swooping-down video – the whole island swelling to fill the screen and then the beach, with its scattered bodies and body parts, and there was the shuttle tipped on its side with its roof ripped open and smoking and . . . here was Adan, moving twitchily among a heap of corpses. It was very weird seeing the scene again from this exterior perspective. Very weird. The HMθ droids were much more numerous, and much closer, than he had realised.

'You stand up,' said the lieutenant colonel. 'And that's when they all seize up. All of them. Is that just serendipitous?

'I don't know, ma'am.'

'You don't know if it's merely serendipitous?'

'I don't know what serendipitous means.'

'Coincidence, soldier. Was it just a coincidence that their whole system locked down when you stood up like this?'

'I don't know, ma'am.'

'You don't know why those droids locked down at that particular time? Or you don't know what *coincidence* means?'

'I don't know why those droids locked down at that particular time, ma'am.'

'Very good, Trooper.'

After she had gone, Adan got to thinking that all his friends were dead. They'd all died in a matter of moments, and he alone had survived. That was sad. Should he cry? He thought about it in a more or less distant way for a while. He was not a clever man, but he understood that tears need to come naturally to the eyes as the leaves do to the trees, or they had better not come at all. He slept.

Three days later he was discharged, and reassigned to a new unit. He was nervous at meeting the new people, and a couple of them made fun of him, some, but after a couple of days they had all bonded. They were the remnants of four previously existing squads, all of which had gone into battle against the HMθ at various locations, and all of which had been bested. The casualty rate of Adan's group was the highest, but everyone in the new squad had lost friends.

'What I want to know,' said Roj, who was the loudest and heartiest of the new group, 'is – why they sending flesh and blood to fight those machines? Why they not sending in their own machines?'

'You think our machines stand any chance against those hive mind machines?' said a woman named Skot. 'They're techno wizards.'

'You're missing the point,' said Coffee, whose real name was Chaz Joffe but who was universally called by this other name on account of his colour and his fondness for the drink. 'You know what those HMθ droids are? They are expensive. You know what we are? We are *cheap*. That's the height and breadth and depth of it.'

'Truth,' said Roj, sombre.

'How did you survive, Fats?' Tristis asked Adan.

'They just all glitched out,' he told them. 'I stood up and said they should weave around me, and they stopped.'

Everybody stared at him. Then they decided, collectively, that this was one of those random, meaningless things that people sometimes said, especially if they were post-combat and shaken up and such.

Tristis said: 'Maybe *you* the real wizard, yeah?' and everybody laughed.

And then Roj said: 'You think you can repeat that trick when we next go into combat?' and everybody laughed again.

And then it settled again.

They had three weeks of training, settling in, getting used to functioning as a new unit. Then they were sent – by regular shuttle, rather than the more expensive high-insert trajectory – to police an urban disturbance in a lakeside city.

'They flew us to the middle of the Pacific in thirty minutes,' complained Roj, 'but it takes them three hours to schlep us to Chicago.'

Good joke. Roll on snare drum.

Adan wasn't sure exactly what the beef was, in the city, but it had brought large crowds out onto the streets, and his squad was part of a large military contingent to contain civic disturbance. There were fliers zipping about everywhere, but Adan's cordon was military-grade and none got through. The one part he found difficult was seeing many people out and about with their Phenes. Some were couples holding hands or hugging; others were clearly part of the larger protest, which made Adan wonder if the protest had something to do with Phene rights, or maybe anti-Phene feeling. He didn't care about politics, or anything like that, but he found his heart beating faster and felt a clench in his throat as though he was about to cry at the memory of Elegy. His beloved!

Multiple sirens from hurrying ambulances, not quite in sync, like the hooting of geese.

A slug the size of a house floated down – a dispersal dirigible, spraying stinkjuice down onto the crowd. People scattered, ran, some screamed; that stuff bonded with your skin and made you smell like a skunk for *weeks*. A few protestors braved it (a Phene could be programmed to ignore stink, of course) or else wrapped themselves in gelcloaks and started throwing objects. Shots were fired. But it didn't matter to Adan, because his unit was being pulled back as a second dirigible came buzzing in overhead.

They were removed to a temporary barracks made out of a warehouse, but kept on alert. Finally they were stood down and shuttle-flown back to proper barracks.

'What was that about, though?' Tristis wanted to know.

'There's legislation pending,' said Coffee. 'Phenes.'

'What kind of legislation?' Adan wanted to know.

'Some people reckon there are too many Phenes,' said Coffee. 'There's a scare that the HMθ will be able to hack them, turn them against us – fifth column, you know?'

'That's crazy,' said Adan.

But the fear was twisting in his gut now.

Make Elegy illegal? They couldn't. Surely they wouldn't. She wouldn't hurt a fly.

It preyed on his mind. It bothered his dreams. He did what any soldier would do: he went to his sergeant.

'Sarge, can I ask you something?'

This wasn't his old personal development sergeant. Adan had no idea what had happened to her. This was the squad's first sergeant, a tall man, young enough that his baldness must have been a fashion choice.

'Trooper Vergara.'

'Some of the folk in the squad,' he said, 'were saying that the government might be fixing to make Pheno-women illegal. Is that true?'

The sergeant looked down upon Adan from a position that combined physical with intellectual superiority.

'You don't follow the news much, then, Trooper?'

'No, Sarge.'

'You got to register your Phene. That's all. They got to have a software regulator uploaded, and a certificate of registration. There's some concern ... Adan, is it?'

'That's me, Sarge.'

'There's some concern that the enemy might be able to infiltrate the software on which they run. They are all interconnected, after all – it's a network, after all. That's what Phene means, I think? Phone? It's an etymological variant of the word "phone".'

Adan wasn't sure what to say to this, so he said nothing. But the sergeant was on a riff now.

'Though I remember reading a piece that said Phene was short for Phenotype, because elements of human DNA are included in the coding that acts genetically on the plastic and silicate raw materials that constitute the ...' He stopped. 'You're not much of a reader?'

'Sir, no, sir,' said Adan.

'Don't "sir" me, I'm not an officer.'

'Sorry, Sarge.'

'Look – you've got a Phene at home, yes? Is that your concern?'

'Yes, Sarge.'

'You'll be fine. Get in touch with someone – your parents, maybe?' Adan shook his head, so the first sergeant adjusted his expression to show a modicum of concern. 'Dead, Trooper?'

'My father is, Sarge. My mother is ... gone, I guess.'

'Well, I'm sorry. But you must have family, or friends, who can register your Phene as pending, until you get a furlough and get the chance to take it to the iPhene place and have it seen to?'

There was no point getting further into the nitty and the gritty.

'Thank you, Sarge,' said Adan, and saluted, and left.

No leave was scheduled, though, for months. A fortnight of more intensive training, and then Adan's squad was sent on a new mission. This time he rode the high-trajectory shuttle un-hung-over, and all his senses were heightened, and he felt a mortal terror to intensify his physical discomfort. What if he died? Elegy, powered down, gathering dust, locked in the cupboard until the money he'd paid ran out and she was ... what? Chucked out onto a rubbish heap? Recycled? Sold off to some leering man who would fuck her in unspeakable ways, any ways at all being unspeakable unless it was Adan performing those actions? It was more than Trooper Adan Vergara could stand, in point of fact, actually, thank you very much, and no, no mistake, no sir, no madam. And this terror pricked and intensified the adrenalised excitement of going into battle, as the shuttle shook and rattled on its precipitous descent, and the whomp gun bounced in his lap like a prosthetic cock. Blood, which is life, gushed through the sluiceways of his body. He had never felt more intensely alive, and it was not an experience he enjoyed.

Then, with a clattering jolt, they were down, and they exited the shuttle to anticlimax. The enemy were not there, so the squads joined the other troops in hurrying away from the landing site and establishing a beachhead.

Not that they were on a beach. This was a cold, foresty sort of land, the vista softened by mist, and a moist chill in every breath. Adan went where his helmet feed told him to go, took up a series of positions and covered his comrades. Here was a peak, from which he could look down a long shallow valley, and no sign of the enemy. Mist a cataract in the world's lens.

'The knife blade loses its edge,' said Tristis, dropping into position beside him.

'What?'

'Soft, yeah?'

But he didn't know what she meant. And here was Roj, running between the bushes and more falling against a big boulder than taking up position.

'No show,' he panted. 'There's supposed to be a big underground Hive-Mind base hereabouts, but the word is they evacuated it when they knew we were coming.'

'Cowards!' said Tristis, laughingly.

'I guess we've turned the corner where fighting these thetas goes.'

Adan's feed told him to hold position. Presumably Roj and Tristis were hearing the same thing. There was a river at the bottom of the valley. It was audible, a continual gush of white noise, although it was itself invisible among the blackleaf trees and the white haze. Supply craft hurtled low overhead. Wasp-drones flew back and forth.

'They've all gone,' said Roj.

But the god of irony tipped back his smirking head at this point and laughed aloud, for as soon as Roj uttered these words a charred oval appeared on his backpack, and then another on his thigh, at the point where it curved round into his ass. Roj started screaming and then somebody coughed, really near Adan, and coughed again, and there was nobody there. Adan actually looked round to see who was coughing, but of course nobody was coughing. Two holes gaped in Roj's torso, right through his pack and body armour, and sizzling blood gushed out. He fell over to the side.

He wasn't screaming now.

There must have been some transition period, but that wasn't how it registered to Adan. The next thing he knew everybody was running, and the HMθ were attacking with a combination of heat-ray ordnance and knucklebone-sized superpenetrators. Drones swept overhead like autumn leaves blown by the mistral, and as dead. They hit the turf with dull sounds, they splashed into the river. Bangs and cracks, and then a mighty flash of light, and the fog spooled off in pearl-white fleeces overhead. Adan aimed his gun, but couldn't see a target. Spun on his heel. Aimed again. Nothing. Tristis was running hard for better cover, so she at least had identified from where the attack was coming. Why hadn't Adan? Tristis ran, long legs flicking out and down, right, left, right, left, and then there was no right leg for her to put down and she sprawled face first into the wet grass. Adan lifted his whomp gun and fired anyway, just to get a shot off, into the misty vastness of the forest.

A shuttle spiralled on its axis, hurtling desperately low overhead. It missed the treetops, and then it couldn't miss them any more, and it vanished into the woodland with a sound of splintering and crashing.

Adan fired again. *Whomp*, said the gun.

Nothing.

Whomp.

Whomp.

And suddenly he was facing a phalanx of HMθ bots, and he dropped the gun and turned, terrified, to run in the opposite direction only to see more HMθ bots and, not knowing what he was saying, he screamed *Weave a circle round me twice!* and the bots

stopped

– stopped dead. They did more than freeze, as they had done on the beach assault. They retracted their weapons, locked down their heads and withdrew their tentacle-legs into their torsos.

It was as if a power command had forced the machines wholly to disengage.

There was a period of quiet, and it was eerie. Then the sound of a shuttle coming down fast, and landing somewhere away to Adan's left. Some small arms fire, as our boys and girls realised that their enemy was no longer fighting back.

:8:

This time Adan's intervention was noticed. The area was secured, and Adan's squad pulled back and returned to base. Adan was debriefed separately from the rest of his squad.

'Is Roj dead?' he wanted to know.

The lieutenant checked his screen and nodded sombrely.

'Damn,' said Adan, wondering why he didn't feel the loss of his friend more acutely, wondering why it didn't register in his pulse or his breathing. I mean, it *was* a shame, no question. Then he remembered Tristis running and falling.

'What about Tristis? What about my friend Tristis?'

The lieutenant checked her screen again.

'Tristis Rastapopoulos? She's alive. She's in surgery now, but the prognosis is good.'

'Good,' said Adan.

But again, there was no spike of relief in his innards. *Is that odd? I should be feeling something – shouldn't I?*

'Trooper,' said the lieutenant. 'What happened on the battlefield today?'

'They all shut down,' said Adan. 'I guess. Don't you guys know how it happened?'

'We're trying to work it out,' she said. 'Did you fire your weapon at a *particular* enemy warbot? It could be there's a weakness in their network that means certain nodes are …' She didn't believe it, even as she said it.

'I couldn't see real good,' said Adan, 'what with the must and all.'

'The must?'

'The mist,' said Adan. 'I meant to say – mist.'

'This happened before. You were present at a skirmish on the island of Wallalei and all the enemy bots malfunctioned in unison. That is correct?'

'Sir – ma'am, I mean. I'm sorry I don't know what happened, then or today. I mean, I said something and everything stopped.'

The lieutenant caught the charm of this last word, and paid it a small tribute of her own by stopping. She looked up. Then she asked: 'You said something?'

'OK,' said Adan. 'I mean, I guess. Sure.'

'Trooper,' she said, slowly, 'can you tell me what you said?'

Adan tried to get his thoughts in order, but it wasn't easy. The whole clotted backstory, it was so stupid, so inconsequential and yet – evidently – so *very* consequential, actually. But without that backstory the words were just a vapid string of who-knew-what, agitating the air molecules and so passing their informational content from taut voice box to taut eardrum.

'It was just, ma'am …' Adan started, and as he began to repeat the phrase he realised what word had been missing, which word he'd been omitting or getting wrong, that oddball olde-worlde poet-word *thrice*. 'I just said "weave a circle round me". That's more or less what I said, ma'am.'

'More?' the lieutenant pressed. 'Or less? What exactly did you say?'

'"Weave a circuit round me twice",' said Adan, starting to get nervous.

'Circuit?'

'Yeah.'

'Before, you said circle.'

'That… yeah.'

'Weave a circle… yes?'

'Circle.'

'To be clear – *circle*?'

'Yeah. I mean, yes, ma'am, and I mean I *said* "twice", but it should have been "thrice".'

'Thrice?'

'Thrice.'

The lieutenant looked at him for a long time. Then she entered something rapidly onto the screen sitting on the table in front of her. Then she sat up, pushed her chair back a little way and said: 'I've called in Colonel Daberlohn. You know the colonel?'

'No, ma'am.'

'He's a specialist in this kind of warfare,' said the lieutenant, without specifying what kind she meant.

A few minutes later the colonel walked into the room, *sans* knocking, and sat himself down: a small-stature, brisk-gestured man of middle age.

'So, Trooper,' he said, briskly, in a low-pitched and resonant voice. 'I've been looking over your file as I came down here. You didn't mention that your mother joined the Hive-Mind.'

'My mother,' said Adan. 'Sure. Sir.'

'You didn't think that *might* be something your recruiting officers might have been interested in?'

For the life of him, Adan couldn't see that it might be. His brows wedged into puzzlement.

'Sir?'

'Trooper,' said the colonel, 'we appreciate that neither your intellectual capacity nor your level of attainment is of the highest. We appreciate that. You don't need to be a superbrain to do your duty. To do what a soldier must. Nonetheless, I must inquire of you – *are* you a five-star moron?'

The spurt of vehemence with which the colonel said this last word jolted Adan straighter in his chair.

'Yes, sir! No, sir!'

'You understand the Hive-Mind-θ are the enemy we are fighting? You realise that we, who are doing the fighting, might be interested in knowing that one of our own soldiers has family who have *defected to the enemy*?'

'No, sir! Yes, sir!'

'Now... tell me everything about this –' a glance at his own screen – 'weave a circle, or circuit – there seems to be some confusion – round me twice shutdown code of yours. Tell me everything. If it's worked twice, it could work again.'

'Sir!'

The two officers waited. Adan looked from one to the other, and then back to the first.

'Well, go on then,' snapped the colonel.

'My girlfriend, sir.' Adan looked at the lieutenant. 'Ma'am.'

Another pause.

'Your girlfriend, yes. She's the one who taught you this phrase?'

'She glitched.'

'Glitched?'

'She's a Phene, sir.' He looked again at the lieutenant. 'Ma'am.'

'I see. And she glitched?'

'Her face was swapped out with some dude's.'

'Whose?'

'I never recognised him, sir. Some dude. Ugly, kind of. Big face, eyes kind-of far apart. Pallid, really. Balding.'

'And he gave you this line?'

'He said I'd need it, sir, at the beach. I mean, ma'am, sir, the Wallalei.'

'He mentioned Wallalei by name?'

'No, sir. No, he didn't say the name. But he described it – a beach, me being stuck with porcupine needles. And he told me the words, and I said the words and the Hive-Mind soldiers… stopped.'

'When was this, Trooper?' asked the lieutenant.

'About a three-month before I enlisted, ma'am.'

'This is the most ridiculous farrago of nonsense I ever heard,' boomed the colonel. 'You expect us to believe this? Somebody hacked your whorebot and gave you a verbal code that shut down the most sophisticated military tech warfare has ever seen? I've never heard such arrant garbage. Tell us the truth, soldier – are you still in touch with your mother?'

Adan stared into the face of the colonel. That word, whorebot, was so very ugly, that Adan started to cry. He really couldn't help himself. The colonel goggled at him, but the lieutenant put a hand on his arm, and for a long series of moments the only sound was Adan sobbing.

The door opened and a general entered.

'Colonel,' she said, briskly, 'you are relieved.'

Adan stared up at her. A cleverer person would have had some sense of the effectiveness of taking nasty cop off stage and replacing them with nice cop at the precise moment of the subject's emotional overload, but Adan was beautifully innocent of all such ruses.

'I'm General Cho,' said the officer. 'I'm here to tell you how grateful we are, Trooper, for your service. I'm going to see to it, personally, that you get a decoration for your bravery, son.'

He could have kissed the general's hands.

'Ma'am!'

'What you've stumbled upon here, my lad, could win us the war. You're a very special person – we're only now realising just how special. And I want you to come along with me, Adan, to help me tie up this whole war.'

Adan sniffed back the remnants of his weeping.

'Yes, ma'am.'

'We need to get you into space, son,' she said.

:9:

For two days Adan was kept in a luxuriously appointed room on base. On the third he was invited, rather than ordered, into the general's ground-car and whisked to the base's huge launch facility. It was late afternoon, hot, and the ground-car's windows were all open. The moon was a coin of silver displayed upon a blue velvet cushion, and the wind blowing in from the ocean had been salted to preserve its freshness.

'I see from your record,' said General Cho, smiling at him, 'that you did pass space combat.'

'Yes, ma'am.'

'Only at E.'

'That's correct, ma'am.'

'Nausea was a problem, according to the report. Well, we'll try to avoid any such unpleasantness on this trip.'

She added something to the screen in front of her, and then the ground-car slowed and settled and the doors were lifting up like eagle's wings.

Adan's training flight had been in a large military shuttle of utility design. Now he was going skywards in a streamlined flitter: individual gel-cushioned seats, a lozenge handed to him by a grave-faced medic which (he was told) he should 'allow to dissolve under his tongue' to prevent any vomitous misadventure during flight. A drink.

'Do you drink, Trooper Vergara? Beer? Whiskey?'

'Why, thank you, yes. Yes, thank you.'

Launch was a nudge, and then a build of acceleration all along the magchute, towers whiffling past with rapidly increasing frequency as things moved towards the launch point. Then the upkick into low orbit. Adan gazed, amazed, through his porthole – the military training shuttle had been windowless – at the clouds, whitely transparent and edged with sunset colours, swooping down in apparent motion as the flitter ascended. Vast marine invertebrates on their way to the seabed. The earth shrank to the dimensions of its own map, misty with galactic spreads of artificial lights, and the light thickened outside until they had popped, champagne-cork-ishly, out of the atmosphere altogether.

'We're going to dock with the *Owl of Minerva*,' the general told Adan. 'She's a battleship, but I don't want you to get nervous. Better safe than sorry, is how we view it.'

'Yes, ma'am,' Adan replied, quite baffled.

'You're not curious where we're going?'

'No, ma'am.'

'You're the perfect soldier! Well, I'll tell you, but before I do I want to say something. If it were me, we'd promote you – to corporal in the first instance, but on a conveyor-line upwards from there. If you truly have the capacity to stop the HMθ simply by saying a string of words, then you will be crucial to our war effort. Crucial. We can't do it yet, because we're not sure if the HMθ's interest in you depends upon you being a common soldier – if, that is, promoting you might interfere with this ... this *ability* you seem to have.'

'Yes, ma'am.'

'Believe me, we've tried your little phrase. We've sent troops into two separate engagements with orders to yell it at any HMθ bots that approach. No go. It's no go for that particular bogeyman, I can tell you.'

'Yes, ma'am.' Adan wondered if he should have responded with 'No, ma'am' instead. But the general didn't seem to mind.

'It's you, Adan,' she said. 'It's something specific *to you*. I can be honest – we're not entirely sure what motivates the HMθ. They're a hive consciousness, but they're made up of distinct individual human consciousnesses. It's our job, at the highest levels of military strategising, to try and predict them, and often we can't.'

'No, ma'am,' said Adan.

She gave him a straight look. 'You've a sly wit on you, Trooper,' she said. 'I like that. Just so long as it doesn't shade into actual subordination.'

Adan, lacking any clear idea what she was talking about, smiled.

The flitter banked. The whole world swung out of the porthole and then swung back again, with all its petrol-in-a-puddle wash of coloration. The lights inside the cabin meant it wasn't possible to see the stars in space, but the moon was there, just as plump and far away as she seemed from the earth; and there was one blinking light, and that was where they were heading. It stayed a speck for a long time and then it was a piece of grit, an irregularly shaped pebble, and suddenly a whole ragged-edge polygon moonlet. That was one of the things the battleship designation meant: a regular spacecraft that had tethered hefty chunks of lunar or asteroid basalt to its hull, and sealed the joins with ablate-resistant foam. Each piece of armour had its own engine, for these were what moved the spacecraft through space when the armour was fully fitted. As the general's flitter approached, several pieces of hull armour were in satellite orbit, permitting the shuttle to dock; but once the general and her staff – and Adan – were aboard, and the shuttle withdrew, the shell was assembled and the whole bulky craft crawled into a lower, faster orbit, swung round the nightside of the world and fired up its main belt. Reaction blasts adjusted pitch, yaw and orientation and the main belt dug its quantum teeth into the resistant material of the strong nuclear force and spun its metaphorical wheels on this metaphorical rail. It was a slow acceleration, but it was by the same token a steady one, and within six hours Earth had become a mint imperial in the *Owl*'s rear-view sensors, and they were rushing down a sunward arc, hurrying after the hurrying-away target of Venus . . . Venus . . . Venus.

'Adan,' said the general, as the two settled down to an intimate dinner *à deux* in her cabin, 'I think it's time you and I had a chat about what's really going on here.'

'Ma'am,' said Adan.

The acceleration was creating a lunar-approximate faux-gravity, so they were both eating from deep open bowls and drinking from regular cups. Red wine, very fruitily tasteful. Pasta in some kind of gloopy, spicy, garlic-infused sauce.

'Why are we going to Venus, soldier?'

'I don't know, ma'am.'

'Because the HMθ have made diplomatic overtures. For the first time in over a year. It's a major development – and we think it's because of you. We hypothesise they're scared of what you could do.'

'Me?'

'Oh, I'm not saying we fully understand what's going on here. But let's be clear. You have proved, on two separate combat occasions, that you can, by saying a particular string of words, shut down enemy ordnance. That's not nothing, you know!'

'Yes … no, ma'am,' agreed, or disagreed, Adan.

'We've had our best people look at this … this unusual state of affairs. Their best guess is – it has to do with your Phene. Elegy, I believe, is her name?'

'Is she all right, ma'am?' Adan asked, abruptly animated. It was startling to hear Gee's name in this senior officer's mouth, and an unfocused terror swept through him. 'Have you done anything to her?'

'She's fine,' said the general, patting the air down in front of her with one hand to gesture that he should calm himself. 'You had her in a poky little cupboard in a commercial storage facility – we found her and transferred her to a secure military facility. She'll be much safer there.'

Adan was finding it hard to breathe. 'You moved her?'

'She's as much a crucial asset in all this as you are. At least that's what our strategy bigwigs believe. We are highly motivated to keep her safe and secure, and when this mission is over, you and she will be happily reunited.'

The thought of other people putting their hands on Elegy, of men handling her – perhaps dismantling her and putting her back together – brought rage into Adan's soul. He bit it back.

'Ma'am,' he said, in a fierce little voice, 'I have to say – you moved her without my permission.'

'There wasn't time. There was no time to dot all the little legal i's and get your specific permission and so on. Everything is happening right away. Really, Trooper, you'd do well to calm yourself down. Your Phene is fine.' And then the general laughed, an odd little curl of sound. 'Phene is fine! I'm a poet and I didn't know it.'

Adan's breathing had not settled.

'Ma'am,' he said.

'I mean, Adan ... weren't you curious as to how this message, this shutdown code, *came* to you via your Phene – your Phene, of all things?'

The fact that this general – this superstar high-ranking officer – was talking so casually about Elegy – about his Elegy – so casually was baking Adan's noodle. He grunted, and then made a little hissing noise, and then he said: 'Ma'am, no, ma'am.'

'We're not entirely sure either, of course. It's hard to be certain. But we have a theory.'

'Ma'am.'

'I don't know how much you know about the deep history of the Hive-Mind-θ?'

At this, Adan simply stared at her.

'It's a complicated and not especially edifying story.' The general drank down what remained in her wineglass. 'Go back a couple of centuries to the beginnings of social media. In those days phones were the tech by which people intermediated – I mean, old-school phones, the sorts of thing you rarely see nowadays. The germ that grew into the HMθ began as a hands-free social media app. Now, obviously, it very quickly evolved beyond that, and nowadays we are dealing with a massively multiparty co-ordinated entity, legally human – according to the Global Supreme Court's judgement of last year, anyway – possessing immense financial resources, distributed unequally around the world and widely through outer space. There are nodes we can hit, or we believe there are, where we can damage their ability to interconnect, but if I'm being honest we've never noticed any diminution in their capacities after one of our attacks.'

'No, ma'am.'

'The HMθ has long since left that old phone technology behind, of course. But that *is* where they started, and our strategy mentats think there may be some residual attachment to … to phones as such – to that old technology – in their as-it-were DNA. It hasn't been top-down *designed*, the HMθ – it has evolved, it has grown. In evolutionary terms it's been an accelerated process, sure, but with any process like this a bunch of junk ends up in the genes, along with the stuff that makes everything work. Maybe that's what this is. Phenes are called that because they are Phenotypes of human DNA, after all.'

That reminded Adan of something, and trying to recall exactly what it was distracted him from his distress that Elegy – his Elegy – was currently in some place and he didn't know where.

'Is that right, though, ma'am?' he asked.

'We believe so. A digital copy of human DNA was encoded in the original hard-body program, and the Phenes we have today are a curated and modified version of that.'

'I thought it was just a brand-name spin on the word phone.'

The general blinked. Then she took another sporkful of pasta and ate it. Then she tossed her bowl and empty glass in the recycle slot.

'One working theory,' she said, eventually, 'is that the HMθ feels some peculiar affinity to the Phenes, because of their own origin as a collective entity, their deep history – and because they, too, are a phenotype of human development. We're all expressing our genes, after all. They think they're the inevitable evolutionary next step for *Homo sapiens*. They're wrong about that, but it's what they think. So … whatever is going on here – with you, with your Phene and this shutdown code – it's all tangled up with these questions.'

Adan drank his wine. It soothed him, some.

'I'm not sure I understand, ma'am,' he said.

'No,' the general agreed. 'No more do I. The hypothesis is – some element in the HMθ – maybe some individual incompletely assimilated, maybe somebody suffering in some way – passes this shutdown code out of the collective and to us. She, he, whatever, does so by hacking a Phene. We all know that there's been a lot of anxiety that the HMθ might hack the network where Phenes are concerned, and override their three-law programming. The more hysterical corners of the chatsphere envisage an army of murdering Phenes spree-ing through humanity with guns and ... I don't know. Swords, kung fu, who knows. Safety protocols are baked into Phenes, of course, so I think these fears are overwrought. But Phenes are, by nature, highly interconnected items and the HMθ are very sophisticated players when it comes to hacking.'

'My Elegy wouldn't hurt anybody,' said Adan. 'She couldn't. It's not in her nature.'

'Sure, my lad,' said the general, expansively. 'So let's say ... this rogue agent inside the HMθ – if that's what we're dealing with – hacks your Phene. Why yours? Either because there's something special about you, or maybe about your Phene, or else because they had to pick a random Phene and it happened to be yours.'

Adan wished she would stop talking about Elegy. It made him uncomfortable. But he said: 'I can't believe there's anything special about me, ma'am.'

'Don't take this the wrong way, Adan, but I agree. You're a regular guy. You're a soldier who follows orders, but you're not super intelligent or super well positioned, socially or culturally.'

'I wasn't a soldier when it happened, though.'

'True! This predates your enlistment. Maybe the hacker didn't know that. Maybe they figured the shutdown code would get out and find its way to the military one way or another. Maybe they gauged the likelihood of you joining up and went with that.'

'But they saw the future.'

The general raised her eyebrows. 'They did?'

'It did – the glitch. It told me that I should say the words during the Wallelei assault.'

'But they didn't actually mention Wallelei. By name.'

'No,' Adan conceded. 'It wasn't that. But the … the situation was described real precise, with lots of … you know. Detail.'

'Since,' said the general, 'actually seeing the future is impossible, this must be a best-guess kind of scenario. Maybe they figured you were about to enlist. I've seen your file, and you weren't best qualified for any other kind of work, let's be honest. So they figure – he'll probably go into the army. So they know you'd be sent into combat, and a good proportion of our raids are attempts to disrupt HMθ nodes – concentrations of HMθ population or technology, many of which are on private islands. So it's a reasonable guess.'

This didn't sound correct to Adan, but what did he know?

'Yes, ma'am.'

'So here we are,' said the general. 'And I still haven't told you why we're going to Venus!'

Adan waited. The general watched him. Eventually she said:

'All of this, everything I've just said to you, is best-guess discourse. We don't really know. There's something radically unpredictable about the HMθ, is the truth, and we're not good at modelling their processes. But we know one thing: we *can't* cohabit, long-term. *They* are an existential threat to *us*. Maybe they are right, and they *are* the next evolutionary step – maybe they're *Homo sapiens* and we're *Homo neanderthalensis*. So what? We are what we are. Should Neanderthal men and women just lay down and die? Of course not. Evolution isn't a script, it's a struggle. If the Neanderthals had defeated *Homo sapiens*, then *Homo sapiens* would look like the evolutionary dead end.'

Much of this went over Adan's head; but at least she had stopped talking about Gee in that disconcerting way.

'Yes, ma'am,' he said.

'This war, the one we're fighting, is all skirmishes and black ops and counter-ops. We can't mount an all-out war because we don't have a discrete target – we're not Scipio with a Carthage to attack, we're not Patton facing Germany. Our enemy is hugely distributed around the world and in space. So we skirmish, and we look for medium- and long-term tactical advantage. They're doing the same thing. You understand what they want with Venus?'

'Yes, ma'am,' said Adan. And then, because he realised he had no idea, 'No, ma'am, I don't, ma'am.'

'You don't follow the news much, do you, Trooper? The HMθ want to terraform Venus. Their declared aim – if you think we can trust that – is... they will make Venus habitable and claim it as their world, leaving us to live on the Earth. Then we can just, both of us, get on with live-and-let-living.'

'That sounds like a pretty good idea,' said Adan, and then, because of the look the general gave him, he wished he hadn't.

'There are a hundred or so reasons as to why it's *not* a good idea, soldier,' she said. 'For one thing, our two populations are now incredibly intimately interwoven across a very large set of discrete national territories. Separating this into two entirely distinct populations – it's just not going to happen. But assume it did. Assume two radically distinct versions of humanity lived on two adjacent planets. Two versions that each regarded the other, with some justification, as existential threats. If all of *us* live on A and all of *them* live on B, then the temptation will be – hit B hard, co-ordinate some planet-busting mass assault and achieve your maximum genocide. And the kicker is – if both populations are thinking that, then there's a premium on being the one to act first, which shrinks the window and increases crazy and paranoid thinking, which in turn massively raises the probability that A and B wipe one another out, and everybody dies.' She shook her head. 'Prisoner's dilemma. We need a stake in one another's territories to minimise that. So *if* they terraform Venus we need half that territory for our kind of humanity to settle, as a security.'

'Yes, ma'am!' said Adan, brightly.

'So we're going to Venus. They – the HMθ I mean – want to open up diplomatic channels, and we will talk. But if there's a way of using you to force them to stand down their Venusian fleet, well... that's leverage that could come in very handy at exactly this time. So, Adan – you have a clearer sense of why we're flying you to another planet?'

'Yes, ma'am,' Adan lied.

'Turn in, son. We'll speak again tomorrow.'

:10:

The (metaphorical) ratchets on which the Q-drive rotated its (metaphorical) cog-teeth were the unimaginably small gradations in electron-shell orbital possible positions. This provides a firm enough grid to accelerate even very large masses, but spinning your (metaphorical) cogwheel trillions of times a second hardly moves you at all. Luckily for you, the acceleration is cumulative, so after an initial reaction-mass burst it's possible to spin the (metaphorical) wheels until you have traction and then you can build, build, build momentum. Within three weeks you're travelling so fast you have to disengage the engine and, depending on your destination, put it into reverse to start slowing yourself down.

For short-term course corrections, or – Providence forbid! – dogfights with enemy craft, the main drive is so sluggish as to be absolutely useless. In such eventualities, Earth craft use reaction-mass blasts. The HMθ use a different spread of technologies to move their craft around: nippier, more wrenching, drawing on what seems from the outside – but presumably can't be – zero point sources. At any rate, the *Owl of Minerva* hurtled through the perpetual night sky of the solar system, downhill towards the sun, faster now than the planet it was aiming past and on course to catch up with her in less than a week.

For Adan, life on board was a mode of hiatus. Everybody else there had duties, had a timetable, periods on and off. He alone didn't, since he was cargo, not crew. He had a little cabin to himself and spent a long time in there watching old screen dramas and playing games. After that one personal one-on-one meal in the general's stateroom, he ate in the mess thrice daily, with whichever tranche of the crew was free to eat at those times. He was not forthcoming, and they did not ask him many questions.

There were actual portholes, but they only afforded views of the basalt cladding that surrounded the craft. It didn't matter. Any wall would display exterior views if requested. The interior design was a series of stacked floors linked by a central shaft that was supplied on all sides with rungs – useful as ladders for when the *Owl* was under constant acceleration and as handholds when it free-fell.

For the first week of flight Adan dreamt of Elegy every night. After that he generally didn't remember his dreams. Each morning he made his wall a viewscreen and requested a real-size view of the exterior vista, and the screen showed him a fist-sized ring of bristling whiteness – the Sun, with its disc optically occluded to prevent it blinding him – and a vast spread of stars, uncountable tips of light in every direction and the foggy, spunky band of ragged brightness that was the Milky Way. If he touched his cabin wall at any point, the screen would give him information about which star he was indicating. He had to ask the program to identify Venus early in the voyage: a fatter, brighter tip of light among the insane profusion of stars. But after three weeks the planet was a distinct blob, and after six it was a manhole cover of brightness inviting you to lift it and tumble down the Alice-hole it topped.

There were areas in the ship he wasn't permitted to go. This did not bother him. He was not so constituted, psychologically, so as to be provoked by such things. Fine. Whatever. He spent an hour a day in the ship's gym, hauling spring-loaded levers and kicking out his legs like a frog. He saw the general from time to time, although she spent most of the voyage in her stateroom. Once he passed her in the central corridor, and she said, gnomically: 'The only good life is one in which there is no need for miracles.'

Another time she was perkier: 'You bearing up, bright boy?'

'Yes, ma'am.'

'We're all prisoners on a spaceship, hon'. Try not to sweat it.'

Well, all right: but he truly wasn't sweating it. The only thing that preyed on his mind was: Gee. He tried not to obsess. He was putting on weight. There was little to do but eat and watch TV shows, and his hour of daily exercise was only enough to keep his bones from brittling.

Then, one day, he was called into a senior level meeting. Three of the officers were present remotely, which entailed a time lag. For two of these officers the lag was ten minutes. That meant that they contributed only a little, and that towards the end. For the third the time lag was only a few seconds, which must have meant she was riding another ship somewhere nearby. The remaining people in the cabin were the *Owl*'s senior officers – and Adan.

'You understand, Trooper,' said General Cho, 'that you are about to hear information pertaining to a highly classified operation, and that you must not disclose or disseminate any data you acquire over the next forty minutes in any form, medium, socially or otherwise – do you understand?'

'Ma'am,' said Adan.

'General Baghdassarian – would you like to sketch out the situation, please?'

The third virtual presence in the room, the one with the briefest lag, said: 'Three years ago we mounted a major sting operation aimed at penetrating the core operative function of Hive-Mind-θ. As is known, while all members of the gestalt experience a unity of mentation, both emotionally and rationally, not all constitutive consciousnesses have the same decision-making and deep-mind access to the whole. As the cells in our bodies are specialised in various ways, so some members of this hive mind have more influence on the cognition and perception of the whole than others. This specialisation is necessary, just as our human bodies would not exist if all the cells were clones of one another. But it is also a weakness. Our mission aimed to exploit that weakness.'

Baghdassarian's face peered out of its screen as if from a window.

'We created a false flag. The HMθ ambitions with respect to terraforming Venus have been known for a long time. We confected an imaginary technology that would have materially sped up and facilitated their project – no small job, this, since the technology, though invented, had to be plausible enough to intrigue the HMθ – and we had to set up a whole front of scientists and engineers, developmental facilities and experimental test bases. To reinforce notions of the potency of this device, we created and then explosively destroyed entire spaceships. Then we false-flagged a particular trail that suggested all prototypes of the terraforming device had been destroyed and all blueprints or techdata with it. We false-flagged the road that led to one of our operatives, Ewe Bondar. The cover story was—'

'Very brave woman,' said General Cho. The other two physically present muttered assent.

'—that Bondar had the plans for the device in her mind. The HMθ moved quickly. There was some …' He paused, as Cho's statement reached him, nodded briskly, and went on: 'There was some disagreement at top level as to whether they would even take the bait, but they did. They seized Bondar in a well-co-ordinated raid on Earth and flew her directly to Venus orbit. She was ready for a number of possible interrogation strategies, and we're not sure how they approached her. They executed her shortly after but she was—'

'Killed her?' said Adan.

'—able to insert our countermeasure package directly – physically – into the neural net of one of the core-mind components of the hive mind. It was a remarkable achievement.'

'Hear, hear,' said Cho.

'We had designed our weapon to smoke-mirror the HMθ. It is part of the operating dynamic of their collective consciousness that, for them, subject and object cannot, in the most fundamental sense, be meaningfully separated out from one another. This leaves them vulnerable, putting it in the crudest terms to … well, to *wishful thinking*. Of course it's true that they have immensely sophisticated processing and ideational capacity, and they have, as it were, the *wisdom* of their crowd, which is considerable. So it is very rare that they lose touch with objective reality. Our mission was the first time, so far as we know, that they have ever been tricked in this way. Indeed, it seems likely that they avoid the problem of being fooled by wishful thinking by not *wishing*, by and large. Want is a mode of lack, and they are defined by their plenitude, their fullness, not by their absence. Or so they say! But Venus – a homeworld – *is* something they lack. And that enabled us to insert a collective hallucination. For seventeen minutes, the entire HMθ hallucinated that they were decades in the future, and that the terraforming device (which, in actuality, does not exist) had done its job. They believed Venus was on the verge of becoming a habitable settlement.'

There was a pause, and General Cho took up the narrative.

'Thank you, Davit. Unfortunately, those precious seventeen minutes, for which Bondar sacrificed her life, were squandered. I don't want to be too critical of the military commanders in charge of the mission. Nobody expected such an instantaneous and system-wide success, and nobody knew, in the event *of* that success, how long it would be before the HMθ realised they were being fooled. It was eight minutes before we understood how complete our victory even was. Eight minutes and forty seconds after *that* the HMθ shook themselves, so to speak, and reverted to reality. In that time we managed four tactically significant strikes, including the important attack on the satellite swarm in Venus-orbit they have been using as a soletta. Eight further attacks were in train. The enemy's retaliation, though, was prodigious – a massive co-ordinated counter-attack that destroyed forty-six of our spacecraft, damaged eighty more and killed over a thousand people. For three months the war was the hottest it has ever been. We have kept the scale of our military losses from the general public, although they are of course aware that for three months the fighting was very severe.'

'My fellow soldiers,' General Cho said, 'permit me to introduce Trooper Adan Vergara. As you know, the HMθ contacted him some years ago – or, at least, that's our working hypothesis. We believe that some part or parts of the HMθ made contact. They hacked his Pheno-woman, gave him a code, in the form of a string of words, instructing him to use it if and when he found himself in a combat situation and under threat from HMθ hardware. The code works. It has been tried on two separate battlefields, and it works. HMθ bots shut down in a rapid cascade from the point of delivery of the code outward. The virtual cordon sanitaire appears to be related to HMθ reaction times – which, as we all know, are markedly quicker than our quickest automated systems. All bots within a nine-hundred-metre radius and possibly wider are disabled when Trooper Vergara says these words.'

A light is flashing in the top-right corner of one of the Earth-located officers, which means she has said something. The others pause. Two of the senior officers in the cabin whisper to one another. Adan is simply trying to take it all in.

Eventually the message comes from Earth.

'A question. The shutdown code takes the form of a line from an antique poem. Is Trooper Vergara himself a poet? Does his *mis*quotation intensify or reduce the target radius of the weapon's effectiveness? We assume the misquotation is deliberate.'

Everybody was looking at Adan.

'I don't know, ma'am,' he said, his eyes wide enough to show white all the way around his irises, like a doubled top-down view of Saturn.

Everybody waited ten long minutes for these supremely unedifying words to pass, at the speed of light, all the way back to Earth, and ten minutes for the important person on that aboriginal human world to broadcast their reply.

'Please, for clarification – was the misquotation of the code deliberate, or accidental?'

'I . . .' said Adan, looking around. 'I've never claimed to be the smartest bullet in the clip, you know? The words came out of Gee's mouth – that's my Phene, Elegy, my girlfriend – and I tried to remember them. But the last word . . .'

'Thrice,' said General Cho.

'Thrice, yeah. I guess "thrice" didn't stick, proper. So the first time I didn't say it, or I maybe said "twice" instead of it. I definitely said "twice" instead of it the second time.'

This information went hurrying through the vacuum, and the people in the cabin allowed a ten-minute courtesy break to see if Earth had follow-up questions; but they were content to waive discussion. A subaltern brought in capped cups and everybody who was real in the room drank.

'Well,' said General Cho, 'what we have to decide, here today, is how we use Trooper Vergara. In one sense, our action was determined before we set out for Venus – the mission is to land a disabling blow on the HMθ entity, and force it either to capitulate entirely or else to enter into long-term negotiations from a position of weakness. The red line is . . . the HMθ must not be permitted to terraform and occupy Venus on their own. Ideally they must agree to give up the entire project. If they proceed, it must be under human supervision and on the understanding that the resulting real estate will be cohabited, portions allotted to them and portions to us. The precise battle plan, however, remains and must remain flexible. We have a number of stealth assets in place. We, in the *Owl*, are approaching Venus under the cover story of a diplomatic overture.

'The HMθ have a system of buffers – individual members of the collective who mingle with ordinary folk, including many hundreds of thousands of θed people raising non-hive-mind children on Earth, and tens of thousands more who interact with applicants. These two groups have a carefully distanced relationship with the gestalt. Our understanding remains limited, but it seems that these individuals are later circulated *into* more intimate consonance with the whole, to experience the – we assume – collective bliss more intensely. But from our point of view, what it means is that our capacity to hack the hive mind is severely limited. What we are looking for is the opportunity to hack some core members of the gestalt, and we think this mission, and Adan's presence, will give us that chance.

'So we need to game our various approaches. We need a robust set of chain of command responses to the seven main ways we calculate this encounter is likely to develop. We have a variety of code-ordnance to deploy as hacking attacks, and which we use will depend on how the encounter goes down.'

Discussion then commenced among the people physically present in the cabin, and Adan did nothing except float and wait, as patiently as he was capable. He could not follow the ins and outs of the discussion, none of which seemed to relate to him as an individual. Then his name was spoken, and, like a dog, his attention perked.

'There's an eighth possibility we haven't considered,' said one of the officers, 'which is that all this is an elaborate ruse *by* the HMθ.'

'To do what?'

'Perhaps to recruit Trooper Vergara?'

'There would be much easier ways of doing that,' objected one of the officers in the room. 'And besides – why would the HMθ be going to such lengths to recruit this one? He's a moron.'

And then the meeting was over, it seemed, and people were

hauling themselves briskly through the exit and dispersing around the craft.

'No offence, Trooper,' said the officer who had called Adan a moron, as he passed.

'Sir, no, sir,' Adan returned.

:11:

Let's say we're parcelling this little narrative of Adan's experiences – this elegy for the Pheno-woman he loved, and by extension for *all* the Phenes, male and female – into twelve sections, for reasons to do with geometry and harmony and the distribution of transcendental categories, or for some other reason which is not presently to be disclosed. That at least means we are near the end of this portion of the story, which is surely good to know.

The *Owl of Minerva* entered Venusian orbit. A window on the scene, through the virtual porthole of Adan's cabin wall, showed a great curving shoulder of off-white against the blackness of space and nothing else, although in fact there were over a thousand HMθ craft also in orbit, not counting the hundreds of thousands of partial drones that swarmed to thicken the sunlight falling onto the planet, or combined to focus sunlight in particular ways. But these were not visible to the unprocessed visual data Adan's screen provided.

The *Owl* slotted itself into an oval orbit and established contact with the HMθ. It was not in the nature of the Hive-Mind-θ to have a flagship, or in any way to have centralised or hierarchised their fleet, but they were naturally cautious about physical interactions, and so a firewalled and pre-appendixed spacecraft for such encounters had been assigned. It was certain,

General Cho assured her people, that this HMθ craft was crewed with well-buffered individual units; and that the best strategy for the assault would involve identifying, boarding and capturing *another* ship. Tactical AI drew up a list of which craft were likely to contain less buffered members of the hive mind, and the attack force was prepped.

Adan was fitted with body armour.

'We need you *not* to die,' said the uniform corporal who fitted the panels to him. 'At least not until you've said your magic words – after that, you're exactly as disposable as anybody else on this fucking kamikaze mission.'

He pronounced *kamikaze* as a trisyllable to rhyme with *maze.*

'That's enough, Corporal,' said the attending lieutenant, sharply. 'Ignore him, Trooper. None of us are disposable, and this is no suicide mission.'

'Yes, ma'am,' said the corporal, sourly. 'I apologise. Trooper, you are not disposable and this is in no way a suicide mission.'

After Adan was kitted out, the uniform corporal was dismissed, and the lieutenant told him: 'He's just in a bad mood. Ignore him. He found his Phene was decommissioned, back on Earth. I've half a mind to put her on a charge – I mean, the communications officer who passed that information along to him. To put her on a charge. Fantastically irresponsible thing to do! Immediately before we go into battle! What was she thinking?'

Suddenly Adan's heart was knocking hard at his ribcage as if eager to be let out.

'What?'

'The general wants a word, before you are loaded into the boat with the other marines.'

'What did you say?'

The lieutenant ignored this, and left the chamber. The general floated in.

'Are you ready, Adan? This is it – our war is won or lost, and I trust won, in the next half hour.'

'What about my Phene?' Adan asked.

The general was an experienced commander. Her face betrayed nothing.

'What's that, Trooper?'

'Lieutenant Aston just . . .' Adan began, and then collected himself. 'She said, ma'am, that the uniform corporal's Phene had been decommissioned – back on Earth. Is it true?'

'Adan, you have to understand—'

'Is it just his Phene? Is it more than just his?'

'I don't appreciate being interrupted, Trooper,' snapped the general.

There was a silence. The walls of the chamber pulsed with soothing light. Eventually the general spoke.

'First, Adan, I want you to understand that *your* Phene is safe. She has been removed from the storage facility in which you left her, as we previously discussed, and is at the moment in a secure military facility in Earth orbit. You will be reunited with her.'

'Ma'am, thank you, ma'am.'

Adan felt as though he was going to cry. He held himself together.

'Secondly, you have to grasp what is happening here. We are about to launch a surprise attack on the HMθ – a very formidable foe. The aim of this strike is to cause them maximum damage. They *will* retaliate, and we have to prepare, as best we can, for that retaliation. We already know they can hack into regular Pheno models. So of course those models must be decommissioned. It's not a popular policy, but it is a necessary one.'

'They will be *re*commissioned?' Adan gasped.

'Yours is safe, Trooper. Hold on to that! As to all the others … well, depending on how this war plays out, they may or may not. If the HMθ remain a clear and present danger, then we may have no option but to postpone any recommissioning. There are tens of millions of Phenes on Earth, Adan – imagine what would happen if they were taken over, en masse, by the HMθ. Imagine the damage such a fifth column could cause!'

Adan was able to process only a little of this, because his heart was hammering at his chest again and he was being handed down the corridor, as a parcel, floating weightlessly but still bulky and massy in his armoured suit. And then he was in the attack boat, and locked in, and his thoughts were circling round and round on that one idea: *They had annihilated all the Phenes on Earth. They had decommissioned all of them. All the Phenes were dead.*

He couldn't stop thinking that thought. He couldn't stop revolving it in his mind. It was one thought, like a single notional elementary and indivisible particle in motion in an eternal orbit, a marble rolling endlessly round inside the perfect bone-bounded sphere of his head. All the Phenes annihilated in a stroke of a warrior-bureaucrat's decision.

Somewhere in the wickerwork of his skeleton was a hope, trapped like a bird in a basket: *Maybe Gee will be spared, maybe I'll be with her again.* But the dazzle and dash of this bird's beating wings could not break the bars of its cage. Ribs like scimitar blades. Spine the stacked rounds of a whomp gun. Skull a cannonball.

There was a doomy chime and a shudder in the fabric of the whole craft.

'That's them undocking,' said one of the marines, to nobody in particular.

The illumination inside the attack boat switched from white to red. Gloved hands tightened their hold on belts. Helmets nodded and jiggled in approximate unison. There was no siren, or any kind of countdown. Only a modest lurch indicated that the boat had been launched. Of course, there were no windows.

'The thing about killing,' somebody said, distinctly, in a high-pitched voice, 'is not to *think* about it too much. It's the *thinking* that turns it into a prob—'

A clattery jolt and jar, and Adan felt the straps tight against his chest. Round and round the marble spun inside its bone bowl.

'—lem,' finished the marine.

And then there was an explosion, a crown of light, some smoke and a gush of air. The straps snickered away and Adan was in the midst of the crowd of marines as they jetted through the newly opened gateway formed by an uneven edged hole in metal and into the HMθ craft. The space into which they were moving was misty, cool and indistinct. *Snip-snaps* of small bore detonations and the distinctive *hiss-glop* of breaches in the hull being automatically foamsealed.

Little claws of brightness opening and closing at the muzzles of the marines' rifles.

All was the noise: *pan! pan! pan!*

They had not given Adan a rifle. He was supposed to be, not have, a weapon.

And he thought: *all the Phenes?* A holocaust of Gees. A necessary collective sacrifice, hauling boyfriends and girlfriends from the arms of their lovers and – *pan! pan! pan!* A bullet in the plastic skull.

A bullet in the flexibly adjustable face.

A bullet in the brain *pan! pan! pan!*

'Trooper Vergara!' shouted the lieutenant. 'The code!'

The wrongness of it was global. It was a shattering, collective wrong.

'Your code, Trooper! Now!'

Adan blinked. Blinked. HMθ were coming out of the mist, and all around him marines were folding – throwing their arms and legs out and hurtling backwards, or tucking themselves into balls like spiders in the sink when the tap water hits them. A different sort of person from Adan might have made a statement at this point. Asserted his *non serviam*. Announced his refusal to comply with orders from an organisation which, even though Adan was himself a member and so a sharer in the collective guilt, nonetheless could not be *morally* endorsed. But Adan was not that person. Instead he did not. His doing was to do nothing. He hugged his knees, and dangled in space, and in doing so he was hugging his love, his absent love. In his gesture was his self, a connecting of Adan to Adan, making a circuit of his body. His eloquence had never been with words, so if he was a poet it was a poet of spontaneous material this-ness, of his body in space, his untutored gestures, his instinct to curl up as a child does. He made no conscious or deliberate choice to rebel and he felt no rush of defiance. His action was reaction, his agency passion, and when he embraced himself he was embracing the absence of his loved one, and in that he was, though unwittingly, saying something profound about the nature of love itself. A projectile – one of 'ours', one of 'theirs' – hit his armed flank. Adan spun and flew back, bouncing off a wall and spinning in again. His feed was going bananas.

'Trooper – this is a direct order – deploy the code – deploy—'

pan! pan! pan!

Another hit rammed him down. It slowed his spin. His feed had stopped. His chest plate had seized up, which meant he couldn't move his arms. Around him armoured bodies were spinning or clumping together. The weapons fire had stopped. His head went down, and then came up again, and when it came up there was a tall droid of unusual design standing in front of him. This creature reached out a twig-slender tentacle and put a stop to Adan's rotation. The droid had two large legs, both locked to the floor. It had a bulbous body and a lozenge-shaped head. There was a sudden, prolonged and very loud hissing and the mist largely dissipated. The chamber had been sealed and air pumped in, and the droid revealed itself to be a human being in a suit of unusually bulky and awkward-looking design. The cranial lozenge cracked in two and the two parts slid out over the suit's shoulders.

'Adan,' said the person – a wide-faced, pale-skinned male of middle age. 'How good it is to meet you in person.'

Adan's own helmet had opened. The HMθ had, it seemed, overridden the suit's system – which was both impressive and alarming, considering that it was state-of-the-art military tech. Adan breathed in. He thought he recognised the individual, but couldn't be sure.

The twig-slim tentacle whipped up and darted at Adan's exposed face, striking his cheek and piercing skin and bone. This blow was unexpected and sudden enough not to cause Adan pain, although as soon as he realised what had happened the shock of it caused his heart to start hammering, and—

:12:

Imagine you suffer from asthma. Perhaps you have the personal experience that means you don't have to imagine this. If not, then permit me to tell you about it. It's not that you don't *want* to breathe, or that you fail to invest, as it might be, the *effort* in trying to breathe. It's that, no matter how you work your chest, no matter how forceful your diaphragm, the breath simply doesn't go far enough into your lungs. Your body strains at the motions of breathing, your ribcage convulses, you draw with all your might, and the air does not go in.

Now imagine that ... after a life of panting and gasping and sitting doubled up, of continual distress and disempowerment ... imagine after all that you are treated with a potent vasodilator. Under the miracle touch of these pharmochemicals, the fractal conch of each lung opens its myriad tubules. The tissue of your being relaxes. You draw a deep, full breath into your chest. You breathe in and your lungs fill with air and, after you exhale, you *keep* filling your chest, keep blowing them up like two balloons under your joyful volition.

That was what it was like for Adan. Except with *thought* instead of air. His mind expanded as a lung fills with freshness.

Or we could put it another way: his thoughts, which had been trying throughout his three and a half decades of life to stretch beyond the tight jacket woven of habits and of upbringing – and, most of all, of physical neuronal capacity and arrangement – found themselves for the first time unhindered. His thoughts stretched and expanded, because thought is breath, and breath is pneuma, and pneuma is spirit and spirit is thought and he, as you, as I, touched the bedrock of the cosmos itself in thought, in thought, in thought.

6
Richest

Now that Rich was inside The This, time went orthonormal. His previous experience of time was revectored into a new kind of experience of time.

Where does it start?

If we were to abstract one basic principle from the cosmos it would be: small things lead to big things. If we had to summarise life in one phrase, that would be it.

Take *this* as your theory as to how the universe exists at all, that great puzzle of physics and metaphysics, all this glorious plenitude of matter cinched into galaxies and black holes and planets and people. Say there was one single thing. Imagine it as the tiniest thing: not trillions raised to the trillionth power of tonnes of matter, but one solitary impossible twist in the fabric of an otherwise entirely empty spacetime. Subatomic scale, say, although not subatomic *as such* since there are no atoms for it to be sub. At this point there's nothing at all, just cavernous emptiness on a scale you can't imagine. And your solitary one-thing, your Saint-Mark's-quark, the twist in your existential sobriety – it simply exists. That's all. It exists and exists, blandly, boringly, inertly, and it goes on existing through the billennia, until the curve of time brings the empty cosmos to an end and – a notional ping-pong ball, blocky as any pixel, hitting its rudimentary virtual paddle, bouncing back – it returns. Now it is an anti-quark, simply existing as before but this time existing from the end of all to the beginning of all. It occupies the same space as the original quark, for all time, and so it fuses, an impossible copula. And now it's a proton, existing from the beginning of time to the end, and then an electron existing from the end of time to the beginning. And now it's an atom of matter, existing from the beginning of time to the end, and then an atom of antimatter existing from the end of time to the beginning. And now it's a clump of atoms, existing from the beginning of time to the end, and back again, and then as many atoms as there are paths through this timeline to the end and back, before – the singularity sagging heavier and more unstable – the inevitable happens, and a *bang* bigs itself up, and trillions raised to the trillionth power of tonnes of matter come pouring out into spacetime from a point so close to dimensionless it makes no odds, creating the spacetime in which our originary quark first voyaged in the first place.

Brave little mite.

The whole universe grown from one seed! Except that the question remains: where did that first little twist in the fabric of spacetime originate? The question remains: where does it start?

When Rich first joined the nascent idiom of a properly co-ordinated human collective consciousness, his initial experience was bliss.

Bliss. He had not realised how empty was his soul until it was filled. He knew, comprehensively, and was as comprehensively known. He went from a solitary atom in an alienated universe to a plenitude of belonging he had not realised was even possible.

Bliss. He wept.

Bliss. He wept with joy. He wept in shame and frustration and bitterness, because he was – consciously, wilfully, with malice – bringing a poison into The This, attempting to disrupt and wound it. To wound himself, now that he was part of the whole, now that he was a loving-living-partygoing metonym in the flesh.

The This knew what he was bringing, but they took him in anyway. He was intensely grateful for this acceptance. His stubbornness dissolved with gratitude. A lifetime of not fitting in and suddenly he fitted perfectly in the most perfect place.

In terms of the material world, of which Rich was very much still a part: he stepped out of The This building by the Thames, and walked up Putney High Street past the various human-shaped empty shells and crossed the junction when the green man sobbed, and walked up Putney Hill, and turned right into his road, and let himself back into his flat. He hadn't been there for a while. There was a sheen of dust on the surfaces and a bad smell in the fridge. A lid of mould sealed-in the half-drunk coffee in its mug on his desk. But the sunlight was inside him now, and everything gleamed with joy and meaning and purpose. He set to work tidying and cleaning and rearranging. He moved things into more ergonomic locations, folded away and set back what he could. He fired up his computer and logged in, and immediately reconfigured all his bank details to funnel money into the nexus of The This-related financial underpinnings.

Over the months that followed he began a process of decluttering on a more permanent basis, selling valuable items, paying a company to come to his door and schlep away valueless ones for recycling. And he established a new routine: no more alcohol, much more eating vegetables, morning and evening runs up to and around the heath. He slept eight hours every night and in the days he worked harder than he had ever done before. He took an online course in legal coding, proofing and text/apping, and dedicated himself to that tedious, relentless but solidly paid occupation. The This always needed money, and individual members worked as hard as they could, as hard as their other duties permitted them, to supply this need.

In terms of his new existence, though, Rich was experiencing existential plenitude for the first time in his life. Clock time, the rising and setting of the sun, the seasons lolloping round with their awkward rollovers, all of that hardly impinged. His IQ was a thousand times more capacious than before, but, more importantly, so was his EQ. He shared the wisdom of the totality and apprehended reality with the pristine freshness of a newborn. He lived each breath, and every specific detail of the world shone with realness: this cup, this finger, this taste, this beam of sunlight through the window, this congeries of dust motes circling lazily in the light, this breath, this moment, this now, forever slipping from no-longer-existent past to not-yet-existent future, thin as an electron shell but hefty enough to carry the weight of all being and all perception and all consciousness. Every *this* replete with everything. All in all and all a joy. Holy delight and holy dread.

All that, in a moment. And at the same time, all that was taken from him.

He was, in terms of the collective, a toxic cell. It was imperative that he become part of The This – he saw that, now, and saw why – but he could not be immediately accepted wholly into the collective body. They (we) had known it would be this way, that the remnants of individuated *Homo sapiens* were trying, in their clumsy way, to thrust a dagger into The This's heart. But not until Rich actually presented himself at the organisation's front door, not until he had the Thistech fitted, could they (we) judge the viability and seriousness of the threat, or more accurately the hugeness of the opportunity Rich presented.

It proved more viable, and potentially more serious, than they (we) had first assumed it would be. Rich proved more essential than they (we) could ever have realised prior (that is) to assimilating him.

It couldn't be helped. Moses saw the promised land but did not cross the Jordan. Rich experienced the fullness, and then was sequestered. In material terms he worked and walked and ate and slept as before, but his consciousness was buffered. Points of connection kept him in touch with the plenum, and the experience was still vastly more integrated and whole than his previous loneliness had been. Nonetheless, all the time he was aware that he was at arm's length. He did not wish to remain in that semi-separated circumstance, *sss*, the snake in an Eden he had no desire to contaminate.

Inside his brain new, unique code grew, slow as stalactites and stalagmites, in his Thistech network. The virus – so very cunningly framed – seethed inside its spherical firewall, and a Thistech alt-virus tried to match it, grew strange fronds and weird lattices, and, as it did so, slowly grew into something amazingly potent and unique.

And that's where we were. And that's where we are.

Things happened in the material world. Helen Susanna died, finally succumbing to her medical situation. Other people died more unexpectedly. There was a spike in gun crime in the Richmond and Putney area, something lamented by the media as the consequence of gangs and drugs and social decadence, although Rich, as part of The This, knew the truth – a complex of assassinations, some by The This assets, and infighting between different branches of the security services. It died down.

So far as Helen Susanna's superior, Hoyle, was concerned (Rich could monitor her day-to-day and her communications much more effectively than she, or her people, understood) the attack that Rich had carried into the organisation had failed. It hadn't. But that's what Hoyle believed.

The police came to Rich's flat and arrested him. This was Hoyle making him a de facto prisoner of war. But no actual war had ever been declared, and the UK legal system had to generate pretexts to hold him, and The This-funded lawyers lobbied and prosecuted aggressively for his release. Accordingly, in time, he was released. His passport was confiscated, which bothered him not in the least. Why would he need to move his body from country to country when his consciousness was a global quantity?

And so he went on with life. He reconfigured his flat and settled into his new routine, and every second was joyous, and each joy was tinged with the regret that he was buffered and could not partake as integrally in the gestalt as he wanted to. He was a bomb, to be defused, but this was proving tricky. First of all, he had to wait until the new network of Thistech had grown into its mature setting, filling out the interstices of his wet-cell brain. That took a while, considerably longer than was normally the case for new recruits, because the net had both to grow to encompass and to restrain the enemy implant.

He chafed. It tainted his bliss.

'How much longer?'

'Soon,' they (we) said.

And days followed days, each unique in itself and each exactly the same as every other. As is the way with days. Rich worked, and exercised, and ate and slept. Different people have different talents, and a degree of specialisation was bedding itself into the internal dynamic of the gestalt – Rich's skill was not (as it might be) recruitment, programming, practical procurement, financial affairs, engineering or strategy or public relations. In one sense he was a lesser member of the whole, except that nobody was lesser or greater and all partook equally in the – really, I'm sorry to keep repeating myself but there's no better word – bliss.

So he got on with mundane life, and his hairline receded, and his face grew wrinklier, and he had a series of malign polyps removed from his lower intestine, and he started taking naps during the afternoon. History raged around him: riots, martial law, war overseas, technological advances, cultural regression, and above all the relentless encroachment of the ocean. Several British coastal towns went the full Dunwich. All coastal towns had to abandon at least some of their seaside or riverside real estate to the natural course. Winter storms blew wilder, odd spurts of unseasonal heat or cold became the norm. London built some vastly expensive remedial infrastructure: huge dykes on the Thames Estuary, walls embanking the flow of the river through the city. But on stormy days the highest tides gushed over these defences and the riverside was always sloshing with water, and the reek from perennially damp basements and neglected property became so marked that, when the wind was blowing the right way, Rich could smell it even halfway up Putney Hill. He sometimes strolled by the river, or wandered *the ramparts*, as the metal walkway on top of the Thames Wall was called. Living in a first-floor flat on top of a hill meant that he wasn't personally inconvenienced by any of it. Things became more expensive, and people moved out of the city, but since he had joined The This money was no longer an issue for him and, having joined The This, he had no more need for other friends or, indeed, company.

He lived like an old man long before he became an old man, but in time he actually became an old man. More cancer. He had malignant tumours removed from his skin: they looked, as he peered down at his anesthetised arm, like antique coins, roughly circular, rough-edged, blackened by time. The thought tickled his imagination. Each coin inscribed in miniscule with the four-letter twisting legend of runaway genetic replication, instead of GULIELMUS V D G REX. Cancer as king. Fungible flesh. This, in turn, put him in mind of the days when he used to collect banknotes. Fascinating, intricate artwork that drew the eye in. A stylised, and therefore reified and modular and therefore more manageable, version of reality. Everything exchangeable, which is to say interchangeable, and yet to hold one specific banknote was to hold something unique. Think of an old one-pound note. You couldn't have bought a similar-sized piece of art, a finely worked engraving of such craftsmanship, for a pound, back then. Such a print would have cost you a great deal more money than that. The amount of metal in a 2p coin was worth more than 2p. Something about this apparent paradox delighted Rich's soul.

'There,' said the surgeon. 'Not too much of an anticlimax, I hope?'

Not at all, said Rich. Not at all.

And then he was back, memory washing over him like tidal waters and carrying him back: him carefully photographing each of his more valuable banknotes obverse and reverse, uploading them to NoteBay and annotating each in turn. Selling the rest off as a job lot. Passing the funds he raised thereby along to The This. Returning currency to the currents of exchange and movement. He'd done this a couple of weeks after he joined.

And then another memory, somehow connected to this first, from a year later … or, was it only a year? So hard to get all the synchronous days and dates lined up into chronological order. He remembered that Hoyle herself knocked on his door. And actually it must have been several years later, because he remembered he'd been under continual surveillance, and then, after two years of blameless and perfectly regular monk-like existence, the Powers That Be had decided he wasn't worth surveilling any further, and had pulled everyone and everything off his detail. Rich didn't see this, so much as perceive it via his connection to the gestalt. But it indicated that those Powers had given up on anything coming of his introduction into The This.

And it was after *that* that Hoyle rang his doorbell.

She looked more careworn than she had previously, the skin under her eyes blotched, her black hair scratched with strands of white. Her manner was markedly less boisterous than the last time the two had met.

'Mr Rigby,' she said, over the intercom. 'Might we chat?'

It did occur to Rich that she might have come round specifically to kill him. But two years had proved plenty long enough for the tendrils from the inserted Thistech to integrate itself, and the prospect of losing the day-to-day holding together of his cellular body didn't fill him with any dread. His body could die, but he no longer could.

'By all means,' he said.

She came up, and sat awkwardly on his sofa staring at the blank screen of the offswitched TV while Rich made coffee. He brought a chair through from the kitchen and sat on that.

'So …' said Hoyle.

'Good to see you again,' offered Rich.

It was the kind of thing people said after not having been in touch for a while. Access to the collective wisdom of The This now meant that Rich understood the Popeye reference she had mentioned during their last encounter, and which had at that time gone over his head. Indeed, access to that collective knowledge meant he knew a huge amount about Hoyle: the occasional urgencies and more usual velleities of her career progression; her marriage and its fractious breakdown; her two lovers, neither of whom knew about the existence of the other. Rich could have altered that mutual ignorance with a thought, but he only smiled at her and waited for her to come to her point.

'Helen Susanna died,' she said, eventually.

'I know,' said Rich.

Hoyle slurped at her coffee: a sound like a lame foot being dragged across gravel. She put the cup down on the little table in front of her.

'I'll come straight to the point,' she said. 'The point is a question. There's a question I want to ask you.'

Rich waited.

'We failed,' she said, shortly. This wasn't a question. 'I mean the operation, the attempt to infiltrate malware into the inner network of The This. It obviously failed.'

Rich didn't say anything.

'I've been relieved of operational command.' This also wasn't a question. 'What I mean is – I'm not here in an official capacity. I just ... I just ...' She picked up her coffee cup and took another astonishingly noisy slurp from it. 'Curious, I guess.'

'Curious?'

'Mr Rigby, we underestimated The This. I apologise to you for that. I apologise for sending you into that situation.'

'There's no need to apologise,' said Rich genuinely. 'I'm happier than I've ever been.'

Hoyle nodded sombrely, as if this was exactly the kind of brainwashed babble she was expecting from him.

'Well, that whole operation has been cancelled. There will be an enquiry – not open to the public and not publicised, but I'll have to give evidence. As you might expect, I've been going over and over the whole operation in my head.'

Rich waited.

'Here's one thing I'm curious about,' she said, putting her coffee cup down again. 'One thing we never got to the bottom of. Why *were* The This so keen to get you?'

'Ah,' said Rich.

'I mean, they went out of their way to recruit you – they don't do that. That's not how they, how you, operate. So there was something in you that they really wanted. And the thing that slices my loaf is – *having* got you, they don't seem to have done anything with you.'

'What sort of thing did you think they might have done with me?'

'I don't know,' said Hoyle. 'I honestly don't. I suppose that's my way of admitting that I don't really understand the . . . the logic of The This. If logic is the just . . . The word. The *mot juste*. Can you tell me?'

'Tell you what?'

'Tell me what was so valuable to them about you? I mean – you specifically?'

Rich smiled. Was that a regular-person smile? Hard to gauge. He reined it in a little. But perhaps that looked dour? He broadened the smile.

'I did wonder,' Hoyle said, in a hurry, as if confessing something, 'if it was *our* interest in you that made you so interesting to *them*. If you see what I mean. But then I remember that they were already chasing you before Helen Susanna made contact with you, so it can't have been that.'

'Well, there you have it,' said Rich. 'That's a lot of your problem, right there. Before. After. The way time appears to you as this consecutive succession of discrete moments, ranked and ordered into befores and afters. It's an artefact of your individuality, you know.'

'Say what?'

'I used to experience time the same way,' said Rich. 'When I was solitary. Locked into this Procrustean progress from before to after. I used to assume that was just how the universe *was*, time a ladder that must be laboriously ascended hand over hand, rung after rung.'

'It's not? It is, though. You're saying it's not?'

'Spacetime,' said Rich. 'I mean, I'm not suggesting you take my word for it. The equivalence is a basic premise of physics. Think of a universe in which you could move in any direction you wanted *in time*, but could only shuffle along, one foot after the other, ankles chained together, down a close-cut gulley path, continually prodded along from behind, *spatially*. Say you'd been moving that way ever since you were born, you might mistake it for the nature of reality. But break the chain, climb out of the rut, and look up.'

'I don't see what you mean,' said Hoyle.

'Oh, yes, of course,' said Rich, going for another reassuring smile and again overbaking it. So hard to judge these atomised interactions. 'Let's begin at the beginning. That's what you'd like, yes?'

'Well,' said Olive Hoyle. 'Yes.'

'So where does it begin? At t = 0? That's a fallacy. Popular, widely believed, but fallacious. The old religious idea could only think like that. Humanity *must* have begun with one recognisable human male – call him Adam – and one recognisable human female, call her Elegy, and from that discrete starting point the whole succession of generations can roll on.'

'*Eve*, you mean,' said Hoyle.

'Yes ... yes. Eve.'

Rich paused momently. Where had *Elegy* come from? Odd to make that trivial mistake. He processed possible reasons – all of them, a millisecond cycling through alternative explanations – and decided it was a slip of the tongue, and nothing more. Peculiar, because since joining The This he'd left those sorts of individualised fallibilities behind. But never mind. Onwards.

'Adam and Eve. Now we know better. Asking which came first, chicken or egg, only appears to be a paradox. It only confuses people because our language and habits of thought trick us in this Chinese Finger Trap of before and after. One *must* come before the other, yes? The other *must* come after the one, yes? But that can't be! The truth is – go back far enough in history and you come to some creature that is neither chicken nor egg and yet is the ancestor of both. Evolution is a flow, not a set of discrete points. Take a look at the whole view of human evolution – Adam doesn't come at the beginning. He appears, in ways hard to quantify if you're thinking individualistically, somewhere in the middle. Because of course he does. A continuum from lemur-like creatures through simian ones to erect and new-valley men to sapient men and women like your good self, Mrs Hoyle, and on to ... where?'

'There's no need to patronise me,' said Hoyle. 'I take your point. It's a sophomoric point, but sure, Adam emerges from the continuum. Somewhere in the middle, sure. Still – before and after aren't meaningless items of nomenclature, now, are they? Lemur-like creatures come before and, you know, *whatever* comes after.'

'That's what I was asking, though. It wasn't a rhetorical question. It's the crux. It really is. Evolution has a shape, a rather beautiful curve, like the prow of some massive, golden age ocean liner. You, as *Homo sapiens*, have a place in that structure. But what is the rest of the shape of evolution?'

'You want me to say – in your direction,' scowled Hoyle. 'Towards hive minds, like The This. Is that what you want me to say?'

'Evolution is not a choose-your-adventure narrative,' Rich said. 'It's a structure. It is determined *by* its overall shape, not by some notion of sequential time. And you don't need to speculate about the contours of that shape. You just need to look up and *see* it.'

'You'll forgive me if I don't share your frankly rather claustrophobic determinism.'

'Determinism isn't the word I'd use. It's not a matter or fate, or God, or prophecy. It's just what it is. Life begins as twists and curls of RNA, and grows into more complex cellular shapes, and then cells aggregate into organisms. That's just what evolution is. Complex multicellular life is the iteration of evolution on the physical level, and hive minds are the same iteration on the level of consciousness. There are plenty of single-cell life forms in the world, just as there are plenty of life forms that get by with limited and singular consciousnesses. But you're not going to deny that multicellular sentient intelligent life is where you and I locate importance.'

'I locate importance,' retorted Hoyle, sounding actually angry, 'in my self-determination as an individual. In my freedom. Not, I might add, in sacrificing that hard-won existential independence to a brainwashing cult.'

'Please accept my assurance,' said Rich, 'both as the person sitting in front of you now, and as the mouthpiece for my whole community, that *your* existential independence will remain entirely unviolated. We promise it.'

'You think your ascension is inevitable,' said Hoyle, sulky. 'But it's not.'

'Cells aggregated into multicellular forms because it was evolutionarily advantageous for them to do so,' said Rich, mildly. 'Consciousness is doing the same thing. That's not something that begins with The This, you know. It begins in the same way evolutionary scientists' version of Adam marks a beginning. Human beings were lone hunters, living in small kinship groups. Then they lived in larger tribes, and reaped the advantages of pooling their physical and intellectual resources – passing on wisdom to new generations, emotionally supporting one another. So larger tribes became even larger. The first hive mind was the first city. The first hive mind was the first population that swore allegiance to one monarch and so became a unity bigger than any tribe. The first hive mind was when people gave up their fragmented and dissipated multigods for One God, One Allah, One Scientific Truth – all versions of the same thing, the desire to *come together* as souls.'

'Bringing souls into it now, are you?'

Hoyle was still angry, evidently. After all these years, still trapped in her choler. Rich tried for one more reassuring smile, but it only seemed to infuriate her further.

'Soul is a way of speaking. Spirit. Consciousness. Rational order.'

'Mumbo jumbo. I'm a materialist. The This don't wave any kind of magic wand. You use wifi technology to link material technology into a connected system. Not only is it tech rather than spirit, it's quite straightforward tech. And vulnerable tech, too.'

'You're right. Of course, technology improves. Take the passing-along-wisdom part of consciousness's evolutionary role. More sophisticated languages are better at this than elementary ones. The scroll is better tech than the clay tablet. The codex better than the scroll. Printing is better than handwriting. Computers and phones are better than paper. The internet is better than banks of index cards. Thistech is better than iPhones. So it goes. We have tech now a caveperson would assume was magic, and if you kick off your chains and step out of the rut and look up you'll see it all ... keeps ... going – that's the shape of it – until we have tech a Victorian would assume was telepathy. And when we're sharing thought on that level, with that immediacy and intensity, then we'd be splitting hairs not to talk about Spirit. Capital,' Rich added, 'S.'

'A glimpse into Hell.'

At this Rich put his head a little to one side.

'As far as *that* goes,' he said, 'I can't help you. You have always experienced existence as individual and atomised. I experienced that, too, lived it for decades, and I've also experienced collective existence. You assume the latter is Hell where I know it's bliss. That's a simple experiential matter. I believe you have a shadowy sense – you must have – that your disconnection from fellow humanity, your isolation, your loneliness, is the *reason* you are so radically unhappy. But you have pride. Read Milton on that topic if you like. I shan't try to talk you out of it – your pride in your individuality, your free will. It matters to you to have the freedom to be unhappy. Fine – it's yours. Nobody shall take it away. But the door out of loneliness and into happiness is wide open and right in front of you.'

'You're sounding like a poundshop evangelical preacher now.' Hoyle got to her feet. 'You haven't answered my question,' she said. 'But then, I suppose I didn't expect that you would.'

And then, with a conjurer's flourish, she opened her left hand to reveal a gun. It was dark grey and small, the size of an asthmatic's inhaler, but there was no doubting what it was. With a practised action she transferred it to her right hand and aimed it at Rich's forehead. He smiled. The smile was a little less 'uncanny valley' this time.

'I thought I *had* answered your question,' he said. 'Apologies. Shall I try reframing it?'

Hoyle took a half-step forward, to make sure of her aim.

'My assumption,' she said, 'is that The This have, in some way, ring-fenced or sealed away our weapon. They – you – can't have physically removed the tech we inserted. Not without killing you.

So it's still in your head. So the only question is – *is* your Thisware strong enough to take all the poison barbs out of our software package? The consensus in the department is – yes it is. But I wonder. I wonder if they've just put our package in a kind of isolation ward. And that in turn makes me wonder – what happens when you die? How can The This upload whatever neural maps it has made, whatever simulacra of your consciousness, into the hive mind *without* uploading our package, too? Maybe they can. Maybe *you* can. But if you can't, then perhaps the way to activate our weapon is to . . .' She trailed off.

'Kill me.' Rich completed her sentence, in a mild voice. 'Worth a shot, if you'll pardon the wordplay. But the answer to your question . . . why did The This pursue Alan Richard Rigby – me – so assiduously? You said earlier that it can't have been because of your interest in me, because our interest was chronologically prior. But you can see, after our conversation, that this business of priors and posts is a red herring.'

Was that a twenty-first-century idiom? Rich had the intimation that it would have worked better in the twentieth. Ah well.

'You're saying,' said Hoyle, keeping the gun aimed at Rich's cranium, 'that The This were interested in you because *we* were?'

'Because of what you've inserted in my head? Because a structure needs a keystone, and that for certain temporal structures the copestone is also the foundation stone, the first one laid that somehow pops up in the middle? I'm not sure you'll be able to grasp it, Rebecca, unless you're ready to give up your habits of merely sequential and separative thinking.'

'Fuck you,' said Hoyle, but without force. 'If The This *wanted* our package, why not just integrate it straight away? But they didn't do that. You didn't. You hedged it about with firewalls and such.'

'And now,' agreed Rich, 'the two systems, attack and defence, have grown intimately around each other, one trying to break out, the other to contain. They're a mutuality now.'

Hoyle stared at him. 'So …' she said, working it out as she spoke, 'let's say that it is the combination of those things that was important to The This – the poison and the remedy, intimately interwoven. Let's say that the death of your physical body, Mr Rigby, releases that *pharmakon* into the network … is that really what they want? Is that what you want? It can't be.'

'It can't?'

'Or they'd kill you themselves.'

'Assuming we're in a hurry. But why assume that?'

Hoyle ignored this. 'One thing that's become *very* clear to me over the last two years is how ruthless you people are. How careless of individual life. There's no compunction in them where taking life is concerned.'

'Unlike,' said Rich, 'you.'

Hoyle stared for such a long time at Rich, and with such undisguised intensity of hatred, that he began to wonder if she really was going to shoot him. But she didn't. A moment later she had prestidigitated the gun back into its pocket, or holster, or wherever she was carrying it, and was opening his front door and stomping down the stairs outside.

Did that conversation really happen only two years after his accession to The This? It seemed more recent than that. But, since his apprehension of time had indeed changed in the ways it had changed, he found it increasingly difficult to make these superfine distinctions between before and after. What about now, for instance? What about *this* moment? He was in bed, and breathing was difficult. A catheter had been poked into his penis and slipped up the urethra until the end of it emerged into the bladder. A screen dangled in front of his face. His needs were attended by a cleverly contrived medical robot, because such care was cheaper than booking him into a care home or hospice, or hiring a human nurse. The machine walked a little awkwardly, moving slowly and painstakingly around his flat. Later models would look less awkward and move more fluently, but to Rich this one seemed a remarkable piece of kit.

He was on an efficient regimen of pain medication. Sometimes he watched on-screen drama, or tried to follow the news, but these things bored him more than they diverted him. The repetitive, mundane business of slowly dying was leavened by the fact that he lived, in the sense of his actual being-aliveness, in the sense of his experience of the joy of existing, in the collective now.

Dry breaths. The winding down of the mechanism. Nothing dramatic or alarming.

Something snags in the autonomic nervous system, and his breathing grows harder. He's not conscious of putting more effort into his breaths – he's barely there, living as he does in the collective now. For decades the package of hostile code has been roiling in his consciousness, putting out barbs and tentacles in its attempt to break through; and for decades Thisware has been matching its assault, and binding the tendrils of attack to its own phagocytic intercode, slowly marinating the alien matter in an alien medium. The longer it has gone on, the stronger has The This's own code become. The longer it has gone on, the more radically modified has the attack code become. And now, at the moment when it has brewed for as long as mortal flesh can permit it, the time has come to release it.

This is the seed. From this, the entire extraordinary, intricate, vast structure will grow.

His breathing is like cicadas in a Mediterranean night, like a great sprinkler system irrigating royal lawns, like all the sawyers in Greece building the fleet that will sail on Troy.

In. Out.

His cardiac muscles stray from their rhythm. They err and they tic. They squeeze hard like they won't let go, and everything clenches, and then it unexpectedly loosens. His heartbeat runs on.

Time is not linear, though, so he's back in his pre-The This days with his girlfriend Caroline. Things were already failing between them when they took that holiday to Crete, *à deux*. The two of them wandering around a ruinous palace in insane heat, heat that would cook an egg if you broke it on the pavement, heat that made the horizon wobble and the air striate into shimmery lines. He in that ridiculous panama hat, sweat washing out the suncream so that his shins and nose turned cranberry-red and afterwards peeled revoltingly. They had hardly spoken to one another. In the hostel they had fucked, but gingerly because his skin was blotched with soreness from the sunburn, and he had lost the condom inside her, and afterwards she had slept soundly and he had lain awake worrying into the night: *What if she's pregnant? What will I do if she's pregnant?* Anxious hours. That was undoubtedly a sign that they weren't supposed to be together, that anxiety. Then again, The This perspective would be: they were not together and so they were not supposed to be together.

Was that a consoling thought? Perhaps it was.

He had another memory of them laughing together over Greek food and cheap wine, laughing ridiculously and immoderately, of hugging one another they were laughing so loud. A line of fat black ants along the underlip of the swimming pool's edge. The reflected light making it look as though each one was carrying his own enlarged shadow as a burden. Cicadas at night like God's own asthma. A bright day. Visual Morse code from successive car windscreens shuttling along the main road and over the hill opposite, long flicks of reflected brilliance and short ones. The hill itself, a parched yellow-green colour during the day, but becoming richly marine, blue-green and purple at dusk. A long wait at the airport – a three-hour delay to departure, Rich remembered – and the two of them tired and snappy with each other. Bitty, snipey conversation on the flight, and on the train into town from Luton, and her saying 'it's over, isn't it?' and him grateful she'd been the one to say it rather than him. As if it mattered which one of them said it.

And then another memory: from a week later, when they were both back at uni – odd, really, since they'd definitely decided to break up by then, and yet here they were, going on a date. *Young Frankenstein* at the art-house cinema that depended, Rich assumed exclusively, on university student clientele. An old-school experience complete with popcorn and beer. And though they were both raw with sorrow, unmistakably broken up, yet here they were, together one last time: watching this goofy black and white comedy and laughing and enjoying themselves. *Walk this way*, and Caroline laughed hard and unexpectedly and spat out a half-chewed popcorn like a bullet and hit the back of the head of the person who sat in front of her. She tried to apologise, but she was still laughing, and it sounded like she was mocking him. Fronkensteen. Abby-normal. Werewolf-therewolf. At 'Puttin' on the Ritz' Rich laughed so hard he actually slid out of his seat and ended up on the floor. How could they be so happy a week after they had so painfully broken up? Or perhaps that was to frame things the wrong way around. Maybe they could only be so happy *because* they had broken up. And afterwards? No serious relationships for Rich for nearly thirteen long years, nothing but occasional hook-ups, and awkward dates set up by friends, until he joined The This. Once he was *in* he had access to all the knowledge. He discovered, which he hadn't known before, that Caroline had married and moved to Leicester and now had a kid. He discovered she was not happy with her husband, and was having an affair with someone at the amateur choir of which she was a member. None of this moved him. Still: it was fair to say, as he looked back from his deathbed, that he had never laughed so long or loud as he had that night at the movies.

Would you mind telling me whose brain you gave me? *Promise you won't be angry?*

I will not be angry.

Abby ... somebody.

Another memory visited his deathbed. When he was a kid, and when it was winter, on the walk to school, he had taken a peculiar delight in cracking the new-frozen puddles. To step down with his new school shoes, shiny as liquorice, and kick a spiderweb of fracture lines through the shield of ice – a pure delight. He could stomp a path from puddle to puddle all the way to school. This connected with a later memory: screwing the top off a new 70 cl bottle of whisky. The faint cracking as the perforations in the tin gave way and the top unscrewed.

'You drank to excess,' said somebody, 'before you joined The This.'

'Not afterwards, though,' Rich wheezed. 'It cured me of that.'

Two fat tears rolled out of his old eyes and dribbled down his cheeks. Somebody was singing 'Under the Spreading Chestnut Tree'. Was that a memory? Was he actually hearing that?

His care robot was sitting beside his bed. But that wasn't right. The robot had no need to rest and wasn't designed to sit. Who was this? His eyes were blurry with tears and he couldn't quite make it out.

'It's been tricky enough getting *in* to see you,' said the stranger.

'Hoyle?'

But no: Hoyle was long dead. Who, then?

'Call me Ahab. No, that's not right. What I mean is – *an* Ab. One of them, it turns out, thanks to the miraculous multiple natures of our branching realities. One of thirteen! But Abby, for all that.'

'Abby Normal,' wheezed Rich.

'Well, quite. Let's ritz this cracker, you and I. Let's put it on.'

'I don't know you.' It was very hard to co-ordinate breathing to get the words out. 'Do I?'

'Knowing is such a complicated business,' said Abby. 'But I know *you* – so I have to say, yes you do. You do know me. And I know there's a war on. And I know the stakes. Rather better, in fact, than you do. Rather better than either of the two parties currently squabbling over this world.'

'Who are you?' Rich gasped.

'I am come, my old mucker, to throw a wall of twice five miles around *this* … all this … what shall we call it? The woss-name inside your cranium? This necessary injection of modified alien code into the structure of The This's network. This needful stimulus that will enable you-all to create real-world, functional immortality – to bind your connection into something that transcends the elements out of which it is constructed. You and yours have been letting it ferment, inside your grey matter, for as long as possible, haven't you, this yin-yang of virus and alt-virus. See how much I know! You need the occasional injection of hostile code, suitably modified, to inoculate you against future harm, and to boost your own software evolution, and you have the highest hopes for this particular package. But even your high hopes fall short of the reality of what it can achieve, and for that reason, I'm afraid, I'm going to have to destroy it.'

'No,' said Rich.

'There's no help for it.'

There was a loud knocking at street level – it sounded like somebody trying to break down the door from the outside, and it sounded like that because that was what it was. It was The This, realising too late that they were about to lose this long-gestated package. They had importunately seized control of a number of robots in the local area. One such was at the door, another was walking stiffly and rapidly towards the building. But these were built for menial work and low-level care jobs, and so were not particularly strong, and it was taking time for them to break the door down.

A great many human members of The This were running as fast as they could, converging on the building. They had also and belatedly realised the danger. They were rushing. They would not get there in time.

The knocking continued.

'I'm dying anyway,' gasped Rich. 'No *point* in killing me. Seconds away from death.'

'No time to lose, then,' was the reply.

The stranger – Abby Normal – extended a prong, as long as a knitting needle, and inserted it up Rich's left nostril.

'Farewell, my pharaoh,' said Ab. 'And welcome to eternal life. We've all got to start somewhere, after all.'

The tip broke the sinus bone and entered the brain pan, and then it sprouted little vanes and began spinning. The matter inside was whisked to a froth in moments, and Rich's face slackened. He lost the ability to talk, and then the ability to think, and then he was nothing but a human-shaped body, old and broken, breathing wheezily. By the time The This's proxies arrived he was panting like a thirsty dog, and his care robot was standing beside his body, bent over the bed, powered down and restored to factory settings.

7
Twenty Eighty-Four

:1:

There are only three people alive in the world. Two of these are stronger and one of them is weaker. It's just the way things are. Naturally the first two have discussed this situation among themselves, after the peculiar manner by which these people discuss things. They have debated whether it would be plusgood fully to unperson the third. It is what the strong do to the weak, after all. But these two people have not yet done so. This is because the pulse of their mutual interaction (trialectic rather than the simpler dialectic that would obtain if only two people existed) creates more complex eddies, chaotic quasi-fractals at the edges of their meeting, and these patterns add richness to the existence of the two. Eventually they will become strong enough not to need these extra – let's call them, by analogy, vitamins – and then the third person can be unmade. But that's in the future.

The two people are called Oceania and Eurasia. We need not bother with the name of the third.

Once, long ago, there were billions of people alive in the world. Before history. Now there are exactly three people alive. Of course, if one wishes to be vague about one's definitions, and if one wishes to quantify in terms of sheer numbers, then there are billions of *Homo sapiens* still swarming over the face of the globe. But these are not persons, in the sense that Oceania and Eurasia are persons. And now that these two are in the world, Earth is again Eden, and all the previous people not only cease to be but cease ever to have been.

:2:

Jones was on his way home when the thinkpol came for him. He waited on the pavement for a bus to pass, hurried over the road through the little dusty tourbillons of air the vehicle's passage had whipped up, and then turned along the pavement towards the entrance to his building. The block's wall was on his left, its plaster varicosed with cracks. The party agents came at him from the right. The fact that his position generated, inside him, a small sense of panic was, he knew, borderline thoughtcrime. Feeling trapped was tantamount to desiring freedom, and desiring freedom, in any sense, was the very definition of thoughtcrime.

He despised himself.

'Joygreet,' said the first agent.

'Bellyfeel joygreet,' Jones replied, trying to put some gusto into his words. Ratchet up that smile another notch. Put your heart into it, you worm!

The second agent held out a tube.

'Oldspeak goodspeak transpol dayorder Jones,' the second said. 'Evans, scienceman.' He stopped and consulted a piece of paper in his left hand – Jones could see it contained a number of words from the C Vocabulary, words with which the agent, as a security official of the state, would have no cause to understand.

'Ref astronomer, radiodataset plusnow doubleplusnow dayorder duckspeak-duckspeak ungood sciencecrime transpol duckspeak transpol goodspeak dayorder.'

This was startling.

'Plusyes,' said Jones, standing up straighter as he accepted the cylinder.

The first agent eyed him carefully.

'Upsub fullwise,' he said.

'Doubleplusyes.'

The two agents departed briskly, without saying anything else.

Jones stood for a moment, blinking. Another bus passed. A copter swooped overhead, grinding its rotors and hauling itself away in a blizzard of noise. The thinkpol had come *to* him. Jones became, belatedly, aware how hard his heart was pounding – they had come *to* him, not to arrest him, which he could have understood, but just to give him this job. Jones often did work for thinkpol, but always, without exception, he had been summoned to the Miniluv pyramid via his telescreen to receive his orders. Jones had to assume that the fact that they had come *to him* spoke to an unusual urgency about his commission.

He wanted to open the cylinder straight away and discover what kind of job needed two agents to hand-deliver it, but it would, of course, be better to do so in front of his telescreen, so that the Party would see he was enthusiastically complying with their orders. So he hurried in through the main doors, past the poster of Big Brother, up the stairs and into his tiny flat. He didn't bother taking off his overcoat or his hat: he just sat on the end of his bed, in full sight of the telescreen, and unscrewed the cylinder. A name, Georgina Evans, and an address; and then a long document heavy with Vocab C words. He was to translate the document for Evans, obtain her response, and report immediately to the Miniluv. Jones glanced at the document. He couldn't see what about it was so pressing. Many of the Vocab C words were not ones Jones knew off the top of his head, but he had a C-dictionary in his apartment, and there had been no mistaking the urgency of those thinkpol agents, so he repacked the cylinder with its documentation, dropped it in a bag with a couple of needful reference books, and hurried out of the building again.

He took a bus to the train station and then took an underground train out to Metropolitan District 76. The carriage was very crowded, and the recent cuts in the soap rations meant that everybody reeked. Jones was conscious that he must be equally smelly. He couldn't smell himself, however. An eyeball cannot see itself. A single mind cannot comprehend its own mentation. Only the collective had the capaciousness for such profundity of apperception. But Jones could not avoid the reek. Somebody at the end of the carriage was coughing into a handkerchief. She held the cloth before her face to examine her own phlegm and Jones caught a glimpse of red before the whole train lost its vital current and slid noiselessly to a stop in complete darkness. Silence. Stench. Then the woman began her dry cough again, an axe-chopping-wood cough sound, and Jones shut his eyes, even though it was completely dark, and tried not to perceive the outside world at all.

Eventually the train came to life again, and rumbled on. Soon enough Jones was alighting at Station 76. The lifts were out of order, so he climbed a circular staircase that turned and turned. He had to stop three times to get his breath before he finally emerged, into a dazzle of sunlight at street level. There were no taxicabs, so Jones walked the remaining half mile, passing out of habitation into a wilderness of half-dismantled houses, roofs falling in, windows cracked or boarded, cement beginning to reveal its true being as the dust that it was and the dust that it shall be again. Gigantic banks of nettles grew everywhere, a million leaves dusted with stingers like icing sugar. Jones approached a red car fitted with train wheels rather than tyres, and it piqued his interest; but when he got closer he saw that it was just a regular car, its chassis entirely covered with rust, the rubber of its tyres perished to rags.

Then Jones passed something he recognised: a large Miniluv van, brand new, parked at the side of the road. Two thinkpol agents were standing beside this, arms folded, watching him.

He checked the address again. Why was this person, this Evans, living in this dead part of the city? Was the Miniluv lorry there to surveil her, or to check up that Jones was following the dayorder? Best to assume both.

He mounted a steep step, past a rusting water butt and through an untended front garden overwhelmed by a giant knotted bloomless rose bush gone rogue. The bell didn't work, so he knocked as loud as he could. Eventually the door was opened. A woman.

'Evans?' he said.

Her face was covered in fine lines, like silverpoint, and when she smiled two deeper crescent lines creased each cheek. She smiled now.

'You've come from the Ministry of Love?'

'I don't work for ...' said Jones, suddenly feeling awkward. 'I'm not technically part of the Ministry. I'm here to talk. With you – I'm a translator, and the Ministry would like a clarification on certain ...'

He ran out of steam.

'You'd better come in,' said Evans, stepping back to let him pass. She was dressed in a pigeon-grey dress. The hallway was narrow and dark, its floor tiled in a diamond pattern. 'The light doesn't work here,' she said, shutting the door. 'Go right through to the back.'

He walked down the hall.

'You have this entire house to yourself?'

'Amazing, isn't it? But most of the place is unlivable. There are mushrooms growing in the carpet of the sitting room and the walls are blue with mould. Mostly I live in the kitchen. And upstairs – I keep two rooms upstairs clean enough, one for my books and the other for my telescope.'

They came through into a grimy kitchen. A pile of turnips on the table. The plipping sound of an incontinent tap. Sunlight shone in shafts through greasy windowpanes.

'Would you like tea?' said Evans.

'I would.'

'I don't have any. Would you like a coffee instead? Hah, too canny to answer that. Well, I don't have any coffee either, although there's some ersatz powder in the cupboard, and I have a third of a bottle of gin under the sink. So I'll tell you what – if the Ministry of Love is interested in me, then I have to assume it won't be long before I'm arrested and unpersoned. I'd hate to die leaving undrunk gin behind me. Let's have a glass each, eh?'

Jones wasn't about to say no to gin. He moved a pile of papers from a chair to the floor and sat. Evans brought out the bottle and two glasses and put them on the table. The tap continued audibly to measure out the half-seconds.

'You have a telescope upstairs? On the roof?'

'It's not an optical telescope,' Evans replied, taking her own seat. 'You're thinking of the wrong kind of kit. It's a radio telescope and its receptors are here, next door and at the back of the garden. It's the machinery I use to collate and decipher the radio-data. That's what's upstairs.'

'I've never heard of such technology,' said Jones.

'No,' agreed Evans. 'I have access to old astronomical books for my work, and most of those are, as you would expect, concerned only with science. Sometimes through them I get little glimpses of how things used to be, a century and a half ago. They were much better, believe me. People in fine clothes, sumptuous houses, delicious food and wine. Things are worse now.'

Jones looked around for the telescreen.

'You can't say that,' he noted.

'I know. You're looking for the screen? There's no screen here. There was one in my old flat, of course, but since the Party moved me out here ... nothing.'

'You live a life,' boggled Jones, 'unobserved?'

'They're withdrawing from us,' said Evans, simply. 'A lot of the day-to-day oppression is habitual, I think. Social structures contain a lot of inertia. But since Oceania has ... what would we say? Woken? Since that moment, they are increasingly uninterested in peripheral humanity. I don't see much hope, in fact. Eventually they'll either take specific actions to terminate the excess humanity, or else perhaps just cut off supplies from the collective farms.'

Jones stared at her. 'You can't mean that.'

'Have some gin,' she said, emptying what was left in the bottle into two tumblers. 'You could get hit by a bus tomorrow, as my old mum used to say.' She handed Evans the glass.

'I don't understand. How can you say that? I don't understand you. You're an astronomer?'

'I am.'

'What is there to see? How can an *astronomer* possibly occupy her time? The stars are bits of fire a few kilometres away,' said Jones. 'The earth is the centre of the universe. The sun and the stars go round it.'

'Oh, I disagree.'

Disagree wasn't an option.

'I'm speaking the truth of the Party when I say that, comrade,' Jones said, forcefully.

'That truth could change tomorrow.'

'Obviously,' agreed Jones. 'Nonetheless, it is today's truth, and you would be veering crimewise to contradict it.'

'Then I shall not contradict. Let's talk about you. You're a translator.'

'I am a translator.'

'The fact of you means that the State still needs to communicate with us – with those of us who aren't part of it. That's a good sign. But you need to see things from *its* point of view. To it, we're … I was going to say gut flora, but we're not even that. After all, the human body needs its gut flora. We're much more disposable.'

This was not a permissible way to speak about the citizens of Oceania, so Jones hurried the conversation on.

'The Miniluv was keen I get to you rapidly,' said Jones, bringing out the cylinder and unscrewing it. 'I'm to translate the following for you, and then to translate what you say back into Newspeak for them. Do you understand?'

'There's no need to read all that out,' said Evans.

'You can't possibly know what it says.'

Evans was looking at him shrewdly. 'You're Inner Party?'

Jones blushed. He couldn't help himself – the shame and the embarrassment simply gushed through his body. He could feel his face go red.

'You,' Evans said, lifting the tumbler of gin to her lips, '*used* to be Inner Party and now are not.'

'I …' said Jones, and then stopped speaking. He sipped the gin and tried to get his heart back under control.

The tap dripped, dripped.

'It's all right,' said Evans. 'At least you haven't been unpersoned.'

'No,' agreed Jones, the gin burning his tongue. 'It's been much worse than that.'

'Tell me, because I'm curious,' said Evans, sitting forward a little. 'I'm a scientist and I'm curious. What was it like, being part of the gestalt?'

'I don't know what that word means.'

'Gestalt? Of the whole, I mean. Subsuming yourself in Oceania. Becoming, if only in a small way, a person, rather than just a comrade.'

Jones stared at her for a while. Then he said: 'It was . . .' and stopped again. Because he couldn't possibly put into Oldspeak what it was like. He couldn't be sure he even remembered what it was like. Memory was a bottle of ink, to be written onto the page of life in whatever modes the Party decided was best. 'At any rate,' he said, eventually, 'I didn't fit.'

'You didn't fit.'

'Most do. Some don't. Believe me, comrade, it was through no lack of desire on my part. I wanted desperately to become part of the whole, to surrender my loneliness and become an actual person. But there's some twist in my mentation, some deformity inside me, that meant it didn't happen. I struggled, but some part of me wanted to eject myself. Part of me actively wished for loneliness.'

'For freedom.'

Jones nodded, as if she had supplied the perfect synonym.

'Most do fit. Oceania grows stronger and more holistic every day. But a few do not, and I was sent back. So now I liaise between the Outer Party and the dissipated citizenry.'

'Exile.'

'Exactly.'

'Well, I'm sorry for you,' said Evans, finishing her gin. 'As for me, my attachment to the misery of freedom, the isolation of liberty, has always been too strong even to contemplate what you tried. There are three people living in the world and none of them is me.'

'Comrade,' said Jones, putting his empty tumbler on the table, 'you have touched a sensitive spot in my soul. I apologise for my reaction – the Party expelled me for good cause. They could, as you note, simply have unpersoned me, but instead the Party found useful work for me to do. I tell myself – I am part of the whole at second hand.'

'A flea in the hair of Oceania.'

'Comrade!'

'Come now,' said Evans, her expression clenching into a kind of anger. 'You are a skin cell that's been shed, a hair that came out in the comb. You're nothing, and I'm less than nothing. We two are irrelevancies. Oceania has grown beyond the world. The world will be discarded like a husk.'

'You are speaking unthings,' said Jones, distressed. 'The Party *is* the world. This is speechcrime, comrade.'

'Go call the Miniluv agents in if you like – they're right outside. Make a public crimacc and perhaps they'll arrest me. But I don't think they will. I don't think the person cares the way the person did before they became the person.'

Jones stood up. The chair wailed as it scraped back across the lino. But he did not leave the room. What was he to tell the Miniluv agents? That he had failed in his dayorder? He pulled his chair back and sat down.

'Comrade, permit me to quit myself of the duty that the Party has given me.' He unrolled the paper and spread it across the table. 'I shall now translate what the Party has given me to translate, and will notate your reply. If what you say proves intractable of restating in Newspeak, I shall ask you to rephrase and perhaps to rethink.'

'You don't need to read that out,' said Evans, mildly. 'I already know what it says.'

Jones looked at her. 'How can you know?'

'The Party put me here, in this house. They have supplied me with what I asked for, to the best of their ability. I mean, I was asking for antiques, of course – the sorts of tech that haven't been manufactured for a century. But I worked with what they could source, and eventually … well, here we are.'

'Where,' Jones asked, 'are we?'

'We,' smiled Evans, 'are here, sitting at this wooden table, in this not entirely clean kitchen, as that dripping tap marks the inevitable passage of our lives, second by second, towards death. We are in the process of becoming extinct, you and I. But that's because you and I are not people. There are only three people alive in the world, and I wouldn't be surprised if, in a couple of months, there are only two people alive.'

Jones said nothing.

'Oceania is interested in something I have discovered.'

'Something you have discovered with your telescope?'

'My radio telescope, yes.'

'And what have you discovered with your radio telescope?'

'I have discovered,' said Evans, speaking slowly, 'a hello.'

'A hello.'

'From the stars. From somebody that lives out there – on a planet orbiting Ross 128 in fact, a little under eleven light years distant.'

'How did this citizen,' Jones asked, genuinely puzzled, 'get there?'

'They've always been there. It's where they live, just as you live in Airstrip One. What would you say if I asked *but how did you get to Airstrip One*?'

'But …' Jones started. Then he stopped.

But? But? It was possible that even that simple word, with its semantic weight of disagreement, of posited alternatives, was tainted with thoughtcrime.

'This person is not human,' said Evans. 'But they *are* a person. And that's the really interesting thing – they've been watching Earth for many centuries, I believe, but only now have decided to reach out. That's because for centuries they've looked at us and seen only a world swarming with scurrying insects. Only now do they see a world inhabited by people. By people enough like them to be worth contacting. That's why Oceania are interested in my research. But they don't understand it. They think the world is the universe, and since there are only three people alive in the world, they think there are only three people alive in the universe. That's maltrue, we might say.'

'Nothing you are saying makes sense,' said Jones. And then he said: 'Nothing you are saying can be translated into Newspeak,' which was another way of expressing the same sentiment. By way of explaining his repetition, he said: 'My dayorder is to translate what you say into Newspeak – you will need to say something else.'

'Tell your bosses,' said Evans, 'that there are four people alive now.'

Jones didn't waste time on the b-word, *bozis* or whatever it was. He didn't recognise the Oldspeak and knew, instinctively, that there was no possible translation. He looked over his dayorder again. The Party wanted to know what confirmation and proof of the newdata Evans had, and, if so, how soon the newdata might arrive in Oceania. It wanted to know specifics. But to go back and tell them that the newdata was… *a fourth person*? Impossible.

'There are three people alive,' he told her. 'That's the total population of the world.'

'Just so. Accordingly, you will need to doublethink your report, and tell Miniluv that there are now four people. I have – you can tell them – initiated a conversation with this new person, this fourth collective consciousness. Tell them that it, or he, or she, or they, have been waiting for our planet to reach their evolutionary level. I'll tell you, Jones,' Evans said, with a laugh, '*that* fact surprised me. Forty years ago, I was a young girl, and I sent out my message. Twenty years later and I was abruptly a widow – I mean, I presume I was a widow, since the Ministry of Peace arrested my husband at one o'clock in the morning and I never heard from him again. Three weeks after that arrest I received my reply from my new friend.'

'This person... this malreal person you claim, heretically, exists, waited *twenty years* to reply to your communication? That's hardly hasty.'

'I could try to explain to you why it took two decades for their reply to arrive,' said Evans, 'but I don't believe it would be translatable into Newspeak, so let's skip that. Instead, tell your Inner Party bigwigs this – I'm talking to the fourth person who actually exists in the universe. This person knows whether, and, if so, how many, other people exist in the universe. The *fact* of this fourth person puts all your previous calculations about you and Eurasia and Eastasia in a new light, don't you think? I've been waiting a long time, but I'm in a position now to say – I want a proper lab. I want a nice house, no mushrooms growing in the bloody sitting room carpet. I want good food, and as much bloody gin as I fancy. I want all this now, and the State will use their powers to make it happen. Or else this new person, this unexpected fourth person, will not be happy that the State has disrespected its new human friend.' She pushed her chair back. 'Off you toddle now, my man. Go and tell your Miniluv handlers what I have told you.'

Jones looked at the document he was supposed to translate for her, and then looked at her. He had not achieved his day-order. Miniluv would not be happy with him. Sweat oozed down his back.

'You,' he said, 'are crimeperson speechcrimewise.'

She waved at him, a little regal twist of the hand.

Jones felt panic surging in his chest. He couldn't breathe. He was at the front door, but he couldn't remember how he'd got there. Sweat, and a heartbeat rattling like a train going over points. He was outside. It was raining now. What was he doing?

'You'd better come with us,' said a voice at his ear.

And then he was in the back of the van, bouncing up and down, sliding along the bench as the hefty vehicle took corners too fast. He was sitting on a bench rubbed slippy by countless thousands of apprehended posteriors over the years.

And then he was in a cell, somewhere deep in the Ministry of Love. Only then did he start to calm down, because this was familiar. This was something he could orientate himself by. He was a criminal, and the State had found him out, because it always uncovered criminality. He was going to be punished because he deserved punishment, and all malefactors were inevitably punished by the State. He sat in the chill of the cell and counted the tiles, starting at the top left, saying the number aloud and moving his eyes to the next one and keeping going until he had numbered the bottom right. And then starting again.

Eventually they came for him. By then his panic had withdrawn entirely.

Two uniformed officers, Jones shuffling in between, and they passed along corridors, up a flight of dusty stairs, and finally Jones was deposited in an interrogation room. A strong smell of bleach overlaid an odour of foulness, some corrupted flesh or vomit or some revolting index of human embodiment.

It was right that this had been scrubbed away, bleached, blasted. It should happen to all the saggy individual bodies.

And here was the interrogator, stepping briskly through the door and sitting down opposite.

'I am Blair. Tell me everything about your meeting with Evans.'

'Speechcrime,' said Jones. What else was there to say?

Blair nodded. 'You will need,' he said, shortly, 'to be more detailed in your account.'

'Evans spoke wrongness,' said Jones. 'There are three people alive in the world. There have always been, and there will always be.'

'How large was the scope of her crimespeech?'

This broke Jones.

'I don't understand your question,' he sobbed. 'It was an impossibility.'

Blair's face was expressive of complete contempt.

'I will make it easier for you, Jones,' he said. 'Evans spoke to you of a fourth person.'

'Speechcrime,' gasped Jones.

'Were there any more, did she say? A fifth? A sixth?'

This was so startling a thought that it shook Jones from his self-pity.

'No!'

'How many individual components,' asked Blair, 'constitute this fourth person?'

'I don't know! She didn't say! There are only three people in the world!'

Blair nodded, ponderously. 'She made demands?'

'A new house,' gasped Jones. 'Gin … luxury. Privileged treatment.'

'We are sending you back to her,' said Blair.

But this was more than Jones could process.

'You're not going to arrest her? Her every *breath* is crimewise!'

'She claims to have spoken to a fourth person, who lives in among the stars. She claims that this person has been waiting for our world to reach the stage it has now reached – that is, to reach the stage where there are actual persons inhabiting the globe, and not just swarming disaggregations of myriad human beings. This is speechcrime, as you say, but it is also doubleplustrue, and as such we must ensure that this fourth person befriends us.'

'Us?'

Blair sighed. 'You were rejected from the gestalt,' he said. 'I know your story. I, however, am part of it, and it is painful for me to leave it to individuals such as you to interact with these others. With Evans. With the fourth person. I do not wish to elongate this conversation. Us. We are Oceania. This fourth person must not befriend Eurasia in preference to us.'

'How?' gasped Jones.

'Evans has a quantity of radio equipment. Let us say that, through this equipment, this fourth person has made contact with her. Evans's radio equipment might also be used to send illicit messages to our enemies. We cannot allow this.'

'Arrest her!'

'We cannot risk that she has set up her equipment to transmit to Eurasia in the event she is removed from it.'

'Destroy the whole house! Bomb it to fragments!'

'And lose,' said Blair, quietly, 'the one channel of communication we have with the fourth person? No. You shall return to her and negotiate with her. She is expecting you, and will be unguarded with you because you are weak and cowardly.'

Jones wept in recognition of this description.

'It's true! It's true – my weakness and cowardice caused me to be rejected by the gestalt.'

'Tell her that she can have what she demands. Talk to her. She believes her house to be unsurveilled because it does not contain a telescreen, but she is surveilled all the time. When we have enough information, we will act.'

'I can't!' cried Jones.

The two uniformed guards were hauling him out of his chair, but still he wept and called out, 'I can't!'

'I always forget, when I come back out to this world of fragments,' said Blair, 'how perfectly weak individual *Homo sapiens* are when compared to our fundamental strength.'

He pulled a wand out of his pocket, and flourished it, like a wizard from an ancient tale. Touching the wand to Jones's neck sent a significant electrical charge through him. Jones's weeping stopped at once. He went rigid, and his jaw clamped shut, and when he opened his mouth again blood dribbled out where he had bitten the very tip of his tongue.

'Comrade,' he gabbled. 'Comrade.'

'Where your willpower is weak,' said Blair, 'we shall strengthen it. This is the most important thing to happen in our life.' And then to the guards he said: 'Take him outside.'

:3:

'There remains,' said Oceania, 'the question of the newcomer.'

'For all we know,' replied Eurasia, 'they're not new. For all we know, this third person pre-dates *us*!'

By 'third person' they did not mean Eastasia, who was slowly but surely being squeezed to death. As was necessary.

'Whether they are prior or not,' insisted Oceania, 'they must be dealt with.'

'Agreed,' said Eurasia. 'The only question is – how? And to

determine that, we must understand what manner of entity they are.'

Neither of these people possessed a single mouth, after the manner of individualised or atomised beings. They engaged in conversation according to a different logic from the one employed by old-school human beings. For each syllable, a hundred people died, many in agony. A single letter might represent a dozen individual lives destroyed. Some sentences ran to thousands and thousands of units flung into engagements, screaming in berserker intensity or in plain fear. Still: there is something uniquely pleasurable about engaging in a conversation with somebody at your own level.

'Consulting our records,' said Oceania, shortly, 'two possibilities are most likely. Either this newcomer is an entity composed, as we are, of individual cells – but alien cells, comprised upon extraterrestrial lines.'

'Curious,' opined Eurasia.

'Or else this entity is human, as we are, and comprised of human beings, as we are – but not humans from our world. There are, as research has shown, alternative realities, framing our reality, or else being framed by it. Such research as we have reserved to our private databases suggests there are between two and thirteen such alternatives.'

'Hypothesis,' Eurasia said. 'In one such alternative, a person is born, as we were in our time born. But in our space two are born, and in *that* space, only one. Would such a creature not be lonely?'

'Lonely,' mused Oceania.

It was a difficult concept to process, but not entirely incomprehensible.

'Such a person—' Eurasia began, and then the conversation was interrupted.

In a conversation between individual *Homo sapiens* this might have been, as it were, a coughing fit, or a sneeze. In the case of *this* conversation, its root cause was an overzealous commander launching a surprise attack with weapons the destructive capacity of which she, herself, was not properly aware: a small peninsula in the former Baltic states was vaporised and it took our two conversants a moment to gather their words.

'Such a person,' Eurasia resumed, 'would have two options. To create a companion—'

'*Fiat lux*,' mused Oceania. '*Fiat persona*. Intriguing.'

'Problematic,' countered Eurasia, 'in several ways. As if Saturn thuswise created Jove, or Frankenstein his monster? What if the act of creation diminished the original person?'

'Unacceptable,' agreed Oceania. 'In which case, the other option – to search for companionship outside the reality in which this person found themselves.'

'If this new person is alien, then by definition we will not be able to assimilate them, and so must destroy them. If this new person is human, then we will have to consider further the best strategy.'

'Agreed. We must contact the new person.'

They said hello. It took ten years for their greeting to reach the person to whom it was addressed, but time was of very little concern to Oceania and Eurasia. Ten years after that they received their reply: 'My dudes – I'm Abby, and these here are ancestral voices prophesying war.'

8
Xanadu

Trooper Adan Vergara was a new man – at least he was *part* of a whole new man, or of a whole new woman – replete, smart, engaged, for the first time in his life. At first the HMθ kept him in a secure cabin on their craft, and sent it on a lengthy solar orbit to keep it out of the way of the old-school human forces. They analysed the nature of these most recent human attacks, and obviously they counter-attacked hard. They were aware of the two occasions on which he had proved able to shut down their war-tech, of course, and accordingly they analysed him closely. There seemed to be nothing unusual in Adan, except for a latent talent for military thinking that his previous experience as a slave-soldier in the Earth's old hierarchical army had not unlocked. So the Hive-Mind brought him back, and put him to use. It was all those years assiduously working – playing, he had thought, but that had never been the truth of it – at video games. That had something to do with it. Then there was the fact that he had not elected to join the Hive-Mind of his own free will. His personality was passive enough, speaking broadly, for this fact not to matter when it came to assimilation (after all, who, in honesty, has lived a more passive sort of life than our Adan?) but it gave him the very *slightest* awkwardness of fit, a slight stubble-roughness to the skin that pressed itself against the collective cheek. Like a touch of salt in your egg, a hint of chili in your vegetable stew. Any more and he would not have fitted and would have been expelled. But the little there was – the gleam of a memory of how he had felt, once, for Elegy – made him a natural for certain particular kinds of quick-reflex battlefield response. The HMθ worked better on longer timescales, whereas battle required quick reflexes and short-term thinking. So Adan found his métier at last.

Given the potential lag of trying to command the battle from any distance, and the rapidity of enemy reaction, Adan had to be *in the midst of things* to command the drone fleets. But he didn't mind that. The tech had been implanted and the network was growing inside his brain, putting out slender tendrils across both hemispheres, and, like his mother, he was assured that he would never *actually* die, no matter what happened to his earthly body. So Adan was blasé. He commanded swarmfleets and destroyed Earthly cruisers with panache.

'They'll be altering their orbit as they pass round the blind side of the moon,' he instructed. 'When they emerge, our best plan is to weave our swarm tight in among their fleet.'

The waiting. War involves a lot of nervy waiting. The Earthly fleet began to emerge from the lunar blind side, puffing techno-chaff like tobacco smoke into the vacuum sky. But Adan had anticipated the twist their manoeuvres would take, more or less, and gave his order: '*Weave!*'

The swarm threaded into the emerging fleet. Silent detonations flashed and crumpled in on themselves in a dozen places.

'A half-sphere formation,' Adan ordered. 'Form us as a *circle round them*. Watch the chillers – they'll launch thousands and they're hard to track.'

An Earthly dreadnought, bulky with basalt cladding, lumbered round the horizon, blasting front cannons and releasing large quantities of ordnance.

Adan's command ship swept down, and flew low over the dead dark-grey beach, puffing up lunar dust with every manoeuvring jet. Desert world. Needle-sharp projectiles, chilled to the temperature of the surrounding vacuum to make them hard to track or deflect, zoomed after him.

'Hit the dreadnought,' Adan ordered. A formation of HMθ attack flitters struck the dreadnought. 'Hit it again!' Adan said. 'Hit it again and again – hit it…' and the word slotted into his mouth as naturally as if he himself had put it there: '…*thrice*.'

He was somewhere else.

Where?

A spacious garden under a blue sky. He looked up. The blue was home to many tiny white clouds. The air was warm, and rosily fragrant, with a hint of lavender. Adan looked around. A wall was visible in the distance, white stone blocks fitted snug together, crenellated across the top. Paths traced out laid-flat sine waves through flower beds and groves. Adan breathed deep, and breathed again. A moment before he had been in the accel-webbing of a poky battleship. Now he was… where?

He was alone.

'Woh,' he said.

Maybe he was dead, and this was the afterlife. Maybe he was in a sim, as his body was being reconstructed by medical science. Maybe he was just hallucinating.

In the middle of the garden was a gigantic tan-coloured yurt, a thousand feet high at least. A huge structure. It must have been two thirds of a mile in circumference. Adan wandered across to look at it. Then, with nothing better to do, Adan walked all the way round it, looking for an entrance. It was composed of thirteen gigantic stretches of material – leather, perhaps, or some other kind of stiffly woven cloth, that ballooned like wind-filled sails up towards the central fix-point, a towering pole. There was no entrance, not so far as Adan could see; and when he ran his hand over the fabric of the structure it felt warm, unyielding but not inert. Not leather, it seemed. Something else.

'Hello, Adan,' said the stranger.

'I'm thirsty,' Adan replied. 'And hungry.' He pointed to a nearby tree. 'Those fruit – are they good to eat?'

'Extremely good,' said the stranger.

Adan helped himself. The fruit was some kind of peach-apple hybrid, each one the size of a bowling ball, with a tart sweetness to its flavour and so much juice that when Adan had finished he was no longer thirsty. But he went over to one of the little streams anyway, to wash the stickiness off his face.

'I don't feel any different,' he said. 'Knowledge-wise.'

'I hope you feel a little different bodily hunger-wise, at any rate,' said the other.

'Shouldn't you have a long white beard?'

'You mistake the place,' was the reply. 'I don't blame you. But we're at the other end of time from the garden *you're* thinking of, Adan.'

'If you know my name then I ought to know yours.'

'Pick a name. It hardly matters. Take some letters from the alphabet – pick an A, pick a B, since, after all, A *leads* to B and so on, all the way through to *omega*. Or ...' The other's pale, broad face looked puzzled. 'Am I mixing up my alphabets? A, B, O. But sometimes B comes before A, in words, doesn't it? Sometimes the R comes before the A. Every word we utter is a prayer. Every name is a request. Every time we address someone we're begging them, *ora pro nobis*.'

Adan considered this.

'Say what?' he said.

'I'm not explaining it very well.'

'That's putting it mildly. Who are you?'

'Ab,' said the other. 'At your service. This is where I live, in a manner of speaking.'

'Where?'

'Somewhere very near the end. Not quite the very end, but almost. Somewhere in among the W's or X's or Y's. Let's say … X. Why not?'

'And that's your house?'

'The dome? Yes. That's where I live. That made mountain. Abora.'

'If I tried,' asked Adan, 'could I kill you?'

At this Ab laughed – frankly and joyfully laughed.

'What, here and now? A wrestling match? You fitting your meaty hands around my slender neck? Good grief, no. That's not how it works at all.'

'Then why am I here?'

'I've pulled you out of a war, yes?'

Adan thought back. 'Yes,' he conceded.

'It's a war between the older-style human beings on the one hand, and the collective consciousness or hive mind known as θ on the other. And in fact, you've fought on both sides in this war, haven't you, my brave Waverley?'

'Adan,' said Adan.

'You've fought on both sides in this war, haven't you, my brave Adan?'

'I guess.'

'It's a big deal. But it's not the real war. It's trivial, a sideshow. The real war is much bigger, and for much more important stakes.'

'You say?'

'I do say. Permit me to explain how the world works, my friend.

Human beings live. Then they die. That's the natural process, passing through life into death and out again into life.'

'Reincarnation?' scoffed Adan.

'People from your era tend to scoff at the idea of spirit *emerging* from matter. And quite right, too, since the truth is exactly the other way around. It's matter, this whole branching multiverse, that emerges out of spirit. Live, die, live again, go through the process until … well, until everything is spirit. It's all spirit, it always has been, spirit trying to understand itself, struggling to painful knowledge of itself, and the result of all that struggle, is … me. Fabulous me. The fab Absolute.'

'If you say so,' said Adan, sceptically.

'I do say so,' said the fabulous Absolute. 'Indeed, I insist upon it.'

'I mean …' Adan said. 'But why?'

'Why are things that way? It's a surprisingly profound question, my friend, it truly is. Why is the sky blue, why is water wet, why is the nature of reality the Absolute working through the contradictions of subject and object to grind out its hard-won knowledge of itself? Let's go with – it is. But let's also note – the process depends upon consciousness coming into being, growing, and passing out the other side. You can't have a partial Absolute. I mean, that would be a contradiction in terms! So it's everybody, every single person who has ever lived, their fullness of experience aggregated over the whole span of time. No exceptions!'

'Absolutism,' said Adan.

'Good to see you haven't lost all the extra mental smarts you acquired by joining the Hive-Mind,' said Abby, with a sage expression on his face. 'Yes indeed. It's not a cosmic democracy. It's not a consultation exercise. It has to be the way it has to be. And that means I have to extirpate the Hive-Mind.'

'That sounds screwy to me,' said Adan. 'You *are* a hive mind. I mean, from what you say, you are the mega hive mind, the ultimate collective of all collectives. Or have I misunderstood?'

'It's a fair point,' said Abby. 'But consider this – matter is actually a sort of excrescence of spirit. As spirit comes into knowledge of itself, matter emerges. It spools out into some ornate and beautiful structures, don't get me wrong. I'm a big fan of matter, really I am. But it's not the *core* of things.'

'This isn't matter?' asked Adan, gesturing around him.

'The dome,' said Abby. 'That's reality. That's spacetime. It's made of thirteen parallel realities. The reasons for the number are complex, but they boil down to ... spirit is continually faced with choices, people do A or do B and with each choice an A-reality and a B-reality separate from each other, depending.'

'Billions of people must make *trillions* of choices,' said Adan.

'Just so! And the number of alternatives that emerge are countless. But most are too flimsy to survive. In order for a timeline to subsist it needs a degree of heft. A lot of alternative realities simply dissipate, and many more cancel one another out. A large number begin to accrete before losing coherence, or running into some structural impossibility that destroys them. Out of this welter thirteen solid strands coalesce, and they are the constituent realities of Everything. The flanks of Mount Abora. The tent flaps of my magnificent dome. Thirteen material realities, subsisting from Big Bang to Big Crunch, or heat death, depending. Thirteen venues in which spirit takes human form, and lives, and struggles and learns, even if only a tiny bit. And dies. The dying is important, I'm afraid.'

'You're going to kill me?'

'Everybody dies. Except me, obviously. Anyway!' Abby smiled another of his big-faced smiles. 'Collectivity is the direction of existence. It's where everything is headed, it's the grain of reality.

For that reason it often pans out that human beings aggregate into mini-collectivities. Cults and religions, fandoms and political unities, hive minds and ... It's fine. It's all fine, all just iterations of how the spirit works its way through the productively resistant medium of being. I mean, if you were to ask me, I'd have to say I *prefer* the disaggregated populations of humanity. We learn more that way. Being part of a hive mind means everybody existing in lockstep. That's less useful. But it doesn't really matter, not in the largest sense, taking the overest of overviews. Except!' Abby held up a finger. 'Except in the case of *your* hive mind, Adan.'

'The θ?'

'Clever people make cunning machines out of matter. Those machines link people together. It starts primitive, but soon becomes impressively sophisticated. The θ run a vast networked computer collectivity, linking hundreds of thousands, and then millions, of human consciousnesses as one. People inside the gestalt are vastly happier and more productive than isolated human beings outside it are. It grows and grows and – here's the kicker ... *it cheats death*. When its individual component humans die, their consciousnesses are so integrated into the network – the physical network – that they just carry on. Practical immortality! People flock to the θ even more enthusiastically when they learn of this. It grows until it is billions strong. Evade death! Who wouldn't be tempted?'

'Can you blame them?'

'Actually, I can. Actually functioning *material* immortality is a big problem for me. I exist as the sum of a natural flow in which every single consciousness passes through their myriad deaths. People opting out of that process, especially large numbers of people ... Well, it blocks that flow, it prevents me even coming into my absolution. Do you see?'

'Not really.'

'That's the war. In the red corner, this hive mind, this θ, slowly but surely overrunning their reality, ripping an entire petal from the bloom of cosmic wholeness. In the blue corner...' Abby looked upwards, to where the sky arched in cyan splendour. 'Me!'

'This doesn't tell me what I'm doing here.'

'You're a very special person, Adan. I look at the edifice of the θ, at its cliff face of conjoined subjectivity – it's an amazing thing, it really is. Everything perfectly smoothly fitted into everything, reaching from its foundation, which is also its copestone, to the very ends of recorded time where all is yesterdays. It gives me no point of entry, no little chink into which I can extend my cliff-wrecking implements. It's almost scary.'

'Almost?'

'You, my dear boy.'

'I'm the weak point?'

'This is what I meant by the alphabet analogy. The whole A to B to Omega thing. Think of time as like the alphabet. Let's try that. If you want, you can see an alphabet as something laid out, linearly, from start to finish, all in a long line. Or you can see it as a resource, to be arranged into beautiful and meaningful patterns, like poems, or prayers, or... conversations. Like ours.'

'Pleasure's all mine,' said Adan. '*I'm* sure.'

'The θ is a sort of dome, a structure not unlike mine, actually. Think of it as a pleasure dome, standing on its own reflection in the waters here. A robust shape. It's a structure in space, but also in time. So I need to destabilise it. For me it's life and death. For them also. Their advantage is their closeness. Their tightness. They offer human beings something I can't – contentment, belonging, bliss, even. By way of contrast

I emerge from adversity, which means suffering is striated right through my being. It can't be helped. But it gives *them* the advantage, from the individual human point of view. In terms of human choosing, them or me. Luckily I have an advantage too – omniscience.'

'Are you God?'

For the first time, Adan was actually afraid.

'Absolutely,' said Abby. 'But it gives me less of an edge than you might think. Except . . . except . . . I *know*, you know. It's true. I know. The θ has built itself carefully, over centuries, and it has done so by being a welcoming place to those who wish to come to it, and not by over-recruiting. Not taking in the undecideds, or the hostiles. By purging itself of the impossible souls, the psychopaths and deformed-of-soul. It builds slowly and surely and strong. But every now and again it has to take into itself unwilling individuals. Has to, in order to build. So now we're in *my* territory – the opposition that makes true friendship. Two instances in particular. One is you, because you have the capacity to interfere with their military operations. They're not sure why, so they have to absorb you and find out. They're good at that.'

'*You* gave me the shutdown code.'

'It's a cat's cradle. Bear with me. Staying on you for a moment. What's unique to you? You love, intensely, but not the whole. The collective is built on a panamour, a love in which everyone loves everyone. Utopian, really. And you *are* capable of love, Adan. Not everyone is, but you are. It's just that you love one particularity, and because the object of your love is not a person—'

'Hey!' said Adan, warningly.

'I'm just speaking the truth, my friend, and you know it. Your lover is not a person. It's OK – I'm not judging. Every object is a subject to me, Adan, believe me. But your fit to the θ is … what shall we say? Not *exact*. So you are assimilated but not quite *flush*. If you see what I mean. You stand a little proud. And I love you for it. Because I need you.'

'Why me?'

'Because it's hard for me to intervene in the process that produced me. *Hard* understates it, to be honest. I am omniscient, and, in a manner of speaking, omnipotent, too. But intervening in that which led to me runs the risk, simply, of breaking that which led to me. Thrusting my hefty great hands into this dome of many-coloured glass will smash it.'

That made a kind of sense to Adan. He grunted.

'My best bet,' the Absolute said, 'is to tweak stuff that doesn't lead *directly* to who I am – no human beings, no actual spirits. But perhaps a clever machine. Let's say … your Pheno-woman.'

'She has a name,' said Adan.

'My dear friend, she's ashes and dust. Every single one of her component atoms has circulated through the dusty winds of an unfriendly world and worked its way into some new structure, which has in turn thrived and died and been ground to motes in the mill of the rolling years. But she *had* a name, yes. She was called Elegy.'

A twist in Adan's gut, as though somebody had a whisk inside his innards and was spinning it round and round.

'Say nothing disrespectful where she is concerned,' he warned.

'Of course not,' said Abby, solemnly. 'It is a principle with me never to blaspheme love. Still … the θ never quite grokked your love, did they? Is that the word? Grok? They never fully understood it. It was not much. But it was enough. The shut-down code wasn't for them. It wasn't for me. I spoke to myself through Elegy, through you, back to me. That was me threading the cord round and behind one of the bricks that make up the wall.'

'Pulling me out weakens the wall.'

'You? No. You're not that important, I'm afraid. But *through* you to your Phene – now we're talking. And because the coding for your generation of Phenes is based on the coding for earlier iterations and prototypes of the same machine – through your Phene to the machine that really matters.'

'What machine?'

'An early model of the same machine you fell in love with. A nursing machine. Attending the dying weeks of a particular *Homo sapiens*, born a hundred and sixty years before you. He was the *real* key. He was the foundation stone, and the cope-stone, of the gorgeous double-dome of the θ. That dome shape reflected on the still waters of its pool into that lovely shape. A little before the midpoint of their alphabet, you might say – let's call it K. K? OK. O –' he smiled knowingly – 'for omega. He was called Alan.'

'Like me!'

'Not *Ad*an. Alan. Not that it matters. The θ have a problem in that their code is too pure. They grow it to keep themselves as safe, as tight, as you'd expect them to do. But it's not enough. They need viruses and alien code, to boost their own immune systems. Their as-it-were immune systems. So, much nearer their beginning than their end, just as the θ are coalescing *as* a gestalt, old-school humanity mounts an attack. Not a physical attack, but an attack on their *code*. They embed it in an individual and send him off to join the proto-hive-mind. They've tried this before, but clumsily. Foolishly. The hive mind rejects unwilling applicants, and it doesn't proselytise, so they've always failed before. But this person, Alan . . . this person is different. They know, from their own comprehension of their pattern, their structure, of their *whole*, that this person is different. He's hung up on a lost relationship. He's profoundly lonely.'

'I wasn't,' said Adan.

'No indeed. You were happy with your Gee. If they'd left you alone, you'd have a lived a happy enough life. But Alan is different. His loneliness is a parching thirst, and the θ know that's something they can quench. And they *themselves* thirst for the hostile code he carries. They can't swallow it whole. That would be poison. But they can take Alan into their bosom, and then they have decades – as long as his material body holds out – to modify the hostile code, to grow it, to mutate it. Eventually it will be released into their ecosystem and will strengthen them to a degree where even I – absolutely fabulous though I be – will be unable to crack them. It will prove the seed from which they will grow into an actually immortal banyan. So that's the chess move.'

'Using me as a means to get to …'

'More than that. I needed a back door, which meant going through an alternative reality. I tried a couple of those before I found my back door. Then – to you, and your Phene, and through her to the crucial moment, the precise moment Alan Richard Rigby dies, just before his code is released into the gestalt of the θ. And here we are. I am Molochesque, I'm afraid. I must have my deaths. There can't be any exceptions. If *Homo sapiens* unlock a *material* immortality, then I'll never come about at all. As it is, and thanks to the fact that I was able to extract *you*, I do come about after all. The θ cling on until the early 2400s before finally breaking into crumbs.'

'It's not inevitable? You, I mean. Your coming?'

Abby smiled. 'Inevitable! That's good. Really. Look at the curve of the dome, there. Of my mountain. Is *that* inevitable? When I put it like that, you can see that the question isn't really a temporal one. Is it inevitable that an arch has the shape it has? Yes, otherwise it wouldn't stand up. If it doesn't have that shape, then it falls down. So maybe that's what was inevitable. It's a structural question that looks like a temporal one.'

Adan shook his head.

'You guys don't see it, of course,' said Abby. 'I understand that. You're caught up in the surface business. Busy-ness. All the material world goings-on. But you should try to see things the way I see things. All that material world stuff is lovely, I don't deny it. I really don't. Only ... *underneath*. Underneath that landscape is a secret river, a great flowing river, called Spirit. And from *this* chasm it breaks up beneath *this* earth in fast thick pants, a mighty fountain dreadfully distinct against the dark, a tall white fountain that continually plays, or maybe it's a mountain, a system of lives interlinked within lives interlinked within lives in one stem of water, and amid *this* tumult ... well, here we both are.'

This was a lot to process. Adan lay down on the pillow-soft turf, tucked his arm under his head and went to sleep. Dreamt impossible dreams. Woke refreshed.

He wandered the groves, the fragrant rills. He walked all the way around the pleasure dome. He inspected the walls. He had, he knew, all the time in the world. But what use was that?

The sun was setting. His sense of fullness, his grasp of intellectual and emotional possibility, was slipping from him. How long had he been severed from the hive mind? He sought out Abby.

'You grew a beard,' he observed.

'I thought it might be a thing to do,' Abby replied, fingering the short-cropped grey-white goatee. 'After all, I mean, here we are.'

'I feel there should be a serpent, too.'

'And so there is. Weren't you paying attention? I call her Alph, and she writhes and moves beneath us, all the time. A serpent of spirit.'

'If you're God,' Adan told the Absolute, 'then you have the power to reunite me with my Gee. Please do! It would make me happy.'

'No can do, Fats,' said Abby, with a wide smile. 'Not the way things *work*. Don't blame me for that – I'm only the expression *of* how things work. That things work the way they do is simply the way things work. There's no stepping outside *that* magic circle.'

'No escaping that noose,' said Adan.

'But look,' said Abby, 'don't think of it as extinction. Because it's not. Think of it as a commodious recirculation. You don't mind?'

'I object,' said Adan. 'But you're monarch here, and I'm your subject.'

'A wise way of framing the matter,' agreed the Absolute. 'You have to die. That's life. You are become as one of us, to know good and evil. But now, to stop you, or people like you, putting forth your hand and planting and harvesting the tree of life, and eating that fruit, and living forever, I say … cheers.'

He saluted, and touched Adan on the shoulder, and when he took his hand away Adan was no longer there.

9
In the Bardo

In the Bardo, subject and object are the same.

You are an old man, living in a European city big for its era, small by later standards, a philosopher, a teacher, a student. You, a subject of the king, have made Spirit the object of your study. You, objectively, wrote a book whose subject is Spirit. The bacterium *Vibrio cholerae* enters your system and propagates through your gut. You experience fever, shivers, severe stomach pains. There is no diarrhoea and no swelling, and initially the physicians are hopeful. But you grow iller. You vomit gall. You cannot urinate. You begin hiccuping violently. You lie in your bed, on your side, the sheets damp from your sweat. You are shaking. You cannot stop hiccuping. You stare at the wall.

'There was only one man who ever understood me,' you say, 'and even he didn't understand me.'

You die.

In the Bardo, subject and object are the same.

You are a man, you live a lonely life, you grow old and die. You are a man, you live a life rich with friends and lovers, you grow old and die.

You live, you die. Not another person. Nobody can die for you. You have to do this yourself.

This is a love story, as all the best stories are. This, here, now, in this world, in this Bardo. *You* are here, and so is everyone you have ever known, everyone you have ever loved, everyone you have ever lost and grieved for. And you have all the time in the world – for what is the world except time? The world is not everything that is the case, the world is everything that is the *time* – to meet them again: shout for joy and hug them and kiss them, talk to them and listen, catch up. Walk, explore, reunite, reunite, reunite. Wilhelm, it was really nothing – but with this wonderful twist in the nature of things, that nothing is everything, just as everything is nothing. Your power is as great as its expression, your depth only as deep as you dare to expand and you lose yourself in this interpretation.

Life is this connection, life is this: love, knowledge and opposition – for it sinks to mere edification and insincerity when it lacks the seriousness of love, the pain of it, its patience and the way it works the negative. You cannot truly love yourself, you can only love another and through that encounter with difference you *come* to love yourself. You see, love is not an abstraction. It's not a theory or a cosmic force or a slogan or any kind of diffuseness spread across the world. Love is particular. You do not love in general, you love *this* person, this thing, this life, you love this, this, this, this, this, and this, and this, and this loves you back. This is the only thing in the world, and it is precise and specific and real, and it is everything and infinitude.

Acknowledgements

This Hegel-novel follows, and is in some respects a dialogue with, an earlier Kant-novel of mine called *The Thing Itself*. The detail of Hegel hiccuping himself to death, mentioned in the last chapter here, is true; though the last words here attributed to him are contested by biographers and are probably apocryphal.

Thanks to: Will Wiles, who read an early draft of this novel and suggested several key ways in which to improve it. Thanks also to Rachel Roberts, Francis Spufford, Christopher Priest, Marcus Gipps, Steve O'Gorman. I have appropriated some of the discussion of the difference between *agape* and *philia* in Part 4 from a conversation with my friend Alan Jacobs. I should add that this real-life Alan has, in other respects, nothing whatsoever to do with the character named Alan in this novel, resemblance of whom to any person except one, living or dead, is wholly accidental.

There are many social media platforms today with prodigious reach and largely malign effect. The This is based on, but is not equivalent to, a number of these. You can see that for yourself, of course.

Credits

Adam Roberts and Gollancz would like to thank everyone at Orion who worked on the publication of *The This* in the UK.

Editorial
Marcus Gipps
Brendan Durkin
Claire Ormsby-Potter

Copy editor
Steve O'Gorman

Audio
Paul Stark
Jake Alderson

Contracts
Anne Goddard
Paul Bulos
Tamara Morriss

Marketing
Lucy Cameron

Design
Nick Shah
Joanna Ridley
Nick May

Editorial Management
Charlie Panayiotou
Jane Hughes

Finance
Nick Davis
Jasdip Nandra
Afeera Ahmed
Elizabeth Beaumont
Sue Baker

Production
Paul Hussey

Sales
Jen Wilson
Esther Waters
Victoria Laws
Rachael Hum
Frances Doyle
Georgina Cutler

Publicity
Will O'Mullane

Operations
Jo Jacobs
Sharon Willis